For my brother, Alex

Saskia Sarginson was awarded a distinction in her MA in Creative Writing at Royal Holloway after a BA in English Literature from Cambridge University and a BA in Fashion Design & Communications. Before becoming a full-time author, Saskia's writing experience included being a health and beauty editor on women's magazines, a ghost writer for the BBC and HarperCollins and copy-writing and script editing. Saskia lives in south London with her partner and four children.

Visit Saskia online:
www.saskiasarginson.co.uk
www.facebook.com/saskiasarginsonbooks
www.twitter.com/@SaskiaSarginson

By Saskia Sarginson

The Central Line

Saskia Sarginson

PIATKUS

PIATKUS

First published in Great Britain in 2022 by Piatkus

1 3 5 7 9 10 8 6 4 2

Epigraph on p. vii from A. C. Grayling, *The Meaning of Things:
Applying Philosophy to Life* (London: Weidenfeld & Nicolson, 2001)

A CIP catalogue record for this book is available from the British Library.

ISBN 978-0-349-42869-7

Typeset in Goudy by M Rules
Printed and bound in Great Britain by Clays Ltd, Elcograf S.p.A.

Papers used by Piatkus are from well-managed forests and other responsible sources.

Piatkus
An imprint of
Little, Brown Book Group
Carmelite House
50 Victoria Embankment
London EC4Y 0DZ

An Hachette UK Company
www.hachette.co.uk

www.littlebrown.co.uk

'People attempt love as climbers attempt Everest;
they scramble along, and end by camping in the foothills,
or half-way up, wherever their compromises leave them.
Some get high enough to see the view, which we know
is magnificent, for we have all glimpsed it in dreams.'

A. C. Grayling, *The Meaning of Things*

Spring

Notting Hill Gate

Cora pushes her chair back with a jolt and stumbles to her feet, napkin falling to the floor. Her date – Felix, his name's Felix, she remembers – stops with his spoon hovering halfway between his mouth and his chocolate mousse. His startled expression is so comical she has to stop herself from giving a snort of laughter. She stands, ready for flight, trapped behind the crammed tables. The couples sitting on either side are practically in their laps. There's a gap of about three inches to squeeze through. She can make it if she turns to the side, sucks everything in.

She clears her throat. 'Sorry. I've got a . . . a terrible headache. I have to go.'

Felix puts his spoon down and for the first time seems to be really looking at her. His gaze hardens.

'The thing is,' she says quickly, 'it's been all about you this evening, hasn't it? And I'm a bit tired of listening.'

This is hardly an exaggeration. Since they sat down, he

hasn't asked her a single question about herself, just gone on about his divorce. But still, her heart races at her own words, heat colouring her cheeks. Oh God. Not a hot flush, she thinks. Not now. She grabs her coat from the back of her chair and, clutching her bag to her chest, endeavours to slide through the gap. Her trailing coat snags on something, and as she tugs it free, an object clatters to the floor. She doesn't look back. 'Sorry,' she mutters as she passes Felix. 'This was a bad idea. My fault. Sorry.'

From the corner of her eye, she sees Felix half raise himself from his chair, his mouth opening and closing. Then she's at the exit, shoving the glass so hard that she almost falls onto the cold, dark pavement.

She's walking fast, alert to the sound of footsteps. But when he hasn't appeared by the time she reaches the end of the street, she slows down. He's probably ordering a brandy with a hearty laugh and a dismissive wave, explaining away her absence to the concerned waiter.

She opens her collar to the night air, wafting the breeze closer with flapping hands. Why did nature or God or whoever have to be quite so cruel as to add hot flushes to all the other ignominies of ageing?

'Damn,' she says out loud, 'Such a stupid waste of time. What an idiot he turned out to be.' She bites the corners of her mouth. No, she thinks. I'm the idiot. A blind date? When I could have been at home finishing my book. That was the problem with listening to advice from a twenty-three-year-old.

She enters Notting Hill Gate Tube station, squeezing her eyes against the gritty rush of air from the tunnels. On the crowded Central Line platform, a train is approaching. She's swept onto a carriage in a press of passengers. Everyone appears to be on their way out for the night, and it looks as if most people have already started drinking. Cora hangs on to a pole and watches them surreptitiously; they stand, tightly packed together, swaying and juddering with the movement of the train, bodies loose, gestures exaggerated, as they shout over the roar, their loud, slurred voices competing with each other. The whole experience is so unlike the prim silence of weekday commuter mornings, it makes her want to laugh. A young woman catches her eye and gets up to offer her her seat. 'Don't mind them,' she says, patting Cora's arm. 'Rowdy but harmless.'

Cora is at once grateful and irritated; she almost refuses, but she's wearing heels for the first time in months and her feet are killing her, so she slinks into the seat with a nod of thanks. This ageing thing is disorientating – feeling the same and looking different; the converging and separating self. She sits upright, bag on her lap, and decides that the whole dating enterprise is a non-starter. Emotionally she's not ready, and even if she were, the few men available are likely to be damaged from divorce or bereavement, or worse, long-term bachelors. And how can she expect to find another man as wonderful as Andrew?

The train gives a violent lurch. Some of the drunks are thrown sideways, tumbling against each other, snatching at the overhead bars just in time. They find the whole thing hilarious, although she's quite sure they probably travel by Tube all the time, and normally sit in bored silence, staring at their phones.

Someone at the other end of the carriage is revealed in glimpses between bodies moving apart. It's his stillness that catches her attention. The only other sober passenger, she thinks. He sits with a book in his lap, seemingly unperturbed by the milling chaos and loud voices. She wonders what he's reading, what story has captivated him so completely.

She gets out at Shepherd's Bush, pulling her coat closer as she mounts the steps to the street. A March wind is blowing. Litter scuffs along the gutter; the lofty plane trees creak, shedding a puzzle of small branches and twigs onto the pavement below. It's nearly the anniversary of Andrew's death. Six years. Her friend Helena keeps telling her that it's time to move on. But the idea of exposing her naked body to a stranger is terrifying.

It was her daughter who signed her up to the dating site, who scrolled through the likely candidates, swiping right, flicking through one profile after another. 'Look at this one,' she said. 'He looks all right.'

Felix: 5'8", slim. Once dark, now salt and pepper. Blue eyes. Partner in architect firm. Liberal. Plays piano. I'm looking for a slender, good-humoured woman to share long walks, and afterwards a whisky by a log fire – someone who loves art galleries and fringe theatre, who isn't afraid to try something new.

Yes. He sounded all right. More than all right. And it was fun earlier, before she met him, choosing what to wear with Fran, both of them laughing at Cora's unkempt nails and the way all her old pots of varnish had turned to gloop. It was lovely to sit close together, feeling Fran's breath on her cheeks as she stippled bronze shadow over Cora's eyelids, exclaiming over the state of her unplucked brows.

'I can't actually see my eyebrows any more,' Cora admitted. 'That's one of the good things about getting short-sighted – you can't see the ruin of your looks, and all the details like spots and blackheads that used to stress you out when you were young.'

Fran sighed. 'God, Mum. Anyone would think you're a hundred and five instead of fifty, the way you go on. There are loads of men out there who'd be blown away by you – you're still pretty hot, you know. Lots of younger men fancy older women – haven't you heard of cougars?' She held up a hand sternly. 'Don't come back with a comment about big cats. You know what I mean.'

Then there was a kind of tickling match between them and Fran fell off the edge of Cora's bed, giggling. Cora smiles; it was worth the boredom of the date to share that uncomplicated happiness with her daughter. Those moments are too rare.

Her mobile beeps and she looks at the screen, worried it'll be Felix, berating her, or begging her to come back. Helena's name flashes up. *How's it going? Hope you're having wild sex right now!!! Call me tomorrow!!! Xxx*, then a string of emoji hearts and kissy faces. Cora sighs and drops the phone into her pocket. Helena will call tomorrow and demand that Cora give her every single detail of the evening.

She closes the front door, tossing her keys into the bowl on the hall table, kicking off the heels, peeling off her tights. She wanders into the kitchen and makes a cup of tea. Releasing her feet from bondage feels good. She wriggles her toes against the cool floor. It's still early, but the house is silent. The kids must be in their rooms.

Upstairs, she knocks on Francesca's door. Usually her daughter would be out on a Saturday night, but Cora had to ground her after she took the car without asking and backed it into a lamp post. There were suspicious dents on the bonnet too, as if someone had been standing on it.

'Fran?' She peers into the dark bedroom. 'Are you awake?'

She was expecting to find her daughter lounging against pillows watching something on her laptop; hoped that Fran would be in the mood to allow her to climb in beside her and zone out in front of Netflix. In her head, she has already turned the disastrous date into a funny story. But even in the half-light from the landing, it's obvious that the room is empty. She flicks the main switch, revealing a bed that Tracey Emin would be proud of, surrounded by piles of clothes, a twist of damp towel, silver Doc Martens lying on their sides. A pair of black tights and a lacy bra dangle from a lampshade. On the dressing table, make-up spills around a collection of opened beer bottles and a lipstick-imprinted mug.

Along the landing, Cora opens her son's door. Luke is sitting at his desk with his back to her, headphones clamped over his ears. In contrast to his sister's room, his is like a monk's cell: minimal, neat, with detailed revision charts for his A levels tacked up on the pinboard. She suspects he has a tendency towards mild OCD. 'Luke!' she yells. He doesn't stir.

She goes over to him, leaning over his shoulder. He starts.

'Jesus, Mum! You gave me a shock,' he says. 'Can't you knock?'

She points to his earphones. He slips them off.

'Where's Fran?'

He shrugs, pushing at the bridge of his glasses. 'Dunno.'

'She hasn't gone out, has she?'

He shrugs again. 'I guess.'

Cora rolls her eyes. 'She promised me she'd stay in ... and she's supposed to be practising for that audition next week.'

Luke sighs. 'Maybe she's, you know, a bit old?' He's staring at his knees as if talking and making eye contact are an impossible combination. 'To be, like, actually *grounded*. I don't think that's, um, a thing any more.'

'Yes, but she's living here without paying rent. The deal is that she tries to get acting jobs. She knows there have to be rules . . .'

Cora stops. She may as well be talking to herself. 'Did you eat supper?'

He nods.

She sniffs the air. He never opens his window, and the room is thick with the stench of adolescent boy. She stretches out a hand to push a strand of hair from his eyes, and he flinches. He was a beautiful baby, round and smiley, fitting perfectly onto her hip, pressing his little fingers inside her mouth, laughing, puckering up for kisses she couldn't stop giving.

'So she didn't say anything to you?' she persists.

'About what?'

'Oh, I don't know . . . maybe about where she was going? Who she was going with? When she'd be back?'

Luke looks confused. 'She doesn't tell me anything, Mum.'

'No,' Cora says, relenting. 'That makes two of us.'

Cora goes downstairs, takes her tea, already going cold, and a family-size packet of crisps and makes herself comfortable on the sofa, sitting cross-legged, feet tucked up. She guesses that Fran will sneak in before twelve, thinking she can slip into bed unnoticed.

She gulps down some lukewarm tea, switches on the TV and stares at the screen without really seeing it. How do you manage a twenty-three-year-old? Fran's an adult, even if she doesn't behave like one. Luke's right. Of course she can't ground her. Andrew used to have the knack of laughing her out of her moods, or he'd be stern and serious, which always made her fall into line. Cora's face contorts, pulled out of shape by grief, and a familiar howling rage welling up from her centre. So much of her anger is for Andrew himself, for putting himself in danger, for thinking he was somehow immortal, god-like, able to joust with lightning and come out victorious. She digs her fingers into her thighs and squeezes hard enough to feel an edge of pain.

'I miss you,' she says quietly, and then repeats it louder into the empty room. 'I miss you, you bastard. God, I miss you.'

Liverpool Street

Fran stomps her boots with everyone else. She lifts her arms, waving them like seaweed underwater; this low and smoky darkness could almost be the bottom of the ocean. The music is so loud it inhabits her, shaking her bones, punching through vital organs, hammering against her heart. She has fulfilled her ambition to get totally wasted. The vodkas she downed earlier perform the magic trick of erasing edges, letting her escape herself to go flickering through the jostling clubbers, so that she's everywhere and nowhere at once. She loves each person dancing around her. Every. Single. Person. In. The. Universe. And it's wonderful. It's profound. There's no loss, no failure. It's like they're all part of some amazing pattern. Suddenly Fran is certain she understands what it's all about. The big question. It's simple! She laughs.

A woman steps into the space before her, grinning, sharing in her delight. She has beautiful green glitter over her cheeks, like a lizard-elf creature. She's echoing Fran's dance movements, shoulders dipping, hips swinging. The two of them close the gap between them. The woman's arms are twined around Fran's neck, chest against sticky chest, and Fran exits her body, flying through space and time, untouchable, her hair straggling down her back in ropes of fire. *Yes!* she shouts into the noise, into the stranger's neck, and it feels better than an orgasm, this hurtling straight down into oblivion.

'You all right?' Someone bangs on the cubicle door. 'There are other people out here, you know.'

Fran lifts her head from the bowl, wipes her lips with the back of her hand. Her mouth is revolting, full of bitter aftertaste. Her face itches with dried perspiration. She scrubs at her forehead with the hem of her top, then pushes herself up from the filthy floor and leans against the stall, shivering. The walls and door are covered with writing in different colours and sizes. Drawings, too. Under a picture of a pair of boobs, there's smudged black writing: *Don't hate me because I'm beautiful,* she reads, *hate me because I did your dad.* Another scrawl of graffiti just below in different handwriting says, *You are a child of the universe no less than the trees and the stars. You have a right to be here.*

Fran starts to cry. She sniffs, unravelling loo paper to blow her nose. God, look at her! She gives a short laugh. Stupid cow. Crying at something scrawled on a toilet door. She staggers out of the cubicle and splashes her face with water. A blurry stranger confronts her in the mirror: panda eyes, black holes inside a waxy mask of despair, red lipstick smeared across her mouth. She fumbles in her pocket for her mobile and squints at the time. She remembers that she has to get home before Mum. The numbers on her phone blink. She sees she has a missed call from her. Three missed calls. Damn.

*

The dark Shoreditch street smells wet, surfaces luminous with reflections. She smiles at the pretty shapes the puddles make in the road: liquid darkness streaked with rainbow colour. Her eardrums pound with the after-effects of the club's sound system. It makes everything echoey, muffled, as if she's underwater. She's trying to walk in a straight line, stick to the middle of the pavement, but time keeps jumping, and with a jolt she finds herself pressed against a grainy wall, the brick-work damp on her cheek. She begins again, one foot and then the other, staring hard at the cracks in the pavement, hoping to outwit them, the way they persist in moving beneath her. Sneaky little buggers. She giggles. The street lurches onto its side, and Fran staggers, an arm flung out. A woman steps around her, tut-tutting.

When she gets to a crossing, she leaves the kerb without looking, walking straight in front of a car. There's a screech of brakes and the blare of a horn. She presses her hands over her heart. 'Whoops.' She giggles again. Outside a corner shop, three men stand close together like a three-headed monster. She sniffs cannabis. The creature turns its heads in her direction. Fran tenses, makes an effort to stand upright. She moves on, feeling their collective gaze at her back, feeling them pinning her down with sudden feral interest.

'Oi! Love . . . need any help?'

Laughter. The horrible laughter of hunters. Even inside the haze of alcohol, she feels a prickle of danger along her spine. Mum goes on at her all the time: 'When you're drunk, you're an easy victim.' Fran's heart bangs against her ribcage: a stark drumbeat of fear. Breath hisses in and out of her lungs.

Then the moment is over; she's already forgotten the rush of adrenalin, only knows how tired she is, how her legs don't want to keep battling with the shifting pavement, how her eyes are sore and can't stay open any longer.

An Underground station rears before her, and she staggers down the steps, remembering to swipe her card, and somehow finds a platform. She pushes onto the train with a crowd of other drunks, all of them riding the night Tube with beer cans and winey breath. It's hot, the air compressed and thin. She finds a seat and collapses onto it, slumping back against the window. Her mobile vibrates in her pocket. Stops and starts again, but she doesn't hear it. Doesn't even hear the whine and squeal of the train as it hurtles through the tunnel. Her head hangs awkwardly to the side, legs splayed out in front, hands dangling at her sides. She gives a snore.

She wakes like a drowning person surfacing. Someone is shaking her shoulder. She stares up. She has no idea where she is. There's a rush of movement, sliding black windows. The world makes no sense. A man is close, too close, his face peering into hers. He frowns. 'You can't sleep here,' he says.

She tries to move her tongue. She remembers that she's on a train. But the carriage that was so full before is nearly empty. An urgent voice has started up inside her head. It tells her not to talk to strange men. It tells her she was due home hours ago. She thinks she should run away from the man, perhaps shout for help, but she knows her legs won't be up to the task, and it seems rude to scream. Exhaustion clouds her with a muddled weight of hopelessness. She remembers the words scrawled on the cubicle door.

'I . . . I have . . . a right to be here . . .' she mutters. 'Like a tree.'

He nods, as if he understands.

She blinks, giving herself up to the moment, to fate, as he encourages her onto her feet, hooks an arm around her ribs.

3

Shepherd's Bush

Cora's face is squashed into the arm of the sofa, her cheek damp with dribble. She wipes it on her sleeve. Sitting up in a rush, she runs her fingers through her hair, encountering something sticky. Crisp crumbs. The TV is still on. She clicks the remote, fumbles for her mobile, checks the time and gasps. Upstairs, she flings open Fran's door. The bed stands cold and empty. Anger is replaced by anxiety. She takes out her mobile and jabs at it, listening to the ringtone and then Fran's voice: 'Hey, leave a message. I'll get back to you. If you're lucky.'

Cora shivers. The heating's off. She stumbles into a pair of pyjama bottoms, pulls an old cardigan on top and goes back downstairs, trying Fran's number again and again; each time it goes to voicemail. She stands by the sitting-room window and opens the blind so that she can stare into the street, turning her head to look in each direction, hoping to see her errant daughter's tall frame loping into view, feet laced into her favourite boots painted with red roses and green thorns, her long titian hair a halo under the street lights.

She leaves a text message. *Where are you? Call me! BTW you weren't supposed to go out. Remember?!!!*

Another: *Call me! Just tell me you're okay!*

Another: *Where ARE you? Please let me know that you're all right. I'm worried.*

She waits at the window. No floral boots stomp into view. They live in a quiet side street. There is little passing traffic, few pedestrians, especially at this time in the morning. She gives up her post to pace the house. She thinks of calling Helena, but it's 2 a.m., and it's not really an emergency. She reassures herself that Fran goes out all the time and is often home late; on the other hand, Cora has no idea where she is or who she's with, never mind that she's not supposed to have left the house in the first place. But most of all, she has an instinct that something's not right.

She wanders around from room to room, not bothering to switch lights on, padding through shadowy spaces. In the kitchen, she opens the fridge, staring into the lit-up interior. Why is she looking at jars of pesto and a bag of carrots? She shakes her head. She makes another cup of tea and carries it around with her, not drinking it.

She tries to think what Andrew would say, and it's almost as if she can feel the weight of his large hand on her shoulder. She knows exactly what the expression on his face would be: patient, knowing, hiding his own small fear for Cora's sake, because of course he'd be worried too. He just wouldn't show it. Andrew took charge of situations – always knew what to do. A man of action. A man who'd climb a ladder in a storm to fix a leaking roof. She listens hard, as if she might catch his voice, but there's another sound. Knuckles on wood, the rap-rap of their metal knocker. Fran! She must have lost her keys.

Cora yanks the door wide. Relief flares. Her daughter is home. But she's not alone. Fran leans against a man, her head tilted back, eyes rolling. Her mouth is a smudge of red; strands of hair stick to her cheeks. Cora stares at the wreck of her child, and fear slides quick and cold through her body. Then her gaze moves to the man who's holding her up. He's taller than her lofty daughter. He has untidy wavy brown hair, skin that looks as though he spends time outdoors, and startling hazel eyes. Something about him tugs at her memory – as if she knows him from another part of her life. But nothing tangible comes to her. He must just have one of those faces.

She shakes her head. Why is he sober and alert when her child is a drunken mess? She tightens her lips with distrust. His expression seems deliberately neutral. She can't read it at all.

'What are you doing with my daughter?' she demands. 'Who are you?'

'Jacob,' he says, tightening his grip on Fran's arm and using his other hand to clasp her waist, preventing a sudden slither downwards. They look intimate leaning against each other.

Cora steps forward. 'I can manage now.' She shoves him with her elbow as she positions herself between the two of them. He lets go immediately, stepping off to the side, and Fran's entire weight descends on Cora's shoulder, unbalancing her.

How could Fran have done this to herself? What made her do it? Or who? Cora peers up at the stranger from under the drooping body of her child. Is he Fran's boyfriend, or someone she met in a club? It occurs to her that he's at least ten years older than her daughter. The realisation angers her even more. 'How dare you bring her home in this state!'

A flicker of something crosses his face – irritation? Surprise? But still he lingers, hesitating on the doorstep as Cora attempts to guide Fran inside. 'Go away!' she tells him. 'We don't need you.' But her daughter is heavy, and has no control of her limbs. She steps on Cora's bare toes in her heavy boot. Cora gasps and staggers, stopping just inside the hall, leaning Fran's weight against the little table.

'She was passed out,' the stranger says. 'Fast asleep. I found her on the night Tube.'

'What?' Cora cranes her neck round to look at him.

'A tree . . . a star . . .' Fran murmurs, and laughs.

'Here, let me help you.' The man steps across the threshold, takes Fran's arm on her other side, slides it across his shoulders, and together they get her into the sitting room. They lower her onto the sofa, where she sprawls, grinning up at them. 'Hello!' Her eyelids close. Her complexion is the colour of old Brie.

Cora straightens and pushes her hair out of her eyes. Fran smells like a brewery. She catches another tang on her breath: the whiff of vomit.

'The Tube?' she asks. 'You found her on a train?'

'The Central Line,' he says.

She gives a small gasp. 'Oh God.' She screws up her forehead. 'You . . . haven't spent the evening with her. You don't know her at all?'

He clears his throat. 'No.'

'I see.' Heat rages into her cheeks. 'Thank you . . . for rescuing her. I'm . . . I'm so sorry to have taken up your time.' She breathes slowly, trying to prevent the oven of her body switching into overdrive.

'No.' He holds up a hand. 'No need.'

'I'm Cora,' she says, standing up straighter. 'And this is my daughter. Fran. Francesca. She . . . she's not always like this.'

She gestures towards her child lolling with mouth agape and eyeliner smeared across her cheeks, and becomes aware of her own baggy PJ bottoms, the saggy grey cardigan drooping around her thighs. She puts a hand up to her hair and finds more greasy remains of crisp crumbs inside the tangles.

'Of course not.' His forehead is crinkling earnestly. 'She's young. It's Saturday night.'

'Yes,' Cora says, gratefully.

'Well.' He nods, his movements slow as he takes a step backwards and turns. 'Goodnight.'

And just like that, Cora thinks, Fran's been got out of yet another scrape. This time by a stranger – someone she won't even remember tomorrow morning, let alone thank.

'Wait!'

He turns back at the threshold, expectant.

'Um.' She swallows. 'I'd like Fran to thank you herself.'

He glances at the comatose figure on the sofa, then turns to Cora with a puzzled eyebrow raised.

'I don't mean now,' Cora says quickly. 'I mean … if it's not an imposition, could you come back? Maybe tomorrow?' He doesn't reply, so she adds, 'I'd … I'd like her to meet you when she's sober, to thank you. She should, I think.' She twists her hands together. 'It's important to take responsibility for your actions, isn't it?'

He gives a small, sorrowful shake of his head. 'It's not necessary, honestly.'

'No.' She's cringing inside. 'Of course not.'

Why on earth would he want to go out of his way twice for a complete stranger? What was she thinking? He's silent, a small crease between his eyebrows. Probably trying to come up with a tactful way of refusing. 'I'm sorry,' she hurries on, flustered, hoping she's not as red as she feels. 'Forget I said anything. I don't know why I asked . . . of course you can't—'

'No,' he interrupts her, 'it's okay. If you'd like me to . . .' He gives her a questioning look. 'I live . . . well, on the same line, so yeah, I could call in tomorrow. No problem. What time?'

His kindness makes her feel like crying. She swallows hard. 'Four o'clock? For tea?'

'Tea?' He smiles. 'That sounds very civilised. I'll see you then.' He glances at Fran. 'Hope she feels better in the morning. Lots of water, I think.'

'Oh, I hope she won't feel better,' Cora says grimly. 'She certainly doesn't deserve to.'

He laughs then, his face widening into an extravagant smile, so broad it's almost too big for his face, his eyes narrowing in creases. The sound comes from his belly. It makes her smile too.

Then he's gone. Quiet as a cat, she thinks. The Good Samaritan. It's only then that she realises where she's seen him before. He's the man she noticed earlier in the evening, lost in his novel on the Central Line.

Shepherd's Bush

Fran slumps at the kitchen table, spooning sugary cereal into her mouth, interspersed with sips of strong sweet tea. She woke at noon with a thick head and a raging thirst, and could barely organise her limbs to stumble down the stairs to make break-fast. She hasn't seen Mum yet, thank God. Her mother doesn't ever get drunk, so how can she understand a hangover?

She wonders how Cora's date went last night. She can't imagine her mother flirting – she's so controlled all the time. It's a mystery how she's managed without sex for so long. No wonder she's uptight. Sex is a cure for lots of things, Fran has discovered, but not hangovers. She's already taken the last of the aspirin from the bathroom medicine cabinet, but the hammering inside her skull hasn't stopped. She's rubbing her forehead with both hands as Cora walks into the kitchen, neat and bright in jeans and a white shirt.

'You're up,' she says. 'We need to talk.' She pauses to draw a breath. 'You're not a teenager any more, Fran. At your age

I'd met your dad and we were living together. You know you weren't even supposed to go out.' She grimaces. 'I thought I could trust you, that . . . that you were mature enough to understand what you'd done.' Her voice rises. 'The car's still at the garage, for heaven's sake.'

Fran drops her head onto her chest, waiting for the lecture to wash over her. She's pretty certain the date with the architect was a failure, judging from her mother's buttoned-up body language.

'Are you listening?' Cora asks.

Fran sighs. 'Look, I'm sorry, okay? I said I was sorry about the car, too. It was an accident. I didn't mean to do it.'

'But you weren't just drunk last night – you were paralytic.' Cora's voice wavers and drops. 'I don't understand why you'd do that to yourself. It's terrifying to think that you were walking around London in that state. Anything could have happened.'

'But it didn't. Right?'

Cora stares at her with an odd expression on her face. 'You don't remember?'

'What?' A bolt of fear unleashes a memory of a man standing close, his fingers on her waist. She swallows, touching her breasts and arms as if checking for evidence. Did some creep molest her last night? Her look of puzzlement seems to be the answer Cora needs.

'A stranger found you on the Tube,' she says, more gently. 'You were asleep. He brought you home.'

Fran blinks. Her memory stirs again. This time she can make out a man's face. But she can't recall precise features, just a blur of eyes, a shine of teeth. She shifts on the chair, squeezing her forehead into a concertina of concentration, but nothing emerges, nothing but fragments that seem more like a dream:

an uncoiling of dark, wet streets; the stranger's arm around her waist, an unfamiliar perfume. Male, spicy, warm.

'So . . . this man . . . we weren't . . . together?'

Cora shakes her head. 'I misunderstood at first. Thought it was his fault you were in that state.' She makes a little puffing noise of exasperation. 'But he wasn't. He just brought you home.'

Fran breathes a sigh of relief.

'Anyway, he's coming here at four,' Cora's saying. 'So you need to have a shower and put on some clean clothes. If you can find any in your bedroom.'

'What?' Fran pushes her half-finished cereal away. 'He's coming here?'

'Yes. For tea. So you can say thank you.'

'No way!'

'Yes way.'

'That's so embarrassing . . . Jesus, Mum, what were you thinking?'

'It's because of his kindness that you're safe. If he'd left you there, God knows what might have happened . . . or if he'd been a different kind of man, someone predatory . . .' Cora closes her eyes briefly and holds up her hand as Fran begins to speak. 'This isn't negotiable, so don't waste your breath. Be ready at four. Actually, make that quarter to. And be polite.'

'You're so over the top. I'm not a child. It's a stupid idea.'

Cora raises one eyebrow.

'Bitch,' Fran hisses under her breath.

As she watches her mother leave the kitchen, she wants to run after her yelling, 'I didn't mean it! I'm sorry!' Only last night, she was pulling tiny hairs out of Cora's eyebrows and discussing what colour lipstick she should wear.

She clatters her dirty cup and bowl into the dishwasher and

leaves the reproachful kitchen. Closing her bedroom door, she shuts herself into her own space. Her taste and Cora's are completely different – her mother favours pale, neutral colours, stripped wooden floors, a spill of green plants in every corner, faded rugs, ornaments in natural textures. If it was up to Fran, she'd have all the rooms in the house decked out in different bold shades, the sofa would be covered in rich velvet with plump tasselled cushions, and vintage chandeliers would glitter from the ceilings. As it is, she's had to settle for painting her room deep pink. Her bed is draped with Indian silks.

All around her are the mantras she's written out in bright felt pen: *I AM STRONG. I AM BEAUTIFUL. I AM ENOUGH*, stuck to her mirror. *MY CURRENT SITUATION IS NOT MY PERMANENT DESTINATION*, right above her bed. *I HAVE MANAGED THIS BEFORE. I CAN MANAGE IT AGAIN*, inside her wardrobe door. *I DESERVE TO BE HAPPY AND I SHALL BE HAPPY* is taped to the inside of her bedroom door.

Her crystals are arranged on her dressing table: amethyst for anxiety, rose quartz for love, and her favourite black obsidian to use as a shield against negative energy and to help her find her true sense of self. She is trying her best. Sometimes she wonders if Dad is watching her – and she wants to tell him, *Look, see, even without you here, I haven't given up. I still want to make you proud.*

The problem is, she can't erase a sense of dread that she's somehow missed the moment, missed the chance of getting her acting career off the ground, that even at her age, she's too late. Worse, that she's just not good enough. The thought makes her feel bruised and dark – makes her snap and snarl at everyone, especially Cora and Luke.

When she left drama college, she was electric with

anticipation, dreaming of roles in the West End. She had her headshots ready. She even made her own website. She got an agent. A decent one. But the promised starring roles never materialised. The decent agent dropped her. Another, less impressive, took her on. There was a hair advert. A lot of promo jobs. She knows how to work a penguin suit.

She squeezes her eyes shut against the midday glare. She can't give up. She can't. Dad believed in her. She takes her pack of well-worn tarot cards and deals herself five, turning them over slowly. She catches her breath as the Wheel of Fortune reveals itself, then she turns over the Fool and sighs with relief. The Fool means a new beginning, and that's exactly what she needs. The dark, bruising cloud in her head begins to shift and lighten. She flips the last card, and gets the Lovers. Right on cue, her phone beeps in her pocket. She glances at the screen. *Later?* Hugo.

She stares at the one-word message. When Fran first met Hugo, she thought he must be gay. Standing among the throng of his admirers at a party, she was thrilled by his bored belittling of everything and everyone. He seemed wildly sophisticated. But then it turned out he liked women too, and she fell into bed with him gratefully, feeling singled out as special. He's like a cat with his slinky elegance, his unpredictability. He never commits the crime of being boring.

She focuses on her phone, rereading his message as if it might contain clues, then she types back, *Sure*, adds a devil's face, deletes it and puts a kiss. Deletes that too. She types, *What time?* But that makes her look needy, so she ends up just sending *Sure*.

After a shower, she FaceTimes her friend Alesha, to complain about her ridiculous punishment and to joke about the kind of man her 'rescuer' will turn out to be. But Alesha is in the middle of having her weave done and isn't in a sympathetic mood. In fact, she's upset that Fran went dancing without her. 'Going out on your own and getting trashed isn't clever, Fran. So now you've just got to suck it up – you brought this on yourself. Ouch!' She winces in genuine pain. Her image snaps off.

Luke, locked in his bedroom, his attention fixed on his laptop screen, is also unsympathetic. 'It's no big deal,' he says, and then covers his ears with his noise-cancelling headphones. He's not required to come down to meet the stranger. 'Don't be silly,' Cora said, when Fran complained he was getting preferential treatment. 'This has nothing to do with him. And I don't want to break his concentration,' she added. 'He's studying hard. Exams start in a couple of months.'

So it's Fran and her mother waiting in the living room, hanging about for some boring do-gooder so that she can grovel in front of him until she's been thoroughly humiliated. Christ. She only got pissed. It's not a fucking crime. The only good thing to come out of this is the batch of Cora's home-made biscuits arranged on a plate on the coffee table, warm from the oven.

Fran checks her mobile. Three minutes past. 'He's probably not even going to turn up,' she says. 'I mean, why would he?' She picks up an oatmeal and raisin cookie and stuffs most of it into her mouth. Just then, the doorbell rings.

Cora shoots Francesca a look that says *behave* as she gets up and goes into the hall. Fran, still chewing, pushes the rest of the cookie in, filling her mouth with delicious buttery sweetness. Her cheeks bulge.

There's a muffled sound of polite greeting, and Cora reappears, leading the way into the room like a fussy parent.

A man follows her. Fran stares. She wasn't expecting him to be good-looking. He stands in a wash of sunlight, calm and slim-hipped in dark jeans and a well-worn jumper, and looks at her with eyes that seem to catch the light and throw it back. She chews quickly, but masticated oatmeal is coating her teeth, obstructing her tongue. She works her jaws desperately.

'Hi,' he says, stepping forward with hand outstretched. 'I'm Jacob.'

She gulps, forcing the remains down her throat, and stands up, brushing crumbs from her lap. At the feel of his fingers, firm around her own sticky ones, she blurts out, 'Sorry. About last night. Thanks for bringing me home.'

On the edge of her consciousness, she's aware of her mother's twitch of surprise, her relieved expression, but Fran is dizzy with the sudden flip-flop of her heart as she looks at Jacob. The man who rescued her. And suddenly she understands that this is meant to be. She's lost inside the thunder roaring in her chest as she falls – not just any old fall, but a terrifying, exhilarating tumble off the edge of the world – all before he's said more than two words to her. And she's panicking like crazy because she doesn't know if he feels it too, this smiling man standing in their living room, negating all embarrassment with one casual shrug.

Shepherd's Bush

'You said you live close by?' Cora folds her feet under her, sitting cross-legged on her chair.

Jacob puts his empty cup on the coffee table, and makes a non-committal noise. 'Not exactly as the crow flies. Bethnal Green.'

'Bethnal Green ... but that's the other side of town!' Cora widens her eyes.

He tilts his head. 'It's on the same line, though. Just enough time to read a couple of chapters of my book.'

'Well, the least I can do is feed you now you're here. Biscuit?'

Jacob grins and accepts a cookie. Their hands brush, and she feels the touch of his skin as a shock. He takes a bite. 'These are delicious,' he says, brandishing it. 'London's so diverse, isn't it? Bethnal Green and Shepherd's Bush are like different cities. Yet all these "villages" add up to one huge metropolis.'

'Yes,' Cora smiles, 'I always think that too. It's one of the things I love about London.' She leans forward. 'Do you live anywhere near the canal?'

'You could say that,' he says with a wry grin. 'I'm in one of the narrowboats.'

'A *boat?*' Fran interjects, sitting forward in her chair.

He smiles and nods.

Cora thinks that he doesn't look like the kind of person who lives in a narrowboat, while realising that she has no idea what she means by that. If anyone had asked her, she would have presumed he lived in a bachelor flat – something modern and airy. But, she checks herself, it could just as easily be a rambling mansion inhabited by a wife and ten children. She tries to stop herself looking at his finger to see if he wears a ring.

'What's it like living there?' she asks.

He crosses one ankle over the other knee. She sees a flash of mulberry-coloured sock. 'I never fail to appreciate being surrounded by nature in the middle of a city. And,' he raises an eyebrow humorously, 'it makes a good talking point.'

Cora thought Fran would start asking questions, but she's fiddling with the ends of her hair, staring into her lap. When she was little, she loved to show off in front of people, leaping up to do impromptu dances. Andrew encouraged her, making a fuss, clapping.

Cora and Jacob are the ones keeping the conversation afloat; they mention the weather (warming into spring at last) and the gas works that seem to be turning every street into a building site. Fran isn't contributing. But what's important, Cora thinks, is her initial reaction, her remorse and gratitude. Meeting Jacob has had exactly the effect on her daughter she hoped it would. She had last-minute doubts – worrying that dragging him back had been selfish, anxious that Fran might behave badly – but

Jacob seems content to sit in the front room, eating a biscuit and sipping his tea. And Fran – her sulky, difficult daughter – is transformed, contrite. She actually blushes when she looks directly at Jacob. No doubt she's embarrassed, although Jacob is doing everything he can to make her comfortable. He hasn't once mentioned her intoxicated state. And he's funny, with the kind of deadpan humour that's delivered without pause, taking Cora by surprise. He listens, too. Which she considers the most attractive thing in the world.

She studies him while he's turned towards Fran. He has a strong face, dominated in profile by a generous nose. In fact, all his features are generous, including his long hazel eyes with heavy lashes and plump lids, framed by mobile eyebrows that swoop and crinkle, lending drama to his expressions. Realising that she's staring, she blinks and looks away.

'That postcard,' he says suddenly, peering intently at a card propped on the mantelpiece. 'Is it from the Pre-Raphaelite exhibition at the V&A?' He smiles. 'I took my mother to see it. It was good, wasn't it?'

Cora's eyes slide towards the image of the Lady of Shalott floating down the river in a barge, romantic and tragic in her white dress.

'Oh yes,' she says, and glances at her daughter. 'You came with me, Fran, do you remember? And we laughed at how much you look like the heroines in the paintings.'

'Mum,' Fran mutters, scowling.

'Yes.' Jacob nods. 'I can see it.'

Fran has turned puce and is staring at her DMs. But a secret smile curls the edges of her lips.

'So what do you do, Jacob?' Cora asks quickly, changing the subject so that Fran can recover.

'Funnily enough,' he says, 'I work for Transport for London.'

'Were you working, then, when you found Fran on the Tube?'

'No,' he says. 'I was just a regular passenger. What about you? What's your line of work?'

'I'm in TV. An editor.'

He nods, opening his mouth as if to ask another question, but his gaze has fallen on the framed photo of Andrew on the sideboard. 'My husband,' Cora says, adding quickly, 'My late husband.'

Jacob starts. 'I'm sorry.'

'He died six years ago,' Cora adds, hoping to make him feel better. She touches her wedding band. She can't bring herself to take it off.

She braces herself, but there's none of the usual hesitant but hungry curiosity as to how Andrew died – Jacob sits in silence, contemplating Andrew's beaming face with a thoughtful expression. It's not exactly an uncomfortable silence, only Cora isn't sure how to break it. She would like to ask him what he was reading on the Tube, but then she'd have to admit she'd noticed him, and that might seem odd. Particularly as she hasn't mentioned it before.

'Where were you going,' Fran blurts out, 'when you found me?'

Jacob's head jerks up. For the first time, Cora sees a flicker of discomfort cross his face. 'I'd been ... visiting ... uh, a friend.' He rubs his nose.

He seems fascinated by the mantelpiece again, taking in the pale feathers arranged in the vintage green glass medicine bottle, the ammonites Cora collected from the beach on a visit to Lyme Regis, framed photos of the kids. She imagines that he's probably wondering how he can politely extricate himself. She's interested to know where he stands on Brexit, although she's sick of that subject. Lots of other questions swirl around her mind too: who his favourite film directors are, whether he has any siblings, what his job actually entails. But there are limits to what you can ask a complete stranger who's doing you a favour, especially one you'll never see again. She doesn't want to be nosy. She shifts on her knees, leaning forward. 'Well,' she says. 'It was so kind of you to come back.' She gives Fran a look. 'Wasn't it?'

'Yeah.' Fran clears her throat and stares at the floor.

He takes the cue and gets to his feet. 'No problem. It was worth it,' he says, eyes sparkling, 'for the biscuits alone.'

Cora unfolds her legs and stands up, running her palms over her jeans. Jacob remains almost as mysterious as he was when he turned up on the doorstep as Fran's saviour. Strange, she thinks, this small crossing of their lives. A tiny spark of chance bringing the three of them together for this brief moment.

'Thanks again,' she says, indicating that he should follow her to the door.

'Bye,' Fran croaks.

Then he's in the street, and with one quick wave, he's gone. Cora shuts the door. Okay, she thinks, breathing out. That's that.

'So,' she says, going back into the living room, 'wasn't so bad, was it? And he was lovely about the whole thing—'

She stops abruptly. The space is empty. There's just a whiff of Coco Mademoiselle, a scattering of crumbs on Fran's chair. Shaking her head, Cora plumps up the pillows on the sofa, sweeps the crumbs into her palm.

'Fran?' she calls from the bottom of the stairs. 'Francesca?'

No answer. She puts the empty plate and cups in the kitchen and goes up, tapping on Fran's door with her knuckles before entering. Fran is sprawled on her bed, talking on her mobile. She stops mid sentence and frowns at her mother. 'Sorry, Lesh,' she mutters into the phone. 'Just a minute ... Mum, do you want something?' She raises one brow questioningly.

'No. Nothing,' Cora says, backing out of the room.

As she shuts the door, she hears Fran laugh.

Cora feels a tug of disappointment. She was curious to know how it made Fran feel to see her Good Samaritan face to face. Wasn't she curious about his life, the mysterious 'friend' he was visiting so late at night? She sighs. Fran's obviously got more important things to discuss with Alesha. She hears the muffled sound of her daughter's voice through the closed door as she moves away down the stairs.

By Fran's age, all of Cora's contemporaries had moved into flat shares, or had been paying instalments towards their first mortgage, but it seems to be almost normal nowadays for young adults to remain in their parents' homes; Cora can see that the world is harder than it was for her generation, but how can Fran grow up when she never takes responsibility for anything?

As she gets ingredients out of the fridge for supper, she can't stop thinking about Jacob. Something about him makes her guess that he had a fulfilled, happy childhood. She imagines noisy siblings, contented parents, a friendly house welcoming to relatives and friends. Maybe that's where his quiet confidence comes from, his lack of mansplaining, no need to prove himself. She stops chopping celery and touches her skin in the place where his hand brushed hers, remembering the sudden tingle. Even now, her cheeks flush, her eyes widening. Silly. She smiles at herself, and moves the knife again. She needs to get out more. Meeting Jacob has reminded her that there's another world beyond her own small routine. She begins to hum.

6

Marble Arch

Before her mother interrupted, Fran was on a joyful roll: a breathless stream of urgent words down the phone, laughing about the unexpectedness of it, explaining the shock of her feelings to Alesha, exactly how amazing Jacob was, floating inside that buoyant rush of hope that only happens at the beginning of something wonderful.

Then Alesha's voice dropped. 'Tall, dark and handsome. Sounds like he's the typical heart-throb type.'

'I admit he's totally fucking gorgeous.' Fran rolls onto her stomach on the bed, keeping the mobile pressed to her ear. 'Taller than me, too, which makes a nice change. But he's not conventional-looking. He has a big nose. Kind of noble, like that guy in *The Pianist*? What's his name?'

'Adrien Brody?'

'That's him. Maybe crossed with Bradley Cooper. Anyway, the point is that Jacob's intelligent. Confident. A real grown-up. But meeting him with Mum there put me off. I couldn't get my shit together. I never even got his number,' she wails.

'He could be a player,' Alesha says. 'Good-looking, affluent. Alpha male.'

'Stop being so judgy. You haven't even met him.' Fran is annoyed. 'He's not some arrogant twenty-something. He's in his thirties. Maybe late thirties.'

Alesha hisses, 'Nooooo – he's too old, Fran. And what's wrong with him, anyway, if he's still single at his age? He's probably got a wife tucked away somewhere.'

'Uh-uh. No ring on his finger,' Fran says triumphantly. 'And trust me, there's nothing wrong with him.'

'I'm just looking out for you, Fran. Older men. They're trouble.'

'What's your problem? Why can't you be happy for me?' Fran says, feeling let down by Alesha in a way she hasn't experienced before. Maybe she's jealous? They often come at things from different perspectives: Lesh is a balanced Libra, whereas Fran is a dreamy Pisces. They're not really compatible, not on paper. 'Anyway, in case you forgot, I don't even know his surname. All I know is that he lives in Bethnal Green.' Her voice is sulky and cross. 'So I'll never see him again.'

'Just as well,' Alesha says. 'Aren't you seeing that other guy – the one in Marble Arch? Although, to be fair, I've never liked the sound of him.'

'Hmm.' Fran rolls onto her back, remembering Jacob's eyes – not just their brilliant hazel, but how kind and steady they were one minute, and then a spark of something else, something more dangerous, more exciting. Did he like her? She couldn't tell. She could normally tell straight away if there was sexual chemistry, but Jacob didn't give away a thing – keeping up a polite facade, sipping his tea and smiling in the right places. Well, Fran supposed he had to really, in front of Cora.

Her phone buzzes. 'Got to go, Lesh,' she says, sitting up. 'Hugo's trying to get hold of me.'

She stares at her screen. *Come over now.*

She licks her lips, her mouth dry. How much has changed in the last hour. She just wants to lie on her bed and think about Jacob, and how he basically said she looked like a Pre-Raphaelite painting. It occurs to her now that the Lovers card wasn't about Hugo at all. It was predicting Jacob. If only she could relive the moments when he was sitting opposite her; but this time she'd be witty and charming, and he'd find her irresistible; this time she'd get his number. She sighs. Hugo doesn't like to be kept waiting. She pushes her feet onto the floor, reaching for her wardrobe, wondering what to wear.

Walking from Marble Arch station, Fran sees a magpie. It hops on the pavement, turning its head to look at her with a crafty eye. One for sorrow, she thinks, and salutes quickly, whispering words of greeting. The bird flies off with a flurry of squawking towards Hyde Park.

'Hey,' says Hugo, pulling her inside the flat. 'Want a drink?'

She follows his slim hips as he leads her along the corridor into a white, stripped-back kitchen, so clinical that it could be an operating theatre. Knives, gleaming and sword-sharp, are arranged in size order on a magnetic strip, evidence that this could after all be a space for preparing a meal – or a body. Everything else is hidden behind doors without handles.

Electronic music pulses in surround sound. Hugo loves his techno classics – it's like walking into a club in Ibiza.

'Margarita?' He pushes a heavy glass across the counter towards her.

She picks it up and licks salt crystals from the rim.

'Drink up,' he says, nodding at her. 'You look like a poor imitation of yourself. All droopy around the mouth.' He sniffs. 'You know I expect you to sing for your supper, sweetheart.'

It's strange how the endearment, one of Hugo's favourites, always sounds like a threat. 'Oh, piss off.' She sips bitter liquid, screwing up her face. 'Anyway, you never feed me. Not actual food.'

'Ah,' he says softly. 'There she is.'

And despite herself, she feels pleasure leap in her belly.

She never knows what she'll find when she comes over – sometimes there are other people, different and yet the same, hanging around the flat, snorting coke and languishing on Hugo's long leather sofas. Usually she hopes that it will just be the two of them – that she'll be the chosen one again. But today she wishes there was a crowd of strangers to hide amongst.

He keeps his clothes on while he undresses her, sliding her knickers down. 'Your legs go on for ever,' he murmurs. 'You really turn me on . . . you're an Amazonian warrior. Christ, you could crush my head between your thighs.' She used to worry that her size would count against her in getting roles, but Tilda Swinton and Uma Thurman haven't let it hold them back. So what *is* the problem? Why is she finding it so hard to get a decent part? As Hugo clasps her hips and pulls her towards him, she remembers her first ever audition, how they cut her off after only four lines: the director's 'next' a punch in her guts, Chekov's Nina popping like a balloon. She was so sure that that was the role that would propel her into stardom.

After she'd recovered from the shock of her failure, she convinced herself that it had merely been a test, a humbling precursor before her certain eventual triumph. That was two years ago.

'Turn over,' Hugo tells her.

She flips onto her belly, her fingers reaching for the sheets, bracing herself. There's nowhere to hide. Hugo likes to keep the light on, and she stares into the folds of the silk pillow, stares at her own hands, noticing every flaw. Stupid. Stupid. How could she ever have let herself believe that she was better, that she was different, special? Because she has to, a voice in her head counters, because there's nothing else. It can't be too late. She's only twenty-three. And she's beautiful, she knows she is. All that beauty – it has to be for something. She just needs to try harder.

She squeezes her eyes tight, gasping as Hugo grabs her hair, yanking her head back. And behind her lids, a thousand stars.

Oxford Circus

On Monday, Cora takes the Tube to Oxford Circus. It's a brisk, gleaming spring day, and she is filled with a bright sense of purpose as she orders a takeaway cappuccino in her reusable cup, smiling at the man behind the till in the Italian café. As she passes Liberty, glass doors slide open and she breathes in the jumble of scents wafting from the perfumery department. Hurrying down Carnaby Street, she can't help glancing into a boutique window, checking her mirrored self, neat in cropped narrow trousers and short jacket, feet laced into practical stylish white plimsolls. She touches her hair, straightens the collar of her shirt. The TV business seems to be run by children – she's older by ten or even twenty years than most of her contemporaries. It's not vanity that makes her choose her clothes with care, more a nagging insecurity. She turns down a narrow passage leading to the post production house. Tapping in the code, she angles her shoulder against the door and pushes inside the pale expanse of the reception area. A few people sit on white sofas, looking at their phones or chatting in low voices. The receptionist gives her a smile and nods at the basket of fruit on the desk. 'Peaches today,' she says.

'Thanks.' Cora chooses one, rosy and firm, and drops it into her bag.

In the windowless suite, she puts her coffee on her desk, shrugs off her jacket and switches on three screens. She brings up the rushes from yesterday, featuring the all-important final reveal, and settles into her chair. The door swishes open, and edit producer Lotte comes in, a bottle of water in hand. She sits at her own desk behind Cora's and takes a swig. 'My head,' she moans, 'Sunday-night pub quiz turned out to be a heavy one – who would have thought?' She rubs her nose. 'It's the competition. Really gets to me. I was downing lagers without even noticing.'

Cora smiles. 'I hate quizzes. Far too nerve-racking.'

'That's because you're competitive,' Lotte says. 'Same as me.'

'Shall we begin?' Cora moves her mouse and clicks open a sequence of a woman crying in a red dress.

'Hmm.' Lotte crosses her legs, hitching up her baggy jeans. 'How was your weekend, by the way?'

'Oh, fine,' Cora says. 'Actually, a bit weird.'

Lotte sips her water, waiting.

'This guy brought my daughter home on Saturday night.' Cora swivels around in her chair. 'No. Not like that.' She shakes her head. 'He'd found her passed out drunk on the night Tube.' She shrugs her shoulders. 'You know Fran can be . . . a bit wild sometimes. And, well, he was a Good Samaritan. Got her home safe.'

'Reassuring to know there are still decent people in the world.'

'Yeah. I asked him to come back the next day, so Fran could

thank him. I suppose I knew it would be embarrassing for her, but I wanted her to confront her actions – to take some kind of responsibility.'

'And he came?' Lotte raises her eyebrows.

Cora nods. 'It was . . .'

'Above and beyond the call of duty?' Lotte laughs. 'He must have liked you.'

Startled, Cora spills a splash of coffee on her hand. She licks it off. 'What?'

'I mean, Good Samaritan or not – to come back? That's a potentially embarrassing situation for him – or just a pain in the arse. He must have had another reason. Not purely altruistic?'

Cora is quiet. 'But he wouldn't be interested in me . . . I'm too old, for a start.'

'Don't be ridiculous, Cora – it's not the number that matters, it's how you look and behave that counts. And you're youthful. Attractive.' Lotte pauses. 'How old was he, anyway?'

'Not sure.' Cora fiddles with her wedding ring, twisting it around. 'Mid to late thirties, maybe?'

'I'd put money down that he fancies you.'

'Lotte! He was just a nice person. It was a one-off. A rare moment when people's lives intersect, before they go back into their separate grooves.'

'Separate grooves, huh?' Lotte scratches her head. 'But you know there's no such thing as just a nice person, right? People are more complicated than that.'

Cora glances at the clock on the wall. 'Maybe. But we have a rough cut to finish. And—'

'Yeah. I know. Let's run the bit where they all come out of the dressing room and we get the tears.'

*

41

They've finished the cut and called it a day. The film's working, tempo just right, moments of humour, plenty of emotion in the final reveal. They'll be starting the fine cut tomorrow. Cora runs to Poland Street to pick up a pair of shoes she's had re-heeled, then heads back towards the Tube station. There's hardly any evidence of the old seedy Soho left. Crossing Marshall Street, where Cranks used to be, she has a lurch of nostalgia for the Soho she knew when she had her first job in the film business.

She joins the crowd gathered at the entrance of Oxford Street station, shuffling down the grimy stairs into the dirty, busy ticket hall; then she's through the barrier, onto the escalator. Normally she hurries down the moving steps, impatient to get home. But today, her conversation with Lotte about Jacob has left her reflective. She's gazing at the people around her without really seeing them, until a profile snags her vision. She refocuses. Her body is suddenly hot. That nose is unmistakable. Jacob is standing on the next escalator. He's travelling in the same direction as her. If he turns his head, he will see her. She has an instinct to duck down, to hide. Should she call his name? If she doesn't, what if he catches sight of her and thinks she's being rude by ignoring him – or worse, scurries away, hoping she hasn't seen him? Lotte's voice sounds in her head: *He must have liked you.*

Nonsense, she tells herself. Ridiculous. But her heart is loud in her ears. The escalator reaches the bottom. When she looks up, Jacob isn't there. Instead, there's an impatient crowd blocking the entrance to the platforms. She can't get through. People push her from behind, muttering. The wall of bodies is impenetrable.

Due to an earlier incident, there is no service on the Central

Line. The tannoy system crackles. *All Central Line trains are cancelled. Use an alternative route.*

Cora sighs, holding her bag tight to her side, wondering what to do.

'Probably someone on the tracks,' a girl says to her friend, who shudders theatrically. 'Talk about picking your time,' the first girl says. 'Sodding rush hour!'

There's no other route she can use. Shepherd's Bush can only be accessed by the Central Line. Some people are fighting their way out towards the exit, others attempting to push through to other lines. Claustrophobia takes her by the throat. She can't see Jacob among the throng of strangers. Maybe it wasn't him after all. Someone steps on her foot. She'll find a bus – or buses; maybe she'll have to take two.

She pushes onto the escalator, walking up, squeezing past people, needing to breathe the fumes of Oxford Street, to feel daylight on her face, hear the rumble of the outside world.

'Cora?' A voice comes from behind her. 'Cora?'

She pauses, causing a traffic jam of irritated people. She moves to the right, holds on to the handrail and looks round.

'It *is* you!' Jacob squeezes onto the step below her, grinning, breathless. He sounds delighted. 'Is this your usual station?'

She's startled by the nearness of him. She's standing above him, his face just inches from her shoulder. She can see the hairs in his eyebrows. The flecks of gold in his irises. She nods.

'I had a meeting nearby,' he continues.

They're in the ticket hall. Cora turns to face him, looking up. To cover her uncertainty, she tries for humour. 'There seems to be a pattern here involving you and the Central Line!'

He looks thoughtful. 'I do spend *some* of my time above ground.'

Cora laughs, tension expelled. They're standing in a horde of impatient people. She clears her throat. 'So . . . I think I'm going to find a bus . . .'

He closes his eyes for a moment. 'Going back to Shepherd's Bush? I'm pretty certain you'll need the 94.'

'How on earth do you know that?'

'I have the inner London bus timetable by heart,' he says. 'Doesn't everyone?' He raises an eyebrow playfully.

Cora tilts her head, remembering that he said he worked for TFL. 'Are you a bus driver, then?' She wonders if she's been rude.

'No,' he says mildly. 'I sit behind a desk, not a wheel.'

'Oh,' she says, not really understanding. But now is not the time for polite discussion. 'I should go . . .'

Shaking his hand seems too formal. She hesitates for a moment, poised to walk away.

'Cora . . . do you want to get a drink?' he says quickly. 'If you're not in a hurry?'

'Sorry?' She wonders if she's misheard.

He gestures towards the exit. 'It's going to be even more hectic on the street than usual – we could wait it out for an hour in a bar, if you like?'

'Thanks, but I don't actually—'

Someone's bag slams into her hip, hard and heavy, as if they've swung a sack of rocks at her.

'Okay. Just a quick one,' she gasps. 'Somewhere close.'

He's already moving towards the exit. 'Follow me.'

Tottenham Court Road

Every morning, Fran does her voice exercises, opening her throat and sounding out vowels, then a series of physical stretches. The session ends by practising a couple of her monologues. One that she never rehearses any more is Chekhov's Nina. Since that first audition, she's become superstitious about it, remembering Nina's lines: *he laughed at all my dreams, then little by little, I stopped believing too.* It feels like a curse now, a prediction.

This morning, she's waiting in a small room with a group of about ten other girls, all trying out for a fringe production in a pub; no pay for the actors, just the chance to notch up experience. *I am strong. I am beautiful. I am enough,* she tells herself, as she sits and stares into the middle distance. *I have managed this before. I can manage it again.* The play is *The House of Bernarda Alba,* and Fran is up for Amelia, a sister with fewer lines than the others.

Her phone bleeps. *Go for it!*

Damn. She shouldn't have told anyone where she was going – not even Lesh. Going to auditions and go-sees used to make her feel excited, professional, hopeful. Now she can imagine what it's like to be a farm animal, herded into the sale ring, at the mercy of strangers, with no power over her own future. At her last callback, for a low-fat yoghurt advert, she stood alone on the taped X on the floor while three people on a sofa stared at her from behind their laptops. 'Can you be more sexy?' the director asked, as she delivered the line *My waist will thank me* over and over into the blank eye of the camera. 'Don't shrug your shoulders,' he said in a bored voice. 'Try to look empowered. Warm. Wholesome.' She could tell he thought she was useless. But she smiled into the camera until her cheeks ached. She didn't get the job.

She's sick of being the girl in the corner whispering 'Pick me, pick me.' It makes her feel desperate and insignificant. Invisible. And it's not easy to make a red-haired girl of five foot ten with big bones feel invisible. But this business has succeeded.

'Francesca Pollen?'

She walks into an airless, windowless rehearsal room, and glances at the hunched figures gathered around a small table littered with takeaway coffees and sandwich wrappers. None of them bothers to introduce themselves; a young man in spectacles nods at her to begin.

Fran takes up her position, puts her shoulders back, raises her chin. She's done her research; not just read the play, but googled Franco's Spain. She understands that the play is a metaphor for the repressive fascist regime. As she stares at the unsmiling, expectant faces behind the table, they slide further and further away from her, becoming tiny blobs at the end of a tunnel, distant planets seen through a telescope. A sense of dread has invaded her – an icy darkness creeping, creeping along her limbs. She clears her throat, but there's no saliva in her mouth. Her lips are dry as dead leaves.

'Do you need a prompt?' a voice says.

She shakes her head. The faces have snapped back into focus, but the lines inside her skull are stuck; she can't get them out. She knows she won't get the part. That's it. The problem. She understands with a calm and certain clarity that there's no point in trying. Another girl is already destined to play Amelia. Not her – not Fran. Her chest is squeezed tight around her lungs, and she can't breathe, can't move. She's been through this process so many times, been scrutinised and whispered about, prodded and poked, and every time it ends in failure.

'Fuck this,' she mutters.

None of them speaks as she turns and walks out of the dingy space, through the door, past the other actors sitting waiting their turn, expressions closed in concentration as they do their breathing exercises, go over their lines, lips moving quietly. Nobody looks up as she passes.

She gets home before Mum and Luke. In her room, she strips off her clothes, trampling them into tangled piles, and pulls on a pair of old leggings and a faded band T-shirt. In the bathroom, she fills the sink with cold water and plunges her face into it, holding her breath for as long as she can, letting out a silent, lung-clenching scream. She surfaces, gasping, and scrubs her face with a stringy massage mitt. Then she stares at herself in the mirror – at her wet, raw skin and big, blank eyes.

There was a time when she was happy; a time before it all went wrong.

Riding her bicycle in their garden in Suffolk as a child, pom-poms dangling from silver handlebars. She got the hang of it

47

quickly, with Dad running behind, holding on to the saddle, his breath in her ears, before he gave a push and fell behind. 'Keep going! That's it, angel!'

She was riding fast across the lawn, the wind in her hair, the wheels of the bike swishing through the grass, sun dapples making her blink as she pedalled under the trees, sure as a horse, skimming the air.

Far behind, she heard a crumpled sound from the drive, a crunch of gravel and Luke's wail. He'd fallen off. Again. Even with stabilisers. She closed her fingers over the brakes, put her sandals on the ground, turning to check on him.

Mummy had him in her arms and he was sobbing against her shoulder. There was a dribble of blood on his knee. It didn't look bad. But he was a cry-baby.

Fran started back across the space between them, pedalling fast, pompoms swinging. Her parents glanced up, smiling, watching as she raced over the grass towards them. She pushed on the pedals, leant over the handlebars, getting closer and closer. She would help Luke find his balance. She'd be patient, because he wasn't as fast or as brave as her. It gave her a warm, tingly feeling in her tummy. Daddy said she was the best big sister in the world.

She hears the front door close, and Luke moving about downstairs.

She tidies her hair, runs a finger under her lashes to catch any mascara smudges and practises a shaky smile in the mirror. She hopes he won't be in an inquisitive mood. Sometimes he goes straight to his freakishly tidy room and sits at his desk.

As she enters the kitchen, he gives her a glance. 'Been anywhere today?' He's carving hunks of bread from a disintegrating loaf.

She leans against a cabinet, watching him. 'No.'

He makes himself a Marmite sandwich and takes a large bite, then, still chewing, gulps from a carton of oat milk. He swallows. 'What have you been up to, then?' He wipes a pale tideline from his top lip.

'Nothing.' She shrugs. 'Not really.' Her mobile vibrates in her pocket and she takes it out. Mum. She can't face any more questions – she's too tired to lie. She slips the phone back into her pocket unanswered.

'Who was that?'

'Nobody.'

Luke's phone rings. 'Mum?' He listens, nodding. 'Cool.' He ends the call.

'Well?'

'She's having a drink after work.' He takes another bite of his sandwich. 'Somewhere busy. I could hardly hear her. That's good, though, right? She's having a life for once.'

'What did she say?'

'She says there's a jar of pesto and we should make ourselves pasta.'

'I'll cook,' Fran says. 'You've been at school all day.'

'Thanks.' Luke raises surprised eyebrows; they appear in half-moons above the frame of his glasses. 'You okay?'

'Of course,' she says. 'Why wouldn't I be?'

She digs out a packet of dry pasta from the cupboard, fills a pan with water and sets it on the stove to boil. Her understanding that she is never going to get a role has come like a kind of revelation. Walking out of the audition is the first empowering thing she's done for years. She feels almost elated. Her acting dreams are over, she tells herself. She says it again a few times, testing it out, the sound of it, the reality of it. *Enough. It's over.* Dad couldn't blame her, not if he's watching in spirit form, seeing how hard these last couple of years have been. Every rejection and disappointment has taken a little more from her, until there's nothing left. This is what people must feel like when they're lost in a blizzard up a mountain and they stop battling. They just lie down, letting the snow cover them. She can totally get it – how it feels, the comfort of an ending, the peace of surrender.

Closing her eyes, she thinks about the texture of snow – tiny crystal petals, flecks of rainbow caught inside the white – but instead of snow flowers, the image of Jacob blossoms before her. The world sending her a message. She hangs on to the thought of him. He would never put himself through the humiliation of a casting. He has purpose in life. Dignity. She has such an ache to be loved, to be worthy of being loved by someone like him.

'Jacob,' she breathes. Jacob will change her luck.

9

Oxford Circus

While Jacob's getting them drinks at the bar, Cora tries Fran's phone, but it goes to voicemail. She calls Luke instead, explaining that she'll be late, and for them to make supper without her. She has to shout over buzzing voices.

Jacob is back; he puts a chilled glass of white wine in front of her.

She takes a sip, remembering how good it feels to unwind with a drink after work, something she hasn't done since forever. 'Explain what you do,' she says. 'What you meant when you said you worked for public transport?'

'Ah, wait for it.' He does a little drum roll with his fingers on the table. 'My official title is ... Chief Safety, Health and Environment Officer for Transport for London.' He finishes with a self-deprecating flourish, and tilts his head to one side, generous eyebrows wrinkling. 'Please don't run away. I promise I'm not as dull as my job makes me sound.'

She scrunches her forehead. 'It doesn't sound dull. Just ...'

she pauses, 'it's a lot of words.' She smiles. 'And I have no idea what all of that really means.'

'The short explanation is that we make the regulations that help to keep London moving as safely as possible—'

'We?'

'My team and me.'

'Ah, you have a team? How many?'

'What?'

'How many in your team?'

She realises with a small jolt that she's flirting, and a blush rises in her cheeks. But it's fun. Just fun. It's what people do, she thinks, when they're out for a drink with someone of the opposite sex. Something she'd almost forgotten about.

He looks embarrassed, rubs his chin. 'Well. There are a few different teams. But altogether . . . about two hundred or so.'

'Now I *am* impressed!'

He laughs. 'I didn't realise you were a woman I needed to impress with numbers.'

She touches his sleeve. 'Seriously, I mean it. Keeping this city moving must be a big job. A tough one. And I interrupted you before. I'm sorry. You were saying, about your job . . .'

He sips his drink, puts it down and leans towards her, 'Okay. For example, I have one team that just looks at data on road accidents, so we can see where accidents are happening. Then we work out what the problem is and try and fix it.' Despite his humour, his eyes are alive when he talks; he cares about what he does.

'And what about the Underground? What's the most dangerous thing about that?'

'Apart from finding sleeping girls on the night Tube? It's falling down escalators. People are always falling down escalators.'

She laughs. 'And the environment bit?'

'That's my passion. I did an environmental science degree. So trying to manage our carbon footprint, transitioning buses to electric, creating cycle paths, all of that's really important.'

She opens her mouth, thinking of another question for him, but he's holding up his hand. 'My turn. What TV programme are you working on at the moment?'

He remembered, she thinks. 'The entertaining kind. Nothing too heavy.' She crosses one leg over the other, pushes her hair behind her ear. She hasn't even finished her drink, so she can't be drunk, but she feels dizzy, her body electric with anticipation, and at the same time she's amazed by how comfortable she is. They're only batting the usual getting-to-know-you questions and answers back and forth, but it's making her feel alive. She's been missing this: fun, connection, playful flirtation.

'Do you always take public transport?' she asks. 'Is it a kind of duty?'

'Sort of. I don't keep a car in London. And travelling by bus and Tube means I get to see things from a passenger's point of view, read my book – and meet new and interesting people.' He smiles. 'But really, I like my bike best.'

She wrinkles her nose. 'That makes me feel guilty. I used to cycle, but my bike's got something wrong with its front brake, and I've been too lazy to take it to the bike shop.'

'Do you know what the matter is?'

She shakes her head. 'Apart from the fact that it's getting rusty from being chained to my front railings? No.'

He turns his half-empty glass in slow circles on the table. 'I could always take a look at it.' He glances up at her. 'I'm a bit of a nerd when it comes to bikes.'

Cora's heart kicks into a new, fast rhythm. Has she pressured him into this without meaning to? Is he just being nice? Does he want to see her again? She feels out of her depth.

She takes a breath. 'That's . . . kind of you,' she says slowly.

'It's not kind. I like fixing bikes.' He's looking at her expectantly.

They hold each other's gaze, and her stomach lurches. She looks down, 'Maybe . . . Saturday afternoon?' she suggests.

'Ah, no. Sorry – I can't do that.' He sits back in his chair.

'Oh.' She's confused. His voice dropped, went flat. 'The . . . the morning, then?'

'Okay. About ten?' He nods and drains his drink. He smiles, but she can sense that he's not quite as present as he was before, and a worry line has appeared between his eyebrows.

Cora sits on the top deck of the bus, her bag on her lap. She looks at the pavement below, busy with people, the atmosphere of the working day replaced by the unfolding evening. Bars and pubs are full. People walk with more of a relaxed, unhurried roll, less of the stressed, purposeful Oxford Street scurry.

She can still feel the graze of his skin as he pressed his cheek lightly to hers to say goodbye. Why did he invite himself over and then go cold on her when she suggested a time and day? What does it mean? She thinks of the disastrous dinner with Felix, and before that, years of nights spent alone, or being the extra woman at a supper party. The best evenings were those sharing a bottle of wine with Helena. She's out of practice at social interaction – especially with a single man. She has no idea how to behave in those situations. 'Just be cool,' Fran told her before the date with Felix. Easier said than done. She's not sure why she was so . . . excitable in the bar. What would anyone else have seen? An older woman

54

flirting with a younger man who was going along with it to be polite? Her cheeks burn and she bites her lip. Marriage to Andrew protected her from all that. But you're not here, she wants to wail. You left me. You left me alone, and I still can't forgive you.

That morning, the vigil was over. She hadn't moved from his side since the accident, spending days and nights at the hospital; but he would never recover. She'd given permission to end life support.

The machines had been switched off. The breathing tube removed. Fran and Luke had said their farewells and been taken, sobbing, into a waiting room – 'Better for them not to witness the end,' a nurse had whispered. So it was just the two of them, as it had been in the beginning.

She held Andrew's hand, stroking his fingers. 'The first time we met in the kitchen at uni, you were annoyed with me,' she said. 'Do you remember? So, you're the slob who never washes up, you said. Then you invited me to a concert.'

Despite herself, she looked for a sign of understanding in his impassive, swollen face; but there was only a flicker of involuntary movement behind his closed eyes. She noticed a violet shadow creeping across his lips, oxygen drawing back.

'I loved you from that moment, while you were explaining that my unwashed mugs were a health hazard. You took my hand at the concert. I can't recall the name of the group, but I'll never forget the way your body felt against mine when we danced. You were so handsome. My head only reached your chest.'

He was disappearing. She could feel him going – slipping away without looking back. She wanted to climb onto the bed, grab his shoulders, hold him to her. She wanted to howl: stay! Suddenly, his hands clenched, his body juddered, a spasm moving through his legs and arms. She pressed her palm over her mouth to stop the cry in her throat. The doctor had warned her this might happen – 'Sometimes there are convulsions,' he'd said.

The trembling in Andrew's limbs stopped. His fingers were blue.

'I've . . . I've loved every moment we've spent together.' She forced herself to go on, to keep talking, in case he could still hear. 'I've loved the life we made, the care you've taken of me, our arguments, our jokes, and . . . and I promise to do my best to see Fran and Luke through this.' She swallowed, controlling her voice. 'You'll be in my heart for ever. Thank you for loving me . . . thank you for our children . . . I hope you find peace, wherever you go, wherever you are . . . after this.' She put her mouth to her husband's forehead; his skin already smelt strange, not him any more. 'Goodbye,' she whispered. 'Goodbye, my love.'

She stares out of the bus window, and a noise like thunder sounds in her head. The crashing makes her blink and curl her fingers tight. She opens her bag to get out her phone as distraction. She'll call Helena. Scroll through Instagram looking at rescue dogs and vegan boots.

As she slips her fingers into the bag, they make contact with something slippery and rotten, like wet flesh. Horrified, she whips her hand out and looks inside. A rich, tangy smell hits her. The peach. She feels annoyance and relief. She must have squashed it. There's juice all over her things. It's a mess. She shuts the bag, licking her fingers, wiping them on her trousers. The stickiness clings.

Holland Park

The initial rush of relief, the sense of lightness, has gone. Without her ambition, without direction, the world is dull and pointless. Fran lingers in bed, eats breakfast at lunchtime in her dressing gown, making herself coffee after coffee, having illicit rollies near an open window, wafting the smoke away with one hand. She spends hours online looking through social media, searching Instagram and Facebook and Twitter, checking how many likes she has (never enough), scrolling through endless posts as if she's looking for something, something that will save her, but instead, when she shuts her laptop or puts down her overheated mobile, she feels sick and empty, her eyes red and sore.

There's no point in watching self-empowerment and self-awareness videos online any more. None of them did her any good. She finds her old checklists written in her notebooks: Her Life Vision Mission: *Be a star. Get a good acting role. Be the person Dad said I was. Prove I have talent.* Most Important Tasks: *Keep doing voice exercises. Go to auditions. Be nicer to Mum and*

Luke. Get my shit together. Don't forget that I can achieve anything if I set out to succeed. Funeral Test: *To be remembered as fun, likeable, inspiring, talented.* She cringes in embarrassment, rips the pages out, scrunching them up and dropping them in the recycling.

On Wednesday evening, she slips out of the house before Cora gets back from work. She's been avoiding her mother all week. As usual, she won't stop nagging about 'plans'.

It's all right for Cora. She has a job she loves; a job she's good at. Fran can see how contented she is, how she enjoys sitting in a poky dark room staring at screens all day.

'Hey.' Alesha rises from her seat at the bar and embraces Fran, pushes a beer, sliver of lime jammed in the neck, towards her.

'Cheers.' Fran hoists herself onto a stool, squeezes juice into the beer, tilts the bottle and drinks. Cold bubbles slide across her tongue. The thump of bass vibrates through the room into the foot she has resting on the floor. The place is crammed with people out after work with collars undone and determined smiles. She glances around. Groups huddle together laughing, clapping each other's shoulders, leaning their faces close. Her bones shrink. Her breath catches.

Alesha touches her arm. 'All right?'

Fran wants to tell Lesh that she's in trouble – that she's totally fucked up. She wants to explain that she has no future, and she's terrified. But if she speaks the words, then it'll be real. She'll start to cry and she may not be able to stop. She just needs to focus on her friend's familiar face and breathe deeply, fill her lungs. She can do this.

'Sorry. Just to flag it, but I can't stay long,' Alesha goes on. 'Got lessons to prepare for tomorrow and reports to write.'

'When did you get this boring?'

'When I got a job.' Alesha laughs. 'And rent to pay.'

'Damn,' says Fran, gaining traction now. 'I keep forgetting. You're like a regular adult. That's scary.'

Alesha puts her head on one side, 'Mum already had two kids by my age.'

Fran shudders, 'That's not going to be happening to me for a long time.'

Alesha sips her glass of red wine and wrinkles her forehead. 'So?'

Fran's pulse jumps; she looks into the amber depths of the bottle.

'The part you were up for?'

'I didn't take it,' she lies. 'They weren't paying. I can't work for free, can I?'

Lesh wags her finger, 'Not with all your training!'

'Exactly.'

'Any other auditions coming up?'

'I'm taking a bit of a break.'

'Babe,' Alesha says softly. 'Don't tell me you've given up on your dream? You love the theatre, right? You still want to play all those Shakespearean roles in the West End?'

'Of course.' Fran makes a face. 'No way I'm giving up. Just need to get my mojo back. And then watch out, agents and casting directors, you will not know what's hit you. Here comes the next Beatrice.'

'Amen to that!' Alesha clinks her glass against Fran's bottle. 'Just hurry up and nail that starring role, then you can move in with us. We're looking for someone to take Marsha's room. Wish it could be you.'

Fran sighs. 'Wish it could too. Actually ...' she swallows,

59

'I was wondering. If I ever wanted to do something different. Like. I don't know. Maybe teaching. Like you. What kind of qualifications would I need?'

'Teaching Year 6? Just your basic GCSE English and maths.' Lesh frowns. 'You're not really thinking of being a teacher, are you?'

'No.' Fran laughs. Looks at her knees. 'Course not.'

Maths has always been a mystery to her. Numbers never do what she expects. They trick her, elude her. She has no qualifications worth shit.

'You still seeing that guy Hugo?' Lesh is asking.

Fran shrugs. 'For now, but … I don't know.' She takes another swig of beer. 'I'd drop him in a heartbeat if I could see Jacob. If only I had his details. Fuck. Fuck. Why didn't I get his full name? I messed up so badly. I can't even stalk him on Instagram.'

Alesha gives her shoulder a gentle shove. 'Probably a good job. You have the worst taste in men.'

'And you always go for the obvious. Look at Carl. Handsome and solvent. I mean, what's wrong with you, Lesh?' Fran rolls her eyes. 'Couldn't you go for someone a little fucked up, like a normal person would?'

Alesha laughs. 'I'm not looking for drama. And Carl knows not to touch my hair.' She taps her painted nails on the bar rail, each one striped like a stick of rock in pink and white. 'I like to be fussed over. Have my man buy me flowers and shit. You should try it sometime.'

Fran concentrates on her jeans, rubbing a finger over a small stain. Dad used to arrive through the front door with armfuls of roses and lilies. Cora would always say something irritating like *Oh, you shouldn't have.* Or *Andrew darling, the garden's full*

of flowers. Or, the most stupid comment of all, *My goodness,
what are these for?*

Dad would smile and say, 'Just because.'

And Fran knew. He gave because he could, for the joy of
giving. For love.

She misses him so much. But if he was here, she couldn't bear
the disappointment in his eyes. She applied to drama school
just before his accident. He cracked open a bottle of champagne
to celebrate the beginning of her career, never doubting she'd
be accepted.

Her scalp has begun to itch. She hasn't washed her hair since
she walked out of the audition. She gives in to the urge and
scratches. Alesha throws her a sideways glance, brow furrowed.
Jesus, that look again. A mirror image of Cora's. Fran can't get
away from it. Even her best friend is a reminder. She may as
well have 'failure' tattooed on her forehead.

'So, Friday night?' Lesh says brightly. 'That new club in
Dalston? We could invite Marsha and Lucy.'

'Sure,' Fran says, knowing she can't afford the entrance fee.
She can't even afford to buy a drink. 'Sounds good.'

'Great. You need cheering up.'

They hug before parting, Fran breathing in her friend's particular scent, the mix of coconut oil and lavender essence. She
feels guilty about all the lies she's been telling – Lesh doesn't
deserve it. She promises herself she'll do better. A swinging
braid tickles her cheek.

She gets on a Central Line train. She's using Luke's Oyster
card. The boy never goes anywhere, except school, so he won't
miss it. She leans against the end of the carriage, near the
dividing door. The window is open and she inhales a rush of
air, dense with shed skin and mouldy dust. She observes the

other passengers, the ones sitting down, all of them staring at phones or folded pages of the *Standard*, and imagines herself in one of the seats, passed out, imagines Jacob coming over to her sprawled body, touching her shoulder. She has a horrible thought. Was her mouth open? Was she snoring? Or dribbling? God, she hopes he doesn't think of her like that.

The train screeches to a halt at a station, and she lurches to the side, banging her elbow. Who is she kidding? He doesn't think of her at all.

Queensway

Every Friday before work, Cora gets the Tube to Queensway to meet Helena for a jog around Hyde Park. They're stretching to warm up. Cora shivers inside her yellow running anorak as she kicks her foot up behind her, and pulls. There's a light drizzle blurring the air, catching in her eyelashes. She holds the pose, enjoying the sense of lengthening in her right quad.

Helena, sleek as a seal in black exercise tights and top, is windmilling her arms vigorously. 'We doing five K today, then?'

Cora grimaces. 'I suppose we'd better.'

At this early hour, there are only a few other joggers and dog-walkers around. The two women set off together down the path towards the Albert Memorial, keeping a steady pace. They usually loop around the perimeter of the park before doing a circuit of the lake.

'God, I hate running,' Cora says.

Helena laughs, 'You say that every time. Maybe we should do something more entertaining to keep fit.'

'Like what?'

'I don't know. Salsa dancing? Bouldering?'

'I vote for Salsa. Best outfits.'

As they near the Gothic extravaganza of the memorial, the sound of traffic from Kensington Road gets louder, and Cora feels a stitch starting under her ribs. She glances up at the lonely figure of Prince Albert on his plinth, washed with rain. 'He was only about forty when he died, wasn't he?' she pants, as they run past.

'Forty-two, I think. Poor Victoria. Left a widow when she was still young—' Helena turns her head towards Cora. 'God. Sorry, Cora! That was thoughtless of me.'

'Don't be silly. Lots of women lose their husbands too young. I'm not the only one.'

The path is slightly uphill and both women lean into the gradient, arms pumping. 'Are you going back to internet dating?' Helena asks breathlessly. 'I know that last date was a disaster, but—'

'No,' Cora says. 'It's not for me.'

'Then how will you meet someone?' Helena leaps across a puddle. 'You shouldn't be put off by one wanker.'

'London's full of people. You can meet someone anywhere.' She waves a hand. 'The Tube, even.'

'Nobody *ever* met anyone on the Tube.'

They run on in silence, their breath coming harder, feet keeping time as they cross the top of the lake at Long Water and head down Buckhill Walk. Cora's stitch has become a tight pain cramping her side; she grits her teeth. 'Actually, I have,' she gasps. 'Met someone on the Tube. Fran met him first.' Her feet thud over the path, 'Well. He found her. Brought her home and—'

'Stop.' Helena slows to a walk, her hands on her hips. Her cheeks are flushed. 'What are you talking about? You've met someone?'

Cora slows too, panting, and digs her thumb between her ribs. 'No.' She winces. 'I mean, he's too young for me. But he just kind of turned up in our lives. Because of the Central Line, of all things.'

'What?' Helena shakes her head. 'You're not making any sense. Let's forget the rest of the run. Get out of the rain and have a coffee. This sounds way more important.'

'Nothing's open yet . . .' Cora protests, wishing she hadn't said anything. Helena is on a mission to get Cora paired up. She's not going to let this go without an interrogation.

'The Lodge Café is. Come on. Race you there.'

Helena dashes off, her dark ponytail swinging behind her. Cora sighs, and follows. All her energy has dissipated and she can hardly keep up with Helena's determined figure.

Over her cappuccino, Helena leans forward, eyes wide. 'Tell me the whole story,' she orders. 'From the beginning.'

Cora explains everything, leaving out her feelings, because how can she explain something she doesn't have words for?

'God, that's exciting.' Helena sits back, looking pleased. 'A toy boy. Just what you need, some energetic sex.'

'Stop it!' Cora shakes her head. 'We bumped into each other and went for a drink. It's not a big deal. And anyway, I'm pretty certain I made an idiot of myself. I was flirting. He was probably mortified.'

'Rubbish. You might be out of practice, but you're a catch for any man, and don't forget it.'

'He's coming over on Saturday to fix my bike.'

'Aha!' Helena raises her eyebrows. 'Now you tell me!' She

swirls her teaspoon through the froth on her drink and licks it. 'That's such an obvious excuse to see you again.'

Cora makes an annoyed noise. 'Or he just wants to mend my bike.'

Helena shakes her head sorrowfully, 'Darling, you're in denial, and I understand. You're scared. It's not surprising. It's been a long time since you've had a man in your life. But don't be. It's obvious he's interested. He's going out of his way to see you.'

'I can't honestly tell if he likes me or not.' Cora looks into her cup, 'But I . . . I do like him. And you're right . . . it's the most frightening thing that's happened to me for a long time.'

Helena's eyebrows arch. 'Admitting it is the first step. So this is progress. Good.' She tilts her head to one side. 'And how is Fran in all of this? Do you think she's learnt something from having to confront her rescuer?'

'I hope so.' Cora sits up straight. Her leggings are damp. Her top sticks uncomfortably to her skin. 'She was quiet around him. I think she was embarrassed.'

'So she should be!' Helena snorts. 'You're too lenient on her.'

Cora shakes her head. 'I know it might seem that way, but she's had a difficult time since Andrew died. You know how close they were. He meant the world to her.'

'But you can't mollycoddle her for ever, Cora.'

'I don't . . .' Cora sighs, breaking off. 'She's always been young for her age. Impetuous. Volatile. But something's going on with her at the moment. I'm worried. She's avoiding me, just mopes in her room.' She bites a fingernail. 'She hasn't had any kind of acting job for ages. It's hard – all those rejections. She seems to have lost her sense of direction. Her ambition.'

Helena smiles, 'She'll sort herself out. Don't worry. Not everyone can be as driven or efficient as you.'

'I'm not driven.'

'It's not an insult!' She grins. 'When you lived in Suffolk, you made your own jam from fruit grown in your own garden. In my book, that's efficient. And now look at you – after everything you went through, you've reinvented yourself. You've got a great job and you're managing as a single mother.'

'Badly.'

'Just accept the compliment. You're the most capable person I know.'

'That's not true. I wasn't always like that . . . you know what happened after I had Fran,' Cora says in a low voice.

'You were ill. That's different.'

'You sound like Andrew used to.'

Helena smiles. 'Because it's true.' She puts her hand across the table to rest it over Cora's, and squeezes.

On her way home, Cora stands with the other commuters in the swaying carriage. Telling Helena about Jacob has made her anxious, made her feel somehow exposed. Since Andrew, she hasn't looked at another man, until now. She'd forgotten how vulnerable it makes you feel.

Just thinking about a new relationship is exhausting. She was with Andrew for such a long time, it was as if they were one person. He became her whole family after her parents died, and he understood why she wanted to have a baby as soon as possible. It seemed a simple thing. She took it for granted that she'd be a good mother.

Cora opened her eyes into darkness. Warmth was spreading under her, wet between her thighs, a circle of damp on the sheet. Her back ached. Bands of steel tightened around her stomach.

'Andrew,' she shook his shoulder, 'wake up, I think . . . it's started.'

He turned, groggy with sleep. 'But . . . you're four weeks early.'

They got to the hospital just in time; no chance of birthing pools or epidurals, the birth was fast and brutal. When they placed a creature on her chest, red-scrunched, slippery with white, Cora had only moments to stare into her baby's face before they took her away. In the premature ward, days had no edges and the endless nights drifted on. Fran wasn't strong enough to feed; they put a tube up her nose held down with pieces of tape that puckered her skin. She developed jaundice, and they placed her in a heat box, naked on her tummy, a blindfold around her eyes. Cora watched her inside that Perspex container. It looked like a tiny coffin.

When she could hold Fran at last and they placed her in her arms, Cora sat stiffly, balancing the heavy head with its thumb-print pulse. Fran stared up, her no-colour pupils sliding in opposite directions, eye muscles too weak to focus.

'It'll be lovely to have her at home with you,' the nurses cooed, but Cora felt only terror at the thought.

Cora just has time to shower and change before work. As she pulls on her clothes, she thinks how presumptuous she's been to think of Jacob in that way. Poor man. Falling prey to the overactive imagination of a middle-aged woman. She gives herself a stern look in the mirror. Don't get ahead of yourself, Cora Pollen.

Fran is in bed. Cora thinks she should warn her about Jacob coming over on Saturday. She might still be embarrassed about meeting him. She knocks and puts her head into the room, 'Fran? Darling? I need to talk to you . . .'

Fran remains unmoving, insensible under the covers. The room smells stale. Piles of dirty clothes litter the floor. 'Fran?' Cora waits for a second, sighs, and closes the door.

Luke's at the kitchen table eating his cornflakes with a physics book propped up in front of him. He pushes at the bridge of his glasses.

'How's the revision going?'

He shrugs. 'Good.'

'Darling, can you tell Fran I need to talk to her this evening? Tell her it's important. Okay?'

Luke grunts and turns a page.

'Luke? Okay?'

He sighs. 'Okay. I heard you.'

She drops a kiss on his hair. There's no time for breakfast. She'll pick something up on her way in.

The rain has cleared and the sky is a milky blue. Early pink and white blossom shines through sunlight. Cora is tired. She didn't sleep well last night, excited about Jacob coming over and worried about Fran. She takes a last gulp of loveliness before going down into the Underground.

On the train, she wonders what to do about Fran. Everything she said to Helena is true. Her daughter seems to be stuck. But how can she help her when Fran avoids being in the same room? Cora's tried to explain that success doesn't usually come easily – that it's not just about talent, it takes perseverance and self-belief and luck. But in her heart, she knows Fran is on the wrong career path. She's afraid her daughter doesn't have enough acting ability to make it. But how can she tell that to someone who's spent her whole life planning to be a star?

Uxorious. A man who loves his wife too much. Is there a

word for a father who loves his daughter too much? By being a doting father, Andrew unwittingly set Fran up for a fall. And now he's not here to catch her.

12

Marble Arch

With Cora at work, and Luke at school, Fran is alone during the day. She wanders the echoing rooms, grateful for the lack of expectation, the privacy of the empty house. Luke has left his breakfast bowl in the sink, a mush of leftover cornflakes gloopy in the bottom. Weird how he's so anal about his room, but in the rest of the house he's a slob. Fran grabs a carton of orange juice from the fridge and swigs a gulp. She wipes a dribble off her chin. There's a note on the table in Luke's neat writing: *Mum wants to talk to you tonight. She says it's urgent.* He's underlined the word urgent.

Fran crumples the paper into a ball and drops it in the bin.

She opens the kitchen window a crack and lights up a rollie. She takes a drag and blows the smoke towards the dazzle of blossom beyond the glass.

Her phone beeps. It's Alesha. *See you tonight! Shall we meet in Zuzu's Bar by the station at 8.30?*

Fran takes another drag. She can't bail too soon. Lesh will be suspicious. She sends: *Yes! Can't wait.*

Her phone pings again. Hugo on WhatsApp. *My place. Tonight.*

An order, not a question. Fran shuts the window, stubs out the disintegrating remains of the cigarette. At least she'll be out of the house. Going to Hugo's doesn't cost money. She might even be able to stay over. He sometimes lets her.

She runs a bath, washes her hair and soaks until there's no more hot water in the cistern. She tugs a comb through the tangles, blasts it with Cora's hairdryer and chooses a red silk mini dress with a Chinese collar, purple tights and her DMs. She draws on dark eyeliner and red lipstick. In the mirror, she sees that she is transformed. She remembers that she's attractive. Fanciable. She wishes Jacob could see her like this.

She judges that she can dip out of her plans with Lesh now. *Sorry, babe. I'm PMS-ing. Feeling awful. Going to bed with hot water bottle. Have a good one!*

Alesha sends back a concerned, disappointed message and lots of tiny hugging emojis and hearts. Fran thinks she should feel worse about lying to her best friend. But it's hard to feel anything at the moment. Her emotions are blanketed with something dense and woolly and suffocating. The only thing that's got through the fuzz is him – the only feelings she has are the ones for him. She asked the cards about him, and the answer she got was pretty clear: the Lovers and the Two of Cups: the union of two people, the joining of one with another. But where is he? How is she going to find him in this sprawling city? Can she really rely on fate to deliver him to her again? She writes his name on the bathroom mirror, using her lipstick, and then scrubs it out with her palm, leaving magenta smears across the glass.

Luke puts his head round her bedroom door. She's in the middle of spritzing herself with perfume. He holds his nose. 'What happened to the mirror?' he asks without real curiosity. 'Mum will go apeshit. She wants to talk to you.'

'I know, dummy. You wrote it in your note.'

He wrinkles his forehead, looking weary. 'Nobody can say I didn't pass the message on.'

Friday-night rush hour. The Underground is busy. She squeezes onto the first train that arrives and pushes her way inside. At each stop, passengers cram in behind her, and she's forced to shuffle further into the carriage. Something sharp catches her calf. She lets out a gasp and glances down to find a home-made placard resting on her leg. Gingerly she stretches her hand down past her knee, pushing the object away. The corner is splintered. She feels a tiny opening in the fabric of her tights; her finger touches skin. She huffs, straightening and glaring at the boy holding the pole attached to the placard. 'Your sign just ripped my tights.'

He's standing too, hanging on to an overhead bar with his other hand. 'Sorry.'

'You shouldn't leave it where it can trip people up.'

'Difficult to manage in here.' He smiles. There is a gap between his teeth. He has curly light brown hair, a short beard and blue eyes. His clothes are stylishly scruffy: workman's jacket, a scarf tied around his neck.

'Bloody hipster,' Fran mutters under her breath.

'You should join us.'

'What?'

'You should come along to one of our demonstrations.'

'Are you in a cult or something?'

73

He shakes his head, 'We were protesting against fur farms today.'

He looks so righteous that she snaps, 'And what about people's rights? Don't those matter?'

'Of course,' he says easily. 'There's a march for refugees next Saturday. Meeting at Parliament Square at one o'clock, if you're interested.'

The train pulls in to Marble Arch station with a screech. 'I'm not,' she says, giving him a last glare before turning her back, stepping through the sliding doors.

There are lots of people in the flat, all strangers to her. Hugo gave her bottom a squeeze when she arrived, but since then he's ignored her. House music blasts out of the customised sound system. She sits on one of the sofas with three other people. They're doing coke, taking it in turns to kneel at the glass coffee table. One of the coke-heads – a thin, balding man with an expensive watch on his wrist – turns to her and grins, indicating a line all ready to go. She shrugs and gets onto the floor, bends over, sweeping her hair out of the way, and snorts. The hit is pure. Immediate. A spark igniting behind her eyes. A flood of energy cruising through her blood.

'I fucking love your dress,' a woman tells her, wiping powder from her nostrils.

'I love yours too,' Fran says.

'You're gorgeous,' the balding man says, putting his hand on Fran's purple thigh. She looks down at his soft fingers and manicured nails.

There is dancing. Hours of sweaty, pulsing, frantic dancing. The balding guy grabs her hips and pulls her close. A beautiful creature appears in the crowd. An androgynous angel. 'Maxime, darling,' he says into her ear, when she asks his name. 'I'm Maxime.' He turns and twists around her for a while, sinuous, gorgeous as liquid smoke. Dark eyes and curling hair and thick, sensuous lips. 'Your dancing is fucking amazing!' she calls over the beat. 'I'm with Rambert,' he says, scooping shapes out of the air with his arms. Then he's gone.

She licks powder off her teeth, wipes it off her chin and sucks her hand. After the dancing, people gather in corners and on the sofas, and there's talking. Fast, clever, urgent talking, and everything is just really, really fucking funny. She stares into a blur of faces and mouths. A hollowness opens in her belly, a roiling, as if she might be sick. She wants Hugo. He's the only person here who's familiar. She searches for him, stumbling from room to room. He reappears in the kitchen with his shirt untucked and lipstick on his cheek; Fran slips her thumbs into his belt loops, relieved. 'Stay with me,' she whispers. Her heart is hammering as if she's run a sprint with Usain Bolt. She puts a hand to her left breast, pressing down the surge of blood, the rapid judder of her pulse. The muscle of her heart wants to leap through her chest, burst out of her skin and escape her body. She can almost see it, a squat purple frog jumping across the carpet, leaving a trail of her blood behind. She can't die here, in Hugo's flat, surrounded by wasted strangers.

'Want to make me happy?' Hugo murmurs, kissing her neck. She nods.

'Charlie likes you. He likes you a lot. Could you go and give him a cuddle?'

Fran is confused. 'Charlie?'

Hugo nods. 'The guy who's been giving you powder all night. You could pay him back with some affection. How about it?'

'Oh no, I . . .'

But then Charlie is there, next to her, and he's draped his arm around her shoulders and is nuzzling her neck, just where Hugo was a moment ago. Hugo is moving away, looking back, winking. Is he winking at her, or Charlie?

'Ready for another bump, gorgeous?' Charlie asks.

The sudden snore wakes her. Like someone choking. She turns her head on the pillow, blinking up at the mountain of a shoulder, and realises it's a man with his back to her. There's a concertina of creases at the bottom of his neck, the dome of a head with one ear visible, sticking up. Reddish hair sprouts across his freckled arms and back. He smells of stale alcohol and sweat. She pushes herself away from him across the crumpled sheets, blinking again as if she could change the view.

Her mouth is rancid. Her eyes raw. She gets up as quietly as she can and gathers her clothes from the floor; clutching them to her belly, she opens the door, glancing back at Charlie. His puckered, wet mouth is open; he snores gently, cheeks inflating and deflating with his breath. It would be funny, if she hadn't slept with him.

She pads into the hall. The place is hushed, dark because the blinds are still down, stuffy and fetid with the smell of last night. Hugo's housekeeper can't have come yet. She slips into the bathroom, splashing her face with water, rubbing at the worst of her smudged eyeliner and mascara, then dresses as quickly as she can. She goes to Hugo's room and opens the door a crack. He's in bed, sprawled on his back, naked, his cock a curled creature between his legs. There's someone with him. She looks at the slender, muscular dancer's legs, the curve of ribs etched with a tiger tattoo, the dark head resting on Hugo's chest. He opens one eye, looking right at her, a lazy smile on his lips. Maxime-darling. She blushes, ducking out of the room quickly, as if she's the one caught out.

Of course Maxime would be Hugo's trophy for the night; it's his habit to collect interesting people – there are always a few artists and eccentrics mixed in with the privileged ex-public-school crowd.

She slips out of the flat and into the lift, pressing the ground-floor button. She knew Hugo liked men too. It's not a surprise. He said right at the start that he didn't do conventional relationships. But she can't think about it now. She just needs to get home and take a shower, wash away the stink of the night. Wash away Charlie.

As she leaves the building, squinting into the morning light, she takes out her phone. There are messages from Lesh with pictures from last night. The girls posing for selfies at the bar. Lesh blowing her a kiss. *Missing you!* It's like looking through a portal into a different world. Somewhere innocent and far, far away. Fran clears her throat. She's got several texts from Mum. Shit. Did she tell Cora she wouldn't be back? She's pretty sure she remembers texting to say she was staying over with Lesh. She clicks on Cora's messages, all sent yesterday evening, scrolling to the last one.

Why didn't you wait to speak to me? Luke left you a message. I bumped into Jacob earlier this week. He's coming over Saturday morning to fix my bike. Have a good time with the girls. X

What the fuck? Fran can't believe what her mother is saying. She rereads the message several times. He's coming to fix her bike? Saturday. That's this morning! She didn't think her heart was capable of more. This isn't the drug-induced hammering of last night. This is the alarm of shock. Like a gong, it reverberates through her skeleton. She flushes hot and then cold.

'Shit.' She dithers on the pavement. She doesn't know what to do. She tugs at the tangled mess of her hair, presses the creased silk of her dress over her legs. She sniffs her skin, the residue of sex and coke. She half turns as if to go back to Hugo's. 'Damn. Fuck.' She turns again, and begins to stumble towards the Tube. Cora hasn't said what time he's arriving.

Maybe she can make it home before he gets there.

13

Shepherd's Bush

There are smears of red grease over the bathroom mirror. Lipstick, Cora guesses, as she wipes it off. Jacob is due any minute. She stares at herself in the newly clean glass. Her stomach is in turmoil. She puts her hands either side of her face and stretches the skin upwards and back, giving herself a mini facelift. Helena has Botox in her forehead. Maybe she should get some too. Erase that worry line between her eyebrows that seems to get deeper every day. But Cora doesn't like the idea of snake venom injected next to her brain. The front door slams, and she drops her hands and runs to the top of the stairs.

Below, Fran is kicking off her boots, breathing heavily. She's wearing a dress so short it could be mistaken for a belt, and her purple tights have a ladder running from ankle to thigh.

'Fran.' Cora starts down the stairs. 'Did you get my message?'

Fran stares up at her mother, her hair falling in listless tangles around her pale face. 'He's not here yet?'

Cora shakes her head, surprised by the tension in her

daughter's voice. She must be nervous at the prospect of seeing Jacob. Cora smells the sour stink of alcohol on her, the bitter aftertaste of a wild night.

'Where were you last night?' she asks. 'You smell like . . . like a brothel.'

Fran gives a humourless laugh. 'If you're asking if I had sex, then yeah. But don't use words like brothel, Mother. It makes you sound like you're from the Dark Ages.'

'I thought you were staying with . . .' Cora knows there's no time for this. She bites her lip. 'Oh, never mind. Fran . . .' She hears the pleading note in her own voice. She swallows. 'Let's not argue.'

The doorbell rings.

Fran hisses between her teeth, pushing past to escape upstairs. The house rattles with the force of her door slamming. Cora settles her shoulders, tidies her hair with her fingers and continues down towards the hall, but Luke has got there first.

She grasps the banister, watching her son open the door. Jacob is on the step, smiling, putting out his hand. They shake. She can't hear what's being said, but a burst of easy laughter reaches her, and she releases a breath she didn't even know she was holding.

'Hi,' she says, standing at the foot of the stairs, suddenly shy, and aware of Luke watching her. Jacob is taller than she remembered. Open-faced; energy vibrates around him, shines from his skin. She thinks of her flirtation the last time they met and vows to do better – she will be grown-up, casual. Normal.

'I've brought my tools.' He holds up his rucksack. 'Is it the sad-looking sit-up-and-beg chained to your front railings like a beaten dog?'

She nods, ''Fraid so.'

'That's no way to treat a bike.'

She can't help grinning. 'I know. But otherwise I have to lug it up the steps and through the house, down the steps into the garden and—'

He holds out his open palm, 'If you give me the keys, I'll bring it through. It'll be easier to work on it at the back. If that's okay?'

She nods again. 'Don't you want a coffee or something first?'

'Later would be great, thanks.' He turns to Luke. 'Want to help?'

Luke twitches his mouth. 'Sure.' He trails after Jacob.

Cora watches them through the open front door as they squat to unlock the chain, Jacob checking the tyres and shaking his head. They bring the bike into the hall, Luke clearing objects out of the way, chatting as if they've known each other all their lives. They're talking about football. She stares after them. Luke is actually engaging in a conversation. And she didn't know he still cared about football. He hasn't mentioned it for years, not since Andrew died and they moved to London.

In the back garden, Jacob sets the bike on the paving stones. He asks for a ground sheet or some old newspapers, and she finds him a tarp from the cellar, dank with mildew and alive with spiders. She can't remember what its original purpose was: something to do with Andrew and his machines – his motorbike, or the sit-on lawnmower needed for the Suffolk lawn. In the kitchen, as she puts out home-made flapjacks and taps freshly ground coffee into the moka pot, she watches them from the window, kneeling next to each other by the upside-down bike, sleeves rolled up, heads close. Luke passing tools to Jacob.

The sound of the pump whirs through the water pipes. Fran in the shower. The coffee is ready, and Cora is wondering about taking it out to the garden when Jacob and Luke come into the kitchen. They're laughing, waving oil-stained fingers. Luke has a black smudge on his cheek. It's good to see him behaving like a normal boy.

'Where should we clean up?' Jacob asks.

She points them to the sink and the bar of soap, and fetches a towel from the back of the door.

'Jacob says I'm a natural,' Luke says, rubbing suds between his hands, looking pleased with himself, glancing at Jacob for approval.

'Yeah, Luke fixed the brakes himself,' Jacob tells her as he dries his hands. 'Both sets had gone. We've oiled the chain and pumped the tyres, haven't we, Luke?'

'Now you've left me with no excuse for not cycling to work.'

'You need a cover for it too, Mum,' Luke says. 'It's really rusty.'

'Yes.' She feels a twinge of shame. 'I'm afraid I haven't looked after it very well.'

Jacob sniffs the air. 'Coffee smells good.'

Cora pours him a cup. 'No sugar?' she asks, remembering how he took his tea. 'And is oat milk all right?'

'Yes to both questions.' He takes the cup from her. 'Thanks.'

'I've got homework,' Luke says as he pads out of the kitchen with a fistful of flapjacks. 'See you, Jacob.'

'See you,' Jacob calls after him. 'Don't forget. We're going to thrash you this weekend.'

'Never,' shouts Luke happily.

Cora raises her eyebrows.

'It's a football thing.' Jacob takes a sip. 'Bright boy,' he says. 'He said he wants to study physics at UEA?'

She nods. 'He's got the brains in this family.' She wants to tell Jacob that Luke has missed time with his dad, that messing about with bikes and talking about football has brought colour to her son's cheeks, a new light to his eyes. But that would imply all sorts of things she couldn't possibly voice. She glances at the helmet dangling from his rucksack, says instead, 'My husband bought my bike for me when we lived in the country. I never really used it there either. The narrow lanes terrified me. You never knew when a tractor would be coming at you – or a car driving on the wrong side of the road.'

He clears his throat and puts his cup on the table. 'Cora,' he begins. 'I wondered if—' His mobile starts to ring. He grimaces and fishes it out of his pocket. His expression darkens when he looks at the screen. 'I'm so sorry,' he says. 'I have to take this.'

He walks out of the kitchen into the garden. She watches him talking earnestly as he paces back and forth. Then he puts the phone back in his pocket and turns towards the house. Cora starts guiltily, and moves towards the table. He comes back into the room and sits down, picking up his cup. 'Sorry about that. Thought for a moment I might have to go and sort something out, but it's okay.' He smiles over the rim as he raises it to his lips and sips, puts it down and says, 'Now, where were we? I was going to ask you—'

'Jacob?'

Cora startles at the sound of Fran's voice. She's in the doorway, a fall of freshly washed hair loose over her shoulders. She looks like a Pre-Raphaelite painting come to life. Nobody would know she's the same girl who stormed in wearing ripped tights and the stench of an all-nighter. She's got her boyfriend jeans on, the waistband loose on her slim hips, legs rolled past the ankles. There's a glimpse of naked skin between her jeans and her plain black T-shirt; her feet are bare.

'There's coffee in the pot,' Cora tells her.

Fran pours herself a cup and settles at the table, flicking back her hair with a practised toss. She gives no sign of the hangover that must be crashing through her head.

'I hear Mum's dragged you here to fix her rusty old bike?' she says, crossing her legs. She wiggles the toes of her dangling foot. She's inherited Andrew's long, narrow feet, Cora's high arches.

'It was the other way round,' Jacob says. 'Once I knew a bike was in distress, I had to insist on saving it.'

Fran laughs. She takes a sip of her drink. 'Ouch! Hot!' She licks her lips, and touches her mouth with delicate taps of her fingertips. A sudden tension hums between the three of them. 'By the way, Mum ... Luke said he needed to talk to you,' she says.

'Now?' Cora glances towards the door.

'Yeah.'

'Excuse me a minute,' Cora says to Jacob.

She goes upstairs and puts her head inside Luke's room. He's not at his desk. Across the landing, the bathroom door is closed. She steps towards it and gives a quiet knock. 'Luke? Are you okay?'

There's no answer. She waits on the landing, folding some sheets in the airing cupboard for something to do; the quiet murmur of Jacob and Fran's voices rises from the kitchen. A chain flushes and Luke comes out of the bathroom. He looks surprised. 'Mum? What are you doing?'

'Oh, just hanging around the airing cupboard for fun,' she says brightly.

'Are you joking? Or have you finally gone senile?'

'Fran said you needed me.'

He looks blank. Then puzzled. 'Oh. Has ... has Jacob asked you, then?' he says hesitantly.

'Asked me what?'

'Nothing.' He sighs, looking disappointed.

'Hang on.' Cora frowns, confused. 'What are you talking about? Luke? Asked me what?'

'Just say yes,' Luke mutters. 'When he asks. Please.' He yanks his jeans up higher on his narrow hips and lopes into his bedroom, shutting the door.

Cora makes to follow, questions on her lips, but Fran is shouting from the hallway, 'Mum! Mum, Jacob's going now!'

Jacob is waiting at the door, his rucksack on his shoulders and his bike helmet in his hand. 'Hey,' he says to her. 'We lost you.' His expression is quizzical, his eyes a little wounded. Or perhaps she's imagining things.

'Sorry.' She puts her hands in her jeans pockets.

'Can I talk to you about something?' he says. 'I was about to mention it before Fran came down. Only I need to get going, or I'll be late.'

Her heart skips a beat in anticipation. He's started out towards the pavement, and she follows him. A sleek green racing machine is locked with two different devices to a lamp post nearby. He puts his helmet on, drops to one knee and takes out a small key. 'It's about Luke,' he says over his shoulder.

'Luke?' She's taken aback for a second.

'He told me he'd like to start cycling.'

Now she understands Luke's cryptic mutterings and odd behaviour. 'But ... he doesn't have a bike.'

Jacob stands up. 'He says he has some money saved up. And he asked me if I'd help him find a second-hand one.'

'Oh ... I'm not sure ... I mean ...'

'If you're worried about him on the road, I don't blame you.

But I'm happy to take him out. Show him the ropes. Make sure he knows what he's doing. I'm usually free on Sunday mornings.'

'Luke's not exactly . . . sporty.' She lowers her voice. 'He's a bit clumsy. I'm not sure if he could manage—'

'Cycling's a good sport for people who don't "do" sport.' He smiles. 'And it could do wonders for his confidence.'

She bites her thumbnail, remembering how Fran took to cycling when she was tiny, how she loved to belt around the Suffolk garden on two wheels. But Luke couldn't seem to get his balance. He struggled on a bike with stabilisers, tipping over and getting stuck like a beetle on his back. He was quite old before he eventually learnt. But, she reminds herself, that was a long time ago.

'Maybe . . .' she says, 'but I couldn't possibly ask you—'

'You're not asking me. Luke is. And I'm saying I'm happy to help. Just . . . I wanted to make sure you're okay with it.'

She opens her mouth. Getting Luke out of his room and away from his computer screen is something she's been trying to do for ages. She worries about her quiet, academic son. He seems to have no friends. But can she trust him with Jacob? She doesn't know him yet.

'I can introduce him to a cycle club,' he's saying. 'A friend of mine runs one that meets in Hyde Park – they have different groups for different abilities and ages.'

'A cycle club?' she says. 'That sound good. Thanks. That's . . . kind.'

He grins. 'Not kind. I told you, I'm a bit of a bike nerd. So – can I give you my number?'

'Your number?'

'So we can stay in contact. Luke has it. But we should

exchange details too, don't you think? If you've got your phone with you?'

He recites his details and she taps letters and numbers in haltingly, wishing she had her glasses on. She holds the screen out to him. 'Is that right?'

He nods. 'Give me a missed call and then I've got your details too.' He throws his leg over the crossbar. 'See you next week.'

She watches him pedal away, head down, legs pumping.

In the hallway, everything is the same. But the air is alive with change, and the slight, subtle smell of him. Her pulse jumps and she has a sick feeling in her stomach. It's the first time in years she's experienced the tortures of attraction. But it doesn't mean he feels the same. She has no idea if he likes her, or if she's inventing something just because she wants it to be true. She holds her phone tighter. The phone with his number in it.

Luke thumps down the stairs. 'Did he ask you – about me getting a road bike?'

His enthusiasm makes her smile. 'He did.' She reaches out to push his hair back from his forehead. 'But I'd worry about you.'

He pulls an exasperated face, batting away her hand. 'Mum! I'm seventeen!'

'I know.' She smiles again. 'So – yes, I think it's a great idea.'

'Yessss!' He punches the air.

His uncomplicated happiness makes Cora's heart sing. At least for her son, seeing Jacob again will be a simple pleasure.

Shepherd's Bush

Fran lies on her bed. She should feel knackered, but she's restless with energy. She cradles her mobile to her chest. She was on the point of calling Alesha to tell her everything, before she remembered, just in time, that she fibbed to her yesterday. Anyway, she wants to recall every moment of her time with Jacob. She lights a rollie and takes a drag, shutting her eyes.

After she'd made up an excuse to get Cora to leave the room, there was a short, boring exchange about bikes before he told her he was in training for a triathlon for some charity.

Fran glanced at his arms, the curve of muscle. He was fit. But not in that bulky Mr Universe way. 'Which charity?'

'HeadsUp. They help kids with brain injury.'

'Oh, cool. I have causes I support too,' she told him, the words out of her mouth before she could think. But when she saw his interested expression, she pushed on. 'Refugees, mostly. I'm ... I'm going to a demonstration next weekend. A march. You know, to get better rights and things for them.'

'That's great.'

It was the approval, no, admiration in his voice that got to her. But then he looked at his watch. 'Do you think your mum will be down soon?'

She shrugged. 'She's always got stuff to do. She's a bit of a clean freak.'

He looked at her bare feet then, and smiled. 'You seem to be a barefoot family.'

'No.' She pressed on, thinking they should get off the topic of Cora. 'I prefer my boots. But . . . I just got out of the shower.' She paused, allowing the image of herself naked under a jet of water to resonate; then, fishing her tobacco and Rizlas out of her pocket, she started to skin up, licking a paper with a delicate flick of her tongue. 'Can I tempt you?' she asked.

He shook his head. 'I don't smoke.'

She put her tin back in her pocket. 'By the way, can I ask?' she said. 'I just wondered, with your name and everything . . . are you Jewish?'

He looked surprised. But then nodded.

'Do you go to synagogue and observe Jewish holidays and things?'

'I used to, when I lived with my family. But now,' he cleared his throat, 'I'm not what my father would call a good Jew. Not any more.'

'Really? I suppose our family are lapsed C of E. Not nearly so exotic. I'm interested in religion – the different interpretations of God.'

She thought he seemed impressed. But did he fancy her? She twirled a strand of hair around her finger and leant closer, looking into his eyes. 'I'd like to know more,' she said in a low voice. 'About your faith.'

He shifted in his chair, a slight angle away from her. 'I'm probably not the right person for that discussion.'

It wasn't the reaction she'd hoped for. It was supposed to be his cue for suggesting meeting up. But she shouldn't have used his religion as an excuse for a date. She forced a smile, deciding she had to be bold. 'I think you are,' she said, glancing down and then up. 'I think you're exactly the right person.'

He looked almost puzzled, which could have been frustrating but was actually sweet. He didn't seem to know how gorgeous he was. Then, like a cold drink on a hot day: the relief of his smile.

She smiled back, encouragingly. Her eyes signalling: *I'm all yours.*

'Well, I'm sure we'll talk about this and many other things,' he said, at last.

'I hope so.'

She holds her mobile tighter. The phone that now contains Jacob's details. Jacob da Costa. And his number, which she almost knows off by heart already. She got everything she needed, except his star sign. She would put money on him being a Cancer – sensitive and romantic. She stands up and flicks her cigarette out of the window, taps on Alesha's name.

Lesh picks up at once. 'Babe? How are you feeling?'

'Better now.' Fran speaks quickly, getting the lies over with. 'Just took paracetamol and got an early one.'

She lets Lesh tell her about the night, the cocktails and the dancing, the shit DJ, how she missed Fran. Then she drops her news, casually, and grins when she hears Lesh shriek, 'What? He came to your house again? How come?'

'He came to mend Mum's bike. She bumped into him at

Oxford Circus, and he offered to sort it out for her. It's such an obvious excuse to see me again, don't you think?'

'Yeah. Maybe.'

'He's a bit nervous around me. I think that's a definite sign he likes me. He's not exactly coming on to me, but that's because he has manners, you know? Style.'

'Not your usual type, then.'

'No – he's actually a good one. I'm sure of it. I've never fallen for anyone so sorted and . . . kind before.'

'I hope so,' Lesh says quietly. 'Forget what I said before. He's not too old. He sounds lovely.'

'He is,' Fran says. 'But one slight problem. I told him I was going to a march next Saturday. For refugees.'

Lesh laughs. 'Why did you tell him that?'

'I don't know. He said he was raising money for a charity and I guess it just came into my head to say something he'd be impressed by. I wasn't actually planning on going. But now I think, maybe I should? What if he asks me about it later? Or, shit . . . what if he's there?'

Lesh laughs for so long that Fran has to shout down the phone, 'It's not that funny! Can you stop now? . . . Lesh!'

When she manages to speak, Alesha says, 'I'm loving this guy. He's turned my best friend into Mother Teresa!' She hiccups. 'Yeah. You'd better go, since you've boasted about it. Let's hope it's not raining. And before you ask. No. Sorry. Not happening. You're on your own. I'm seeing Carl. I do my bit for the good of the world when I'm teaching all those little monsters Monday to Friday.'

Fran clicks off her phone. She can't move. Every part of her body is weighted with happy exhaustion. She can imagine his long, slim fingers holding her face, pressing into the dip of her spine, moving skilfully between her legs. He'll be as men are supposed to be in bed but never are. She has a brief flash of last night. Charlie's lips around her nipple, his teeth closing. She flinches, blinking the memory away. Sleeping with Jacob will be different – sensuous and beautiful, like it's supposed to be. She gathers her packet of rolling papers and tin of baccy from the bed, rummages for her spare Rizlas in her top drawer and drops the lot into the bin. From now on, she's giving up smoking. She doesn't want her mouth to taste like ash when he kisses her.

Shepherd's Bush

It's been nearly a week since Jacob came over and mended the bike. Cora dropped him a missed call that day, but as soon as she heard his voice on his answer message, she flung the phone from her as if it was a scorpion.

'What's wrong with me? I'm turning into a teenager,' she complained to Helena over the phone on Monday.

'You just fancy him,' Helena said.

'No. I don't,' Cora insisted. 'Oh God,' she relented. 'I do. I do.'

'It's great. Enjoy the angst. Wish I had some in my life.'

When she asked Fran what she and Jacob had talked about when left alone in the kitchen, Fran smirked as if at a secret joke. 'Nothing much,' she shrugged. 'Bikes. Charity and stuff.'

'Charity?'

'Hmm. He's doing a triathlon to raise money.'

Cora felt deflated. Why hadn't he told her about the triathlon? When she thought about it, they'd hardly said anything at all. She could have had the same exchange with the postman.

Friday. Nothing from Jacob. Cora has a knot in her stomach and a headache. Then a text pings. She feels a flash of excitement when she sees his name on her screen.

Found a possible bike for Luke. Not too far away. East Acton. Is it okay for me to take him to try it out? I can pick him up at 10 a.m. Sunday.

Plain facts about place and time. Nothing personal. Disappointed, she types: *Yes. Fine by me. Thanks.*

While he waits to get his bike, Luke allows himself to be distracted from his revision by short, intense bursts of research into locks and aerodynamic helmets, low-weight Italian shoes and special breathable tops. When Cora overhears him talking to his sister about Jacob, she notices that both of them have developed a slightly proprietorial tone.

Fran comes downstairs on Saturday afternoon, her hair streaming down her back, lips letter-box red.

'Going somewhere nice?'

'A march, actually,' she says. 'For refugees.'

Cora tries to control her amazement. 'That's . . . that's good. Are you going with . . . someone?'

'I don't need to have my hand held, Mum.' Fran looks offended. 'I'm a big girl now.'

'No, I didn't mean—'

But Fran has already gone. The front door closes behind her. Cora shakes her head. Why must they always misunderstand each other?

She spends the afternoon cleaning out the kitchen cupboards. But however ruthless she is in streamlining old pans and chucking away chipped china, she can't stop herself from thinking about Jacob. Does he like her? Or is she just an older woman to him – a charity case, someone who needs help with her neglected bike and shy son?

At least Fran is being proactive and taking an interest in the world. It seems a good sign that she's going on this march. The image of her daughter as she turned to say goodbye is still fixed in Cora's vision. She's unhappy. She's been unhappy for a long time. Cora would sacrifice anything to make her smile again, properly.

She sets herself the task of rearranging and dusting all the books in the house. She begins to pull out spines, shuffling them into the right places, moving others into piles. She stands with a heap of books at her feet, her heart strangely achy; she knows that her daughter is in need of support and guidance and love – things she's stubbornly reluctant to let Cora give her. She has to find a way of connecting with her again.

Bond Street

Before she left for the march, she looked Jacob up on social media for the millionth time, hoping to find something that she could draw hope from. But his page is as lame as her mother's – photos of trees, a post about the brain place he's raising money for, petitions that need signing; nothing revealing about himself and his personal life. No ex-girlfriends to scrutinise. No family to examine. Even after careful sleuthing, she's failed to track him down on any other platform. She feels shut out. As if he's excluded her on purpose.

When she arrives at Parliament Square, she nearly turns around and goes straight home. The sheer number of people takes her breath away. She stares around, looking for Jacob, noticing family groups, women dressed in bright colours as if they're at a festival, kids with faces painted as birds or lions. Fran's the only person not holding a sign or wearing a T-shirt bearing a message in bold writing.

As the march moves off, everyone begins to shout, taking

their cues from organisers who stride past with megaphones, blaring out slogans: 'Stop the drowning!' 'Choose love!' 'No one is illegal!'

Fran hesitates, but the pull of people setting off with purpose tugs at her, and she thinks she'll give it half an hour. She shouts too, just for something to do, to blend in. It feels surprisingly good. She raises her voice louder. A woman next to her turns and smiles.

If Lesh could see her now, she'd kill herself laughing, Fran thinks, lost inside a sea of happy-clappers and knit-your-own-yoghurt enthusiasts. It so isn't her thing. And yet her feet keep shuffling onwards, and her mouth keeps opening to repeat the latest slogan. And when thousands of voices around her sing out the same words, a chill of excitement chases across her skin. Later, when her feet have begun to ache and she's wondering how to escape, one of the men with megaphones glances over, and after a quick double-take, approaches grinning.

He must be heading for someone next to her, or behind her, she thinks. Even when he falls into step beside her, she's convinced he's a weirdo, or he's made a mistake.

'Hi,' he says. 'You came.'

She looks at him sideways, through suspicious eyes, before she recognises the little beard. The earnest expression. It's the man who snagged her tights on the Tube. To her horror, Fran feels a blush spreading across her cheeks. Humiliation painted loud. He suggested the bloody march in the first place – he probably thinks she's come because of him. *For* him.

'Yeah,' she says. 'Big surprise.'

He's wearing a T-shirt that says WE STAND WITH YOU and torn jeans. It makes him less of a hipster. He isn't bad-looking really, behind all that holier-than-thou crap, and the facial hair.

'Tell me something?' he asks.

'What?'

'Are you always angry?'

'Only when I see you.'

He laughs, 'Maybe we can change that.'

She glares at him while she tries to think of a good comeback.

'I'm Zac.'

'Fran,' she says.

'So why did you come today, Fran?'

She thinks of Jacob. She shrugs. 'I was curious.' She snatches a glance at him from the corner of her eye. 'I'm guessing this is something you do all the time? Go to protests? Each weekend something different?'

'No,' he says in a voice you might use with a three-year-old. 'My main interest is trying to help refugees. It's not just about protesting. It's about getting involved in other ways – writing to MPs, raising awareness . . .'

'Hmm.' She's stopped listening. They're heading along St James's towards Piccadilly. Green Park should appear any minute. Her getaway.

'My friend came here from Syria to study. But then his father was killed in a mortar attack, and his home was destroyed.'

'Shit.' Fran's attention is snagged. 'I'm sorry.'

'His mother and sister got out, but now they're somewhere in Greece. We've lost track of them. He worries about them all the time. Bad things happen to women alone in the camps.'

'Sorry,' Fran mutters again, feeling inadequate.

'I just think we all need to help each other,' Zac says. 'If we can.'

'Right,' Fran says. 'Thanks for educating me.'

He grins. 'Words come out of your mouth. But your eyes say something different.'

'Really?'

'Yeah. You try far too hard to be mean for it to be real.'

'So what are my eyes saying, then?'

'Maybe I'll tell you one day. But right now, I've got to get back to the day job.'

He waves his megaphone in a goodbye salute and pushes his way through the crowd. She can just make out the top of his head. 'See you, Fran,' his voice blares out.

There's laughter. 'See you, Fran!' a couple of voices echo.

'Not if I can help it,' she mutters under her breath, ducking her chin.

Then he's in her face again. 'What's your surname?' he asks, panting slightly.

She freezes. 'Pollen,' she admits.

'Like flower pollen?'

She gives a grudging nod.

And he's gone. Hurrying ahead, shouting out slogans, the rest of the crowd parroting him. Fran looks up to see the arches of the Ritz on her left, and immediately, Green Park Tube station. 'Thank Christ,' she whispers, slipping away down onto the platform, grateful for the normality of Saturday afternoon shoppers clutching bags, people staring at their phones or gazing into space, headphones buzzing at their ears.

On the train, she slumps onto a seat, more tired than she can remember, her feet sore, lower back aching. That was a waste of time, she thinks, as she changes onto the Central Line at Bond Street. She never did see Jacob in the crowd.

17

Shepherd's Bush

Sunday morning. True to his word, Jacob arrives early. Standing on the doorstep, he hardly says a thing, his attention all on Luke in the brief seconds he waits for him to shove his feet into trainers. Cora feels awkward. She can't look him in the face.

She watches the two of them disappear down the street, then turns back into the house, determined to get on with something useful. She found an old scratched wooden chair on the pavement a few days ago, lugged it home as a project. It's a good piece of furniture that just needs some love and a lick of paint to give it a new life. Pre-loved. Everything deserves the chance to be loved again.

She takes the chair into the garden and sets it on some newspaper, surrounds herself with equipment – sanding paper, chalk paint and brushes – and puts her earphones on, finding a comedy podcast to keep her amused. She's done the hard preparation work, and is engrossed in applying the first coat of paint – a pretty cornflower blue – when she realises that Luke is back, and he's wheeling a bike.

She slips off the headphones, 'You bought it!'

'Jacob says it's a bargain.' Luke is holding the handlebars of a silver racer, 'He's going to help me sort it out. Get it road-ready.'

'Yeah, it's a good buy.'

She startles, realising Jacob's there. He smiles, nodding. 'And you're pretty handy with a paintbrush.' He's walking forward to look at the chair. She straightens, and they're standing next to each other. He touches her forehead. 'You've got some paint . . .'

Her skin burns under his finger. She looks down, and is confronted with her tatty trainers, her old black leggings covered in dried paint splodges. She's a mess. Maybe she should have made an effort, knowing he might come back to the house. She can't think of anything to say. 'Coffee?' she asks finally. 'Or tea?'

He asks for coffee, but only if she's having one too, so she goes into the house to make it for them both.

'Do you mind if I stay for a bit and help Luke get his bike sorted?'

She jumps. He's come in behind her.

'Of course not. It's . . .' She was going to say *kind of you*, but stops herself.

'You're learning fast,' he smiles.

The coffee hisses, spilling onto the stove, and Cora turns off the heat, pouring it into two cups.

'If you live on a boat,' she says, 'does that mean you go off along the canal network? Travel the countryside?'

'That's a nice idea. But I've never done it.'

'Do you like it? Living on a boat?' She glances around her. 'I'm not sure I could manage in such a small space.'

He puts his cup down. 'You should come over sometime – see it for yourself.'

'Sounds ... good,' she manages.

Luke's voice comes from the garden, calling for Jacob.

'Think I'm needed,' he grins.

Cora joins them. Hours pass in the garden. Fran hasn't appeared. She must be sleeping in as usual. The three of them are engrossed in their separate projects, exchanging idle conversation as they work, calling out across the grass to each other with comments about what they're doing, and in Luke's case, plying Jacob with questions about his work, about the London Underground. He's a boy who collects facts.

'Yes,' Jacob is saying. 'Underground stations were used as air-raid shelters in the Second World War, but what lots of people don't know is that the Central Line was converted into a fighter aircraft factory that stretched for two miles. It was an official secret until the eighties.'

Luke gives an impressed whistle. 'And I've heard stories that the tunnels twist about so much because they're avoiding old plague pits?' he says hopefully.

Cora sits back on her heels, listening.

'Bones have been dug up while tunnels are being built, but no, the main reason for the twists is that the tracks often follow public roads.'

'Why is that?' Cora can't help asking.

'It's cheaper,' Jacob laughs. 'If the Underground want to excavate under private property, it will cost them.'

There's a sudden squawking and a flutter of wings from the

trees at the end of the garden. Three magpies fly out in a dazzle of black and white. Cora shakes her head. 'Up to no good again.'

'I think they get a bad rap,' Jacob says.

Cora says, 'Isn't the collective noun for them a mischief?'

Jacob gives a half-smile and goes back to the puzzle of the bike.

Cora has finished her chair. She stands up, knees aching. It looks good. Now she needs to leave it to dry. She goes across to Luke and Jacob, both hunched over the dismantled bike, the chain lying on newspaper, wheels unbolted. 'I'm going to go in – get cleaned up,' she says.

'Cool,' Luke says, without looking up.

Jacob glances at the chalky-blue chair. 'You're full of surprises. I didn't have you down as a handywoman. That's a professional job.'

'Thanks,' she laughs. 'I like rescuing things. It was a shame to see it abandoned on the pavement.'

It feels natural, she thinks, having Jacob here. But the idea that something romantic could happen between them seems ridiculous. The fact that he suggested she visit the boat was something he could as easily have offered to Fran or Luke, or both of them – probably already has. She thinks of the exact words he used: *You should come over sometime.* Casual. Vague. A throwaway invitation.

In the bathroom, Cora catches a glimpse of her reflection above the sink and shakes her head. 'Just stop this now,' she mutters as she strips off. 'You're behaving like a schoolgirl.' In the shower, she lets the spray hit her upturned face, scrubbing off daubs of blue paint. But as she steps out, grabbing a towel to wrap around her, she remembers the softening of his gaze as he touched her forehead earlier. She begins to hum as she hurries into a clean pair of jeans and T-shirt and goes downstairs.

When she reaches the kitchen and looks out of the window, she sees that her daughter has joined Jacob and Luke in the garden. She's wearing an old kimono and a pair of wellingtons. It's an eccentric outfit, but one that looks amazing on her – as if she's an artist, or a model in *Vogue*, rocking something that no normal woman would ever think of wearing. Her long hair falls down her back like a flame. Sometimes Cora's breath is stilled in her chest by her daughter's beauty. She starts to unload the dishwasher. She can hear the other three outside, their laughter, their easy conversation, and it makes her feel old.

She straightens, watching them through the glass. Fran leans towards Jacob and puts her hand on his arm. It's an intimate gesture. Cora's stomach contracts. Fran seems nearer in age to him than Cora is. Their skin has the shine of youth; their limbs are supple. She closes her eyes. How could she have been so deluded as to think Jacob would be interested in a middle-aged woman, greying at the temples, who needs spectacles to read a text message? She stays in the kitchen, avoiding looking out of the window.

She hears movement in the hall and realises that Jacob is leaving. He comes into the kitchen. 'Hello,' he says. 'I've told Luke I'll swing by next Sunday. The friend I told you about – the one who runs the cycle club – says they've got an open morning in Hyde Park.' He reaches an arm into the sleeve of his jacket, and his T-shirt lifts, showing a glimpse of firm, tanned skin. Cora looks away. 'It's a great opportunity for Luke to meet some of the riders,' he's saying. 'And try his bike in the safety of the park.'

'Thanks.' Her lips stretch, aiming for a smile.

'And what about you – when are you going to come and see the boat?' he says. 'How about next week? I owe you two coffees. And I like to pay my debts.'

'Oh!' She's undone by surprise, buoyant with pleasure. She can't stop a real smile spreading across her face. But she has to check. 'Have you . . . Are the . . . um . . . Fran and Luke . . . are they coming too?'

He looks puzzled. 'They're welcome, of course. But I was thinking it would be . . . nice if you came over – just you.'

She doesn't trust her voice. She clears her throat. 'I'd like that,' she says carefully. 'Thanks.'

'Good.' He leans forwards and kisses her cheek. She inhales the scent of his skin, the tang of oil and rubber, the fresh, earthy smells of her garden.

18

Marble Arch

Fran can't believe she overslept. She was shattered from the day before: hips and feet sore from all that walking. As soon as she opened her eyes and realised the time, she threw on her kimono and rushed downstairs, afraid she'd already missed him, only to find him in the garden with Luke, messing about with bits of bike spread out on the ground. Maybe he'd taken it apart as a delaying tactic, so he could wait for her.

She told him the story of Zac's refugee friend. She wanted him to know she'd been on the march, that she's got principles, like him. She's made it pretty obvious that she's into him. Why hasn't he made a move yet? She bites her nail. Maybe he's worried she's too young. But she's ready to be with an older man – a real grown-up. She needs to end it with Hugo. Their relationship is a lie. He's vain. He never asks about her or seems interested in anything but sex. Sometimes she feels a bit scared of him. She's going to dump him right now; she'll do it by text. He won't care. He's probably seeing other people anyway.

She takes out her phone: *I'm not going to come round again. Sorry. It's not working.*

She sighs with relief. Her whole body feels lighter.

Her phone pings. *8 p.m. My place.*

She sits for a moment, wondering if their texts crossed. She feels a flush of embarrassment. Then she taps: *I meant it. It's over.*

Another ping. Why is Hugo sending her pictures? She opens the photo. Some porno trash of a naked girl giving a blow job. Her breath catches in her chest. It's her, caught in a circle of flash. Coked out of her head. There's enough of her face to recognise, her long red hair flopping all over Hugo's legs, the rose tattoo on her shoulder.

Pretty picture, isn't it? See you at 8.

Her throat constricts. Bile rising. She feels sick. He's got others on his phone. He was always into all that shit – taking photos of them together in bed, asking her to send him pictures of naked body parts. It seemed funny at the time, even flattering. Now she realises how stupid she's been. How careless.

She's dressed in jeans and sweatshirt, face bare of make-up. She refuses to give him the satisfaction of thinking she's made an effort to appear sexy. Hugo opens the door and looks her up and down. One eyebrow rises scornfully, before he jerks his head, turning on his heel for her to follow him.

In the kitchen, she stands apart from him behind the central island, as if it could act as a shield, and grips the cold marble edges of the counter.

'No kiss? No small talk?' He takes down a bottle of vodka and pours it into two glasses, sliding one over to her. 'That's not polite.' He downs a shot and pours another.

'What do you want, Hugo?'

'Thing is, Fran, you've got it all wrong.' He leans against the sleek contours of the cabinet behind him, ankles crossed. 'You're not the one to tell me when this ends.'

'What do you mean?' She frowns. 'You can't force me into seeing you.'

'I have such a lovely array of pictures of you. If I put one of those on the web and tagged you in it, I think the whole world would come calling. Not that they'd be offering you Chekov or Shakespeare. But work's work. Right?'

She pushes her glass away untouched. Her mouth is sour, dry. She can't understand why he's doing this. She knows he doesn't love her. She's not stupid. But she thought he liked her. They were in a relationship.

'Why are you being so ... so cruel? I'm ...' she looks at her feet, 'I'm supposed to be your girlfriend.'

He laughs and shakes his head. 'You're not my girlfriend. But you do belong to me, until I say you don't.'

There's a buzzing inside her head. The room shrinks and folds towards her. She holds one of her wrists and squeezes. How could she not have twigged before that he's a psycho, a control freak? He collects people like other people collect stamps. She's seen the way he plays a room, using his so-called guests like pawns, manipulating them. She let him do it with her, making her sleep with Charlie. It's a game to him.

He steps closer. 'You're not going to cry, are you?' he says with curiosity.

'What if I go to the police?' she asks when she can manage to speak.

'It's your word against mine. And the images aren't on my phone any more. You're not going to risk them going public.

Can you imagine what your mother would think? Your friends?' He grins. 'You know my dad is a high court judge. I'm untouchable, Fran.'

'But when will it end?' She can hardly breathe.

He shrugs. 'Let's just see when I get tired of you, shall we?'

'You bastard.' She feels sick. 'Doesn't it bother you that I don't want to sleep with you? You're ... you're forcing me.'

Hugo smiles. 'I'll message you when I need you. And this time, come when I call. Unless you want the photos going viral.'

Outside his flat, her knees give way and she sinks to her haunches, panting, her hands clasped over her head, as if warding off a blow. People walk past without stopping. She only sees their legs. They probably think she's drunk. She's always known deep down that being with Hugo was a kind of self-punishment – he was all she felt she deserved. He was cruel and controlling. Meeting Jacob was the reason she'd decided enough was enough; that maybe she was worth more than Hugo. But now she sees that it's too late. He'll never let her go.

The moment Mum came back from the consultant, Fran knew. She opened her mouth, sounds gargling out of her. Moon faces turning towards them. Strangers gaping in the quiet of the hospital waiting room. She wanted to scream: why are you alive when he's going to die?

Dad. Her dad. She was the reason he was lying in a bed, a tangle of wires attaching him to machines.

A nurse was at her elbow. They were being led down a corridor, she and Luke and Mum. Then they were shown into a different room – Fran knew it was a special one, for bad news. The nurse closed the door softly.

'I'm sorry, my loves,' Mum said, her skin blotchy red from crying.
'I'm sorry . . . I've had to . . . to agree . . .'

Luke couldn't speak he was crying so much.

'No.' Fran's voice was harsh. It ripped at her throat. 'You can't.
You can't. He might wake up. He . . . he's strong . . .'

Mum shook her head, and her hands trembled as they reached
out to try and hold them both. 'His brain is . . . too damaged . . .
He's never going to be . . . He can't breathe . . . can't eat . . .'

She ducked away from Mum's fingers. Her chest was tight. 'I
hate you,' she whispered. 'You're a murderer.'

She rammed her fists into her eye sockets. She'd killed Dad. It
was her. But she couldn't stop shouting at Mum, the same word,
over and over.

Murderer.

At home, she stares at herself in the mirror. 'Stupid,' she
whispers. 'Stupid, stupid girl. You deserve this. You're nothing. Nothing.'

She slaps herself once, hard. The stinging shock of her fingers
against her cheek feels like a relief. She does it again.

It's as if the world has shut its door on her. She's tumbling
into a void, and she can't see the bottom. Dad, her career, and
now this. She thinks of Jacob. At least he doesn't know what
a failure she is, how weak and thoughtless and frivolous. Then
a thought hits her, and it hurts more than her hand against
her skin. Maybe he does. Maybe he could read it in her face,
or smell it on her, like cigarette smoke. That's why he's not
interested.

Bethnal Green

Cora follows Jacob's directions. She leaves Bethnal Green Tube station, making her way down the traffic-clogged old Roman Road, heady with fumes, turning off down a confusion of side streets in the direction of, she hopes, the canal. There's an abandoned shopping trolley on its side, and a burnt-out scooter smelling of ash and oil. But once she's on the towpath, she walks under branches of oaks into a different world: a country-side tangle of cow parsley, nettles and dandelions, the froth of early hawthorn. The surface of the canal gleams in the early-evening light.

Hard to believe that the noise and bustle of Hackney is so close. A few people walk the bank: a woman with her collie, a couple hand in hand, two boys with fishing rods. A cyclist pedals past. And as she rounds a corner, there are the narrow-boats: low in the water, moored bow to stern along the bank, neatly painted in reds, greens and yellows.

Approaching them, she slows and hesitates; then Jacob

appears, waving at her. Her steps quicken, her smile broadening. There's an awkward moment where neither of them seems to know how to greet each other – a handshake or a polite kiss on the cheek? She raises herself onto the balls of her feet, reaching up to proffer her cheek, but somehow her lips make contact with the edge of his mouth. She gasps, reeling back. His laughter is a relief.

'I always find that particular greeting a minefield,' he smiles. 'It's like a dance, isn't it? Easy to land in the wrong place.'

She grins, 'At least we avoided a nose clash.'

He steps to one side, offering his hand to guide her across the gangplank. 'Welcome aboard,' he says.

As she stands on the back deck, a shape swoops low; her ears are filled with a feathery rustle, and something grazes the top of her head. She gasps, wobbles, nearly loses her balance. Jacob takes her elbow. 'Scout!' he's shouting up into the sky. 'Careful!'

Cora stares into the pale light, confusion making her dizzy.

'Sorry,' Jacob says. 'Are you all right?'

A magpie flutters down and lands on his shoulder.

'This is Scout,' he says. 'She can be a bit of a clown sometimes. A bit cheeky.'

The bird regards Cora with bright eyes, and leans her head towards Jacob's face, pecking gently at his ear. She lets out a questioning squawk.

'No,' he tells her. 'I don't have any treats.'

The bird picks up a strand of his hair, tweaks it, making him laugh, and then launches from his shoulder, flying across the canal and up into the trees on the far bank.

'She's a . . . a pet?' Cora asks.

'No. I found her on the towpath when she was a baby,' he says. 'She was near to death. I nursed her until she was better.'

He gazes into the trees. 'I thought she'd take off for good as soon as she could fly. But she comes back when she feels like it, answers to her name if I call her.'

He leads the way inside the boat. Cora ducks her head and goes down steep steps into a narrow space. She looks around with amazement. On the outside, the craft looks traditional, painted like a gypsy caravan, but inside, it's bigger than she thought, modern and homely, with panelled sides in warm grey, honey parquet flooring, a couple of vintage leather chairs, bookshelves filled with colourful spines, a wood burner in the corner.

She can't stop thinking of the magpie, and touches her head at the place the bird skimmed past. 'She's called Scout?'

'Yeah. You know. Her curious nature – always scouting around.'

'Most people are wary of magpies.'

He grins. 'Well, this one's intelligent and funny, and I know we don't think of birds as being loving, but she's as affectionate as any dog or cat.'

There are sketches pinned up on one wall: an owl, a drawing of a water vole, and a page full of impressions of a magpie, wings spread, nestled on the ground, recognisable as the bird on his shoulder.

'I'm guessing these are Scout?' She goes closer to inspect them. 'Are they your work?'

He nods.

'They're good. Really good.'

He rubs his nose. 'Just doodles.'

They are standing in an impossibly tiny kitchen. There's a shiny red kettle steaming on the gas ring, and red mugs hanging from pegs. He's got an old chambray shirt on, sleeves rolled up to show strong forearms with a dusting of hair. His shoulders are broad. She wonders how a tall man manages in such a confined space, but watching him, she sees that he's learnt to move carefully. She likes the way he dresses in simple, well-worn things. He's wearing his shirt over faded black jeans with sturdy brown boots.

She realises she's staring and pulls her gaze away, her fingers trailing the enamelled worktop as she glances out of a little window at some ducks on the water. She thinks of Scout sitting on his shoulder. He was a natural with her.

He opens a tiny fridge tucked away behind a cupboard door. 'We're in between tea time and wine time. Which would you prefer?'

Being here with him on the boat, she feels a nerve-jangling sense of adventure, a kind of recklessness she hasn't felt in years. 'Wine. Please.'

'Good choice,' he says, pouring Sauvignon into two glasses. He hands her one and indicates a chair, taking the other.

As she gazes around, she remembers that Luke told her yesterday that he'd done some research into Jacob's job, and had been impressed to discover that Jacob earned 'a fat salary'. So he could afford to live pretty much wherever he wanted. But he's chosen this modest space.

'Were you brought up on a boat?' she asks.

'My mother would faint at the idea! My family thought I'd gone mad. I knew nothing about boats, but I liked the idea of living differently, being more self-sufficient. I had to learn fast – to splice ropes, use a pressure washer, change an oil filter.'

'None of that's appealing right now,' Cora laughs.

'I'm not selling it, am I?' He's grinning. 'Okay, how about . . . I wake up to the gentle sound of lapping water, and I might see a kingfisher before I even make myself a coffee. The boating community's tight, too – we look out for each other.' He shrugs. 'Also, I like the puzzle of keeping all my things in a small space. To be honest, I'm a natural slob. So it stops me accumulating too much stuff. Keeps my life . . . streamlined.'

Cora dips her head as she sips her drink. Could 'streamlined' be code for keeping his life uncluttered by relationships?

'You said you haven't taken the boat out of London yet?' she asks. 'Isn't that the point of living on the water – the freedom to travel?'

'Not always. Some houseboats don't ever move from their mooring, but,' he lifts his shoulders, 'you're right, exploring the canal network would be fun. An adventure. I make plans in my head.'

'So what's stopping you?'

He gazes out of the window. 'Too busy at work? I don't know.' He shrugs again. 'Just never the right time.'

'But you could manage the locks? They look terrifying to me.'

He tells her how he got stuck in the first lock he tried to operate on the way to the mooring, and laughs when he recalls how he thought the boat would sink in the rising swell.

She's finding it hard to concentrate. She's certain she's not imagining it: the air is alive with tension; anticipation hums between them. When he turns to her, it's hard to look away, so that their eye contact is becoming more and more intense, at odds with the lightness of their conversation.

She makes an effort to drag her gaze towards the porthole, and the towpath beyond. 'Do you know the other boat people very well? You live so close to each other.'

'Yeah.' He laughs. 'It's difficult to keep secrets when you live on a boat. But somehow it's less claustrophobic than living in a terrace of houses.'

'Do you have secrets that need keeping, then?'

It was a joke, but Jacob jerks upright so quickly he spills wine on his shirt. He grabs a sopping-wet cloth from the sink and swipes at the darkened patch. He's making a mess of it, dampening the wrong bit of shirt, water dripping over his shoes. Cora can't stop herself: she takes the cloth from him. With a quick squeeze over the sink, she gets rid of the excess water, then dabs at the spot. 'There. It won't stain,' she says.

'It . . . it doesn't matter anyway,' he says hoarsely. His body is rigid, hands clenched by his sides. She can see the texture of his skin inside the open neck of his shirt, the dip between his collarbones.

'Well . . .' She clears her throat, gripping the cloth.

'I . . . I invited you here because . . . I like you, Cora.' He rubs his chin. 'God, I sound like a schoolboy. I wasn't going to just blurt it out.'

His words repeat in her head, and her heart swells. She wants to confess, *I like you too*; but she's suddenly afraid. She wanted this to happen with every fibre of her being, but now he's said the words, she's scared. She looks at his open face, and worries that maybe he hasn't understood how much older than him she is. She tilts her chin. 'I'm fifty, Jacob.'

'I'm thirty-eight.'

He didn't flinch at her age. She does the maths. Twelve years. The gap feels like a bottomless pit – something dangerous.

She's still clutching the damp cloth. If she moved her arm, her hand would touch his. Her breath is caught in her chest. 'You don't . . . mind?'

'Why would I?' He takes the cloth from her, tosses it neatly into the sink. 'Cora, I need to ask you something.'

'Yes?'

'Would it be okay . . . if I kissed you?'

She nods. There's a roaring in her ears. But as his mouth meets hers, silence. Like falling underwater, like swimming into another element. Blind. Hushed. Soft. His hands hold her face. She slides her arms around his neck. When they break apart, she's shaking. They stand together without speaking, her head on his shoulder, his arms around her.

She leans into his embrace. He takes her chin and tilts it towards him. They kiss again. Nothing else exists except the two of them, their mouths moving, his fingers in her hair, behind her neck. When they stop, they stand together with their noses and foreheads touching, breath swallowing breath.

'You have no idea how much I wanted to do that,' he says. 'I just wasn't sure if you felt the same way.'

'I didn't know if you liked me either.'

'Thank goodness that's cleared up then.' He hugs her close, his mouth in her hair. She feels a warmth spread across her scalp. Her body is alive with feelings she'd forgotten. Her veins tingle, singing with oxygen and blood – the rushing of life, soaring and swooping through her limbs. Her heart has expanded in her chest, thudding with a new resounding strength.

'Cora.' He says her name slowly. 'I'm glad you're here.'

'I'm glad too.'

Now that they've crossed the line into physical contact, they don't need spoken words. They remain standing together, leaning against each other, exploring with fingers and lips, pressing their noses into the other's neck, inhaling. They sigh, and smile, and kiss some more. Cora has no idea of time passing. She could have been in his arms for moments or hours. But she's aware that the light outside has changed; a glimpse out of a porthole shows the sun slipping towards the tree-lined horizon, a haze behind the distant tower blocks.

There's the sound of heavy wings swooping across the water, and Jacob steps away, looking through glass on the other side of the boat. 'Swans. Look.'

She bends beside him and sees the pale feathering of their flight. The sight catches at her throat. She straightens. 'I told the kids I wouldn't be out long. I should get going.' She's light-headed. She wishes she could stay here with him for ever. The prospect of leaving makes her heavy with loss.

'I'll walk you to the Tube,' he says. 'Next time, I'll make you dinner. Or we can go out. Have a proper date?'

Her heart brightens. Sings. 'It's magical here. Another world,' she says. 'I'd love to come again.' She smiles. 'I'll bring pudding.'

'No.' He takes her hand. 'No. I want to cook for you.'

As they step onto the bank, the trees have become silhouettes against a dark violet sky. A wash of red leaks across the distant city. They walk hip to hip, his arm across her shoulders, hers around his waist.

'When did you first know?' she asks. 'About me.'

'When you opened your front door. You were standing there with bare feet, and crisps in your hair. But you were like a tiger protecting your young – even though she's about a foot taller than you – and afterwards, I ... I kept seeing your face, your eyes, dark and soulful, as if you were telling me something ...' He stops.

Cora's cheeks burn with pleasure; she ducks her head to hide it.

He rubs his nose and gives a brief laugh. 'I wasn't brave enough to ask for your number. I couldn't blame you for being suspicious of me – a stranger bringing Fran home.'

'I ... I liked you too. But I couldn't believe you'd find me attractive. I still can't really believe this is happening,' she says.

'Neither can I.'

'Are you sure you want to date an old lady?' She gives a quick self-conscious laugh.

He stops. 'You should celebrate your age.' He kisses her gently, his voice serious, 'Every year has led up to this moment – to you being you.'

At the entrance to the Tube, they kiss properly, in public, like lovers – like young lovers, she thinks.

On the platform, she stares into the rush and clatter of the oncoming train. She finds a seat inside a busy carriage and settles into it; she's unable to control her smile as she remembers the way his mouth tasted, how his tongue felt against her own. Her lips feel tender from kissing. Avoiding the eyeline of passengers sitting opposite, her gaze finds the Tube map above the window. She's never felt so right, so completely herself. Not for a long time. She looks at the straight red Central Line, thinking that it connects her and Jacob now, like a ribbon tied between them, or an artery taking life from one to the other.

Shepherd's Bush

Fran's phone beeps. It's Alesha, again. Fran ignores her, turning the phone to silent. If she answers, Lesh will suss that something's wrong. Convincing her otherwise, Fran thinks, would require acting skills. The irony twists her mouth into a grimace. Finally she can admit to herself that she only got into drama school because someone dropped out at the last minute. Dad was wrong about her. She isn't talented. He just wanted her to be an actress because he knew she wasn't clever enough to do anything else.

She's not clever enough to get out of Hugo's trap. She's thought about it non-stop since leaving his flat. She's asked the cards for advice. But nothing's helping. There's no solution. She's going to have to go through with it. If he posts those pictures, her life will be over. Mum will be devastated, and even more disappointed in her than she already is. Luke will be traumatised. And Jacob ... She frowns. She'll never be able to look Jacob in the face again.

She lies flat on her bed, staring up at the paintwork above her, and recalls a different ceiling in Suffolk. Closing her eyes, she hears the thunder boom, the crash of lightning. It was exciting at first, staring into the wet dark, waiting for the flares of white revealing the garden as a ghostly other-world, before blackness wiped it out again.

It was as she got into bed that she noticed a quickening above her head, like a giant shadow-spider on the move. She stared up at the newly darkened surface. The stain began to bleed. Drops of liquid fell onto her cheek, wet and cold. She touched her skin. Water! As she watched, the whole ceiling came alive. It rippled, puckered and swelled – bellying out like a fat man's paunch. Then, with a groan, it split open, spewing an ocean into her room.

She ran downstairs, shouting for help. Mum brought up buckets and towels to mop up the mess. Dad came up with his flashlight. Fran's room was in the attic, tucked up under the eaves. Dad crawled into the roof space with a grim expression. After ten minutes, he backed out, trousers ripped at the knee, smudges of dirt on his cheek.

'A big branch from the beech has crashed through the tiles,' he explained. 'I need to get it out before I can patch the roof up.' He had that look on his face, the one he got when he was taking charge, being Superman. 'I can't do it from inside, there's no space. I need to get some leverage on the wood to pull it free.'

'Well, obviously you can't go up there now,' Mum said.

The buckets Mum had set under the worst of the leak were nearly full. The raindrops plopped in rapid percussion. Fran stared at the damage; all her lovely things were spoiled. She picked up dirty shoes and dripping books, twists of sodden clothing – her Topshop stuff bought on a visit to London. Her bedding was sopping. Her brand-new guitar ruined, and she hadn't even learned to play it yet.

'It's not that bad, love,' Mum coaxed. 'It'll dry out tomorrow. We'll call someone first thing to fix the roof.' She patted Fran's shaking shoulders. 'Come on. I'll make up a camp bed in Luke's room for tonight.'

But it was bad. Tears blurred Fran's vision as her fingers fumbled through the mossy damp of the carpet. It was worse than bad.

'Dad,' she wailed, stumbling off the floor and into his arms. 'Everything's spoiled.' She breathed in his wool-and-tobacco smell as she sobbed into his chest.

He stroked her hair with big fingers, whispering endearments. 'Don't cry, angel,' he murmured. 'I'll make it right. The worst of the storm is over.' His words rumbled through his ribcage, the echo of them filtering into her bones. 'I can patch it up now.'

Mum argued against it, but he won. He always did.

Fran and Luke stood barefoot at the threshold of the front door, faces tilted to watch their father perform his heroic deed. For me, Fran thought. This is for me. Mum waited at the bottom of the ladder, holding it steady, disapproving in her silence. Dad was a dark shape ascending, getting smaller as he went up, rung by rung, the torch clamped to his forehead blinking through the rain, tools slotted into his belt like guns, mac flapping.

Did she see him fall? Sometimes she thinks she did. But it happened so fast. She has an image of him stuck in her head, his plummet to earth caught mid dive. He hangs suspended over the wet ground, a flare of lightning picking out his features, the surprise on his face, his yellow coat like useless wings, his hands splayed as if he could stop the rushing ground.

Shepherd's Bush

When Cora wakes on Sunday morning, she can tell she's slept in by the slant of light through her curtains. She blinks, a smile starting at her centre. She never sleeps late. She relives his lips on hers, their kiss at the entrance of the Tube station. She allows herself a luxurious yawn, pointing her toes, stretching her fingers. 'Jacob.' She tries his name on her tongue. Saying it again, louder, slower, into the room.

In the bathroom, she cleans her teeth, spitting, rinsing. She feels like a young girl. It's a surprise to notice the slight loosening of skin on her arms as she reaches to put her toothbrush back on the shelf.

Downstairs, she makes pancakes with the radio on, throwing flour into the bowl, her bare feet sprinkled with white. She can't remember when she felt this hungry.

'You're in a good mood.'

She glances up as Luke sits at the table.

'Morning, darling.' She kisses his hair, and he hardly flinches, just protests weakly out of habit – 'Mum!' – brushing her off. But he's smiling.

She doesn't usually eat much more than a slice of toast, but now she heaps pancakes onto her plate, pouring on maple syrup, licking the sweetness from her fingers. 'God, these are delicious,' she says to herself, to Luke, to nobody in particular.

Her phone beeps.

Good morning. Just to say, I'm thinking of you. To be honest, didn't stop thinking of you all night. Supper at the boat on Wednesday?

Thinking of you too, she types. *Wednesday sounds good.*

She's aware that she's smiling and smiling, as if she's deranged. Her cheeks ache with it. Luke is looking at her strangely. 'Not having a funny turn, are you, Mum?'

'No.' She shakes her head. 'Just happy, that's all.'

'Good.' He scrapes his plate, licking his knife. 'Jacob's coming to pick me up today. He's taking me to a meet at a cycle club.'

She jolts at his name. 'Yes – yes … I know.'

The thought that she'll see him again soon, however briefly, sets a nervous fluttering under her ribs. It strikes her that her shy son is excited about the prospect of being introduced to strangers: a small miracle, she thinks, one somehow brought about by Jacob.

She jumps to her feet, gathering plates, wiping sugar from the table, anything to hide her face.

Luke goes off to get ready, whistling as he passes Fran, who has appeared in the doorway. She trudges to the table, hands hanging limply at her sides. She's wearing a pair of baggy leggings and a stained T-shirt. Cora's happiness drains away, spiralling into nothing.

'Darling, what's the matter? Are you ill?'

Fran grunts and shakes her head.

'You need to eat. Shall I make more pancakes? My special recipe! They're delicious. Luke and I made pigs of ourselves. But there's mix left.'

Fran shakes her head again. 'Not hungry.' She pours herself a coffee and slumps at the table, hair falling around her cheeks.

Cora pulls up a chair next to her, and touches her daughter's hand. 'Talk to me, Fran.' She searches for the right words. 'I know we haven't been getting on lately, but I hate it when we fight. You can tell me anything. Whatever it is, we can sort it out together.'

Fran snatches her hand away. 'You don't understand.'

The optimism of her evening with Jacob is still with her, so Cora takes Fran's hand again and squeezes. She looks at her daughter's fingers, studded with silver rings, remembering them as a toddler's, sticky and clenched. 'If you explain it to me, then maybe I will understand.' She lowers her voice. 'I want to.'

Fran pulls away again and drives the heels of both hands into her eyes. 'I can't.'

'You're scaring me, Fran,' Cora says quietly. 'What could be so bad?'

'Nothing . . . just . . .'

'What?' she whispers.

'I . . . I miss Dad,' Fran says.

Cora reaches out and pulls her daughter to her. 'I know, love.' She tightens her arms around her and presses her nose into her hair, inhaling stale Coco Mademoiselle and the musty traces of sleep-doused skin.

Fran slumps against her shoulder, and Cora is grateful for this physical contact, but a niggling voice inside warns that something's wrong – this is not just about Andrew.

'Is there . . . something else?' she asks softly.

Fran struggles to sit up. She stares down at the table. 'There's . . . this man. It's just . . . I really like him . . . and I don't know if he likes me back. I thought he did. But now I'm not so sure.' She sniffs. 'I don't know if I can handle the rejection. He's the first man I've met that I know I can have a proper relationship with. A grown-up relationship.'

Cora takes a breath, a sense of relief rushing through her. Fran is opening up to her. There's a chance here for a connection. 'Do I know him? This man?'

Fran nods. 'It's Jacob.'

Cora bites back her gasp. The room spins. She curls her fingers around the edge of the table and grips. 'Jacob?'

Fran's nodding. 'It's clear he likes me. He only agreed to come over that time you invited him because he wanted to meet me again. And then offering to come and fix your bike? It was so he could see me. I know there's something between us. But . . . he hasn't asked me out yet.' She licks a finger and rubs it across a stain on her top. 'I can't stop thinking about him.' She draws in a deep breath. 'I don't know what I'm doing wrong. I've given him all the signs. Maybe I should just ask him.' She sighs and shakes her head. 'Normally I would. But I don't know, he makes me feel . . . shy.'

'Oh Fran.' Cora touches her daughter's hand. 'That sounds serious.'

Fran gulps. 'Everything's . . . hopeless at the moment. I'm not getting any parts. I think my agent wants to drop me. If I was with Jacob, it would change everything. I'd start to believe in myself again.'

Cora sinks back into her chair. Why didn't she see this? It was under her nose all the time. How could she have been so blind? She touches her belly. Her stomach hurts. She was greedy. All those pancakes. Serves her right.

Helena rings, and Cora takes the call upstairs in her room, shutting the door.

'So,' Helena asks. 'How did it go? Last night?'

'It was amazing,' Cora says in a flat voice. 'Wonderful. We kissed.'

'Well, don't sound so bloody miserable about it!'

Cora stands by the window, looking into the street. 'I can't go through with it, Helena. I'm . . . I'm in shock. Fran's literally just told me that she likes Jacob. My own daughter likes the same man as me! How could I have missed it? She'll be devastated when she finds out I'm seeing him. I can't do it.'

There's a pause, and then, 'Yes, you can.' Helena's voice is firm. 'I'm not letting you ruin this. He's the first man you've liked since Andrew. I've known Fran since she was a baby, and she's used to getting her own way. I mean, I love her. Of course I do. But her feelings for Jacob are just infatuation. Tell her you're seeing him, and she'll act out for a bit, and then she'll get over it. Find some poor boy her own age to terrorise.'

'I don't know . . . I don't think—'

'Cora!' Helena interrupts. 'Just see him one more time. Give it a chance.'

'He's picking Luke up in a minute. Taking him out on a bike ride.' She's watching the street as she talks, waiting for the first glimpse of him.

'So the kids don't know?'

'No – much too early. And . . . impossible now. With Fran.'

'Think that's best.'

'He messaged me this morning, because he knows we can't

127

talk properly when he gets here. He asked me to have dinner on his boat on Wednesday.'

'Go,' Helena says. 'Or you'll have me to answer to.'

Cora leans her forehead on the glass. She's heavy with her betrayal of Fran. It was unintentional before, but if she sees Jacob now, she'll be hurting her daughter on purpose. It's impossible. Fran is too vulnerable, too fragile. Helena doesn't understand.

Helena's still talking, but Cora loses focus when she spots Jacob turning into the street. He cycles towards their house, unaware of her gaze, and locks his bike to the gate. It's odd to see him as a stranger would, an anonymous cyclist behind his helmet and glasses, and at the same time to know that she's felt the beat of his heart, his lips on hers. She loses sight of him as he goes up the steps to the front door. The bell rings. Luke shouts up the stairs. 'Bye!'

She panics that she's going to miss them. She says goodbye to Helena and clicks off. Below, Fran has come outside onto the street to talk to Jacob. She's wearing a long cardigan; underneath it her legs are bare. Jacob looks distracted, trying to answer Fran's questions and talk to Luke at the same time.

Cora throws open the window and leans out. Jacob's in the middle of pointing out something on the handlebars of Luke's bike; at the sound of the sash, they glance up. Luke's spectacles glint in the light.

'Hi!' Jacob calls, craning his neck. 'We're going to get going. Should be about two hours. Don't worry,' he adds. 'I'll look after him.'

An unspoken understanding passes between them, a warmth in his eyes just for her. It makes her legs weak. Fran's disappeared, into the house, or maybe she's waiting on the top step. Leaning further out of the window, Cora gives Luke a confident wave, and he gives her a thumbs-up. She watches the two of them cycle away until they turn the corner. She trusts Jacob with Luke. She remembers how it felt inside the circle of his arms when he held her on the boat. A belonging. A peace. A beginning.

But she's got to walk away. And somehow, she has to tell him.

Shepherd's Bush

Fran regrets those moments in the kitchen. Now that Mum knows, she'll be like a bloodhound on the scent. She'll ask about Jacob all the time. She'll try to be helpful, offering suggestions and plans, but make everything worse. Like the pep talks she gives before Fran goes to auditions. Cora can't leave things alone – if something's damaged, it must be mended, improved, perfected. Why can't she get it? Fran isn't like her. They couldn't be more different. Fran doesn't write to-do lists. She's not an uptight clean freak. Most of all, she's not cheerleader positive about every bloody thing. *Try your best* is her mother's mantra. *Try your best in everything you do.* But what if you try your best and you still fail?

With Dad, it was different. His belief in Fran was an invisible mantle she wore to protect her from the world. He kept her safe from failure through the power of his faith. Dad, tall, strong, charismatic and clever, was her ally, her supporter. Even when she failed maths and didn't get the starring role in the school play, he would be there with a wink and a hug, and the exact right words to make her feel better, to make her feel that this was a tiny bump in the road to certain success. 'You have something the others don't,' he told her. 'You're a star. Don't ever forget it.'

He built her a stage in the playroom. A platform with a curtain and a couple of changes of scenery commissioned from the local art school. Instead of bedtime stories, he talked through all the famous Shakespeare heroines, explaining their roles. He said she'd be a perfect Beatrice. A few times a year, he took her on special trips to London to see opening nights – they went to the Globe, the Almeida, the National, the Young Vic – and afterwards, in the car on the way home, she'd sit up front with him and they would talk about the performance, pick out the role that she'd play when she was older. She loved those nights. The way it felt to be enclosed inside the leathery warmth of his car, secure and free, flying through the darkness with Dad giving her all his attention.

One night, after coming back from seeing a Tom Stoppard play, Fran heard her parents talking quietly together in their bedroom.

With a small shock, she caught her own name. Careful not to step on a creaky board, she stopped outside the partly closed door, heart racing.

'Darling, I didn't mean it like that . . . It's wonderful that you do so much for Fran.' Mum's voice. 'That you share your love of the theatre with her . . . but don't you think you might be setting her up for a fall?'

'Fran's made for the stage, with her height and her looks.' Dad's voice. 'Like a young Vanessa Redgrave. She's not academic, not like Luke. This is something she could excel at.'

'Just because you want her to be a star, that doesn't mean—'

'Is this about me and Fran going off without you?' he interrupted. 'Because you know you can come too, darling. We'd love you to.'

Fran swallowed a gasp. She didn't want to share her father, not on their special trips to London. Horrified, she listened intently for her mother's reply.

Mum sighed. 'I can't leave Luke. And I know you two like your alone time. I'm not jealous, Andrew, just . . . a bit concerned, for Fran. You're encouraging her to put all her eggs in one basket – I hate that expression, sorry – but it's true.'

'You're wrong, my love. If she's to succeed in this business, she needs to be one-track-minded. She needs to go all out for it, with blinkers on. She must give and hazard all she has for this.'

The Merchant of Venice. Fran recognised the quote, grinning with pleasure, knowing Mum wouldn't understand the reference. She crept softly away, her heart glowing with Dad's words, the certainty of his belief in her. It made her feel invincible.

Even if he got it wrong about her acting abilities, he was always there for her, listening without judgement, thinking the best of her. Well, he's not here to protect her now. There's only Mum, who knows all her failings. The thought of Cora ever finding out about Hugo makes Fran feel sick.

She looks at her phone again, and sees a notification on Facebook. Grateful for the distraction, she clicks on a new friend request. Some random guy. Her finger hovers. She hasn't met most of her Facebook friends – the thousand or so she's acquired. May as well have one more, she thinks; it's all bullshit anyway. Then she squints closer at the profile picture. He looks familiar. The hipster with a megaphone. She squirms as she remembers how he embarrassed her on the march. She closes the page. No way is she going to accept Zac Jessiman as a friend.

Bethnal Green

On Wednesday, Cora finds Fran watching a film in the sitting room. She stands in the doorway, freshly showered, with glossy hair and her best jeans on. She twists her hands together as she explains that she's going out to supper and might be late back. *I'm going to see Jacob*, a voice in her head is shouting. *I'm sorry. I'm sorry.* She waits for the interrogation. But Fran just mutters, 'Have a good one,' and carries on staring at the flickering screen, bouncing her legs off the edge of the sofa.

Luke is in his room, at his desk. He swings around in his chair, giving her his full attention. 'Are you meeting Helena?'

'No,' Cora admits. 'Someone else. Another friend.'

Luke looks puzzled; he pushes at the bridge of his glasses. 'Okay.'

'I've left a salad in the fridge. And there's pizza.'

He nods. His face is open, trusting. He has a new pimple on his chin. 'Have a good time, Mum.' Her easy child.

She has lied to her children. There's a knot in her throat. But she can't tell Jacob that it's over in a text, as if she's a teenager. She owes it to him to see him face to face and explain.

She shuts Luke's door gently behind her. His room is immaculate as usual. It doesn't seem normal for a seventeen-year-old boy to fold his clothes, to keep his pens in a container on his desk, every pencil sharpened, to make his own bed each day, sheets pulled tight, wrinkle-free, as if he's in the army. She worries that his obsessive cleanliness and tidiness is getting worse. It definitely increased after Andrew's accident. But his nascent relationship with Jacob, the bike rides, the exercise, it's all helping, she thinks. He seems more relaxed. He smiles more.

How different her children are: Fran throws her clothes into crumpled piles on the floor, and Luke can't stand to have a pencil out of line. She doesn't know if either of those things is her fault.

On the Central Line, she finds a seat and stares unseeingly at her reflection. She tries to think of the words to tell Jacob she's ending it – ending it before it's even begun. Her mind is muddled with jumbled sentences she can't untangle.

'Text me, and I'll meet you by the gate,' he said.

As she leaves Bethnal Green station, she tries to message as she walks along the busy road, but has to stop and put her glasses on. How anyone stares at a phone while negotiating a busy London pavement is beyond her. She would be the one to twist an ankle or slam into a lamp post.

He's there, waiting at the rusty gate, and despite everything, her breath releases in a burst of happiness at the sight of his profile, at the familiarity of his smile as he greets her. Scout is at his feet, pecking at the grass.

'Hey, you.' He reaches for her, pulling her into a hug.

She closes her eyes, leaning her cheek against his chest: the lithe, muscular shape of him, the woody, outdoorsy smell of him. They break away at the same time, and he grins, rubbing his nose.

She bends over to look at the bird, 'Hello, Scout.'

'You can stroke her if you like.'

She squats down and puts her hand on the magpie's head, wondering at the delicate skull, velvety sleek beneath her fingers. She's not just black and white, as Cora thought. Petrol green and blue shimmers inside her feathers, iridescent in the light. She flutters up and hops onto Cora's back. Cora laughs.

'She likes you,' Jacob says. 'A bird with taste.'

Cora stands slowly, and as she straightens, with a slight push, Scout takes off and glides in a loop around them before she disappears.

She smells their supper before they reach the boat. Spices, the scent of lemon, the zing of chilli. Aboard, she gasps when she sees the flatbreads ready on plates, the saucepan of basmati rice, the yellow and red curries laid out on a bright cloth. Fresh coriander speckling the dishes with green.

'You made all this here?' She looks at the two-ring stove.

He smiles and points her to her seat, picking up a bottle of white. She nods, and he fills a glass and holds up his own. They clink.

She feels sick. She can't tell him, not yet. He's made such an effort. She'll tell him later, after they've eaten. She gulps some wine. 'Thanks for helping Luke with his bike – for taking him out. I haven't seen him so happy since . . . since his dad died.'

He puts a jug of water on the small table. 'It's a pleasure. He's a good kid.'

'He's the easy one, in some ways,' she says. 'Fran's always

been an extrovert. Passionate. But it's his quietness that worries me, his neatness. And he's so shy. To see him talking to you – actually putting several sentences together – it feels a bit like a miracle.'

'I don't know much about kids,' he says, offering her a bowl of rice. 'But I can see that you're a wonderful mother.'

'Thanks, but I'm not sure there's any such thing.' Cora shakes her head as she spoons food onto her plate. 'They saved me after Andrew died. Gave me purpose. A reason to get up in the morning. Luke still lets me mother him, just about.' She laughs. 'But knowing he needs me ... it's a big part of who I am.'

He nods. 'Being needed is like an anchor, isn't it? It weighs you down, but it stops you getting lost, too ...' He gives an embarrassed smile. 'Enough of the sailing metaphors. We should eat.'

'This looks amazing.' She gestures to their plates. 'Do you often cook Indian food?'

'Not when it's just me. But I like cooking different cuisines ... Mexican, Chinese, Lebanese. I grew up eating Friday-night suppers. The chicken soup joke is true, so it was a revelation to me when I discovered other kinds of food.'

'But you were born here?' She forks some food into her mouth.

'Right here. In Hackney.'

'And your family is ... traditional?'

'Yup, I was brought up going to synagogue, doing what was expected. But now ... it's just not for me.'

'Is there a reason for that?' She glances up at him. 'Sorry, I'm being nosy again.'

He waves her apology away with a waft of his long hand. 'I stopped going to synagogue with my father when I was fifteen.

I . . . suppose I began to question why things were the way they were. My parents didn't understand. They felt . . . angry and hurt, especially Dad. Although he's got used to it now.'

'Religion gives a framework, doesn't it? Rules, routine, ritual.' She puts down her fork. 'It offers answers. People need comfort. We all do, I think.'

'Exactly. But it's not really that simple, is it?'

The light-hearted bantering of their first conversation has gone; something more serious has settled between them. They eat in silence for a few minutes. The tastes are too delicious not to give them proper attention: subtle and sweet, tangy, full of flavour. She notices that his tiny kitchen is almost clear of dirty pans.

'Have you always worked in TV?' he asks, offering her some more chutney.

'After university, my first job was a runner in film. Then I moved into TV. But when I got pregnant, I stopped.'

'So you were a full-time mum?'

'Yes. I'd always planned to be one, and we were living in the middle of nowhere in Suffolk. We . . . Andrew and I . . . we moved there just after I got pregnant with Fran. He always wanted a house in the country.'

He gives her a long look. 'Didn't you want that too?'

'At first I did. It seemed the right place to raise a family.' She thinks of those endless days, the numb despair that clouded her head. 'But after Andrew died, I needed to go back to work.'

Their fingers brush as he refills her water glass. A shiver runs through her. She puts her fork and knife on her plate. 'That was completely delicious – but I can't eat another thing.'

'Neither can I.'

They both sit back in their chairs. *Now*, she thinks, her pulse revving into overdrive. This is the moment. 'Jacob, I ...' She stumbles into silence.

'Yes?' His face is expectant.

'I wanted to ...' Her nerve fails. *Coward*, she hisses at herself. But she can't hurt him. Once she speaks the words, she won't be able to take them back. He's still looking at her, waiting for her to finish her sentence.

'I ... wanted to ask you,' she continues, 'where ... um ... where did your family come from originally?'

'On my father's side, Portugal. My grandfather came to England in the early 1900s, so my father was born here.'

'And your mother's family?'

'Russia, way back.' He clears the plates from the small table, gesturing to her to stay sitting down. 'What about you? Your background? Nobody's a hundred per cent English, are they?'

'I think there's some Italian blood in the family.' She tucks her hair behind her ear. 'But my parents both died when I was at university. My father had an aneurysm. With my mother it was cancer. She was dead within six months.'

'I'm sorry,' he whispers.

'Ironically, I wasn't interested in our ancestral tree until I had my own children, but of course by then I'd missed my chance to quiz Mum and Dad.' She doesn't meet his eyes. 'I have no idea if I really have Italian blood. My upbringing was very English. I was an only child. It was a happy childhood. But I suppose our life was suburban. Ordinary.'

'Nothing like you, then.' He sits down, moving his chair closer. Their knees are touching. He runs his finger gently over her face. 'These freckles. Perhaps you have some Scottish blood too? Or Irish? But your eyes ...' He looks into them. 'I'm sure you're right about Mediterranean ancestors. Did you know that your irises are golden-brown in sunshine, but when the light is faint, like now, they're almost black? Olive black.'

She looks down; her throat is tight. She can't speak.

He takes her hand and threads his fingers through hers. She stares at the interweaving of skin, tanned and pale. Her heart is beating fast. She feels the thud echo through her bones, beating at her temples.

'You . . . still wear your wedding ring?'

A shiver goes through her. She looks at the band of gold on her finger. 'Andrew fell from a ladder. In a storm. He went up to fix the roof.'

She feels him stiffen at her words.

'You were there, when he fell? That must have been . . . terrible.'

'He didn't die,' she says quietly. 'Not immediately. He was on life support for weeks. In a coma. But there was no improvement. His brain was too damaged. They told me there was no hope.' She stops, her throat dry. 'I gave them permission to turn off the machines.'

'Cora.' He tightens his fingers around hers. 'God, I'm sorry.'

'Those weeks were the worst of my life. I spent every moment I could with him. Hoping. Playing him music. Talking to him about the past – the future. Waiting.' She shakes her head. 'But it was no good. The smell of hospitals makes me feel sick. Panicky. Brings it all back. I was so grateful to the staff, but . . .' She shudders. 'I had nightmares for years. Still do. I can't stop thinking that . . . that I killed him. I was the one who had to say—'

'No,' he says urgently. 'Don't think that, Cora. It wasn't you who killed him. It was his injuries.' He leans closer. 'It must have been very hard. I'm sorry.' He rubs her fingers. 'Thank you,' his voice is hoarse, 'for telling me.'

She looks at him. All she wants is to kiss him, to put her lips against his, shut her eyes and disappear into the moment. They are very close, their faces almost touching. A small voice tells her to stop, to move away, to explain that she has to leave. *I really must go. I really must go.* 'Thank you,' she says, her voice wobbling. 'For listening. Thank you for tonight.'

A small frown creases his forehead. 'What is it, Cora?'

'Fran,' she whispers. 'It's Fran. She likes you. She told me the other day. It . . . it was such a shock. We can't do this again. It was a mistake. I . . . I can't see you.' Her mouth is dry. 'I'm sorry. But I don't know what this would do to her.'

'Fran?' He pushes his hands across his cheeks, visibly shaken. 'She said that?' His shoulders slump. She can see him collecting himself, thinking it through. 'That's . . . difficult, but . . .' He looks up. 'Cora, I don't want to interfere in your relationship with your daughter, but . . . wouldn't the best thing be to just tell her the truth?'

'I . . . I can't. I'm sorry.' It comes out as a hoarse croak. 'She'd see it as a betrayal. I can't do that to her.' She shifts in her chair. 'I should go home.'

'Wait. This is crazy,' he says. 'Can't we talk about it?'

'Talking won't help, because the problem's not us,' she says slowly. 'It's Fran. I can't stop her from having feelings for you.'

'Doesn't it make any difference that I don't have feelings for her?'

'Yes, of course, but . . .' She frowns. 'Not as far as this goes. It's changed everything, knowing how she thinks of you.'

'Please. Tell her about us,' he says urgently. 'Give her the chance to be happy for you. When I talked to her in your kitchen, it occurred to me that she's looking for a kind of father figure. Maybe she's attracted to me because she's got the two roles mixed up.'

Cora grips her hands in her lap and stares at them. *You are a bad mother*, a voice in her head chants. *Bad. Bad. Bad.*

'If you don't tell her, you won't give anyone a chance, Cora – not us and not Fran.'

A tear rolls down her face, trickling past her nose into her mouth. She licks it away. His words are persuasive. She recognises reason inside them.

She turns. 'I . . . I can't. I don't want to hurt her.'

He sits in silence for what seems like a long time, then, 'Okay.' He stands, resigned. 'I'll call you a cab.'

'The trains will be running.'

'Then I'll come with you,' he says.

They sit side by side, both of them staring ahead without speaking. A strand of hair is caught in the chain of her necklace, pulling at the nape of her neck. She travelled this line with so much hope on her way to see him that first time, but now everything is wrong.

Outside her house, they stand apart from each other.

'Jacob . . . I'm sorry about tonight. I knew I shouldn't see you again, but I still came. I should have told you earlier, but I was greedy. I . . . I wanted the evening to go on for ever.'

'I did too. I still do.'

'But I was wrong. Selfish. I wish things were different. But I'm a mother. My child has to come first. I'm sorry.' She shakes her head.

'I understand . . . I think I understand more than you know. But . . . are you sure, Cora? Are you sure that you want to end this before we've even had a chance to try and work things out?'

Cora bites her lip. Perhaps Fran has already fallen for another man. Her daughter changes her mind all the time. Falls in and out of love like a whirlwind. What if Cora's giving up Jacob needlessly? Her hungry ache for him is the only sensation in her body: her yearning to touch him, kiss him. She wants him so badly. It's wild in her blood, like an addiction.

'I ... I don't know what to do,' she says. 'Maybe ... I don't know ... just ... Maybe I need some time to think.'

'I'm not going anywhere.'

'Thank you,' she manages.

'Except now,' he says. 'Obviously I'm going somewhere now. I'm not standing outside your house indefinitely.'

His humour takes her by surprise. Her mouth lifts and falls.

He doesn't smile. His eyes are very bright, as if there are tears in them. She watches him walk away, and she has to stop herself running after him, hauling him back, hauling back all her hopes. Instead she watches as he rounds the corner out of sight.

Marble Arch

Hugo's message is short. He's given her two hours to get there.

But she's not going. She's better than this. *I am strong,* she tells herself. *I can do this.* She takes her mobile out to text him, to say she's not playing his games. *Fuck you. I'm not coming.* But what if his reaction is to post a picture immediately? She'll call the police instead, she decides. She'll ask to speak to a female officer. But she sits with the phone in her hand, the thought of what she'll have to admit to making her squirm. She tries to imagine how the officer will react when she explains her stupidity, what they'll think of her when they see the photographs. And anyway, even if they take her seriously, Hugo will contradict her. His lies immaculate. His word against hers.

The person she loved best in the world, who knew her and loved her, is dead. She can still see him falling through the rain, through the dark. She always will.

In the mirror, she outlines her eyes with black; her fingers shake as she tries to add mascara. She doesn't understand how it's come to this – how she's made the wrong choices, how she's failed every test since he died. Women are supposed to be sticking together, being strong and brave. The whole #MeToo thing is all over social media, but here she is letting herself be exploited by a man. Things have happened at castings – fingers brushing her bottom, fumbled gropes, knowing looks and suggestive winks – but she was scared of reporting anyone. She thought people wouldn't book her for jobs if she made a fuss. She remembers the therapist she saw after Dad died telling her that she was seeking male approval. She wants men to want her, the woman said, to fill the void left by Dad, to replace his love.

But nothing will ever fill the void, she thinks. Nobody will ever love her the way Dad did. Nobody will ever see her as he saw her.

The aroma of baking filters up the stairs. Cora's been making cakes for days. The moment she's back from work, she starts on a batch of banana muffins or chocolate brownies. Not even Luke could eat so much. Her mother's been acting strangely lately, monosyllabic, manically busy. Probably something to do with being middle-aged. Her hormones going crazy.

Fran puts her head around the kitchen door. Cora is standing at the counter pouring batter into a tin. She's concentrating on what she's doing, her hair scraped back, a splodge of flour on her cheek. She looks up and gives a wavering smile. 'Going out?'

Fran nods.

'But you'll be home tonight?'

'Yeah.'

'Okay.' Cora bends and puts the tin in the oven. She straightens. 'Fran?' Her voice is breathless. Fran half turns, her hand on the door.

'I was thinking that it would be nice to do something

together. See an exhibition and then get some lunch? My treat. Maybe tomorrow?'

Fran's cheeks burn. She wishes with all her heart that she lived in a world where she could stare at paintings and talk about inconsequential things over a bowl of pasta. If only life could be that simple. She swallows and nods. 'Sounds good, Mum.'

'Really? Great!' Cora pulls her in for a hug. 'Then it's a date. We haven't spent any time together for ages. I miss you, Fran.' Her eyes are bright with unshed tears.

Fran buries her face in her mother's neck, breathing in caramelised sugar. It would be so easy to lose control, break down and confess what she's done, but the thought of Mum's horror makes her disentangle herself from the embrace.

'Got to go or I'll be late.' She manages a smile.

Hugo lives between Marble Arch and Baker Street. The lobby of his modern block is sleek and empty, except for the concierge behind his desk. Fran thinks she might throw up on the shiny marble floor. The concierge has lifted his gaze from a newspaper and is giving her a suspicious look. She needs to look normal. She rearranges her hair behind her ears and approaches the lift. But when she raises her hand to press the button, it's as if she's turned to stone.

'Can I help you, miss?' The voice comes from behind her.

She doesn't turn around. Her heart is beating fast. 'No, thanks.' But she can't press the lift button. It's as if there's a force field around it. Her hand drops to her side.

She hears him get up from his desk, feet approaching on the hard floor. 'Who have you come to see?'

The thought that he might buzz up to Hugo makes her panic.

145

'No one,' she says quickly. She swings around to face him, wrinkles her forehead. 'I've . . . I've made a . . . a mistake.'

She clomps across the floor, hurrying towards the exit, feeling his gaze at her back. She pushes through the heavy glass doors onto the pavement. She can hardly breathe. She half expects Hugo to appear, to grab her and force her back in there, hustling her into the lift. Her legs are weak and she stops in the shadow of the building. The street is busy with people going out for the evening, couples walking hand in hand, an immaculately dressed man with a chocolate-brown spaniel on a lead. How long does she have before Hugo realises she's a no-show; how long before he posts a photo?

She takes out her mobile and scrolls through Instagram. Even though it's too soon, she's afraid of seeing a picture of herself pop up – wonders which one he'll post first, what the hashtag will be; wonders if it will go viral. She brings up her list of contacts. None of them can help. Hardly anyone on the list is actually a friend. She's lost touch with most people. She hasn't seen anyone from drama school for months. Too humiliating to admit that she hasn't even had a proper callback since leaving. There's Alesha, but what could she do? As her gaze drifts over the names and numbers, she stops at one. Jacob.

He picks up after two rings, and she realises immediately that he doesn't know who's calling him – he didn't add her as a contact. She nearly hangs up. But she's desperate. 'Jacob. It's me. It's Fran.'

'Fran? Has something happened? Are you okay? Is your mother okay?'

'No.' She swallows. 'I'm not okay.' And then all the failure and pain spill out of her and she can't breathe. She gasps into the receiver, 'I . . . I'm scared. I don't know what to do.' She's aware of curious faces turning in her direction. She stands with the mobile clamped to her ear, teeth chattering, trying to get air into her lungs. 'Please. Help me.'

'Tell me where you are,' he says. 'Stay there. I'm coming.'

She bends over, hands on her knees, collecting herself, easing her lungs into movement. Then she waits anxiously on the corner, biting her nails, her gaze on the entrance. She keeps thinking she sees Hugo coming out into the street, already swiping through the archive of photos – those pictures.

Jacob arrives on his racing bike, skin covered with a sheen of sweat. He must have pedalled hard to get across town so fast. She wants to run into his arms. Her head spins with relief. He locks his bike to a stand and comes over, taking off his helmet. His face is anxious, serious. Noble. He takes her elbow and steers her into the nearest coffee shop, which is still open but empty of customers. She concentrates on the feel of his fingers on her arm, the sense of his body close to hers. He orders two teas and they sit at a corner table.

'What's going on?' he asks.

She tells him. About Hugo and his parties. The drugs. About Charlie. The photos on Hugo's phone. She doesn't try and make it better or less sordid; she doesn't give excuses. She tells it plain and true. She feels a glimmer of pride that she's able to do it, and she watches his face carefully for signs of disgust. But his expression is the same all the way through – grim and concerned.

'And this man Hugo. He's up there now?' He glances across the street to the block of flats.

'I guess.'

His shoulders seem to widen, his body expanding as he pushes his chair back and gets to his feet. 'Right. I won't be long.'

'But . . . but what are you going to do?' She's frightened now that she's unleashed something that will get Jacob hurt.

'Stay here, Fran. I'm going to make some calls first. I'll be back soon.'

He leaves the café. She watches him cross the road, pause outside Hugo's building and take out his phone. He talks into it for a while, and then he goes through the glass doors.

Fran stares at the place where he disappeared. Her body is stiff with tension; nerves make her belly ache. She stands up, not taking her eyes off the entrance. She craves a smoke, wishes she hadn't thrown all her stuff in the bin. She twists her hands together. She scratches her scalp hard. Should she call the police? She thinks of the row of knives arranged on a rack in Hugo's kitchen, his temper, his belief that he's untouchable. She doesn't know how long Jacob's been gone. She didn't check the time he left.

The waitress comes over and pointedly wipes down the adjacent tables. Fran ignores her. She's not leaving until he's back. Then he's there, crossing the road, glancing left and right as he slips between the traffic. He seems unhurt. She goes to the entrance to meet him. 'Are you okay? What happened?'

He nods, and she follows him back to the table. He's breathing hard. He sits down and takes a long drink of his cold tea, wiping his mouth with the back of his hand.

'Jacob? What did you do?'

'You don't have to worry any more, Fran. Hugo won't contact you again. There'll be no photos appearing on the internet.'

'What?' She gasps. 'How? How did you do it?'

'I have contacts in the police. It's part of my job. Like my weekly meetings at City Hall.'

She frowns, confused. 'City Hall?'

'The mayor.' He nods. 'I had a talk with Hugo. I let him know what I knew – and who my friends are. He understood that he was making a mistake. And just to be sure, I've talked to a mate of mine in the force and he's agreed to go round to see him and talk to him about the . . . repercussions of what he's done.'

'So that's it?'

'That's up to you, Fran. You have the option of pressing charges. If you want.' He tilts his head to the side. 'Coercion. Blackmail. I haven't started that process yet, but we can.'

She shakes her head. 'No.'

'Think about it,' he says, and his eyes are steady and kind. 'Take some time. No one's going to force you to do anything.'

She shakes her head again. 'I just want to forget it.' She rubs her eyes. 'Thank you,' she says. She wants to take his hand and kiss his fingers. 'This is the second time you've rescued me.'

Something inside her has softened, gentled. A hard stone, stuck fast in her chest, has become dislodged. She trembles. It feels meant-to-be, this connection she has with Jacob. He makes her feel safe. He makes her feel seen.

'What about Cora?' he asks. 'Does she know . . . about this?'

Fran frowns, jolted out of her thoughts. 'God. No!'

'Think about telling her – about Hugo. You'd be surprised how much she'd understand. How much she'd want to know what you've gone through. She's your mum.' He looks over at the sulking waitress. 'We should go. She wants to close up.'

'Jacob . . .' Fran grabs his arm, sensing a gap closing, an opportunity fading. 'I . . . I need to tell you something.'

He stares at her, at her fingers on his shirt, and he pulls away slightly. 'Fran. You don't have to.'

'I want to,' she insists, leaning across the table. 'I do have to.' She lets go of his arm. 'The thing is . . . I can't stop thinking about you.' She lowers her lashes. 'I felt an attraction between us the moment you walked into my house.' She smiles. 'And don't you think it's weird, how we met . . . how we've been connected again and again? Like . . . like fate or something?'

He glances down, and then he looks at her. She knows it's not good news, because he's keeping very still, his eyes, his mouth all neutral. She wants to put her hands over her ears. She sits back.

'I'm sorry,' he says quietly. 'I don't feel the same way.'

There's a roaring in her head. 'Do you . . . do you have a girlfriend, then?'

'Not exactly.' He rubs his nose. 'But there is someone I like very much.'

'What's her name?' Fran lifts her chin. She's just talking now. Saying anything to give her time to regain her composure.

'It doesn't matter.'

'It does.' She suddenly needs him to give her this one thing. 'Tell me. Please.'

'I can't.' He shifts in his chair. 'I can't tell you.'

'What?' She nearly laughs. 'Why can't you?' She puts a hand over her mouth. 'I don't know her, do I?' Her eyes widen mockingly, 'You're not seeing my friend Alesha, are you?' Lesh would never do that to her.

'I don't know your friend.' His face is wiped blank.

'But there isn't anyone else . . .'

He doesn't speak. He just looks at her. 'We should go,' he says again.

She's desperate for the truth now. What other woman do they both know?

'Wait!' A crazy thought occurs to her. 'It's not my mum, is it? You don't like my mother?' The idea is ridiculous.

150

Jacob gets up. 'Come on. You need to get home.'

'Shit!' Fran pushes onto her feet. 'You are! You're seeing my mother!'

He doesn't deny it. Shock and bitterness collide. 'Seriously?' The walls of the café are melting, the tables and chairs disintegrating, her world shattered. She wants to hurt him. She wants to hurt Cora. 'Is that what you like? Old ladies? Are you into that kind of thing?'

'Enough, Fran,' he says quietly.

Her body is trembling with rejection, her mind spinning. She manages to gather her dignity. 'I'm going now,' she says in a stiff voice.

She turns on her heel and walks out ahead of him. She forces her feet to keep moving, one in front of the other; she's straining to hear his voice, hoping he'll call her back to tell her it's all a bad joke.

She keeps listening for his footsteps as she makes her way to the Underground; or maybe it'll be the sound of his bike braking: *Stop, Fran, I didn't mean it.* She doesn't let go of hope until she's on the train and it's rattling through tunnels.

When she gets home, it's not late, but Cora's already in bed. There's a sliver of light under her door. Fran stands outside the room, her hand flat on the wood, waiting and listening. Cora knew that Fran liked Jacob. And all this time she's been throwing herself at him. Fran's fingers curl into a fist. What kind of mother would do that to her daughter?

She goes into her own room, stumbling over the mess on the floor, and kicks off one of her boots. Cora. With Jacob? Her mother is the least spontaneous person she knows. She does research before she buys a pair of socks. With Jacob? A man who's years and years younger? It doesn't make sense. Fran doesn't bother to undress, or clean her teeth. She falls into crumpled sheets, angry tears juddering through her. The last hours have taken on the feel of a hallucination. The horror of waiting in the lobby. The wonder of Jacob coming to her rescue. But then the perfect ending scratched out, the promise of it disappearing into a black hole, because of Cora. She doesn't know if it's a farce or a tragedy. She just knows that it's not fair – that nothing in her life ever works out.

Bethnal Green

Cora is standing at the kitchen sink, morning light warm on her face, an untouched coffee in her hands. She glances into the small half-paved area beyond the window, recalling without wanting to Jacob kneeling there over a dismantled bike. A spasm of remembering assaults her: Jacob cupping her cheeks, kissing her eyelids, tracing the line of her throat.

Giving him up was the only possible thing. If this were a fairy tale, it would be the forfeit she would have to pay, the test she would have to pass to escape the spell cast by a wicked witch. But she is not the princess in this story – Fran is. She reminds herself that they're having a mother-and-daughter outing today. The thought helps to lift her heart. Her plan is for them to see the new Picasso exhibition; she booked tickets online last night. Afterwards they'll go somewhere nice for lunch, and they can talk properly, have a heart-to-heart, free of miscommunication. It'll be a chance to get closer, to show Fran how much she is loved.

Cora was in bed early last night, staring at a meaningless sitcom on her laptop, when she heard Fran's feet thumping up the stairs, heard them stop outside her bedroom door. She turned the sound down, wondering whether to call out. But Fran went into her own room and shut the door. She hasn't emerged. She needs to get up if they're going to make it to the Tate on time.

Cora goes into the hall. 'Fran?' she calls up the stairs. Sighing, she makes her way up to the landing, checking in on Luke on the way. He's got his headphones on and is staring at his screen. Since getting his new bike, he's started to read *Cycling Weekly*. It's not just physics and maths textbooks any more. He's joined the cycling club. She'll always be grateful to Jacob for that. Tears prick her eyes and she blinks them away.

She puts her hand on Luke's shoulder, and he slips his headphones off, turning to look up at her.

'Can you get yourself some lunch, darling?' she asks. 'Plenty of stuff in the fridge. Remember I told you last night that Fran and I are going out today – I'll have my mobile if you need me.'

'Cool.' He nods.

She pauses outside Fran's door and knocks. No answer. So she turns the handle. 'Fran?'

The room is in darkness. Cora wrinkles her nose against a sour fug. She steps carefully, feeling her way through the gloom, fumbles for the blind cord and tugs. As the blind rises, the morning spills into her eyes and she squints, turning towards the bed. 'Fran! Time to get up. It's late. I've booked tickets for one o'clock.'

Fran is sprawled across the bed like a broken doll. She's dressed in her clothes from the night before, one foot laced into a boot. She doesn't move, even though the sunlight is full on her face. 'Fran?' Cora crosses the room in two strides. Then she sees the half-empty bottle of vodka on the carpet, smells the fumes. She pats Fran's cheeks, shakes her shoulders, urgent now. 'Wake up!'

To her relief, Fran opens one eye and groans. She screws up her face and turns away from Cora, stuffing her head under the pillow, growling, 'Goway.' Cora takes hold of her daughter's hand, 'Come on, Fran. Sit up.'

Fran ignores her, holding the pillow. Cora unpeels her grip as gently as she can, slips her fingers under Fran's shoulder blades and pulls. 'Up you get.' She's determined to manoeuvre her into an upright position.

Fran is a dead weight. But with more tugging, her spine lifts away from the sheet and she slumps forward.

'Fran?' Cora perches on the bed, catching her breath. 'How much did you drink? Can you focus?'

There's something sticky under her toes. Glancing down, she sees a splatter of vomit. Grimacing, she moves her foot away. There's more on the sheet – a yellow trail. She gasps. 'Jesus, Fran! You could have died. What were you thinking?' She holds Fran's arm, fear making her squeeze tight. 'We need to get some liquid into you. Water. Lots of water . . .'

Fran scowls, wrenching her arm away. 'Leave me alone.' She pushes her legs out of the sheets and sways off the mattress onto her feet. Her complexion is bloated and grey, skin smudged with make-up.

Cora bites her lip, struggling with frustration and fury. 'This has to stop – it's out of control, drinking spirits alone. You need to tell me why, Fran – why did you do it?'

Fran opens her lips as if to speak, but instead she retches and stumbles from the room, a hand over her mouth. Cora follows

155

her to the bathroom, where she's on her knees before the toilet, her body heaving as she's sick into the bowl. She kneels beside her, scooping her hair up and holding it back. She rubs Fran's shoulders in slow circles.

When the shuddering stops, Fran sits on her heels and wipes her mouth with the back of her hand.

'I'll get you some water,' Cora says, keeping her voice calm. 'Some sweet tea. I think there's arrowroot in the cupboard—'

'Don't,' Fran says, her voice rough, cracked. 'I don't want your help.'

Cora shakes her head. 'Don't be silly. I'm upset, but I still want to look after you.'

'Get away from me. I don't care what you want . . . I don't care what you think.' Fran shrugs her off and hauls herself to her feet.

Cora reaches for her arm. 'I don't understand . . . What's the matter?' She notices bits of vomit caught in Fran's hair. She wants to run a bath, put her daughter in it, wash her hair, soap away the stink of the alcohol. Put her to bed in clean sheets, feed her tea, keep her safe.

Fran staggers away from her as if she's contagious. 'You don't give a shit about me – never have.'

'What?' It's like a punch. Cora reels. She shakes her head. 'No. That's not true. Don't say that, Fran.' She tries to keep her voice steady. 'I . . . I just don't want to see you hurting yourself like this.'

'Really?' Fran gives a sarcastic laugh. 'So what do *you* think is hurting me?'

Cora's lungs empty of air. She stares at Fran, confused.

'He told me,' Fran hisses.

'Who told you what?' But even as she asks the question, Cora has a cold, jerky sensation, as if she's slipping in mud, falling.

'Jacob,' Fran says. 'He . . . he told me everything. You've been seeing him behind my back.' She pushes a lank strand of hair from her forehead with shaking fingers. 'How could you? When you knew how I felt?'

The light through the window dazzles Cora's eyes. She squints and looks away. 'Jacob? You saw him?' She's finding it hard to process the meaning of Fran's words. 'He said that?'

Fran nods.

'But . . . how . . . I don't understand . . .'

'Yes, you do.'

'It's . . . it's not what you think.' Cora stumbles over her words. 'We did see each other. Twice. And then I ended it.'

'And I'm supposed to thank you for your great sacrifice?'

'No . . .'

Fran makes a sudden gesture with her hand, cutting the air. 'You knew I liked him. Jesus!' She steps back. 'What's wrong with you?'

'I'm sorry,' Cora says. Her mouth is dry. 'I . . . I didn't want you to find out like this. But I had no idea you liked him, Fran. And when you told me, I ended it. Look, let's talk later.' She walks over to the cabinet and opens it. 'We need to get liquids into you first, some aspirin.' She picks up a packet of painkillers and holds it out. 'Take a couple of these. Have a shower. You'll feel better afterwards. Then I'll make you breakfast and we'll sit down and—'

'Just leave me alone!' With one move, Fran dashes the packet out of Cora's hand.

'Fran . . .'

'Get out!' she screams suddenly. 'Get out!'

Cora moves as if she's been stung. She shuts the door behind her and leans against it, eyes closed, fingers trembling. Fran's voice rings in her ears. Why would Jacob seek Fran out – cause this pain, this confusion? She paces the corridor, rubbing her forehead. There's no point in his actions, unless he intended to hurt her, unless he wanted to wound both of them – her *and* Fran. Perhaps it's been a joke to him all along – a mother and daughter wanting him, competing for him. Wouldn't that be the ultimate fantasy for some men? Her skin is hot, her cheeks burn with anger. She takes her mobile out of her back pocket, fingers twitching towards his contact. But she needs to confront him in person. She'll know whether he's telling the truth if she can stand before him and watch his body language, his eyes.

She hears the loo flush from behind the bathroom door.

In Fran's room, she drags soiled sheets from the bed and makes it up with fresh linen. She'll take a chance on him being at the boat. It'll be faster on the Tube, avoiding Saturday lunchtime traffic. She can hear Fran getting into the shower, the slide of the door, the rush of water. She pauses at the head of the stairs – can she leave her daughter alone? She's over the worst of it. She's just got the hangover from hell now, and knowing Fran, she'll sleep it off. Cora runs down to the hall, shoves her feet into shoes, slings her bag across her shoulder and leaves the house.

The boat is empty. A man on the towpath nods at her. 'You looking for Jacob? He's never around on a Saturday afternoon, love.'

Disappointment and anticlimax knock the air out of her lungs.

'You all right?' The man is looking at her with a concerned expression.

She nods, asks when he usually gets back, and the man

raises his palms. 'Couldn't tell you. Sorry.' He comes closer. 'I'm George,' he says. 'You might recognise me from my modelling jobs – menswear catalogues and that.' She looks at his reddened, fleshy cheeks. He's a middle-aged man with a paunch.

'Oh.' She smiles, making an effort to join the joke. 'Yes, I knew I'd seen you somewhere before.'

'And this is Claude,' he adds, tilting his head towards a heavy-set brindled dog, tongue lolling. Cora leans down and puts her palm against the animal's warm, smooth back. 'Hello, Claude.'

'You need anything, give me a shout,' George says, tossing a tennis ball in the air. 'I'm in the boat next door.' He looks at her with curious, kind eyes. 'Right. We're off to get our ten thousand steps.' He takes a battered paperback from his pocket and starts off down the towpath, the book raised before him, his dog trotting behind.

She spots a bench in sight of the boat and sits down. There's a plaque on the back: *To Lucinda, my true love. Wait for me.* She grimaces at the irony. She may have hours to wait for Jacob, but true love doesn't come into it any more. Frustration twists inside. Anger rages through her with nowhere to go. She won't be able to do anything until she's spoken to him. There's a part of her that can't believe he's really told Fran – a fragile hope clings that there's been a misunderstanding, a confusion, and she just needs him to clear it up. But another part is certain that he did tell her, that none of it has been real. He's made a fool of her, and he's hurt her daughter.

It's a beautiful April day – finally there's real warmth in the air – and the towpath is busy with joggers and dog-walkers, the water noisy with ducks and coots, the splish of fish rising. Her fury makes her feel like an intruder into the calm of the moment. Her mind drifts, watching the afternoon, the small dramas of other people's lives, the activity of the canal itself. George and Claude return from their walk. He puts his hand up in greeting, 'Still here? Want a beer?'

She shakes her head. 'I'm fine.'

He disappears inside his boat, his dog padding behind. It's warm in the sunshine, and the rhythm of the afternoon seduces her into a doze. She slumps, neck at an angle, sun on her cheek, thoughts of Fran in her head – remembering how she used to sing to her as an unborn baby, telling her stories, imagining who she'd be, longing for the moment when she could hold her.

'Cora?'

She looks up, startled. The sky has clouded over. She'd almost forgotten where she is. She shivers.

He's standing before her, looking puzzled. 'What are you ...' His face creases with concern. 'Are you all right – has something happened?'

She stands up carefully, stiff from sitting for so long, and her anger rushes back: her righteous anger. 'How dare you tell Fran about us,' she hisses.

His expression changes, and her small hope that this was somehow just a misunderstanding drains away. Her heart shuts.

'I didn't know whether to warn you or not.' He's looking anxious. 'Is she okay? Is she still upset?'

'Don't pretend you give a damn about her.' She scowls. 'I found her comatose on her bed this morning. She'd been drinking vodka alone in her room. What the hell did you say?'

'I had to say something, Cora. She asked.'

She shakes her head. 'I'm trying to understand. You were having a conversation with my daughter last night without telling me? Did you arrange to meet her?' It's as if she's falling through space. All certainty gone. 'Just tell me.'

He runs a hand through his hair. 'Okay,' he says quietly. 'This isn't the place. Let's go into the boat and we can talk.'

She wants to scream into his face, shove his chest with the heels of her hands, but she follows him down into the main cabin. The tight space forces them closer than she would like, and she holds herself rigid, careful not to let their bodies brush together.

'What happened?' she asks.

He pours himself some water and drinks it down in one. He puts the glass on the surface and clears his throat. 'Fran phoned me. Yesterday evening.'

Cora wrinkles her forehead. 'She called you?'

'She said she needed help. I was worried about her. So I cycled over to meet her.'

'But . . . why you?'

He shrugs. 'I don't know.'

Cora's mind struggles to catch up, to make sense of what he's saying. 'Where? Where was she?'

'Marble Arch.'

'What was she doing in Marble Arch?'

'I helped her with her . . . problem. Then she told me how she felt about me. It was difficult. I tried to let her down gently, but she was hurt and . . . angry.' He rubs his chin. 'Then she asked me if I had a girlfriend, so I told her I didn't, but that there was someone I liked.'

'Shit.'

'Yeah. Then she wanted to know the name, and she just wouldn't take no for an answer. I didn't tell her it was you. But she guessed.'

'Oh God.' Cora sinks into a chair.

'Cora.' He folds to his knees in front of her, looking into

161

her face. 'This could be a good thing. She knows now. The worst is over.'

He looks earnest. His gaze direct. Cora shakes her head. 'She was so angry with me, as if I've betrayed her ... and I have, haven't I?'

He places his long hands over hers. 'You haven't betrayed her. You stopped seeing me – tried to do the right thing.'

'But ... but why did she need help? Why did she call you?' She leans closer, her pulse bumping. 'What happened?'

He sits back on his heels, releasing her hands. 'I can't tell you, Cora. It's up to Fran.'

'Really?' She stands up, her fingers twitching. 'You're seriously not going to tell me what terrible thing my own daughter was going through that she had to call you for help?'

He stands up wearily. 'I can't betray her confidence.'

Cora turns away from him, folding her arms. Her shoulders are tight. She stares out of the window at the dark green canal, the glimmers of light that spark and fade, and feels her frustration seeping away. He's in an impossible position. They all are. And she believes him. She trusts him. She can't help it. She shakes her head, begrudging, accepting, and turns back. 'Is she ... is she okay now? Is there something else I need to do to help her with ... whatever it is?'

'No.'

She bites her lip. 'I've got it all wrong, haven't I? I'm not protecting her.'

'You're doing your best. But she's a grown-up. Not a child. I think the only thing to do now is to be honest.' He puts a hand on her shoulder and turns her gently to face him. 'When you walked away, I tried to convince myself I could go back to how I was before I met you – that it would be better for all of us.

But I can't. Even these few times we've been together, you've changed me. If you still feel the same about me, then let's go back to where we left off – see each other again, without any subterfuge or secrecy. We have nothing to be ashamed of, Cora. Fran will get used to the situation, get used to me.'

'Will she?'

He nods. 'In time. She's young. Nothing happened.' He raises his palms and rubs his forehead. 'Maybe it's her pride that's hurting most.'

Cora puts her face in her hands. 'I don't know. I just . . . don't know what to do.'

'I care about Fran. And I'm sorry she drank too much last night.' He puts his hands on her shoulders, rests them there lightly. 'But Cora, something *has* happened between us,' his voice trembles, 'something I didn't hope for, didn't expect. And now . . . now I don't want to lose it. I don't want to lose you.'

She leans into him. His arms wrap around her. Her cheek rubs against his shirt. He smells salty. Her head hurts, her thoughts cloudy with confusion, but Jacob's words feel like the truth.

'All right . . . I'll talk to her,' she says, fumbling for a tissue in her pocket. 'I'll tell her about us. Try and make her understand.'

He squeezes her closer. 'Thank you,' he says.

She moves away, wiping her face. 'And this . . . problem that Fran had last night. She's not in any danger? You're sure she's all right – safe?'

He inclines his head. 'She's safe.'

'I don't know what you did, but . . . thank you.'

'Don't thank me. I was glad I could help.'

'I should go.'

They look into each other's eyes, at each other's mouths, and hesitate. They don't kiss. She wants to, and she thinks he does too, only nothing is settled yet. She has to talk to Fran first. He holds up his hand in a salute, and she nods and moves towards the door, towards the bright tangle of the towpath, and the busy passers-by lost in their own mysterious lives.

Shepherd's Bush

Wet from the shower, Fran watches from the window as Cora strides down the street towards the Tube station, bag bumping at her hip as she disappears from view. Now that the coast is clear, she negotiates the stairs on unsteady legs. She stands at the kitchen sink and drinks several glasses of water, takes a couple of painkillers with more water. Luke slouches in, maths textbook in his hand, and grabs a Coke out of the fridge, closing the door with a bang.

'Do you mind?' she hisses. 'My head's exploding.'

He gives her a look of considered patronisation. 'I don't know why you do it to yourself.'

'Living here, dummy. Nobody could stand it. You're a boring little swot and Mum's a . . . a bitch.'

'Don't say that about Mum.' He swigs his drink and burps. 'You're just pissed off because your head hurts.' He stops at the door, and touches the bridge of his glasses. 'And you don't have to live here. You're twenty-three. You can leave home, you know.'

She turns her back on him, switching on the kettle, listening to him thumping up the stairs back to his precious laptop, his boring physics questions, his maths problems.

Carrying a full mug of tea, she drags herself to her room, slopping liquid onto the carpet as she goes. She pulls the blinds against the mockery of the beautiful afternoon and gets into bed. Lying against the pillows, wet hair dribbling down her neck, she sips the hot drink. She has the urge to confess the whole story to Alesha, cry on her shoulder; but then she'd have to admit that the man she's gone on about, the man she loves, is actually besotted with her mother.

She feels like such a fool.

She picks up the rose quartz crystal from her bedside table and holds it to her lips. It's cool against her skin. The stone of universal love. But it hasn't worked for her; her heart has not been purified, she hasn't attracted unconditional love. She hurts inside, as if everything is bruised – the pain makes her feel sick. Jacob's image flickers before her eyes: his smile as he sat at their kitchen table; the look on his face as he took off his helmet, striding towards her as he came to save her from Hugo; his closed, careful expression in the café when she guessed right about Cora. She opens her fingers and lets the stone drop to the floor.

She's in the middle of thinking that she probably won't be able to sleep when she plummets into unconsciousness.

There's a knock on the door. Her head is fuzzy and her mouth tastes revolting. She can't open her eyes. She ignores the knocking, but her mother breezes into the room. 'How are you feeling? Have you drunk lots of water?'

Fran turns onto her other side, burying her face in the pillow.

'I've brought you up some toast and Marmite and tea. Can I sit down?' Cora seems to take Fran's stony silence for a yes and sits on the edge of the bed, placing the tray next to her. The smell of buttery toast makes Fran's stomach rumble.

'I've been to see Jacob,' Cora says. 'He told me that you called him last night. But he wouldn't tell me why,' she adds quickly. 'He said it was private.'

Fran wishes she had the strength to physically remove her mother from her room. She struggles into a sitting position; she would like to eat the toast, but doesn't want to acknowledge it. She picks up her phone, looking at the screen. Ignoring her mother is the next best thing to kicking her out.

Cora sighs. 'Whatever it was, you know you can talk to me about it. I promise I won't judge or get angry . . .' She leaves a pause. Fran continues to scroll through her phone. 'I love you,' Cora says softly. 'So if there's a time when you change your mind . . .'

Fran's insides clench; a sudden weakness enters her, a longing to be in her mum's arms. But Cora has broken her heart. Her trust.

'I know it was a mess before, with Jacob,' Cora is saying, and Fran hears a catch in her voice. 'I'm sorry . . . so sorry about how it came out. About hurting you. But Jacob and I . . . It's true. We like each other. It happened slowly – wasn't something we planned. I'd already said no to him before you saw him last night. I did it straight after you told me you had feelings for him. But now . . . we've talked about it and we'd . . . we'd like to have a relationship.'

She pauses. Fran's heart is thumping at her ribs. She can't believe what Cora's saying – that after all this, she and Jacob are going to date each other.

167

'It really surprised me, Fran – I never expected anything like this to happen again, after your dad,' her mum's voice goes on. 'But . . . making you unhappy is the last thing I want, which is why it's complicated.' She leans forward. Fran feels the heat of her gaze, but refuses to look at her. 'You're more important to me than anything – you and Luke. So if it'd be too difficult, if it'd cause you . . . pain . . .' she swallows audibly, 'then I'd understand, and I'll tell Jacob no once and for all.'

Fran's cheeks are hot with humiliation. Her mother and Jacob have been discussing her: Fran the problem; Fran the poor deluded failure of a daughter. Her mobile falls onto the duvet. She sits up with her legs bent, hooks her arms around them and speaks into her knees. 'I'll never forgive you for lying to me.' Her voice is muffled. 'But I can't stop you seeing him. What would be the point? You've already made up your mind.'

'No . . . no—'

'Yes!' Fran snaps her head up and fixes her with a fierce glare. 'Yes, Mum. You always get what you want. That's how you are.'

'That's not true!' Cora sighs, glancing down. 'I just . . . I try hard. That's all. But this is different. This is about feelings – about us. Look. I can't bear it when we're fighting. I want us to go back to how we were before Jacob, before we started to argue all the time . . .'

'And when was that? It wasn't perfect before Jacob, was it?' Fran says. 'I can't seem to make you understand me. And I don't understand you.'

Cora stretches out her hand and places it over Fran's. They stay like that for a moment. Mother and daughter. 'Fran,' Cora says in her serious voice, 'would you like me to say no to Jacob? You're my daughter. You come first.'

Fran shifts, pulls away. 'Do what you like, Mum,' she says

quietly. 'I'm over it. I'm over Jacob. He was just a stupid crush anyway – I was bored,' she shrugs, 'and he was there. It was something to do. Something to entertain myself with till someone better came along.'

'Honestly?' Cora's voice is a whisper.

'Yeah. Obviously. God, I'd never really want to go out with him,' Fran lies with a hollow laugh. 'He's way too old for me.'

She knows that if she stops them from seeing each other, it will only make them want each other more, turn them into a weird version of Romeo and Juliet. Better for them to have a relationship, and then Jacob will get bored. Her mother is work-obsessed. Predictable. She has wrinkles. He's not going to keep pink-tinted glasses welded to his face for ever. She can wait it out. She can do this – she's strong enough.

Cora sits back. She looks relieved, but also still worried. 'Okay,' she says slowly, softly. 'We'll take it one day at a time. But I'm here if you need me . . . if you need anything. I do love you, Fran, whatever you think.'

Fran gives a tiny shrug, keeping her expression closed. She stares down at her phone, her hair falling around her like a curtain. She hears Cora leave the room, the quiet click of the door.

She notices that Zac has sent her message requests on Twitter and Instagram. He's persistent, she thinks. She'll give him that. Reliable. Her finger hovers over the screen, but she's not in the mood to exchange meaningless messages. She remembers his scruffy beard and his irritating way of thinking he knows her. She switches her phone to silent, picks up a piece of cold toast and takes a bite.

Bethnal Green

May, and London is incandescent with pink and white blossom shimmering on rowans, crab apples, hawthorn bushes and late-flowering cherry trees. Reflections from a myriad of flowers light up buildings and streets; pavements are hazy with drifts of snowy petals.

Exam season has started. Luke has his A levels spread over two weeks. Cora gets him up in time to eat a proper breakfast before watching him go off with an ashen complexion, clutching his pencil case full of perfectly sharpened pencils, clean rubbers, new pens and a calculator. He dutifully calls her at work when he comes out of the exam room, but his response is confined to a couple of words, and is never exactly a confident affirmation. 'It was all right, I s'pose' is the most he'll admit to. Cora can't get any more out of him, so she feeds him good food, gets him to bed early and keeps her fingers crossed.

May is also the season for lovers, and when Cora doesn't need to be at home for Luke, she and Jacob have been doing the things couples do at the beginning of a relationship: going to exhibitions and films, cooking each other their favourite foods, sitting in cafés, talking and holding hands. They take long walks along the towpath. Jacob points out herons waiting to spear fish with their long beaks; Cora thinks they look like old men with their stooped shoulders: old men in feathery grey scarves. There are black cormorants hanging their wings out to dry, chaffinches singing in alder trees. And apparently there are otters. She had no idea that otters could thrive in a London canal. She's yet to see one, but he showed her his sketch of a mother and her pups he saw early one morning as they played on the bank. The drawing is lively and tender, capturing the expression on the mother's face, the exuberance of the pups.

Cora has already met George next door with his dog, Claude, and now she's been introduced to the other boat-dwellers. Jacob was right when he said it's a close community. It's clear that they all like him – he jokes with them, helps out when they have engine troubles, squatting down with oil on his fingers, offering to lend tools. She notices that he lives frugally. It helps that his home is so small – there's nowhere to store stuff, no room for anything extra. But it's more than that, she thinks. He has what a fashion editor would term a 'capsule wardrobe'. She remembers Andrew's shirts and suits, his rack of bright-coloured silk ties. Jacob has nothing like so many clothes – he usually wears the same old navy fisherman's jumper and blue jeans when he's not at the office – and seems to feel no desire to go shopping. They never do anything that costs money, like eating at expensive restaurants – not that she minds; she prefers the little family-run places where the owners know Jacob by name and sometimes pull up a chair and sit with them, pouring brandies.

Every Saturday morning, Jacob tends to the boat, cleaning the engine and doing other maintenance jobs, and at noon he disappears to visit his parents. He never misses it, and she's already got used to his routine; has stopped having any expectations of seeing him on a Saturday until later in the evening.

Now that they're a couple, she can't help wondering if he'll ask her along to one of these lunches soon.

On Friday, they eat supper early at their favourite little Italian café in Hackney, and then stroll along the towpath towards the boat through the spring air. It's not dark yet, and Scout has kept them company, flitting from branch to branch, sometimes landing on Jacob's shoulder and taking off again.

'You've got lunch with your parents tomorrow?' Cora asks.

He nods.

'Have you,' she tries for a casual tone, 'told them about me yet?'

He keeps walking. The moment extends. He clears his throat. 'Not yet. They're quite traditional and I need to work up to it. But I will. I want to tell the whole world about you! But my parents ...' He makes a sound in his throat. 'I have to find the right moment.'

It hadn't occurred to her that it might be difficult for him to tell them about her. That it might be a problem. It feels as though she's just stubbed her toe on an invisible rock in the road. 'Oh, I hope ... they won't be upset. I suppose I'm not going to be their idea of the right partner for you.'

He squeezes her tighter into his side, kisses the top of her head. 'Don't worry about them. It'll be fine. When they get to know you, they'll love you.'

A part of her wants to laugh. She's fifty, for goodness' sake! And she's nervous about what her boyfriend's parents will think of her. But he's obviously close to his family, and their opinion will matter. As if he knows what she's thinking, he interlaces his fingers with hers and brings the back of her hand to his mouth, pressing softly, his lips warm against her skin.

At the boat, he fishes a dog treat out of his pocket and gives it to Scout; she takes it in her beak with solemn dignity, swallows, and takes off, disappearing into the trees on the opposite bank.

Jacob puts the kettle on to make tea. Cora watches him; the way he moves has become familiar, the tilt of his head under the low ceiling, the slow certainty of his limbs, the way he rubs his nose when he's thoughtful. They haven't slept together yet. Cora is frightened of revealing herself to him. She can't help worrying that he might have expectations of an older woman, expectations that she won't be able to fulfil: her extra twelve years have not resulted in her being more sexually experienced – quite the opposite. She married young, and there was only Andrew, their sex life satisfying and comfortable but hardly experimental. She and Jacob have done a lot of kissing, but Jacob's never pushed for anything more, even when they've been breathless with desire. She knows he's waiting for her to make the first move.

They take their tea onto the deck to enjoy the warm, dusky air, and sit in agreeable silence, listening to George chatting to Claude in his cabin next door, the noises of the night birds on the water. She watches Jacob curl his fingers around his cup, long, tapering fingers, slightly calloused from wielding spanners and gripping handlebars. She thinks of him with Scout, how gentle he is when he strokes her, his smile when she lies on her back to invite tummy rubs as if she's a puppy. She knows he had to wake up throughout the night to feed her in those first touch-and-go weeks, and the thought of him hunched over the scruffy ball of feathers feeding her at first with a pipette of milk, and then mushing up dog food, dropping it little by little into the tiny beak, moves her. He's staring at the water, seemingly hypnotised by the changing colours that roll and glisten in the dying light. She closes her eyes, understanding that this is what it feels like to be happy, happy in a simple and truthful way. And she knows in this instant that she trusts him with her fifty-year-old body. With her heart.

She puts her cup down. 'You haven't shown me where you sleep.' Her voice emerges as a cracked squeak rather than the husky whisper she hoped for.

He gives her a quick look.

She stares back, not dropping her gaze. He answers her question silently, standing and holding out his hand. She takes it, their fingers entwining. She follows him into the boat, through the main cabin, through a door, past the minute bathroom into the end of the boat, where a bed takes up most of the space. It's made up with white linen, plain and clean. There's a skylight right above, letting in the inky wash of night as it falls, sudden and deep.

She looks at the bed. She needs to feel his skin next to hers, to have nothing between them, to know how their shapes fit. The confines of the room mean it's impossible not to brush against each other. Her hand touches his, and he lifts it to his mouth. With her other hand she begins to unbutton her shirt, her fingers clumsy. He reaches out and slips one button free for her. 'Are you sure, Cora? This is what you want?' He's very close.

She looks up and nods. Her mind is wiped clean. All she knows is that there's a deep and exquisite ache in her pelvis and groin. She's hollowed out with painful longing. Nothing will fill it but him. Nothing will make it right but him.

They undress each other, shrugging away their clothes. And then they are kissing, and the bed catches them as they fall.

Afterwards, she can't speak. She is full of the tenderness of his hands, the way he kissed behind her ears, her throat tightening with the force of her gratitude. When he was inside her, she had a moment of fear, remembering that this was the first time for six years, the first man since Andrew. The only other. Jacob stopped moving, looking down at her. 'Are you all right?' Those words. His noticing. It was all she needed.

Now she lies against his chest, sticky and exhausted. She pushes her face into his shoulder, kissing him lazily, a smile on her lips.

Jacob is on his back, one long leg out of the sheet, one arm under her head. 'Look at the stars,' he says.

Through the skylight, the night is punctured with brilliance, tea lights set out on a dark lawn. She looks up, aware of the slight movement of the boat, the lulling of tiny watery movements, the swish of the canal around them.

There are so many things they don't know about each other yet. It will take a while to discover them, to reveal them. She will savour that exploration, she thinks. It takes time to know another person in all their complexities, to work through the human habit of layering truth and fiction, creating an invention of ourselves.

'Jacob . . .' she says.

He turns on his hip to look at her – moonlight has painted them with shadows, but she knows he can see enough of her expression.

'Nothing,' she says. 'Just. I'm happy.'

He takes her hand and kisses it. 'Me too,' he says.

They lie in sleepy silence. Thank God Fran has stopped liking him. Even if Jacob was only a passing crush, it must have been a terrible shock to be rejected by him, to understand that the man she desired wanted her mother instead. Cora doesn't blame her for being angry and confused. But watching her daughter drift through her days, she worries that she's failed her in a different way. Fran is dissatisfied, directionless. Cora doesn't know how to save her. Doesn't know how to help her find the joy that she herself has found. Loving her children isn't enough, she understands. Loving them won't ensure their safety, their happiness.

At least she doesn't have to worry about Luke. He sat his last exam last week, and she's certain he's done well; he'll go to university and excel at his degree. He's shy with his contemporaries, but thanks to Jacob, he's part of the cycling club and even making friends.

'So,' Jacob is saying, his tone playful, 'you should start learning some of the terminology of the boat – now that you're an honorary boat person.'

'An honorary boat person?'

'Uh-huh . . . So the skylight above? It's called a Houdini hatch.'

She laughs. 'I'll remember that!'

'The back of the boat is the stern. The cabin is the midships. The . . .'

She yawns.

He smiles. 'Am I boring you?'

She snuggles into him, his arm lying warm and firm around her waist, his nose pressed into the back of her neck. 'Houdini hatch,' she whispers, and yawns again. 'Midships.'

He spoons her from behind, and she shifts her hips, pressing her back and bottom against the planes of his chest and thighs. He scoops her closer, his arm around her ribs.

She is drifting into sleep. She could sleep the whole night in his arms, in his bed. She never thought she'd be comfortable enough with a new man to be this relaxed. For her and Luke, Jacob has come into their lives like a blessing, she thinks. She sighs and drops her head to kiss his arm. She feels lucky. So very lucky.

Summer

28

St Paul's

Fran is bored and lonely. Luke's not exactly great company. When she asked him if he thought he'd done well in his exams, he just said, 'Maybe.' And when she asked if he liked Jacob and wasn't it weird him being with Mum, he said, 'Jacob's cool.' Then he shrugged. 'It's good to see Mum happy.' Fran screwed up her face. 'I think it's *disgusting* – he's much younger than her.' But Luke wouldn't be drawn. He rolled his eyes and mumbled something about needing to oil his chain.

She misses Alesha. She's been seeing her less, keeping their conversations brief, because she can't face telling her the truth about Jacob and Cora. But she's been lying to Lesh for ages, even before Jacob. She's not sure how to stop, because every lie has webbed her into continuing the deceit. Then she reminds herself that it's not just her fault; Alesha's not always available, busy with her boyfriend and her job.

Zac is the only other person besides Lesh who wants to see her. His friend request has languished on her Facebook page for weeks, along with all his other message requests.

She looks at his latest, and her finger hovers.

She presses the accept button, hoping that he'll want to do other things besides going on marches and standing around with a placard shouting at people shopping.

A message pops up from him: *Hey – are you ignoring me?*

She types: *I was.*

His response comes back instantly: *Past tense. Good.*

She can't help smiling. *But asking to be my FB friend? Definitely lame.*

Him: *Hangs head in shame.*

Her: *So now you've got my attention. What do you want?*

Him: *Ouch. Straight to the point. Do I have to want something?*

Her: *Duh!*

Him: *Okay. How about meeting for a coffee sometime?*

Her: *I'm in need of fun! How about you invite me to a party? Introduce me to fascinating people?*

She waits. Maybe she's gone too far, being so transparent, so bossy. Maybe he took offence over her last remark – but who's that touchy? It was a joke. She stares at her phone. Their flirty banter made her laugh, took her mind off Jacob.

She's just about to give up on him when her mobile pings.

No parties, but how about a walk by the river?

She shakes her head. His idea of a good time is so not hers. But she can't stay cooped up in the house any longer.

Fine, she types. *Where and when?*

This afternoon? Somerset House?

She wasn't expecting him to be quite so desperate.

There's a smell of bleach coming from the bathroom. Cora's bending over the sink, yellow Marigolds on, her denim shorts rolled up to show tanned legs. She's humming as she spritzes limescale remover onto the taps. She's always humming now-adays. Her skin glows. She has the look of someone getting a lot of good sex. It makes Fran queasy to think of it. Mostly Cora goes to Jacob's; sometimes she stays the night at his place. It seems silly for a grown man to live on a boat, as if he's playing at life.

'I'm going out,' Fran tells her. 'Meeting a friend.'

'Oh good.' Cora straightens. 'Anyone I know?'

'No.' Then she relents. 'He's called Zac. He's a bit boring, but I haven't got anything better to do.' She yawns. 'And the sun's out.'

'Boring?' Cora's frowning.

'You know – he's one of those bleeding-heart liberals on a mission to save the world. Stop the ice caps melting. Protect the rainforests. Like he's the second coming or something.'

'Honestly, Fran. He sounds the opposite of boring! I think it's great that he's trying to sort out the mess the world's in.'

'Ha!' Fran snorts. 'He might present himself to the world as an eco-warrior, but I know who he really is – I looked up his birthday on Facebook. It's in April.'

Cora looks puzzled.

'He's an Aries,' Fran says, and makes a shuddering sound. 'I'd usually run a mile. The worst in the whole zodiac. Arrogant and sexist.'

'Arrogant, sexist *and* boring. Well, I hope he turns out to be better than you think.' Cora smiles. 'Text me if you're staying out late.'

Fran notices the creases at the corners of her mother's eyes, the lines on her forehead; strands of silver weave through her brown hair. She's good-looking for someone her age. With her slender bones and delicate features, she's the exact opposite of Fran – but she's *fifty*. What does Jacob see in her? Fran is certain he'll get tired of her soon. He'll come back, begging Fran to forgive him for making the wrong choice. Then she'll humiliate him like he did to her. Or, she falters, maybe not. Because if – when – she gets him back from Cora, she knows she won't really want to punish him. What she longs for more than anything is for him to focus on her, like he did when he came to rescue her from Hugo. At the centre of his attention, her fear subsided. She didn't feel like a failure any more. She felt warm and safe, as if everything was going to be okay.

She gets out at St Paul's and walks to Somerset House. It's busy with tourists. Zac's waiting for her in the cobbled central area. He puts up his hand and comes over. 'Hi.' He smiles. 'Want to go inside? There's a photography exhibition.'

She glances towards the entrance, at the queue snaking up to the ticket desk. 'Too hot to be indoors. Let's just walk around.'

They wander across Waterloo Bridge, across the choppy river, busy with launches. Fran stops and leans over the wall, staring at the London Eye and the Palace of Westminster. 'God, I love London,' she says, spreading her arms wide. 'Feel the energy! Standing here makes me remember how lucky we are to live in this city.' But then, turning her head, she sees the National Theatre, and a heaviness seeps into her chest. Once, she dreamed of walking its boards. She looks away. 'Come on.' She marches ahead towards the South Bank. 'Let's keep moving.'

On the promenade, skaters rattle past on boards, a man with his jacket slung over his shoulder shouts into his mobile. The hot air is dense, heavy. Zac starts to browse at one of the second-hand book stalls. He's leaning against a trestle table, one leg casually crossed over the other ankle, pretending to concentrate on a book. It makes her snort with laughter.

'What's that?' she asks, bumping his elbow with her own.

'This? *Crime and Punishment*. Have you read it?'

She rolls her eyes. 'Too long and old-fashioned.'

He puts the book on the table. 'What do you like, then?'

'Mostly I prefer to read plays. Fewer words, but lots of heart. Guess that makes me a bit weird.'

'No.' He tilts his head. 'Actually, not weird at all.' He shrugs. 'I was going to suggest going to the Poetry Library in the Festival Hall, only . . .' he waves his arms, 'now I think that will involve too many words.'

'Do I hear sarcasm?' She allows herself a smile. 'Didn't think you had it in you.'

'You are one of the rudest people I've met,' he says, falling into step next to her. Her smile broadens, but she doesn't let him see it. He's about the same height. In heels, she'd be taller. 'I should be offended,' he goes on. 'Maybe I'm just thick-skinned. Or . . . maybe this is just your way of protecting yourself?'

'Oh God, don't try and psychoanalyse me.' She bats a hand in his direction, but she's startled by how his words have sounded a bell inside her. She stops smiling. 'I get angry because life is cruel.'

The sky has become heavy and dark. Big drops of rain fall, splattering the dusty pavement, releasing smells of urine and dirt and hot concrete. Summer rain. Fran tilts her face up, letting the softness soak her skin, seep into her mouth. The fabric of her T-shirt is damp, and she feels her nipples rise. She crosses her arms, suddenly embarrassed.

'Come on.' He's pointing to the Festival Hall.

They run across to the entrance, joining a throng of others

wanting to get out of the wet. Inside, they buy takeaway coffees and sit on one of the sofas by the window. The glass is smudged with rain splatters. A jazz band is playing, and the place is busy with people sheltering from the weather, shaking out damp hair and smiling at each other. There's an air of an impromptu party.

'What do you do when you're not trying to save the world?' Fran asks, sipping her drink. 'Because, sorry to break this to you, you know it's all pointless, don't you?'

'First of all,' he says, 'I think this planet is worth fighting for. It's all we've got.' He pauses. 'That's why I try to raise awareness about the environment and climate change, and I'm involved with a charity that provides drama workshops for refugees and asylum seekers. My day job's not exactly exciting. I'm a carer for the elderly.'

Fran nearly spits her drink out. 'So you're telling me you're an eco-warrior who volunteers for refugees *and* cares for old people. You are way too nice for me.'

'I'm not sure I want to be described as nice.' He makes a face. 'And anyway, can someone really be too nice?'

'Maybe. Maybe not.' She makes a considering kind of expression and holds her hand flat, tipping it one way and then the other. 'But seriously, isn't your job depressing?'

'No,' he says. 'Well. Yes. It can be. I help them get through their day. Try and put a smile on their faces while I'm at it.'

She thinks of Jacob running his triathlon for a charity to help brain-damaged kids. But here is someone actually rolling up his sleeves and helping properly, doing the things nobody else wants to do every single day – not just getting sweaty for one afternoon.

'Is that what you always wanted to do? Be a carer?'

He wrinkles his nose. 'No. When I was at school, I wanted

to be a doctor. But then . . . I screwed up. I was an idiot. Messed up my exams, got into trouble with the law. Too much dope. The wrong crowd.' He looks embarrassed. 'I fell into this job. The pay's crap, but I've grown to like it. I feel as if I'm doing something useful.' He gives her a wry look, 'If that doesn't sound too boring.'

Fran looks at him more closely, 'What's stopping you from retaking your exams?'

He looks surprised. 'I . . . well, I never thought . . .'

'You've still got brains, haven't you? And you're not ancient yet.'

'Yeah,' he frowns, 'I suppose. But I have to earn my living. And . . . guess I've just been too busy—'

'Too busy earning a crap salary?'

'Ouch.' He makes a mock-despairing face and gestures towards his worn trousers and scruffy shoes. 'I live in a flat above a disused pub. In my spare time I write poetry. If you're here for my fortune,' he grins, 'better leave now.'

'Oh damn,' she says. 'Now you tell me. Thought you were one of those millionaire eccentrics who likes to dress like a tramp.'

'When you're not killing me with sarcasm, what do you do with your life?' he asks.

'Survive,' she says, the truth coming out without her wanting it to, and she can't help adding, 'Just . . . you know . . . get from one day to the next.'

He turns to look at her. 'That bad, huh?' His voice is low.

She returns his gaze. His eyes are pale blue, the kind she doesn't like because they can be cold, but they are steady, flecked with yellow, and his pupils are huge. She feels a weird sensation, like vertigo, and then she notices his little moustache and beard and thinks how ticklish and unpleasant they'd feel if she kissed him, and she can't even believe she thought of kissing him. He's so not her type.

She clears her throat. 'I used to want to be an actress, but I was deluded. Right now, I need to earn money – don't care how – enough to leave home. My mother's dating ...' she stumbles, thinking of Jacob's face, and forces herself to go on, 'a ... a toy boy, which is embarrassing. I can't live with her any more. She lied to me.'

He sits back from her, a frown crease between his eyebrows.

He's obviously disappointed with her answer, she thinks. Tough. She's not interested in him. She hears herself, hates the meanness of her thoughts. She can't seem to shake off her anger at the world – can't stop it contaminating her.

'You know, you don't have to pretend with me,' he's saying. 'I mean,' he blushes, 'you don't have to be someone you're not.'

His words jolt her, but she scowls, blinking hard. 'Could you just stop trying to tell me who I am? You hardly know me.'

'Whatever you say,' he says, holding up his hands.

She could swear he's laughing at her behind his silly little beard. She gets up, flicking her hair over her shoulders, and puts her hands on her hips. 'I've got to go,' she says.

'Look.' He turns to face the window. 'A rainbow.'

They stand beside each other gazing at the sky, at the slender painted arch suspended over the broken river and the tumbled city. Fran catches a whiff of Zac's warm, slightly musty smell, the damp fibres of his shirt, his wet hair. She feels suddenly very tired. She would like to lean her head on his shoulder. She steps away, putting two strides between them, and shoves her hands into her jeans pockets.

29

Shepherd's Bush

Cora is making supper; she's cooking for all four of them, her and Fran and Luke and Jacob. It feels like an occasion – the first time they've sat down together. Jacob's been over to the house a few times to help Luke with his bike, to drink coffee, share lunch with her. He hasn't spent the night here yet – it feels too soon for that. On his visits, he's spoken to Fran in passing. Cora could see how embarrassed Fran was at first, but Jacob has been steady and kind, and she thinks Fran's become easier in his company. Fran agreed to this supper. Cora takes that as a good sign. She wants to make the food as delicious as possible, set the scene for them to have a relaxed meal around the table.

She dices carrots and celery finely, adding them to the onions in the frying pan, and stirs with a wooden spoon, sprinkling in chopped parsley and sage. When everything is simmering, she lays the table with the best cutlery, and puts a vase of red tulips in the centre. She stands with her hands on her hips, wondering what else needs to be done. The scent of caramelised vegetables is pungent, making her mouth water; there's a bottle of wine chilling in the fridge, along with cans of Luke's favourite fizzy drink. She needs this to be a success. If she can't be with Jacob and her children in the same room at the same time, how can her relationship with him survive? She doesn't want to keep it in a separate box, as if it's an illicit affair. She wants them all to get along. It should be possible. She knows Jacob won't try to replace Andrew; he's not looking to be a father figure to Luke and Fran, just a friend. Her nerves thrum under her skin – she wants this to be the start of a new phase in their lives.

The doorbell rings, and he's there on the step, grinning. Delphiniums, roses and gypsophila spill from his arms. She embraces him, inhaling summer meadows. 'How did you know what my favourite flowers are?'

'Just a lucky guess.' His grin stretches wider. 'How's it going? Anything I can do?'

She shakes her head. 'Help yourself to a drink. Wine? Water? Something fizzy? I'll call the kids.'

Luke bounds down the stairs, and he and Jacob exchange play punches. 'Bet you're pleased to have finished your exams!' Jacob says.

Luke nods. 'Yeah.'

'Still enjoying the club rides?'

Luke nods again. 'Yeah. They're good.'

Cora grins to herself. Even Jacob can't get her quiet son to say more than a few words at a time. But Luke's smile speaks more than any elaborate sentence could.

Fran comes into the room. She's dressed up for the occasion. Her hair is piled in a loose chignon and she's wearing a low-cut vintage green crêpe dress that hugs her waist. Silver hoops hang from her ears. She looks more sophisticated and grown-up than usual. She smiles politely. 'Hello, Jacob.'

Cora lets out a breath, relaxes. It's going to be all right, she thinks. She gestures towards the chairs. 'So,' she says. 'Let's sit down. Who's hungry?'

She and Jacob sit at opposite ends of the table. They snatch smiles and glances between pauses in the conversation, but they're careful not to touch or use endearments. She doesn't want to make the kids feel uncomfortable. They've already discussed taking it slowly – getting Luke and Fran used to Jacob being around as a friend first. Even Luke could feel antagonistic if he thinks Jacob is being too demonstrative with his mother.

Fran picks up her glass of wine and takes a slow sip. 'Tell me, Jacob,' she says, fluttering her lashes. 'How old *are* you exactly?'

Cora's breath catches in her throat.

Jacob's expression doesn't change. 'Exactly? Thirty-eight years and four months,' he says.

'And have all your other girlfriends been older than you? Is it, you know, a *thing*?'

Cora sits up straighter, her eyes on Jacob. He shakes his head. 'I haven't really thought about it . . . but no, I suppose not.'

'Mum's the only older woman, then?'

He nods. 'Not that I think of her like that.'

Fran gives a little smile and looks into her wine glass thoughtfully.

Luke chews his mouthful and puts his fork down. 'I never think of Mum as an older woman either. She's just Mum.'

'And you're just an idiot,' Fran says.

Luke opens his mouth to protest.

'Pudding?' Cora says quickly, pushing her chair back. 'I've made chocolate brownies.'

The rest of the meal passes without incident. They talk about the animals and birds that Jacob has spotted at the canal; the waterways that run from one end of the country to the other. Luke explains why he wants to do the degree course he's applied for at UEA. Afterwards, Fran and Luke help to clear up. Fran gets Spotify on the speakers, finding some music she likes, and turns it up loud. Jacob wipes a cloth over the surfaces and asks Fran a question about the band they're listening to; she answers without a trace of sarcasm.

After the kids have left the kitchen, Jacob pulls Cora close. 'I think that went well, don't you?'

She nods. 'I was worried for a minute. When Fran started to quiz you about your other girlfriends.'

He laughs, 'Your daughter is nothing if not forthright.'

'Is this really what you want, Jacob?' She pulls away from him, a frown creasing her forehead. 'An older woman and two adult children? You could have anyone – someone younger, without all this history, without the difficulties.'

'I like history,' he says, catching hold of her hands. 'I want you, Cora. And that means your children too.' He pulls her closer. 'Nothing worth anything is ever easy.'

'Now I know you're a masochist,' she murmurs.

The kids are upstairs, but just to be sure, Cora glances towards the door before she wraps her arms around his neck. His hands are on the small of her back. They kiss. When they break off, he murmurs, 'I've been waiting to do that all evening.'

Cora smiles, resting her head on his chest. This is working, she tells herself. It seemed impossible before. But they're really doing it – having a relationship in the open with the kids' approval, forming a new kind of family. Fran will always be Fran. But there was no real friction, no tantrums this evening.

In fact, there were moments of laughter and ease. And it will just keep getting easier, she tells herself. Time will work in their favour.

Holborn

Fran gets off the Tube at Holborn and walks towards the pub Zac suggested: cheap beer and a good atmosphere, he said. She weaves through the after-work crowds on autopilot, thinking about last night, the way the four of them sat around the table as if they were pretending to be a family. It took all her resolve, all her acting abilities to behave as if nothing was wrong – as if it was perfectly fine for the man she loves to be sitting there as her mother's boyfriend. He's twelve years younger than her! He would have been a baby when Cora was in secondary school. Her mother's a cradle-snatcher.

Her phone rings, and she takes it out of her pocket. It's Lesh. She sighs and answers. 'Hey, can't talk – just on my way out.'

'Oh. Okay. We haven't had a proper chat for ages. Are you all right?'

'Yeah. Fine.' She stops walking. 'I know we haven't seen much of each other lately. I've been ... working,' she improvises. 'Crap promos. But better than nothing. We'll catch up soon. Promise.'

'I'll hold you to that. I'm organising a night out with the girls next Saturday. Will you come?'

Fran swallows, clears her throat. 'Course.'

'See you then. I'll text you the details.'

'Yeah. Bye.'

She slips the phone into her back pocket. She feels bad. She knows Lesh deserves better. But how can she talk about her life right now? She bites her thumbnail, remembering that Jacob said he'd never been with anyone older than him before, which means this thing with her mother is clearly some kind of experiment. He's just trying something new. He'll get bored soon. At least she hopes he will.

She hurries on, pushing through knots of people. Meeting up with Zac is surprisingly enjoyable. He's more interesting than she originally thought – he doesn't talk about good causes all the time. He talks about normal stuff too. He even makes her laugh.

He's already waiting when she walks in, and he's got two beers on the table. They grin at each other as she slips into her seat. The place is warm and crowded – an old-fashioned pub with worn red carpets and beer mats on dark wooden tables. 'Cheers.' She raises her glass and they clink.

After they've chatted about some music he sent her on Spotify, he leans back in his chair. 'How's it going at home?' he asks, wiping the froth from his top lip.

'What do you mean?'

He laughs. 'Don't be so defensive. I just mean with your mum and her toy boy?'

Fran's drink sticks in her throat. 'None of your business.'

'I'm just curious,' he persists. 'What's the problem? If they're happy? What does it matter that he's younger?'

He's not going to let up. Fran sighs. 'She's making a fool of herself. Obviously he can't really like her. Not really.'

'Why not?' He looks genuinely puzzled. 'Just because there's an age gap?'

'Twelve years.'

He shakes his head, 'That's nothing. I know someone who's married to a man twenty years older. I didn't think you were such a prude, Fran. Age, gender, colour, culture. None of that really matters.' He holds her gaze. 'Love is love. Right?'

'Sounds like one of the slogans you shout at protests.' She grins. 'Love is love.'

'Okay, I won't mention it again.' He narrows his eyes. 'But there's clearly something else going on here . . .'

'Zac!' She pretends to hit him.

He pulls back, laughing, holding up his hands. 'Okay. Okay!'

'Change of subject,' she says, feeling strangely as if she's on the brink of tears, 'Tell me about the charity you said you were involved in – the one for refugees.'

'It's really a theatre group,' he says, his voice becoming serious. 'Cat's Eye. It's been going for about a year now. They do workshops and performances. They're really good. You'd like it.'

'But I'm not acting any more,' she says. 'And I'm not a refugee or asylum seeker.'

'You might like to go to one of their performances, though. Or you could just call in and check out their work – they meet at Boleponds Community Centre at Hanger Lane on Wednesday and Friday evenings.'

'Do you do any performing?'

'Nope, I'm the money man,' he says with an ironic grin. 'I'm in charge of raising funds, and promoting them.' He lifts his glass to his mouth. Puts it down and leans forward. 'Have you really given up acting?'

She stares at him. He seems determined to bring up every painful subject this evening. She shakes her head. 'I just wasn't good enough. I love the theatre, though. Love everything about it.'

'You said you read scripts for pleasure. As if they're novels?'

She nods. 'I picture the play unfolding in front of me – it's like a game. I decide what the characters are wearing and how they speak the lines.'

'Bet you were top of the class in English at school.'

'God, no!' She sits back. 'My teachers thought I was stupid. My spelling and punctuation were hopeless, and that seemed to matter more than my imagination.'

'Are you dyslexic?'

'A bit, I think.' She presses her thumbnail into her finger. 'I love stories, but I'm not that confident about talking about them – about literature. People tell you you're stupid enough times, you come to believe them. My dad was the one who encouraged me to be an actress. We went to see plays in London. It was so exciting. I knew I wanted to work in the theatre then.'

'Is he around now, your dad?'

She has a lump in her throat. 'He's dead.' She shakes her head. 'He fell off a ladder when I was seventeen. Then he was in a coma. My mum had to give permission to turn off life sup-port.' She can't believe she's telling him this stuff. She's never talked about it to anyone before. Not even Lesh.

'Shit!' Zac leans forward and takes one of her hands in his. His fingers are warm and strong. 'I'm so sorry, Fran,' he murmurs. 'That's really tough. But he was right to tell you to

197

dream big – even if you don't become an actress, there are lots of other creative things you could do. You're not stupid. You're perceptive and interesting and passionate. Don't let anyone tell you differently.'

She gazes up at him; his eyes are bright, the colour of a summer sky, of cornflowers, a place she wants to be. 'Thanks,' she whispers.

There's a tightness in the air, a simmering of molecules that gathers around them, shutting out the clamour and clatter of the pub, webbing them together in a moment of silent connection. Just her and Zac. The rest of the world fallen away.

A part of her wants to slip onto his lap, curl her arms around his neck, press her lips to his.

She sits back, pulling her hand away. She shifts in her chair and glances towards the bar. 'Shall we get one more round in? It's my turn.'

She can see a split second of pain cross his features, the blue of his eyes seeming to dim, as if a light's been switched off. But then he's back to being Zac again. He grins. 'Thought you'd never offer.'

31

Bethnal Green

They are lying on his bed, naked, their skin skimmed with sweat, limbs flung out in gestures of surrender, dazed from love-making. It's too hot for covers. The open Houdini hatch above is a dark rectangle, the summer stars cancelled by the brightness of a candle on the shelf beside them. The tiny flame casts long shadows across the cabin, netting them inside trembling shapes. Cora sighs, heavy with contentment.

Jacob finds her hand on the sheet and threads his fingers through hers. 'Hungry?' he asks.

'Mmm. Maybe. A bit.'

'I'll go and find us something. Tea? Toast?'

'Oh, don't leave. Not yet,' she says, rolling her head onto his shoulder.

He presses his lips into her hair, murmuring his agreement.

'By the way,' she says, 'Luke got his results yesterday. He got all A stars. So he'll be off to UEA in October.'

'That's amazing!' Jacob sits up. 'Tell him congratulations from me. You must be so proud.'

'I am.' She smiles. 'He wanted to go out for pizza to celebrate with me and his sister last night. Not one for going over the top, Luke. A Coke and a Margherita was all he wanted. I did try and call you on the off chance, to see if you could join us. I left a message.'

'Oh yeah. You did. Sorry.' He glances away, lying down again. 'It was a long day. I didn't get your voicemail till it was too late – should have replied, though.'

She squeezes his fingers. 'It's fine, you didn't know it was anything special. Luke wanted to surprise you.'

'Now I feel really guilty.'

She puts her hand on his cheek and gently turns his face towards her. 'It's not a problem. He can tell you next time you do a ride.'

'Yeah.' He nods. 'I'll get him something for his bike. He was saying he wanted a nice speedo.' He squeezes her tight. 'Three A stars! Your son's a genius.'

'I can't take any credit.' She smiles. 'I dropped science after my O levels.' She pushes one foot over the side of the bed, hoping to feel a breeze slipping in through the open glass above. 'I'm going to miss Luke when he leaves. Norwich is too far to pop back from. But I suppose that's the point. To get away from home, from your parents.' She rolls onto one elbow to face him. 'You went to Imperial, didn't you? Did you stay in halls or at home?'

'I thought I should move out as I wasn't getting on with Dad,' he says. 'Luckily I managed to get into some student accommodation in Streatham.'

'Are things better with your father now?'

He rubs the end of his nose, as if he has to think about it. 'We love each other, so we've learnt to manage the situation.

He's stopped trying to re-convert me. But I think secretly he's still disappointed.'

She kisses his cheek, lands on his ear instead. 'That must be hard.'

He looks pensive. 'It's just . . . I never wanted to hurt him. My parents are old and they've been through a lot. I want to look after them. Make them happy.'

He still hasn't told his parents about her, and she can see that she may not be the kind of news that would make them happy. And yet she doesn't want to be something he's ashamed of – a guilty secret.

Jacob knows all about Cora's childhood, the shock of her parents' sudden deaths, her lack of siblings; she's told him about Andrew. She's even spoken about her depression after Fran was born. The first time she's told anyone except Helena. He's a good listener, easy to confide in, but he doesn't reciprocate.

'You know, you never talk about your family,' she says. 'I don't even know if you have brothers and sisters?'

There is a tense beat of silence. The candle flickers. He clears his throat. 'One,' he says. 'A younger brother.' His voice sounds completely unlike him: stiff and formal. She's confused, unsure if she should even ask the brother's name.

'Anyway.' He yawns, stretching his long arms, giving a little shake. 'I'm starving. I'll go and make us that toast.' He gets up, pulling a robe from the back of the door.

From the bed, she stares through the half-open door; at the end of the short, narrow passage she can see Jacob in the main section of the boat as he passes to and fro across her view. She smells toast, hears the whine of the kettle. God, he really didn't want to talk about his brother. She supposes that they've fallen out. It must have been a bad row, she thinks – bitter things

201

spoken, a betrayal perhaps, an ongoing feud. Families are complicated. She knows that better than anyone.

When he returns, carrying a laden tray, she kneels on the sheet to help him. The tray is heavy with two cups of tea, a plate piled with toast and Marmite, sliced bananas and apple in a bowl, ginger biscuits, and a bar of dark chocolate. 'You *are* hungry,' she says, sitting back and carefully taking a full mug to cradle.

'That's your doing,' he says. 'And if you don't cover up,' he adds in a mock-threatening voice, 'we'll never leave this bed. Never leave the boat, for that matter!'

She smiles, relieved that his mood has lightened.

They eat, scattering crumbs on their skin, licking their fingers, sharing comments about the food, the sound of the night birds, their plans for the next morning. Afterwards, Jacob runs a shower and they squeeze into the minute wet-room together. Pressed tight against each other's soapy bodies, they kiss under the cool water, and somehow, despite the lack of space, they manage to make love again, Jacob lifting her onto his hips, her shoulders jammed against the walls, her hands grasping for purchase on whatever she can reach: the ceiling, the tiles, tangling in his hair.

Back in bed, they lie under a thin sheet, curled up in each other's arms, exhausted. The muggy August heat is made more bearable by the open hatch, and the soft slap of the canal against the boat.

'Jacob,' Cora murmurs into his neck, 'I was thinking ... maybe we could get out of town ... have a weekend away. Paris or Amsterdam ...'

'Hmm.' He yawns and turns onto his back. 'Nice idea. Let's talk about it another time, when we're not so tired.'

He sounds half asleep, and she nods against his chest, but she felt his muscles clench. Perhaps her voice startled him as he was drifting into a dream. She's sure he's properly asleep now; his lungs rise and fall in a steady rhythm. She leans up on one elbow and smiles, dipping her face towards him, pressing her lips into the hollow of his breastbone. Her feelings for this man have surprised her. Only a few months ago, he was a stranger. What would Andrew think if he could see her now? She rolls onto her back. She's sure he would have liked Jacob if they'd met. And he wouldn't want her to spend the rest of her life alone – he'd be glad for her. Something in her chest releases, a final letting-go of grief and pain, of Andrew himself. A forgiveness. She'll always love him, but she has room in her heart for another.

It's a hot Friday morning, and a haze shimmers over Hyde Park as Cora and Helena jog around their normal route. Cora has fallen behind; every stride hurts. She thought at first that maybe it was the heat, or she was coming down with something, but then she realised that her muscles and tendons are bruised from her gymnastics in the shower. The ridiculousness of this makes her grin, and then she's giggling uncontrollably. The memory of it – how he lifted her, his head between her breasts, her thighs clamped around his hips – makes her stomach contract in pleasure. The fact that she's having energetic, inventive sex at her age is such a wonderful thing – something she never thought possible – she feels a sudden wild joy. Laughter takes hold of her. She stops with her hands on her hips, bending over, gasping for air. A passing woman gives her a puzzled glance before whistling for her Labrador and moving on.

Helena glances over her shoulder, jogging on the spot, and then strides back. 'Cora?' She looks concerned. 'You all right?'

Cora wipes her eyes. 'Sorry. I just . . . I just had a weird realisation. My legs are aching like crazy. Well, all of me is, actually. And then I realised that . . . that it's the sex.'

Helena raises one eyebrow. 'Really?' she says, her voice full of sarcasm. 'All the sex that you won't share the details of with me?'

Cora takes a couple of deep breaths, steadying herself. 'Sometimes I can't believe it's happening to me – that *he's* happening to me. He's funny and kind and clever. He makes me laugh. Brings me snacks in bed . . .'

'And fucks you. A lot. You lucky cow.' Helena sits down on the grass. 'It's too bloody hot to run. If you were a better friend, you'd console me with some salacious details about your sexual exploits. You know my love life is non-existent. Larry just turns over and snores.'

'Sorry.' Cora folds her legs under her and sinks down beside Helena. 'If . . . if it was just a casual fling, you know I wouldn't hold back.' There's a view of the Serpentine below; the park is getting busier with skaters and joggers and dog-walkers. Two riders canter along the sandy horse track.

Helena swigs from the water bottle she's carrying and passes it to Cora. 'Oh, I know. And I know you better than that. I'm just teasing really. I'm green with envy, but I'm happy for you. You look amazing – all shiny and glowing. Orgasms are so rejuvenating. And the ones another actual live human gives are the gold-star kind.'

Cora laughs. 'But the best bit is how relaxed I feel with him, how at home we are together. At first, I was nervous about him seeing my body, wondering if he'd be turned off by my stretch marks, the droopy bits, but he seems to like every bit of me. I can just be my natural self.'

'I hope that's not a euphemism for letting yourself go – he is twelve years younger than you. You'll have to work at keeping yourself looking gorgeous and sleek.'

'If you mean am I having Brazilians all the time, then no. That one time you made me try it was the one and only.'

'But men love it.'

'Not Jacob. And anyway, it was so itchy when it started to grow back. Which was literally about three hours after it all came off. I can't believe you pay to be tortured like that.'

Helena rolls her eyes. 'If you change your mind, I could swing you a discount . . .'

Cora mock-glares at her friend, and Helena holds up her hands. 'Kidding!' She lies back on the grass, looking up into the sky.

'Helena, I . . . I really like Jacob, you know,' Cora says quietly as she lies next to her.

'Hmm. I didn't really get that.'

'No. I mean,' Cora shades the sun with her hand, 'I trust him. There's no game-playing. He understands me.' She closes her eyes. 'It's a bit frightening. But I'm letting myself fall for him.'

'Oh, honey,' Helena says. 'I hate to break it to you, but you fell for this guy a while ago. There's no shutting the stable door now.'

They lie in silence listening to the distant thrum of traffic, birdsong coming from the branches of the trees.

'How's Fran, by the way?' Helena says. 'Do you think she's okay with you and Jacob being together now?'

Cora sits, drawing her knees up and clasping her hands around her shins. 'Yes, I think so. She . . . she seems happier in herself. There's a guy called Zac she's been seeing a lot, but I have no idea if they're dating or just friends. She'd never tell me, of course.'

'I used to wish I had a daughter,' Helena says, raising one leg skywards and pulling it into a hamstring stretch by grabbing the toe of her running shoe. 'But actually I can see that boys are easier.' She's performing the same exercise with her other leg. 'My two are emotionally stunted. But at least there's no hysteria in our house, no dark emotional undercurrents. Just shouting. And some wrestling. Then it's over.'

'God. Yes.' Cora blinks. 'It's not an undercurrent at my place. It's a whirlpool. A rip tide. A constant threat of drowning.'

Helena lets go of her foot and leans on her elbow, looking up at Cora. 'And no sign of her getting a job, or wanting to do a course?'

Cora shrugs. 'I'm not interfering at the moment. And I'm especially not asking her what her plans are. If I do, I just end up pushing her further away.'

'She'll be fine. Of course she will. And she *is* a grown-up.'

Cora plucks at the short grass beside her, rubbing it between her fingers. 'Yes, but we both know that however old they are, they never stop being your child.'

'Come on.' Helena gets to her feet, stretching out a hand. 'Let's do a slow jog to the gate, then at least we've done something.'

That evening, alone in her own bed, Cora googles Airbnbs in Amsterdam – not quite such an obvious romantic getaway as Paris, she thinks. She scrolls through charming flats in the centre, homing in on those overlooking a canal. She finds a loft apartment with stripped wooden floors, full of gorgeous paintings. She bookmarks it, feeling excited. She considers some small boutique hotels, reading about breakfast buffets, bikes to be hired, museums to visit. If she could surreptitiously find out which weekends he's available, she could book it as a surprise. Nobody, she thinks, could be averse to a couple of days in Amsterdam. She closes her laptop and slides it onto the floor. But what about his Saturday afternoons with his parents? Surely he can miss one family lunch? She'll ask, in a subtle way, put out more feelers, see if he'll agree to setting a few days aside soon.

She switches off the bedside lamp, settling down in the dark. Behind closed lids, she imagines them cycling along cobbled streets, across bridges, Jacob stretching out his hand and her wobbling as she lets go of the handlebars to clasp his fingers, both of them laughing. In her vision, they are backlit against the Dutch cityscape. She sees herself from the outside, as if she's a character in a film. One she wants to keep watching.

32

Shepherd's Bush

As she leaves the house, Fran walks into a blaze of early-evening sunshine. This summer is turning out to be one of the hottest on record. Radio presenters are all over it, relaying the latest scorching temperatures, talking about the most crowded beaches in England, sometimes chiming in with warnings about climate change. Fran puts her sunglasses on and heads towards the Tube station. The street gives off the tang of burnt tarmac and fox pee; the big plane trees are listless, branches drooping with dusty leaves. People slouch along in clothes usually saved for beach holidays – flip-flops, shorts, sunhats – and it seems every girl under forty is wearing a strappy floral number.

'Fran!'

The voice, coming from behind, kicks her heart into overdrive. She keeps walking, head down. 'Fran! Wait!'

She knows who it is before she turns.

Alesha hurries to catch up. She's frowning. 'Are you running away from me?'

Fran stares at her, thoughts jangling incoherently. The sight of Lesh makes her want to throw her arms around her in relief; but the urge to disappear is stronger, preferably to teleport to another planet, far away from embarrassment and guilt and her lack of a viable excuse.

Alesha is staring at her, 'What's going on? I know something's up. You keep cancelling on me. And when we do talk, you're weird.'

'Sorry,' Fran says. 'I know I've been a terrible friend. But I've been . . . busy.'

'Seriously?' Alesha has her hands on her hips. 'This has been going on for weeks.' She frowns. 'Months, actually. I feel like you've been hiding things from me since . . . since March.'

'No,' Fran pleads. 'No. I've just been . . . distracted. Especially recently. I was planning on . . . on spending more time with you.'

'Is that right?' Alesha folds her arms. 'Then tell me what's been keeping you so *busy* you sometimes don't even acknowledge my text messages?'

She sounds as though she's giving one of her pupils a tongue-lashing. But it's her friend's obvious hurt, the vulnerability in her dark eyes, that makes Fran's bottom lip tremble. 'Lesh . . . please . . .' She reaches out a hand.

Alesha steps back, shaking her head, 'I know you're lying about something.'

Fran takes her sunglasses off, bangles clattering. Shit. She needs to come up with something. 'It's . . . it's Jacob,' she says slowly, looking at her feet. 'We've been seeing each other . . . and . . . I've been staying on his boat. It's kind of taken over my life.' She forces herself to meet Alesha's gaze. 'I know I should have told you. I'm sorry.'

'Wow!' Alesha's eyebrows jump halfway up her forehead. 'I

wasn't expecting that. Jacob? You've got together with him? Why couldn't you have just told me, for fuck's sake! I was worried about you . . . I even thought you might be ill or something.' Her mouth twitches into a smile. 'I'll forgive you then, this one time. Seriously, I'm happy for you, babe. This is what you wanted.' She shakes her head. 'But don't do it again, okay? We can't let men get between us – girlfriends stick for life.'

They hug, Fran leaning down to hold her smaller friend, pressing her face into Lesh's hair, her chin resting on polished round shoulders.

'Where are you off to?' Lesh asks when they step apart.

'I'm meeting him. Jacob.'

Actually, she's seeing Zac. When did life become this complicated?

A delivery lorry roars past, leaving a stench of diesel. Fran flicks her hair over her shoulder. 'Thanks for coming. You're the best. But I'm running late.' She looks towards the end of the street. 'Are you walking to the Tube station?'

'Carl drove me. He's waiting in the car just over there.'

Fran wrinkles her nose. 'That man will do anything for you.'

Alesha grins. 'I'm a lucky girl.' She winks. 'You'd better go, then. Wouldn't want you to be late.' She smiles. 'See you soon. Dinner, maybe?'

'For sure.'

'Love you.'

'Love you too.' Fran turns and walks away. The sun is burning the top of her head. Her feet are sweating in her DMs. As she replaces her glasses, the plastic rim is slick against her cheek. She's just told the biggest lie of her life. To her best friend. She feels sick.

'I missed you!' Lesh calls out from behind her.

Fran stops and turns, forcing herself to grin. 'Missed you too!'

'We can have double dates now!' Lesh sings over her shoulder. 'Me and Carl, and you and Jacob. It'll be cool!'

Fran waves, the smile stuck to her lips.

As she sets off towards the Tube station, the smile fades from her mouth. A throbbing has started at her temples. Panic presses against her heart. Why did she say that she was with Jacob? It feels all wrong that Mum's dating him. But does that mean she still fancies him herself? She doesn't know what she feels any more, just that she's confused, claustrophobic. Trapped.

On the Tube, she fans herself, standing up in the aisle to avoid creasing her dress or getting it dirty. The carriage smells of sweat. A blast of hot air from an open window tears at her hair, tangling it. She runs her tongue over her lips, tasting soot.

Zac is sitting at a corner table in the busy pub garden. He stands up and waves. She's glad to see him. He's someone she can be honest with, someone she isn't lying to.

'You managed to get a table,' she says. 'Well done!'

'Had to get here at dawn. But hey, anything for you!' He hands her a beer and they clink.

'Cheers,' she says, taking a long gulp.

They talk about small stuff, order a couple more beers, but she's ahead of him, finishing her third with a swig. 'You're going hard,' he says.

'I need it.'

'Maybe you should slow down?'

She scowls, 'Don't tell me what to do. If it's the cost you're worried about—'

'It's not that,' he interrupts. 'Maybe you think it's funny being off your face.' He frowns. 'But it's not. It's bad for you. And it's death to your brain cells.'

She rolls her eyes. 'Fuck off, Mr Know-It-All. If you're going to be like this, I'm leaving.'

'That's what you do, isn't it? Run away as soon as things get difficult.' He gestures towards the exit.

'You know nothing about my life,' she fires back. 'I have my reasons for wanting to drink today.'

'You're right. I don't know much about you, because you don't tell me.' He stretches his fingers wide. 'But if you're drinking to forget, it won't work. I know all about that. I see misery in buckets every day.'

'For God's sake,' she says, leaning back in her chair. 'I'm not an idiot. Of course I know that loads of people are much worse off than me. But you can't tell me *I'm* not hurting just because other people have a more shit life than me.'

'I didn't say that you can't be sad.' He leans towards her, his voice dropping. 'I'm just worried about how fast you're knocking it back.'

She narrows her eyes. 'Careful. You're beginning to sound like my mother.'

'You know,' he grimaces, 'you're really hard to help.'

'And you're a patronising bastard.'

They stare at each other, unblinking, brows furrowed, a staring match of fury. And then suddenly they both begin to grin, and Fran is laughing, a proper from-the-gut guffaw. Zac's howling too, a weird donkey bray.

'God, you have an unsexy laugh,' she giggles, wiping her eyes.

'Can a laugh be sexy?'

'Obviously.'

'Okay.' He shakes his head, still snorting a bit. 'I'd better work on that, then. Try to cultivate a sexy laugh. Whatever that is.'

'Don't bother,' she says. 'I like it the way it is.'

He flashes her a huge smile.

They have another round of beers. She sips hers more slowly, and they share a packet of crisps and chat about inconsequential things. The small garden is rammed with people eating, talking and laughing. There's a smell of hot salty chips and suntan cream. The sun beats down on big green and white umbrellas sheltering each table. A dog sleeps in the shade, a water bowl on the grass.

Zac brings a travel backgammon set out of his pocket and challenges her to a game. 'My dad and I used to play this together,' she says as she moves a checker.

'Now you tell me,' he says, leaning on his elbows and staring at the board. 'You're good.'

They play in concentrated silence until Fran wins. 'You were a tough opponent,' she concedes, helping him to pack up the board.

'You owe me a rematch,' he says.

'No problem. If you want to get thrashed twice.'

He laughs. 'I'll take my chances. But another time. I think we should go. There's a long queue of hopefuls eyeing up our table.'

They leave the pub and walk slowly towards the Tube station. The city has the gritty, stale feel of late summer, the air hot and heavy, the streets emptier than usual. Fran prefers it like this. It feels a bit like a classroom after the teacher's walked out; there's an unsettling liberation, a feeling that anarchy could take over.

Bar and pubs are overflowing with drinkers, spilling out of doorways, glasses in hand, their chatter rising above the noise of traffic. As Fran and Zac wait on the pavement to cross the road, she lifts her hair away from her hot neck to try and catch a breeze. Zac leans across and blows. She closes her eyes, 'Mmm. Feels nice.'

'Mobile air conditioning available any time of day or night,' he says.

They say goodbye at the entrance to the Underground, but as she goes through the turnstile towards the escalator, Fran has a sudden urge not to get on the Tube. She's not ready to go home. She'd like to keep walking the hot streets with Zac, to keep talking, or not-talking – to feel his breath on her neck again. She stops and turns, the suggestion forming on her lips. But he has already walked off. She catches a glimpse of the back of his head as he hesitates at a crossing. The lights change, and he's gone.

33

Bethnal Green

Jacob is standing inside the engine hatch at the back of the boat. Only his top half is visible. He frowns at the machine at his feet, a spanner in his hand.

'Jacob,' Cora says, making her voice casual, 'is there a weekend coming up when you might be free, by any chance?'

He turns to look at her. 'A whole weekend?'

'Yes,' she laughs. 'An actual whole weekend. A Saturday and Sunday at least.'

'Well,' he scratches his cheek, smearing oil on his skin, 'not sure at the moment. Work's pretty full-on.'

She tries to suppress her disappointment. Perhaps this won't be as easy to organise as she thought, especially as in her enthusiasm she's picked the wrong moment to ask. He's not concentrating on anything but the mystery of the generator. He squats down, out of sight. Generator malfunctions, according to Jacob, are a common problem for narrowboat owners.

Cora sits back in her deckchair, positioned on the flat roof. She's podding broad beans into a bowl for their lunch. She continues to ease the beans out of their velvety casing – a calming task, one that makes her feel she could have slipped backwards in time a hundred years. As her hands move, she glances at her naked finger, the pale circle that marks the place her wedding ring used to sit.

The canal bank is busy with dog-walkers, cyclists, and joggers running past those who just want to wander, enjoying the sunshine. Passers-by often stand and stare at the canal dwellers, as if they're specimens in a zoo. 'We should charge,' George laughed when she mentioned it. 'You're a boat person now, mate. Don't let it get to you.'

Cora prefers to go unnoticed. She's not one of life's exhibitionists. Jacob doesn't seem to mind. He always smiles and answers questions about moorings and water supplies politely when someone stops on the path to chat.

Later, sitting together in the cabin, eating fresh beans dressed in lemony mayonnaise with falafels, Cora tries again. 'So, about a possible free weekend – is there one we could circle for a trip somewhere?'

She's longing to tell him about the gorgeous Airbnb in Amsterdam, but she wants to save the surprise until she can book it.

He rubs his nose. 'I'd have to check my diary.'

'Okay.' She swallows her frustration. He's being unusually vague and distracted – probably still puzzling over the workings of the engine. He has oil smudges on his cheek and chin. She leans across and kisses his mouth just above the stain. 'You're in a dream today,' she says softly.

He startles, then kisses her back. 'Sorry,' he smiles.

'I could stay tonight?' she says. 'Fran's home with Luke. But if you'd rather be alone . . .'

'No,' he says, his voice suddenly fierce. 'I want you to stay. Please.'

'Okay,' she says, and it really does feel okay. There was no doubt in his voice, no doubt in his eyes when he looked at her.

They've reached that phase in their relationship where they can be in the same space but doing different things. They don't need to be engaged in constant conversation. He returns to the engine after lunch, and she takes her book and lies on deck in her shorts and T-shirt, enjoying the heat on her back and the sound of water lapping at the hull. She can understand why he likes this life – the simplicity of it, the kindness of the community, the closeness to nature in the middle of a city. She's come to appreciate the boat – her nooks and crannies, the way she creaks, the timber forming its own secret language, the small, clever spaces that insist on being negotiated with care. Aware of the lack of room, she never leaves anything behind. She only keeps a toothbrush here. It sits in the cup on the tiny sink, rubbing bristles with Jacob's. She likes to see the two together, a symbol of their developing relationship, the beginnings of being a couple.

In the middle of the night, lying entwined in his arms, she's woken by the sound of a mobile ringing. She jolts into wakefulness, immediately aware that it's not hers but Jacob's, and that he's fumbled through the darkness for the blinking light. He holds the phone to his ear.

He listens, then says in a heavy voice, 'Okay. Yeah. I'll be there.'

'Jacob?' She sits up, rubbing her eyes. 'What time is it? Is everything all right?'

'Think it's around midnight. I need to go.' He swings his legs off the mattress, and she can hear him scrabbling for his clothes and pulling them on.

'But what's happened? Is something wrong?'

'Nothing for you to worry about.'

'Put the light on – I don't mind.'

'No. It's fine.'

She realises that moonlight is flooding the cabin, silky and pale through the glass above, dissipating her initial blindness. The room is visible in soft, sketchy outlines.

'I don't understand. Has there been an accident?'

He doesn't answer for a moment, and she can see enough to make out the shape of him sitting on the end of the bed, putting on his shoes. 'It's . . . it's my brother,' he says. 'Natan. He's in trouble. I need to sort it out. I'll probably be a couple of hours.'

'Oh . . . Hope it's not serious.'

'It happens sometimes.' He makes his way around the mattress to drop a kiss on her head. 'Go back to sleep.'

She rolls over onto his side of the bed, listening to him making his way through the main cabin. Then the faint sounds of him unlocking his bike and heaving it onto the path, the crunch of stones as he cycles away.

This is why he didn't want to talk about his mysterious brother. She imagines Jacob pedalling through the darkened streets to a police station to bail him out, and wonders what kind of trouble his brother is in. Whatever it is, it's something that's made Jacob resigned. Sad and distant, as if he's used to being woken in the middle of the night to deal with problems.

She's even more determined to get some dates from him; she wants to book that Airbnb. He needs a break. He's been looking tired recently. He works hard, has a demanding job, and now she knows that he's got an errant brother, one he feels responsible for. It's given her a new understanding of him and his life – and the knowledge of that small revelation sits inside her like a flickering light as she drifts back to sleep.

34

Bethnal Green

'We're not ready for double dates yet,' Fran says. She's glad they're talking on the phone, so Lesh can't see her. 'Me and Jacob, we need a bit more time, you know, hanging out together.'

'Yeah, I totally get that, babe. I'm just keen to meet this guy. You've given him quite a build-up.'

Fran manages a laugh. She clears her throat. 'Got to go, Lesh. I'm meeting him at the boat.'

She clicks off the mobile, letting it drop onto her bed, and pushes her face into her hands. What the actual fuck. She can't keep this up much longer.

She pulls on a pair of vintage denim dungarees, adds red lipstick and laces up her favourite DMs.

She puts her head around the kitchen door to say goodbye. Cora's there with Luke. They've been shopping all afternoon to kit Luke out for university, and there are bags piled over the table, spilling contents. Fran notices a shiny saucepan; a mug with a funny picture of a dog. New jeans and sweatshirts. A boxed-up pair of snazzy trainers.

'Oxford Street was a nightmare,' Cora is saying. 'Not sure my feet will ever recover. Or my nerves.'

Fran wanders over to the table. 'Why does he need a saucepan? Isn't he going to be in halls?' She shakes her head. 'And what's wrong with the clothes he has already?' She picks up a navy hoodie and looks at the price tag. 'He wears the same clothes every day.' Fran didn't get a whole load of new stuff bought for her when she went to drama school.

Cora takes the hoodie out of her hands with a gentle nudge. 'There's a kitchen in his hall. And anyway, this is, I don't know, a kind of ritual. It's a big step. Moving out. And also, he deserves it, for doing so well.' She looks at Fran more closely. 'You look nice. Are you going out?'

'Uh-huh.' Fran flicks her hair over her shoulder. 'Meeting Zac for a walk.'

'You should bring him home one day. Introduce us. We'd like to meet him, wouldn't we, Luke?'

Luke rolls his eyes. He's busy making himself a sandwich.

'He's not my boyfriend,' Fran says. 'And I don't know what's worse – introducing him to you, or you to him.'

'That doesn't make sense,' Luke says through a mouthful of sandwich.

'Says the genius.' Fran is already moving towards the door.

Zac's waiting for her at the entrance to Bethnal Green Tube station, his headphones on. When he sees her, he switches his music off and slips his headphones down. He puts up his hand. 'Hey.'

They grin at each other.

'So,' he says as they begin to walk together, 'what made you want to slum it on this side of town?'

'Just fancied a change,' Fran says. 'Thought it would be nice to walk along the canal.'

'It's the right weather for it,' Zac agrees. 'When I was a kid, my dad used to bring me here to fish.'

'Ah, the male bonding ritual – killing defenceless creatures.'

'Actually, I got upset when he caught anything, and made him throw it back.'

Fran laughs. 'Most boys want to destroy things. Nice to know you were a softie.'

They've reached the towpath. Fran smells the weedy, dank scent of the water. The path is busy with joggers and people out for an early-evening walk, and she and Zac move closer together, weaving in and out of the throng. She notices that they have the same instinct for direction, their steps making a pattern, like a dance.

Fran knows that Zac isn't close to his dad, and his mum took off to live with a new man on the Costa Brava years ago. She feels bad for him. 'I expect your dad liked the opportunity to spend time with you,' she says. 'Have you to himself for the afternoon.'

'I'm pretty certain Mum paid him to get me out from under her feet,' Zac says.

There's not a trace of self-pity in his voice. He never complains about his upbringing; he even makes jokes about it, although Fran can sense the hurt beneath the bravado.

She smiles and squeezes his arm, 'Well, I promise I didn't need paying to take you out today.'

As they reach a line of narrowboats tied up end to end, her

pulse jumps. This must be where Jacob lives. She knows he's not here; he'll be with Mum and Luke, having supper. She was curious to see his boat. She wanted to find out which was his, but now she wonders why.

There's a man sitting on top of one of the narrowboats in a deckchair, a can of beer in his hand. A loud bark startles Fran, and a shadow beneath the man's chair unfurls. She catches a glimpse of teeth and lolling tongue as a large dog flies through the air, landing in front of her and bouncing up with front paws against her thighs, making her stumble back. Claws dig into her knees, hot breath on her skin. She tries to push the animal down.

'Oi, Claude!' the man shouts, getting to his feet. 'Sorry about that. He's just being friendly. Long as you don't owe him money, he's a pussycat.'

The large brindled dog gazes up at her, panting, head on one side, seemingly contrite. She glances down and notices a trickle of blood on her shin.

'He's scratched my leg!'

'That happened to a mate of mine,' the man says, straight-faced. 'And the next day his head fell off.'

Fran gives him a hard glare.

Zac's taken her fingers in his. He squeezes in silent support. 'Thanks, mate.' He waves to the man, tugging Fran's hand. 'Come on,' he says softly. 'Let's go.'

He guides her to a bench nearby and, to her surprise, drops to one knee. He's examining her shin, his fingers gentle on her skin. Fran swallows a gasp. His touch feels so intimate. She hasn't shaved her legs recently. She screws up her face, pre-pared to push his hand away or leap up. But he shows no sign of recoiling in disgust; his expression is one of concentration.

He unties the cotton scarf from around his neck. 'It was clean on this morning,' he explains as he dabs at the blood. 'Just a graze,' he says, sitting back.

She manages a smile. 'You must think I'm a wuss. It was just . . . a shock. I'm not used to dogs.'

'I didn't see him under the chair either.' He crumples up his scarf and shoves it in his back pocket. 'But I do like dogs. I plan to have one some day – a rescue mutt preferably.'

'To go with your hipster look. Well,' she says, leaning over to examine the graze, 'thanks for patching me up, Doctor. You shouldn't give up on your dreams, you know. You could be a real doctor if you retook your exams.'

'Yeah,' he says. 'Maybe.'

They walk on. 'Look,' Zac says, pointing through some scrubby bushes to an ice-cream van parked on the lane running parallel to the path. 'My treat.'

She follows him, joining the short queue; he buys an ice lolly for her and a cone for himself. They wander back to the towpath, falling into companionable silence. The evening has turned muggy, the sun dipping low in the sky. But it's still light, and clouds of midges hover, waiting to ambush any bits of exposed skin. Fran brushes them away as she licks the orange-flavoured ice. She'd forgotten the simple joy of a lolly. It makes a nice change not to be drinking, too, she realises – usually anything sociable involves alcohol.

As she drops her stick in a bin, Zac finishes the last mouthful of his ice cream with a satisfied sigh. They're walking back past the narrowboats. She's relieved to see that the man isn't there, and there's no sign of his dog.

Zac's laughing.

'What?'

'Your mouth. It's totally orange.'

She sticks her tongue out and widens her eyes. 'What do you think, Doc? Is it serious?'

He puts his head on one side, considering. 'Hmm. A bad case of orange-itis. The only cure is a dip in a canal. Preferably one with lots of slimy weed . . .'

She runs away from him, 'Don't you dare!'

He springs after her, catching her around the middle, and they stagger across the path, laughing. Fran screams, struggling to get free. She's enjoying the feel of his arms around her. As their bodies sway together, they push and pull against each other, and a sudden hot wanting starts up inside her, unexpected, urgent. She catches her breath.

An elderly man waves his walking stick at them. They break apart, letting him past. 'Sorry,' Zac calls after him, and grabs her hand. 'Let's try not to knock any pensioners over.'

'Audrey Hepburn got an eye disease after she jumped in a canal in Venice doing her own film stunt,' she says.

'You know I'd never really throw you in.' Their fingers interlace. She likes him holding her hand. She doesn't pull away. 'Actually,' he goes on, 'I think it was the other one, the one who had a love affair with Spencer Tracy.'

'Katharine Hepburn?'

'Yeah. I like those old films. We should watch one together sometime. Anyway, meant to say before, there's a party at Hanger Lane tomorrow night. Do you want to come?'

'Sure,' she says. 'Text me the address.'

'There'll be some people there I'd like you to meet.'

'Cool.'

When they get to the Tube station, he smiles. 'Thanks for suggesting this – it's been great.'

'Thanks for coming with me.' She stares down at her feet, suddenly too embarrassed to look at him.

'So ... I'm going to walk home from here,' he says. 'Fran?'

She blinks, raising her eyes. 'What?'

He leans in for a kiss. Her stomach drops, her whole body fizzing with anticipation. But before their mouths make contact, she's pulling back. Their noses collide, faces touching and recoiling. They stand staring at each other, stunned by the glitch, as if time has shifted out of sync. Heat rages in her cheeks. He squints at her in confusion.

'Shit. Sorry,' she says. 'But ... but there's no way I can kiss you with that beard.'

'Seriously?' He has the grace to smile.

She nods, playful now. 'Yup. It has to go. I don't even know what you look like under it.' She screws up her face. 'It's a deal-breaker.'

He puts his hands in his pockets. 'When we went to the South Bank, I thought you were the rudest person I'd ever met.'

'And your point is?'

'I was right. You are.'

She laughs, turning to go into the station, giving him a wave over her shoulder, but her heart is racing. He took her by surprise. 'Damn,' she mutters. 'Damn. Damn.' She wishes she had kissed him, beard or no beard. She forces her feet to keep going through the station, down onto the platform, but all she really wants to do is run back and grab him.

Shepherd's Bush

Jacob makes a great chilli. He's standing in Cora's kitchen, a tea towel draped over his shoulder, stirring a pan on the stove, adding a cube of dark chocolate, a teaspoon more chipotle, as he chats to Luke about mysterious things like Garmins and something called electronic shifting. Luke asks him about the importance of cadence, and if a carbon frame with disc brakes is worth saving for, and Jacob laughs and says only if he wins the lottery. Cora hasn't the slightest idea what they're talking about, but she loves watching them. They are so easy in each other's company – it feels right for Jacob to be here, part of her family. But the optimism she felt after the four of them had supper has dwindled. Fran finds every excuse to avoid being here at the same time as Jacob.

Luke has always been easier than his sister, but then he's only known love and security – he had a mum who could pick him up and hold him properly, who didn't need drugs to get her through each day.

Andrew took her to the doctor. Antidepressants were prescribed – small pills that took away the edge of pain, took away the real colours and shapes and sounds of her life. She was dulled. Numb. It was enough to enable her to pick Fran up, but she couldn't properly see or feel her. She was weak, unable to sleep, exhausted.

Time passed. Cora began to feel better, to manage without drugs. Fran was a sturdy toddler, angry, tearful, demanding. Then a tall child with long, thin white limbs. Andrew swept her up above his head, tickling her tummy; to Cora, Fran's laughter was a relief and an accusation. She was afraid of failing as a mother again – it took her years before she was ready to try for a second baby. But it was different with Luke. She cradled him in her arms, sniffed the curdy warmth of his skin, held his tiny, squirming feet in her hands. When he sucked at her with his milk-blistered mouth, she felt overwhelmed in a new way. Love inhabited her, filling her bones, leaking from her pores, making her soft and fierce at the same time.

Jacob is showing Luke how to juggle with a couple of onions. Luke drops them both and scrabbles under the table to find them. Cora can't help smiling – the evening feels so warm and comfortable. Over supper, passing each other bowls of tomato salsa and avocado, the three of them discuss Luke's imminent departure for university.

'Make sure you do all the things you want to do,' Jacob says. 'Those three years go past very fast.'

Luke takes his glasses off and polishes them on the edge of his shirt. 'I just want to get into the physics lab,' he says, staring hard at his spectacles.

'Darling,' Cora says. 'Jacob's right. University should be fun too. There are so many clubs to join. Things to do. There'll be a cycling club, won't there, Jacob?'

Jacob and Cora laugh as they remember stories from their own student days, and Cora tells the tale of how she met Helena in her first week, and how their friendship began with a misunderstanding over the last piece of chocolate cake in a café frequented by students. 'We practically came to blows,' she smiles. 'Then we sat down and shared it, and discovered we had more than a passion for cake in common. She's been my best friend ever since.'

After they've stacked the dishwasher and Luke has gone off to his room, Jacob and Cora slump on the sofa and flick through films.

'I've already seen that one,' Cora says. 'What about that? Oh no. Too violent.'

'Seems we've seen them all before,' he says.

She sighs and leans back. He slips his arm around her shoulder.

'Did you have lots of girlfriends at university?' she asks.

'No ... not really.'

'Really?' She glances at him to see if he's joking. 'A good-looking boy like you?' she teases.

He seems embarrassed, glancing away.

'Why not?' she asks, curious now.

'I don't know.' He lifts his shoulders. 'I was the first person in my family to go to university. I felt I had to do well – there seemed a lot riding on it.'

She wonders if his brother was a tearaway even then. 'And did your brother follow in your footsteps? Did he go to uni?'

His body stiffens and he sits forward. 'No.' He goes back to scrolling through films. 'What about you? Were there any great student loves?' His voice is strangely remote.

'I met Andrew in my first year,' she says quietly. 'And that was that. We married after I graduated.' She's already told him this. She puts her hands on her knees, takes a steadying breath. 'Jacob, what's going on with your brother? Where did you go the other night? Did you have to . . . to bail him out or something?'

'Bail him out?' He stares at her, then shakes his head. 'He hadn't been arrested. It was more of . . . an emotional thing.'

'Like a breakdown?'

'Yes. He's . . . ill.' He rubs his forehead as if it hurts. 'Do you mind if we don't talk about it?'

She touches his hand, 'Okay,' she says quietly. 'Sorry.'

The atmosphere between them has changed, tightened, become awkward. 'Let's forget the film,' she says, making her voice bright. 'Let's book a weekend away – I was going to keep it a surprise, but I've found an amazing apartment to rent in Amsterdam.' She stands up to fetch her laptop. 'I'll show you.'

'Look,' he says, 'it's a lovely idea. But at the moment, getting away is difficult. I don't want us to book and then have to cancel.'

Cora remains in the centre of the room, motionless, as if she's a thief caught with her pockets full. Her blood thumps with disappointment. 'Really . . . so there's no time at all that you can take?' She tries to keep her voice steady.

'I'm sorry. I just can't promise you a whole weekend.'

Anger leaps inside her. 'You can't promise a whole weekend?'

He doesn't answer, looking at the floor. His shoulders hunch, making him seem uncomfortable, almost furtive. She steps closer. 'Why not? Jacob? What's going on?'

'Cora . . .' He raises his eyes to her, dark with pain. Her fury wavers. 'This is all going too fast for me.'

'What do you mean?' Her throat is suddenly dry.

'Just. This. It's new to me.' He gestures towards her and then

230

himself. 'I've been single for a long time. Being in a couple . . .' he swallows, 'it's out of my comfort zone. This isn't to do with you. It doesn't change my feelings for you . . . but I need . . . I need a bit of breathing space.'

'What's that supposed to mean?' She shakes her head. 'Of course this is to do with me if you're having doubts about . . . about us. I've been alone for a long time . . . you're not the only one having to get used to things.'

Neither of them speaks. She wants to snatch her sentences back, erase the bitterness. If she reached her arm towards him, her fingers could touch his cheek, and yet the air between them has solidified, become impenetrable. How can this be happening? She drags her hair back from her face, pulling it into a tight ponytail. She bites her lip, thinking of how to get back to their connection. 'Jacob . . . the only way to make this work is through honesty. You said that yourself, remember? When you told me to talk to Fran about us?'

He nods, eyes downcast.

'I'm . . . I'm trying to be honest, to share my world with you.' She speaks slowly, keeping still, because she doesn't want him to misinterpret anything she does as a rejection. 'I know it's hard. We have separate homes and jobs and responsibilities. I have the kids.' She tilts her head, her gaze encompassing the room, the two of them. 'But here you are, making chilli, cooking a meal for us. You spend time with my children. And my friend Helena is longing to meet you.' She squeezes her hands together. 'What I'm saying is . . . I've opened the door to my life, but you don't reciprocate. I only know George. The boat people. Not anyone really close to you.'

'I'm sorry.' His gaze is steady. He straightens his spine, broadening his chest. He looks like him again. 'The truth is, I haven't had any long-term relationships and I don't have lots of close friends. I guess you could call me a loner – and maybe that's why this feels . . . I don't know . . . a bit unnerving.' His voice is husky. 'Our intimacy – wonderful and precious – is also strange to me.' He scrunches his face as if in frustration, as if he's failing to explain something properly.

Her throat closes. 'I don't really understand.' She can hardly breathe. It doesn't seem possible that the evening has crashed from the happy comfort of a brief hour ago into this darkness.

'I'm sorry,' he says again, his voice cracking. 'I find it hard to talk about this stuff.'

'You mean your brother?' she says softly.

'It's . . . not easy to explain. But he needs me. Just give me a bit more time . . . I don't want to hide anything from you.'

'Whatever it is,' she moves closer, 'you can tell me.'

He stares at the ground, rubs his knuckles across his cheek. 'All right. If . . . if I try, I'd need you to . . . to just listen. This isn't something—'

'Mum?'

Jacob's head jerks towards the sound. Cora starts.

Luke is at the threshold, his expression expectant. 'Can I take my PS4 to uni?'

'Your PS4?' Cora stares at her son, hardly able to understand what he's saying. 'Um . . . I suppose so. If it fits in the car.'

'Cool.' He nods, disappearing. She hears his footsteps padding up the stairs. She turns back to Jacob. 'Sorry. You were saying?'

He gazes at the empty doorway, then back at her. 'Nothing. It doesn't matter. All that matters is us. I want to share my life with you, Cora. I do. And I'm sorry that we can't have that weekend away. But we could spend it on the boat instead – I could cook something special.'

'Or we could take the boat on a trip?' she suggests, a spark of enthusiasm catching in her voice. 'Explore the canal?'

'Maybe ... but not this weekend,' he says slowly. 'Perhaps. One day.'

She nods, disappointed. Why can't he commit to going away with her, even in England?

'Does anyone in your family know about me yet?' she asks. 'Your brother? Your parents?'

He shakes his head, not meeting her eyes.

'But they live just along the Central Line, don't they? You see them every Saturday afternoon. I used to hope you'd ask me to go with you.' She pauses, her chest tight. 'Now ... now I wonder if it'll ever happen.'

The corners of his mouth twitch downwards, and he passes his palm over his eyes wearily, 'I told you, my father's a traditionalist. It might take him a while to come round. But he will. Both my parents will love you when they meet you.'

'You said that before. That they'll love me when they meet me. But they don't even know of my existence. You're ashamed of me,' she says.

'No.' His eyes shine with earnestness, flecks of gold shimmering. 'That's not it at all.'

'Jacob ... I can understand that I'd be a shock to them,' she says quietly. 'I'm too old. Not the right faith.' She wants to rub out their argument, take it all back; she wants to be as they were before, but the truth has lodged cold and sharp inside her. 'But we're not children. We're independent adults, and how can we have a relationship if you have to hide me from them? It won't work, will it?'

'Cora ...' He strides across the carpet and takes her hands in his. 'Don't say that. Listen, my parents are Isaac and Rachel

233

da Costa, and you're right, they're just along the Central Line, in Leytonstone, at 88 Francis Road. The house I grew up in. And I'm going to introduce you to them soon.' He squeezes her fingers. 'Please trust me.'

She blinks away tears. The warmth of his fingers, clasped firmly around her own, seeps into her. Slowly she nods. He gathers her into his arms, his mouth in her hair. 'Thank you,' he whispers. 'We can do this. One step at a time.'

And she thinks that she can manage that, can go at his pace, not rush headlong into the relationship just because *she's* ready, because *she's* hungry for more. As long as they're together, that's all that matters, and weekends in Amsterdam, exploring the canal, meeting his family can wait.

Hanger Lane

Fran clicks the latch, turning for the stairs, and comes to an abrupt halt. Jacob's bike is parked in the hall. He's still here. She swears softly under her breath; she doesn't want to run into him. Her instinct is to get to the safety of her room. But she hears conversation coming from the sitting room and creeps towards it, listening hard. They're arguing. Cora sounds unhappy. Fran recognises doubt in her mother's voice. Disappointment. Then Jacob talking in a reassuring tone. He tells her the names of his parents, reciting their address like an incantation. She hears the little half-choke Cora makes, a rustle of movement as if bodies are touching, and then silence. Fran frowns. He hasn't told his family about Mum? After all this time? That seems dodgy. She moves away with soft steps.

Lying in bed, she goes over the events of her own evening. Who would have thought walking along a smelly canal through clouds of midges would be so much fun? But she's beginning to realise that just being with Zac is enough to make things better. She hasn't laughed so much for ages; when she's with him, there's a kind of innocence, like being a child again. She recalls their near-kiss outside the Tube station and flinches. That moment their faces collided! She screws up her eyes. Excruciating. But the brief memory of his skin brushing hers makes her shiver with pleasure; the close-up scent of him, musky and warm. But there's the party, she reminds herself. A second chance. This time she'll get it right. She falls asleep considering what she'll wear.

Friday evening. Fran arrives at the address in Hanger Lane. It's a couple of streets away from the main road, one of those suburban fake-Tudor semis built from paper and promises. She hopes Zac's already there – he usually arrives first, but she's a bit late, just to be sure. She's nervous about seeing him. She had a few beers while she was waiting at home, slugged some vodka from the bottle she keeps in her underwear drawer. She adjusts her top as she stands on the doorstep, runs her fingers through her hair. A girl opens up, beckoning her to enter. 'Hope you've brought something to drink,' she says. Fran pulls two beers from her pockets. The girl drifts away. A thudding bass reverberates through the walls, overlaid by the buzz and hum of shouted conversation. Fran sniffs the cloying stink of weed. She finds the kitchen, popping the top of one of the bottles, taking a couple of gulps to set her up as she glances around.

Zac isn't in the kitchen. It's filled with scruffy student types. She discovers a damp-topped table littered with mostly empty cans and bottles, plastic cups rolling on their side and flattened crisp packets. She picks up a bottle with a couple of inches of gin left in the bottom and tucks it under her arm; holding the beer in her other hand, she makes her way to the crowded sitting room. She scans the room for him, her heart bumping under her ribs. She stands at the edge and downs some of the neat spirit with a grimace, followed by another gulp of beer. Where is he? She takes out her mobile and finds a text from him. *Running late. Sorry. Be there soon.*

Sighing, she finishes the beer. The party has the feel of an event that's coming undone, an evening already past its peak. Everyone seems engrossed in their own drama: tight groups and locked-together couples stumble about the middle of the room in an approximation of dancing; private conversations take place in shadowy corners, on sofas and chairs that have been pushed together like a cheap furniture store.

She bites a fingernail. He's not usually late. But he would choose to start now – when she's desperate to see him and is stuck in a place where she knows nobody and the music's terrible. She swigs the remains of the gin and puts the empty bottle on the floor. As she straightens, something grabs her hair, ripping at her scalp. 'Ouch!' Her hands fly to her head as she's tugged to the side. She stares up in confusion. A dancer's bangle has snagged in her hair. She manages to grab the girl's wrist.

The girl swings round and, understanding the situation, tries to pull her bangle away, causing another flare of pain. Fran's fingers fumble to release strands of red from the silver band. With a couple of yanks, she stands up, holding a clump of her own hair. She rubs her scalp, glaring at the girl.

But the dancer has already gone, lost in the sea of bodies.

'That's it,' Fran mutters to nobody. 'I'm leaving.' As she makes her way towards the door, she glimpses someone near the wall. He seems strangely familiar. He's talking to a girl, who stares up at him, nodding.

The man turns his head, giving Fran a better look at his profile. She gasps, and fights her way through the crowd towards him, pushing elbows and hips out of the way. She confronts him, panting. 'Where the fuck have you been?'

She gazes into familiar pale blue eyes, but where there was once a tangle of hair, now there's skin – a jaw and a chin and the generous shape of a mouth.

He's shaved off his beard.

'Fran,' he blinks at her, 'this is Yara.' Her gestures to the girl at his side. She's pretty and petite, with shining black hair and delicate features. She offers a hand as if to shake Fran's.

Fran ignores her. She stares at Zac. 'I've been waiting for ages.'

'Yara is part of the theatre group I told you about – Cat's Eye?' He's speaking slowly, as if she's stupid.

'Whatever.' She shrugs. She's fighting down tears. Her throat is tight. 'Yeah. I remember. Your refugee hobby.' She gestures towards the door. 'Can we leave now?'

Zac turns to the girl. 'I'm sorry, Yara. Excuse us a minute.'

He grabs the top of Fran's arm, fingers pinching, and half pushes her into the kitchen. 'Ouch!' she protests. 'What?'

'What's the matter with you?'

At least now they're on their own. She leans towards him. 'I'm happy to see you too,' she says, aiming to make him laugh. God, he looks so damn hot without his beard. She wonders if she should just kiss him right now.

'I'm not joking, Fran. You were incredibly rude to Yara.'

She realises he's holding her wrist, and twists away. 'So what? You were supposed to be meeting me, not her.'

'You're drunk,' he says.

'What do you expect? I've been waiting for hours with nobody to talk to, not knowing where you were.'

'You're an adult, Fran. You could have introduced yourself. Lots of the theatre group are here . . . it's why I suggested it.'

'I'm not interested in your stupid theatre group!'

His body stiffens and he shakes his head, 'You know what, Fran? I'm tired of trying to think the best of you even when you're behaving like a spoilt brat.'

'You're the one who's rude! You're hours late!'

'Because someone died. One of the old people I look after. Jack. He was a lovely man. It happened late this afternoon.'

She stares at him. For a second, she feels sorry. But then righteousness stings her eyes. So some poor old man died; that doesn't explain why Zac was talking to a pretty girl before he came to find her. Anger flares. She frowns at him. But he looks so handsome. She wishes he would stop being stern and angry, make a joke like he usually does. She doesn't want to argue. She's too tired. Too drunk.

'I didn't mean it,' she says. 'I wasn't being serious.' She puts a placating hand on his arm.

'Exactly,' Zac says, stepping away. 'You don't take anything seriously – except yourself.'

His rejection is like a slap. She puts a hand to her cheek as if she can really feel a sting there.

She draws her shoulders back, sticks out her chin. 'What about you?' she sneers. 'Mr Fucking Goody Two-Shoes, criticising me all the time. You could have been a doctor, but instead you're like, oh poor me,' she makes a mocking whiny voice, 'I've failed . . . I'm broke . . . I'm a victim.' She sways closer, her finger prodding his chest. 'You're too scared to change your life.'

'You're the victim, Fran,' he says, his voice suddenly quiet. 'I've never met anyone in my whole life who's more of a victim than you.'

239

'Fuck off.' Tears clog her throat. She blinks them away. 'I hate you.'

She staggers from the room, out into the hall, and makes it to the front door, pulling it open, escaping into the dark, unfamiliar street.

Fran walks along the pavement towards the rumble and roar of the main road, heading for the Tube station. She hates everything she can see: the pebble-dashed houses, the telegraph poles and street lighting. The skinny fox eating from old take-away cartons. 'Actually, not you,' she whispers as she passes. 'You're just trying to get by in a shitty world.' Above her head, there are no stars; she can't even see the moon. The injustice of Zac's words makes her want to scream. She has to talk to someone about what just happened. She takes out her mobile.

Alesha sounds sleepy. 'Babe, are you okay? It's late.'

Fran takes a deep breath. 'I've just been to a crap party in shitty Hanger Lane, and there's this guy called Zac, and he's such a wanker—'

'Hang on, who's Zac? What about Jacob?'

Fran stops. Her body is ringing with fury. It seems easy now to confess the lie. It's a small thing next to Zac's cruelty. 'I'm not with Jacob, Lesh. I made it up. He's with my mum.'

'What?'

She sits on a low garden wall. 'I'm sorry, I couldn't tell you before. It felt so humiliating. And it was a shock. I mean, Jacob is twelve years younger than Mum. And I thought he liked me. And I'd gone on and on about him to you.'

'Babe. I wish you'd told me.'

'I know. I know I should have. It was unbearable at home. Mum all loved-up with Jacob.' She inhales a deep gulp of air.

240

'And another thing. I've given up acting. I never get any work. I'm sick of it. I feel like such a . . . a failure.'

'You're not a failure.' Lesh's voice is firm. 'You just need to figure out what you want.'

'I thought I wanted to act. I . . . I don't know about anything else.'

'Don't panic. Something will happen. And for now, you have a roof over your head. You're going to be okay.' There's a pause. 'And this bloke – Zac?'

'He's a nobody. Only he's so bloody self-important. He thinks he knows best about everything. He invited me to this party and then never showed up for hours and then he was talking to this other girl before he came to find me, so obviously I was upset, and he was horrible, Lesh. He told me I was a spoilt brat.'

Letting it out is as painful and ugly as throwing up, but afterwards there is the cleansing wash of relief.

Silence. Fran sees that her battery is about to die. 'Lesh?'

'Sounds like you like each other.'

'What?'

'It's clear you guys have a thing for each other.'

'Me and Jacob?'

'No, you idiot. You and Zac.'

Fran wants to tell Lesh that she's got it all wrong, and she could never like anyone as mean as Zac. But her battery finally dies. She's left speaking into a piece of warm plastic and metal, into the rush of traffic moving past, into the empty night.

37

Bethnal Green

They're eating at their favourite Italian café. The plan is for Cora to stay over at Jacob's afterwards and leave for work from the boat the next morning. Fran promised to stay home to keep Luke company.

They sit opposite each other at the corner table they've come to think of as theirs. A red candle flickers between them, casting shadows across their faces.

'I'm glad we're doing this tonight. I'm afraid the rest of the week is going to be full-on,' Cora says, winding spaghetti around her fork. 'It's a tricky edit. I'll be working long hours, so . . .'

'. . . maybe we should leave seeing each other till the weekend?' Jacob finishes her sentence.

Cora gives him a quick glance. He seems almost relieved by her news. 'Yes,' she says quietly. 'Probably safer.'

Jacob nods and picks up his beer.

She has an unnerving sense that she doesn't know him – that there are layers and layers still hidden from her.

'How were your parents on Saturday?' she asks. 'Was your brother there too?'

Jacob looks down at the remains of his pizza. 'Yes,' he says gruffly. 'They were all there, and they're fine.'

She nods, pushing her food around her plate. She's lost her appetite.

'And I wanted to tell you that I spoke to my mother,' he says, fiddling with his spoon. 'She's less traditional than Dad. And when I explained how you made me feel ... she said she was happy for me. She said you sounded wonderful.' He looks up, his expression hopeful.

'That's ... good,' she says, but a voice in her head is whispering, *Too little too late.* 'And your brother? Your dad? When will you tell them?' She hears how tight her voice sounds, hates that it seems as though she's nagging him. She doesn't want it to be like this.

He hesitates. 'I'm going to tell my father next. When the moment is right.'

Cora shakes her head. Hopelessness creeps through her bones. There's too much weighed against them. Why did she set herself up for failure, for pain? She misses Andrew. Misses their long years of familiarity and trust, their memories, their shared family. Being with Jacob is like walking through fog – she's feeling her way, not knowing what's under her feet, wondering if she's about to fall off the edge of a cliff.

She takes a sip of wine, puts her glass down and begins to reach across to take his hand. She can't erase her feelings for him. She loves him. She just hasn't said the words yet.

His mobile starts to ring. She takes her hand back, curling her fingers into her palm. She's noticed that he has two different ringtones: one like a bell. It's this one that's chiming urgently now from his pocket. He grimaces and reaches for it. He answers and stands up, making an apologetic face, holding up his hand to signal that he has to take the call.

She watches him making his way around tables, talking earnestly, the phone clamped to his ear. He comes back almost immediately, breathless, and takes his jacket off the back of the chair.

'Something's come up. It's urgent. Got to go,' he says. 'I'm so sorry, Cora.'

'Your brother?'

He nods. 'I'm sure I won't be too long. Shall I see you back at the boat? I'll give you the keys.'

'No,' she says. 'No, don't worry. I'm going to go home.'

'Cora . . .' His voice falters.

She shakes her head. 'It's all right. I'm tired. I'll see you at the weekend.'

He looks anguished, torn. But she knows he'll go to his brother. He always does. Whatever hold Natan has over Jacob, it's stronger than anything else, stronger than her.

They lean across the table to kiss – a cool, brief touch of lips – and he gives her another apologetic look before he hurries out of the restaurant. She sits at the table alone, her fingers pressed to her heart.

Doubt is like grit in her shoe – tiny but uncomfortable, making it impossible to keep going. Not long ago, she felt they could surmount anything. Now, suddenly, it's all become too much – the way he told her he needed space, the Saturday afternoons she's always excluded from, the phone calls he gets at strange times from his brother. She was prepared to take getting to know him slowly, but this is different. The obstacles are gathering. Doubt has highlighted the age gap between them, made the mismatch of their individual experience and expectations glaringly obvious.

Cora can't sleep. After long days and evenings in the edit, she goes to bed exhausted. Under crumpled sheets, she tosses and turns. Hot flashes come, one after another, setting her skin on fire. She sits up, gulping water, pushing damp hair away from her forehead. Sometimes she gets up to pace the shadowy house. On one four o'clock wander, she flicks on a side light to browse books in the sitting room, stopping with her finger pressed to the spine of *The Importance of Being Earnest*. She slips it out, opening it to the first page and leafing through, remembering how the non-existent Bunbury was used as an excuse for one of the characters to disappear from his life in order to escape to the country. She shuts the play with a snap, a terrible thought occurring: perhaps Natan isn't real? She's never seen any evidence of his existence. Or Jacob's parents', for that matter. Is his entire family a fabrication? An excuse to disappear into another life?

She goes into the kitchen, runs the tap, and leans against the sink drinking glass after glass of water. She's worried that her lack of sleep is making her paranoid. She squats down and rummages through the cupboard where she keeps tins and emergency rations, and there at the back is a bottle of single malt. Andrew loved his single malts – he liked them aged and smoky. She takes it out, dusts it off and looks at it dubiously. But it could help knock her out. She sniffs it, smelling Irish bogs, misty mornings, crackling fires. She pours herself a small measure and lets it lie on her tongue: warm, potent, pungent. She returns the bottle to the cupboard and takes her thimbleful of amber liquid back to bed.

Cora wakes the next morning with the empty, sticky glass on her bedside table. Her clock tells her it's past ten o'clock.

The whisky did its job. She realises that it's raining heavily. Her head is muggy with dreams, or perhaps she has a hangover; she's not used to spirits. She gets into the shower to wake herself up. Downstairs, there are a couple of boxes already waiting in the hallway to be packed into the car for tomorrow, when Luke is off to university. Cora's set to drive him to Norwich.

The house is quiet. Luke will be at the cycling club. He goes off early on Saturday mornings, coming back after lunch exhausted, often mud-splattered. Fran must still be in bed. Her door is closed. Cora sits alone at the kitchen table with a cup of tea and a slice of toast, and decides that she has to speak to Jacob. They haven't seen each other all week. She misses him. They're supposed to be meeting this evening, but they should talk this through as soon as possible. She needs to explain how anxious his secrecy is making her, to make him understand that introducing her to his parents and his mysterious brother is their only chance of succeeding as a couple, even if that means running the risk of his family's disapproval.

She glances at her watch; she must hurry to get to the boat before he leaves for Leytonstone. She clatters her breakfast things into the dishwasher.

The sky is a heavy scrawl of charcoal clouds. A strong wind bends the treetops, scuffs the surface of the canal, whips strands of hair across her eyes and sends rain slanting into her face. She trudges the towpath, hood up, stepping around puddles. But when she reaches Jacob's boat, she sees that the door is locked with a padlock. He must have left early. She doesn't know what to do. The words she wants to say to him are urgent – too urgent to put on hold. She leans across and peers through the porthole into the empty galley, climbs up onto the stern and rattles the door in frustration. 'Jacob!'

She phones him, rain splattering the screen of her mobile. It goes to voicemail. She can't leave a message. There's too much to say. She clicks off, shoves the phone into her coat pocket.

George appears on the path with Claude ambling at his heels. 'You all right, my dear?' His rain-washed face beams at her.

'He's gone.' Cora's lips tremble. 'I needed to see him ...'

George inclines his head towards his own boat. 'If you want to wait out of the rain, I've got his spare key. I can fetch it. Won't cost you much.'

Her eyes widen in gratitude and she forces a smile.

She slips off her dripping mac and hangs it in the entrance, pulls off her boots and pads through in her socks. Jacob has left everything neat and tidy. She runs her fingers over the surfaces of the galley and fills the kettle, puts it on just for something to do; she doesn't really want another cup.

She eases clammy wet jeans over her cold legs and finds a pair of his old jogging bottoms to put on, rolling up the ankles. He won't mind, she thinks. He's left her alone here several times when he's had to rush off after one of his mysterious phone calls, and sometimes he leaves for work before her if she's stayed over on a weekday evening – 'Make yourself at home,' he always says. 'You know where everything is.'

But still. He has no idea she's here. Maybe she should have gone home as soon as she realised she'd missed him; maybe she should have refused the key from George. Rain slaps against the glass, drizzling in crazy patterns across the portholes. Outside, the pockmarked canal is patrolled by ducks and moorhens. The towpath is empty of anything but puddles. She's here now, she thinks. She's dry and warm. It will be a surprise for him, a good surprise. She could see if there's anything to cook for supper – have it ready for him.

He's pinned some new sketches to the corkboard, and she goes closer to examine them: a stooped heron, a darting king-fisher. More drawings of Scout. On the small bookshelf below, she sees a folder sticking out, edges of paper visible. She picks it up, thinking she'll flick through his illustrations. But she soon realises that these are not sketches of animals or birds.

She sits down heavily, numb fingers leafing through sheaves of paper, understanding that these are all portraits of the same boy. He is dark-haired, large-eyed. The drawings seem to span a few years – in one, he's solid-looking, aged five or six perhaps, bending to pick up a football. In another, he's lanky, his hair longer, grinning. At the back of the folder she finds a photo-graph of the child: a formal colour photo of him in a school uniform, his hair combed but his collar undone and an impish smile flashing, bright and challenging. She guesses he's about the same age here as in the last drawing – twelve or thirteen. He bears an unmistakable resemblance to Jacob.

She sits for a long time with the folder on her lap, the photo gripped between her fingers. There is only one explanation that she can think of – this child is his son. Jacob must spend his Saturday afternoons with the boy. She was right about him using his family as an excuse. That's why he's never invited her along to one of his lunches. And what of the child's mother? Considering his single life on the boat, it seems unlikely that Jacob is still with her. But in that case, why does he need to keep his son's existence from Cora?

Looking at the photo of the boy untethers her from everything she thought she knew. She feels as if she's floating.

She can see the unformed beginnings of Jacob in the childish features – there's no mistaking it. She gets up and paces the boat. The small spaces are making her feel trapped, claustrophobic. 'Dammit, Jacob,' she says aloud. 'What's going on? What are you keeping from me?' In the saloon, she stops in front of a chest of drawers and her hand goes to the handle, pulling it before she's processed the thought. She slides her fingers inside, stealthily at first, uncertain, but then more boldly, systematically picking through the objects inside. She takes everything out of every drawer and then replaces it. She's not sure what she's looking for – another photograph of the boy, something that might belong to him? A picture of the child's mother? Her heart skitters inside her ribs, a mix of guilt and fear.

In the bedroom, she searches the tiny shelves, looks under the bed. She can find nothing to confirm her theory, but nothing to contradict it either. There are no children's things on the boat. The space is spare and uncluttered. It occurs to her again that Jacob lives frugally – not like a city dweller with a good job and no real responsibilities. He owns no luxuries, only the essentials for life. His bike is his main expense, but even that is useful, and he's often joked that he got it second-hand; he doesn't have any of the latest expensive specialist equipment that he and Luke discuss after Luke points it out in his cycling magazines.

She sits on the bed, the open folder of drawings spread out next to her. *Who are you?* she whispers. And she's not sure if she's thinking of Jacob or the boy. The sound of rain hammering against the Houdini hatch drowns out her thoughts, bullyingly soporific. She curls on her side, shivering, knees drawn up, and closes her eyes.

*

She's aware of change as she drifts towards consciousness – a shift in air pressure, a lack of sound. The battering of water against glass has stopped. The mattress below her has dipped slightly, as if to accommodate another human weight. She hears the sound of breathing. Her eyes flick open. Jacob is sitting on the bed next to her staring into the middle distance, face twisted, anguish hollowing his eyes, pulling at his long mouth.

'Jacob?' She raises herself onto her elbows. 'What's wrong?' She rubs her forehead. 'I . . . I fell asleep waiting for you.'

He turns to look at her, and she's shocked by the way his eyes are sheeted, his expression closed. 'You've been looking through my stuff.'

Her gaze falls on the folder, the spill of sketches. Guilt stings. But then she remembers: it's Jacob who has the secrets, Jacob who is hiding something from her. She sits up, pushing at her hair, running her tongue over her teeth. 'Who is he?' She blinks at the drawings.

Jacob stiffens, his body rigid. He inclines his head towards the midships. 'How did you get in?'

'George.' Cora is unnerved by his cold tone. 'He gave me the key.'

'And you thought you'd ransack the place while I was out?' His voice rises, anger pushing through.

'No . . . of course not.' She struggles into a sitting position. 'I wanted to talk to you. And then I saw the sketches. He . . . he looks like you.'

Jacob lets out a rasping sigh.

'Is . . . is he your son?' she persists.

He stands up in one abrupt movement. 'I can't do this any more, Cora.'

Disbelief plummets through her, cold and sharp. 'What?'

'I made a mistake. Falling for you. Letting you fall for me.'

She clambers unsteadily to her feet. 'What are you talking about?' They're standing together in the small space between mattress and wall; she can smell the damp in his jacket, see tears glittering in his lashes.

'You once told me you were selfish, wanting to see me when you knew Fran liked me,' he says in a dead voice. 'Well, I was selfish too, thinking that . . . that we could have a relationship. It was irresponsible of me. Stupid.'

'But . . .' Her muscles quiver. 'I don't . . . I don't understand.'

'I'm not in a position to . . . commit to another person. My life isn't my own. I have duties, responsibilities elsewhere. I should never have asked you for that first drink. I should never have come to your house to mend your bike. It was all a mistake.' He chops his hand through the air as if severing some invisible object. 'I'm sorry.'

'Jacob.' She grabs at his hand, holds it tight. 'Just tell me what's going on. We can work it out, I know we can. Whatever it is.'

'Cora,' he whispers. 'Some things can't be mended.' He disengages his hand, slips it from hers. 'Find a man who deserves you. You're a wonderful woman. A wonderful person.' His voice breaks. 'Tell Luke to enjoy university. He's done so well. And remind him to wear his helmet.'

'Jacob . . .' She crosses her hands over her chest in a protective gesture. 'Are you breaking up with me?'

'I . . . It's . . . Yes. Yes. I'm sorry.'

'You can't mean it?' Her throat is squeezed shut. She's having to stop herself from howling. 'It doesn't make sense.'

'I'm sorry.' His voice is almost a whisper. 'I'm not . . . free. I never was.' He draws a deep breath. 'It would be better if you go now.'

'Seriously?' She almost staggers. It feels as if the boat is capsizing, water rushing in, the world turning upside down. 'You're ending it? Like this?'

'There's no other way, is there? No good way – no right words.' He swallows with a gulping sound, and gazes at the floor. 'I . . . I don't have a choice. Forgive me.'

She stares at him. He's a stranger. She has no idea who she's invited into her life, her bed, her children's lives. She can't argue any more. She can't even look at him. She knows she crossed a line when she searched through his stuff, but she only did it because he was hiding something. And now that she's found it, instead of discussing the situation – opening up and telling her about his son – he's throwing her out as if she's a thief. She needs to get away.

She blunders through the doorway into the main cabin. It's as though her eyesight has failed. She can't see properly, can't understand what's beneath her hands as she gropes her way out of the boat.

Leytonstone

Fran hauls herself out of bed. Her mouth is dry, and her eyeballs burn. It's horribly early. But she has to say goodbye to Luke; he'll be off to UEA any minute. The car's already packed and waiting, and Cora will be impatient, stressing about traffic. As she sits on the loo, Fran tries not to remember the party, Zac on his high horse, his gaze glacial as a robot's, trying to make her feel bad. Bastard. It doesn't matter how much she drinks, she can't block out the memory of their row. She splashes her face with cold water, wishing she'd told him exactly what a loser he is.

She smells toast as she fumbles her way downstairs, yawning, wrapped in her old kimono. In the kitchen, her mother is putting the finishing touches to a couple of sandwiches, sprinkling them with salt and slicing them in half. Luke's sitting at the table, shovelling cereal into his mouth as if it's his last meal.

'Hey,' Fran says, ruffling his hair. 'So we finally get rid of you.'

'Gerroff!' He dodges her hand with a jerk.

'Can't you just be nice to each other, for once?' Cora's voice is strained. She turns and gives both her children an accusing stare. Her bottom lip trembles.

She's been crying. Her eyes are swollen-lidded. Her hair looks as though she hasn't pulled a comb through it for weeks. The draining board is piled with pans from last night, the table spotted with spilt milk and the breadboard covered in crumbs and smears of butter. She's obviously upset about Luke going to Norwich – about leaving him at university to fend for himself. He's always been her favourite. The clever one, who never causes a scene or makes a fuss. Fran picks up a crust of toast from a plate and munches it as she boils the kettle for tea.

When Cora has packed the sandwiches into a bag with a flask of coffee, she rattles her car keys. 'Right. This is it. Come on, love.' She motions to Luke. 'We need to get on the road. Beat the traffic. The whole world will be going off to university today.'

Fran has a sudden pang of loss. Luke is endlessly annoying, but he's her brother and she loves him. It's going to be weird in the house without his nerdy presence. She catches him by the sleeve of his jumper and pulls him in for a hug, clasping his bony shoulders, inhaling a whiff of boy pong. 'Give them hell,' she whispers into his hair. 'Get wasted every night. Fuck some hot freshers.' She pulls back, screwing up her face. 'And remember to wash.'

He disentangles himself from her embrace, rubbing his chin. 'Yeah,' he mutters. 'Thanks. Useful advice.'

Cora ushers him towards the door. 'I won't be back till this evening,' she calls over her shoulder. 'Could you clear up the kitchen?'

Fran watches from the doorstep as they get into the car, Luke's bike strapped to the boot, and drive off down the street.

She lifts her hand in farewell, waiting until the car turns the corner before she steps back into the empty house.

She sits at the sticky table in the untidy kitchen and swallows a couple of aspirin with a strong, sugary coffee that makes her head spin. She checks her mobile for messages. Nothing. More than a week has gone by, and not a word. She can't believe Zac hasn't contacted her. Disappointment plummets through her like a stone, dragging her into a swampy darkness – she thought he would have called by now, or messaged or something to apologise. He's probably waiting for her to call – thinks she owes *him* an apology. She should never have let him get under her skin.

In her bedroom, she picks up her pack of cards. The impulse to do a reading – to consult the Tarot about Zac – is strong. But she puts them down. She doesn't need the cards to tell her that she's better off without him. When she really thinks about it, all he does is preach at her and order her about. She remembers the noise Cora made the other night with Jacob, the soft exhale as their bodies came together – the sound of them making up after their row. But their argument had sounded serious. It's a shock to realise that Jacob has been hiding Cora from his family – that he's somehow ashamed of her. Fran feels suddenly protective of her mother. All this time, she'd presumed they were loved-up and happy. But it's clear something's wrong, and Cora's going to get even more hurt. Maybe that was why she was so miserable earlier. Not just about Luke going off to uni.

'Men!' Fran says aloud. 'They're all the same.'

Zac and Jacob have both turned out to be losers. Fran doesn't want to stay here moping. Zac's not worth it. She closes her eyes and concentrates, bringing back the address Jacob recited that evening, and types it into TFL: it's a forty-five-minute journey, all the way on the Central Line. She has an idea. It will take her mind off Zac, and maybe do her mother a favour.

Coming out of Leytonstone Underground station, Fran follows Citymapper down side streets, past rows of houses, cats crouched on fences, dustbins kept in neat alcoves, cars parked bumper to bumper. When she reaches number 88, she looks up at a semi-detached red-brick house with sparkling glass at the windows, peeling paint on the sills. It looks slightly shabby, ordinary. The thought of going inside and delivering bad news to two strangers suddenly seems like a silly idea. She dithers, biting her thumbnail. Maybe she should forget it and go home. But as she begins to back away, the door swings open.

A woman with a mass of frizzy brown-grey hair stands in the opening, holding out her hands as if to catch something or someone, hands that are strangely whitened up to the wrists. Her expression changes, a slight tucking-in of her chin, a closing and refolding of her mouth. She blinks. 'I was expecting . . .' she says. She looks at Fran over the top of small round glasses. 'Can I help you?'

'I . . . I know your son. Jacob,' she says.

'Oh?' The woman wipes her hands on her apron, leaving dusty trails. 'He's not here.'

Fran nods. 'That's okay.'

The woman gives her a searching look. 'Do you want to come in?' She opens the door wider. 'I'm Rachel. His mother.'

'Francesca,' Fran says as she steps warily into the narrow hallway. The woman leads the way towards the back of the house, her generous hips straining the fabric of a long floral skirt, the ties of an apron dangling at her slippered heels. The kitchen is small and hot, fragrant with baking and spices;

Fran notices scuffed beige worktops, splashbacks tiled with an orange and brown pattern, the walls a dull chocolate. She widens her eyes; it looks like a setting for a sitcom from the seventies.

'Take a seat.' Jacob's mother gestures to a chair with an orange and brown crocheted cushion. There are sketches of animals and birds pinned to the fridge with magnets shaped like fruit. Rachel sees where Fran is looking. 'Jacob. He has a gift.' She smiles. 'Since he moved to that boat, he's become a naturalist – like David Attenborough.'

She goes to the oven and takes out a batch of buttery-smelling biscuits. She puts them carefully onto a wire mesh and switches on a kettle. 'You'll have some tea with me?' She bends and brings out a cake tin; dips inside and cuts a large slice and puts it on a plate in front of Fran. 'Apple cake. Eat. Eat. You look as though you need it.'

Fran takes a nibble. It's delicious. Caramelised, gooey and dense. 'Is your . . . your husband here?'

Rachel is busy at the work surface, with her back to Fran, stirring something in a bowl, dipping her finger and tasting. She turns with an expression of mild surprise. 'Isaac? No. He's out this morning. He'll be back in about an hour.' She goes back to mixing. 'How is it you know Jacob again?' she asks over her shoulder.

'Oh.' Fran swallows her mouthful. 'I didn't say. We met . . . on the Underground.'

'Because of his job? He has a very important job, you know.'

'No. He . . . he helped me.'

'He's always been a good boy.' Rachel stops bustling at the surfaces and gives Fran a keen stare. 'But tell me. Why is it that you've come, Francesca? If it's not Jacob you've come to see?'

'Um. Well . . .' Fran sits back, seized by another bout of nerves. 'I'm here . . . I'm here because of my mother. Cora. She—'

'Cora?' Rachel interrupts. 'You're Cora's daughter? You're Fran?'

'Yes,' Fran admits.

'You should have said.' Rachel is beaming. 'Do you look like her?'

Fran's pulse jumps in surprise. 'Not really. I think I look more like my dad. Mum is small, with brown hair and dark eyes.'

'Yes.' Rachel is nodding. 'Yes. That's exactly how I imagined her.'

'You're . . . all right about it? About Jacob being with my mum?' Fran scratches the top of the table with her nail, then folds her hands together, catching them between her knees to keep them still.

Rachel gives a quick nod and goes back to stirring the bowl. 'You think I should disapprove because she's older than him?'

'Well . . .' Fran's chest tightens with confusion. 'Yes. Maybe. I did at first. But it's not just the age gap that's the problem, is it? Your family won't accept her. I overheard the two of them arguing about it the other night, and . . . and Mum was upset. She said Jacob was ashamed of her. I mean, that doesn't seem like a healthy way to start a relationship.'

Rachel swings back to the table and sits down. She leans forward. 'I don't understand. Why are you here, Fran? To help your mother or make trouble for her?'

Fran swallows a gasp. Why *did* she come? She's been a bitch to Mum, she realises. Ever since Jacob came into their lives, her jealousy means she hasn't supported Cora through any of this. It can't have been easy for her all these months, knowing of Jacob's reluctance to tell his family. And she, Fran, has been busy worrying about how *she* feels. Zac's voice pops into her head. He was right. She's selfish. The knowledge shrivels her insides.

Rachel is looking at her expectantly, and Fran rubs her eyes. 'I was angry when they first got together,' she admits. 'But . . . I'm not any more. She looked like she'd been crying this morning. I don't want her to get hurt.'

Rachel takes her glasses off and polishes them on her apron. Her eyes are the same bright hazel as Jacob's. 'No relationship runs smoothly all the time,' she says calmly. 'It's how a couple negotiate their difficulties that makes or breaks them in the end. Cora and Jacob must work this out for themselves. It isn't our business.' She puts her glasses back on. 'You should know that my son has been through hell. He is the most lonely person I know. Cora is the first woman he's let into his heart. If your mother has brought him some joy, if she has brought love into his life,' she gives Fran a direct look, 'I will not let anyone spoil that.'

Fran holds the edge of the table. The lino-covered floor seems to buckle and collapse. She wishes she could fall through it and disappear, or better, reverse time and never set out for Leytonstone in the first place. 'No . . . I didn't mean . . . I . . . I don't want to spoil it either.'

A weird twisting feeling squirms in her belly. Shame. It warms her face. She feels sick. She looks at the plate – at the slab of cake she'll never be able to eat now.

'Cora and Jacob have both known loneliness,' Rachel goes on. 'It's hard for a woman to lose her husband at such a young age – to cope with two children on her own.'

'It was hard for me, too. To lose my dad.' A tear trickles down Fran's cheek. She licks it in surprise. She never cries.

'Ah, so now we come to it.' Rachel's voice is softer. 'You're still grieving, child.' She touches Fran's cheek with warm, dry fingers, leaving them there for a second. 'Grief is confusing. You wait and wait for it to fly away like a big dark bird. But it stays perched on your shoulder. You have to live with it – the pain. You can't patch it up with distractions.'

'I'm trying to live with it,' Fran whispers. Another tear is tickling her face, seeping into her mouth. She tastes it, salty on her tongue. She has a strange, tight ache in her chest. 'But I miss him. Everything's wrong without him.'

'All you can do is be strong. In memory of him. Your father. But most importantly, for the living. The dead look after themselves. Be careful with other people's hearts, Fran,' Rachel says, handing her a tissue. 'Your mother needs your support. Not interference. I'll tell you a secret: kindness is healing. It does something to your insides, something chemical. Sends little atoms of happiness bouncing around you.'

The doorbell peals. 'That will be Natan.' Rachel heaves herself up from the table. 'Jacob's brother.'

'Jacob has a brother?'

Rachel gives her a look that seems touched with pity or sorrow. She leaves the room and Fran hears a scraping sound, a rolling movement against the floor, muffled voices.

Rachel reappears in the doorway. She's pushing a wheelchair. The man sitting in it looks like Jacob and not like Jacob. He's got the same features, big eyes and a generous nose, a wide, mobile mouth. But his head is at an odd angle and his eyes are glazed as if he's looking somewhere else, beyond the kitchen. His fingers jump and tremble on the armrests of the chair.

'This is Natan,' Rachel says, her voice as dark and rich as her cake. 'My younger son.'

'Hello,' Fran says.

260

Natan's eyebrows twitch, and his hands clench into fists.

'It's all right, my darling.' Rachel bends over him, stroking his tightened knuckles, kissing his forehead. 'Natan comes to see us every Saturday afternoon. It's our favourite time of the week. And this weekend is special because we're seeing him twice – today is his birthday.' She glances towards the door. 'Jacob will be paying the taxi.'

The sound of his name is like an electric shock. Fran stiffens, her head jerking towards the doorway, towards a familiar figure.

Jacob stands there, shock widening his eyes. 'Fran?'

'Fran called in to say hello. She was just passing.' Rachel gives her a meaningful look.

Fran swallows, glances at Jacob's mother. 'Thanks. For the cake. Sorry. For . . . you know.'

'You never had your tea.'

'It doesn't matter.'

'I'll walk you out,' Jacob says.

They stride along the pavement together. 'You . . . just happened to be passing?' Jacob asks, his voice neutral but his eyes locked on her.

'Yeah.' She glances down.

'I didn't know you knew where my parents lived.'

'I didn't know you had a brother – Mum never said.'

'She knows I have a brother, but not that he's brain-damaged.' He shakes his head. 'Fran . . . hasn't your mother said anything to you about last night?'

'I haven't talked to her today. She's taking Luke to university. What do you mean?'

He ducks his head. 'I thought . . . I thought maybe you'd come because she'd told you about last night.'

'I have no idea what you're talking about – what happened last night?'

He sighs. 'I'll let your mum tell you.'

'Is she okay? She seemed upset this morning. Did you say something to her?'

He blinks and frowns, looking at his feet. 'Better if she tells you herself.' His mouth twists as if he's trying to control it.

'You're being very mysterious.' She gives him an assessing glance. 'Why is your brother in a wheelchair? Is he ill?'

'He had an accident. When he was a teenager.' Jacob's voice is gruff. 'Natan can't talk or walk. He's in a care home.'

'Oh.' Fran struggles to think of what to say, remembering her father in the bed attached to machines. 'Shit. I'm sorry. But . . . why didn't you tell Mum, why is Natan a secret?'

'He's not a secret.' Jacob's voice rises. He shakes his head. 'I love him. He's my brother. But . . . it's complicated, Fran. I can't discuss it with you.'

Fran is aware of her breathing, the rise and fall of her chest, the need for oxygen. Life is fragile, she thinks. There's a pinching across her feet where she must have tied her laces too tight. The air on her cheeks is weighted, colours moving, slurring as if she's on acid. She slows her steps, blinking into the light. She snatches a glance at the man walking beside her. She hardly recognises him. In her head, he's come to look different. All this time, she's been thinking of him as a different person. A fantasy. She puts a hand on her chest. She feels weird, sort of numb. Why did she think he had the power to change her life? She snatches another glance at him. He looks sad. She feels sorry for him. He's a grown-up and he can't even tell his dad about the person he's dating. It seems kind of pathetic. The tension she sensed before – the attraction she felt – it's gone.

Meeting his mother. Seeing Natan. Jacob's serious face – his sadness. It's the biggest reality check ever.

She's suddenly clumsy, nearly tripping over her feet. There's nothing between them. It's not Jacob, she thinks. It never was.

'I've got to get going,' she says, her voice cracking with urgency. 'I'm late for something.'

He stops on the pavement and nods. His eyes are dull, all the brightness extinguished.

'I like your mum,' she says. 'And . . . I'm sorry about Natan – about his accident, I mean.'

'Goodbye, Fran. Take care of yourself.' His mouth contorts. 'And your mum.'

It's like he's saying goodbye for ever, she thinks, as she turns and hurries away. But she hasn't got time to ask more questions; she has a breathless need to talk to Zac, to make it right between them.

When she gets to the entrance to the Tube station, she slows to a halt, takes out her mobile and presses Zac's number. She waits impatiently for him to answer.

'Fran?' His voice sounds weary.

'We need to talk,' she says. 'Can we meet?'

'There's nothing to talk about.'

'The other night—'

'It doesn't matter. Nothing matters to you. That's the point.' He sounds defeated rather than angry. 'Fran, I can't be friends with someone who doesn't give a shit about anyone else.'

'I . . . I do give a shit,' she says.

'I thought you were special. Underneath your rudeness, underneath all the swearing, I thought there was someone beautiful. Loving and bright. I thought you were just protecting yourself because of the way the world's hurt you.'

She holds her breath, her chest tight.

'But I can't keep waiting for that girl,' he says. 'I don't think she's ever going to show.'

'Zac . . .' Her voice breaks. 'I'm sorry . . . I really am. Please . . . can you stop being angry with me now?'

'I don't know.'

She waits, listening to silence, hoping for more.

'Look, I've got to go, Fran.'

'No,' she says, trying not to cry. Tears mist her eyes. 'Wait.' It's as if someone's turned a tap on inside her body and she can't turn it off. 'Please.'

'It's not that simple.' His voice hardens. 'You can't have everything your own way all the time.' She hears him sigh. 'Man up, Fran.'

'Man up?!' Her body flames with fury, tears evaporating in the blaze. 'Oh, fuck you, Zac! Fuck you! You're not better than me!'

But she's shouting into a void, because he's clicked off. Ahead of her, people go through the barriers, backs of heads disappearing down the escalator. She beats her hands together in frustration. Strangers hurrying past don't give her a glance.

'Well, good riddance,' she says aloud, clutching her mobile. 'Don't think I'll be calling or texting. Fucking arsehole.'

A woman clicks her tongue in annoyance as she steps around her.

'Fuck you too,' Fran says.

The woman doesn't look back.

Shepherd's Bush

The long drive back from Norwich passed in a blur. Afterwards, Cora wonders how she negotiated roundabouts and junctions, how close she might have come to an accident. While Luke was with her, she managed to stay focused. She talked to him about his course; they discussed him seeking out the university cycle club in freshers' week. After she'd seen him to his room, she stayed for a couple of hours to settle him in – made his space look cosy, found the local supermarket and stocked up on some of his favourite snacks. It helped to keep her from remembering last night.

But on the return journey, she couldn't stop going over and over it in her mind. Each hurtful word. Every painful moment. The car made strange tapping noises, as if a stone was trapped in the engine, and she worried it would break down and she'd be stranded on the hard shoulder. But it got her home. Now her back aches from hours spent at the wheel. She parks on the street and gets out with difficulty, her spine tight as a corkscrew.

Slowly, slowly she straightens out the kinks. The hot car ticks, the engine cooling.

Inside the house, she drops her keys in the bowl, kicks off her shoes. She's too exhausted to think of eating. She sniffs, head cocked to one side. She can smell the sharp bite of ammonia. She goes into the kitchen, switches on the light, and gasps. The whole place is immaculate. All the breakfast things have been cleared away, the table wiped clean, the work surfaces tidy. There's a saucepan on the stove with a note propped on the surface: *Hope your trip was okay. I made some soup in case you're hungry. Fran x*

Cora lifts the lid, looking at the liquid. She's not hungry, and her throat is tight with grief. But she can't remember the last time Fran did anything like this, and she doesn't want to be unappreciative, so she heats it up and sits at the table, forcing herself to eat a little. It's good, peppery and yet mild, just what she would have wanted after a long day if she hadn't been sick with loss.

She puts her bowl in the dishwasher and trudges upstairs. On the landing, she turns left instead of right and goes into Luke's room. Through the gloom, she can see his bare corkboards. All his revision charts taken down. His desk cleared of laptop, books and pens. Although he was so quiet in the house, often shut in his room staring at a screen, he was an ally, a smiling face. He needed her. She hopes he'll cope with university – she knows he'll be up to the academic work; it's the social demands that will be difficult for him.

She sits on his stripped bed. She wants to talk to Jacob about Luke, tell him about Luke's new room and the other students they met, how she hopes he'll be able to form friendships, relax a bit, learn how to be untidy for once. Jacob was kind to Luke, seemed genuinely fond of him. But now Cora doesn't know what to think or believe. Jacob has a son – a child he's never owned up to, never talked about – a son only a few years younger than Luke. Why would he keep that a secret? Maybe it's why he never introduced her to his parents and brother, because she would have found out about it through them.

She doesn't know how she'll get through the days. The loss of Jacob has blown a hole in her life, left a gaping crater of desolation; it's as if the explosion has gone right through her insides. She puts her hands over her belly, over the deep, dark pain. She can feel it funnelling into her, digging away her strength.

She feels ancient. Every bone aching. Her worry about being too old for Jacob evaporated when she was with him, because he made her feel beautiful and sensual and unique. Outside, on the street or in shops, she sometimes caught other people looking, saw the question on their faces. They didn't know if she was his mother or sister or girlfriend. She could see them assessing, wondering, judging. And then Jacob would pull her in for a kiss, hold her tight against his side, and it would be obvious that she was his lover, his partner. She'd stopped feeling apologetic about it, stopped caring if anyone was shocked. She and Jacob were happy. Complete.

But all the time, their truth was founded on a lie. He's never been free. Their happiness was false, jinxed by this thing – a bomb, a trap, waiting to explode, to destroy them. Jacob let her believe they had a future. She wants to hate him for that cruelty. But she can't. She misses him. She misses him. She doubles over, rocking, her forehead on her knees.

Her mobile beeps. She grabs it to read the screen, heart skittering. Helena. Cora clicks her phone to silent. She can't talk to Helena now, can't explain any of this – it's too raw, too

267

painful to put into words. And she knows that Helena will leap to her defence, will be angry with Jacob on Cora's behalf, will want to find fault with everything about him.

She rubs her forehead. Perhaps she will sleep here, on Luke's bed, on the bare mattress. Perhaps she won't even take off her clothes. Her body is heavy with inertia. Even moving her fingers seems impossible.

'Mum?' Fran has slipped into the room. 'Are you okay?'

She sits on the bed beside Cora, a fall of shining red hair in Cora's peripheral vision. 'What is it? Are you worried about Luke?' She takes Cora's hand and folds her fingers around it.

Cora manages a nod.

'He'll be fine. He's tougher than he looks.' Fran squeezes her mother's fingers. 'Why don't you call Jacob?' she suggests. 'Ask him to come over?'

Cora can't help flinching – a puckering of nerves and sinews, a twitch of despair. Her mouth is dry. She can't speak. A sob rises and sticks in her throat.

'What is it?' Fran says, more urgently. 'Has something happened?'

'It's over,' Cora says, her voice grating. 'Between me and Jacob. He ended it. Last night.'

'What?' Fran sounds shocked, outraged. 'Oh Mum.' She puts her arm around Cora's shoulders. 'I'm so sorry.'

Cora is undone by Fran's unexpected kindness. One tear slips down her cheek. She shivers, shoulders shaking. Fran tightens her grip, hugging Cora into the warm curve of her ribs. They sit side by side in the dim room, lit by the sulphurous glow from the street light, lungs rising and falling in synchronisation, a slow, secret dance. Fran's strength holds Cora up, stops her sliding onto the floor.

'Did ... did you have an argument?' Fran asks quietly. 'Last night?'

Cora shakes her head, her neck creaking. 'He has a son. Another life. One I didn't know about.'

'A son?' Fran sounds surprised. 'Fuck. I can't believe it. Jesus, Mum. I'm so sorry.'

Cora nods, gulps.

'Did you meet his son? How old is he?'

She shakes her head. 'I just ... saw pictures. A photo. I think he's about twelve or thirteen.' Her voice wobbles, and she clasps her fingers over her mouth. 'It's not the fact that he has a child. Of course that wouldn't have mattered. It's that ... that he lied to me.'

'Another lie.' Fran rubs Cora's back in slow circles. 'It's weird. Why does he have to keep so much hidden ... what's the matter with him?'

The firm feel of her daughter's touch is comforting, steadying. But Cora stops sobbing and clears her throat, wipes her nose on the edge of her sleeve. 'What do you mean? Is there something else I don't know?'

Fran's hand stills. She swallows. 'No. No. Nothing. I just ... I meant, you know, about his son.' She stands up. 'It's late. Let's get you into bed. Make you comfortable.' Her tone is almost matronly. It's so unlike her. In normal circumstances, it would have made Cora laugh. 'You've always told me sleep's the best cure,' she's saying. 'And you must be exhausted.'

Cora doesn't object. She lets her daughter lead her to the bathroom as if she's an invalid; lets her sponge her face with cool water, put toothpaste on her brush and hand it to her. She submits to it all, Fran waiting while Cora has a pee, and then, in the bedroom, kneeling to undress her and slipping a nightdress over her head, drawing the sheets back, fetching her a glass of water. 'All men are bastards,' she says, her voice tight. 'We don't need them. We're better off without them.'

As Cora lies down, Fran straightens the covers, drops a kiss on her forehead. 'Night,' she murmurs.

'Night,' Cora manages to reply, too tired to wonder at the transformation in her daughter, the room already spinning away, a rush of oblivion coming for her.

Autumn

Shepherd's Bush

October is tipping into November. The silvery trunks of the London plane trees gleam in the dusk of early evening. Leaves cling like shadows, dangling seed pods cutting polka-dot patterns into the sky.

Fran's given up checking her phone for missed calls and text messages from Zac. She's deleted him as a friend on Facebook, blocked him on Instagram. She misses him – she hates him. Most of the time she manages to screen him from her thoughts. She has other things to worry about. Like her mother. Cora seems diminished. Her clothes are loose, clavicles jutting. She needs a belt for her jeans. Watching the effort it takes for her to do even the most ordinary things – raise a fork to her mouth, lock a door, hold a conversation – makes Fran understand that her mother is stunned by loss. If it was Fran, she would have given up and stayed in bed with a bottle of Absolut to keep her company, but Cora keeps going.

On weekday mornings, she leaves for the edit suite early.

She skips breakfast, going out dressed in her uniform of narrow trousers, short jacket, white trainers and her cherry-red cross-body bag. She reassures Fran that yes, she picks up a coffee from a café in Carnaby Street, and yes, she has a bagel at work. On Friday mornings, she goes off before Fran's awake to meet Helena for a run in Hyde Park. And one evening a week, she spritzes herself with perfume, changes into a skirt and goes to meet her friend for supper at their favourite Levantine restaurant. Fran thinks it's lucky that Cora's a creature of routine, because it seems to be the only thing that's holding her up.

Fran and Cora have started to frequent the local cinema – they choose the adrenalin buzz of adventure movies, sometimes documentaries, nothing romantic. That's an unspoken rule. Fran cooks for Cora in the evenings and they eat together – meals that Luke would have complained left him hungry, soups and salads, or sometimes just a bowl of hummus with toasted pitta. Afterwards they share a bar of good dark chocolate with cups of tea. They discuss Cora's work, a TV series they're watching, the books they're reading, the latest email from Luke. These are rare. He's never been a communicator. He mostly writes about his lectures and his bike.

Since the night she came back from Norwich, Cora hasn't spoken Jacob's name. Fran thinks it's odd that he has a son and never said. She thinks about Natan in his wheelchair, and how Jacob never told Cora what had happened to him. Why would he leave out such important information? Jacob has hurt Cora. Fran hasn't seen her mother like this since Dad died. She has a prickling anger at the back of her nose, as if she's on the verge of crying; her rage is for Mum. Rachel's words keep replaying in her head – how happy Cora made Jacob, how lonely he'd been before they met. She can't admit to Cora that she's met Rachel, because then she'd have to confess to her visit. And anyway, it doesn't matter now. Jacob's gone. What remains are Rachel's words, and the shame that swallowed Fran up in that orange and brown kitchen.

Cora and Fran are eating breakfast together. Fran got up early to make pancakes using Cora's special recipe, and they've polished off the lot between them. Fran encouraged her mother to have seconds, and then thirds, part of her plan to get Cora to eat more, to put on the weight she's lost. They sit in companionable silence, sipping coffee. Fran groans. 'I've got to undo my jeans.'

Cora smiles. 'It's a weekend treat. We deserve it.' She starts to clear the plates, and then stops and looks at Fran. 'You know, the morning I found you comatose after you drank all that vodka, I still don't know if I did the right thing . . . agreeing to go out with Jacob. It's been bothering me. You said it was just a crush, but it wasn't, was it?'

Fran squirms inside. 'Forget it, Mum. I was being selfish. I made it all up in my head, all that stuff about Jacob.'

Cora leaves the dirty plates on the side and sits down. 'If anyone had ever told me I'd fall for the same man as my daughter, I'd never have believed them.' She gives a shaky smile. 'I'm sorry I hurt you.'

'You were good for each other. It just took me a while to see it.'

Fran sees the shine of tears in her mother's eyes.

'Dad would have approved of Jacob,' she says firmly. 'It was time for you to start living again, and he helped you do that. But there are lots of other men out there. I can help you look through dating websites. Maybe Jacob was just your transition man.'

'Thanks.' Cora shakes her head. 'But I've had enough of emotional upheaval.' She gives a small smile. 'I'm glad you think Dad would have approved of Jacob.'

Fran bites her lip. 'While we're apologising, I . . . I have to tell you that I'm sorry I called you a murderer, you know, when we were in the hospital.'

'Oh Fran,' Cora says. 'You hardly knew what you were saying. We were both stunned by shock and grief.'

'It was me,' Fran whispers. 'I was the murderer. He only climbed the ladder to please me. I asked him to.'

'No.' Cora takes her hand and squeezes. 'He made that decision himself. It was his choice. When he fell, it was a terrible accident.'

'I thought . . . maybe you hated me for it,' Fran says.

'Never.' Cora looks shocked. 'Of course not.'

'But . . . I've always thought you liked Luke more than me. I was difficult. And then . . . Dad died because of me.'

'He didn't die because of you,' Cora says. 'Fran, I had no idea you've been blaming yourself. You two were so close. Andrew was a wonderful dad.' She bites her lip, frowning. 'I've never told you what really happened after you were born.'

'What do you mean?'

'I think I've mentioned my depression, but I've never told you how bad it was, how ill I was. I couldn't function as a mother. I was scared all the time. Everything felt impossible. And then I was numb. On tranquillisers. Unable to give you the care you needed, the warmth, the love.' Cora's voice breaks. 'I let you down.'

Fran remembers the emptiness of her own small hands – fingers stretching into a dazzle of sunlight, bright motes flickering, needing the person behind the gold, the shadow of her mother, distant, blue-edged, unreachable.

She remembers stumbling on unsteady legs across a carpet littered with toys. Her mother on the sofa staring blankly into space. And how suddenly her bladder was full, an urgent need pressing a pain through her tummy, and how she tugged at Cora's unresponsive hands. And then the warm, wet flood making her knickers heavy, the shameful trickling through her woollen tights. The dark stain on the carpet.

'All my life I thought it was me ... I thought I was the problem ...'

A tear slips down Cora's cheek. 'You've never been a problem, my darling. I've always loved you, and always will. You and your brother. But it was you who suffered when you were little.' She wipes her eyes. 'Thank God for Andrew. He did so much with you.'

Fran thinks of this – of her father's throaty laugh, his ready hugs and booming voice making things all right. She always went to him. Sometimes she secretly wished they could live together, just the two of them, without Mum and Luke.

Cora reaches across and holds her fingers. Fran looks at their joined hands on the table, her wrists poking from her jumper, blue veins branching under her pale skin, carrying blood she shares with her mother.

'It must have been awful for you, Mum.' She squeezes Cora's fingers. 'It helps to know about it. A lot of things I didn't understand before suddenly make sense.'

She sits back, touching her pulse, its small drumbeat, its steady insistence on hope.

41

Queensway

'You're too thin,' Helena remarks as they do their stretches on the grass near the Serpentine Gallery, their usual meeting point.

Cora slides into a runner's stretch, one leg extended out behind, a hand resting on the damp, dewy ground, the other on her supporting bent knee. 'I'm fine.'

'I'm not getting at you.' Helena holds up her palms. 'Just. You know. Worried.'

Cora struggles to her feet, and touches the small of her back where she felt a twinge. She performs some cautious pelvic circles, and decides she hasn't done any damage. Since that night on the boat, her body feels fragile, ancient.

'Are you eating?' Helena persists.

Cora windmills her arms. 'Please stop going on, Helena. I'm fine. Really. I've survived the death of my husband, remember? The father of my children, the love of my life. So ... yes, I can survive this.' She tucks a flyaway wisp of hair under her peaked cap. 'Jacob was always a bit of a mystery, to be honest.

But everything else was good, so I suppose I was in denial.' She rolls her shoulders. 'I'm over him. It was an affair. And now it's over.'

'Really?' Helena raises an eyebrow.

'Yes.' Cora looks away.

'Shame about the sex, though,' Helena sighs. 'It suited you to be a sexed-up goddess. Now ... well, you know me. I tell it as it is, and I'm sorry, but you look terrible. I'll keep nagging until you get some colour in your cheeks.'

'I guess that will be in about five minutes then, once we've started the torture.' Cora jogs on the spot, and then turns for the path. 'Come on. Let's get this over with.'

Cora's days are a series of lists and chores. They stretch ahead in an endless etching of scribbled words and numbers. Things to be got through. Things to be ticked off. To be endured. She wonders if she'll ever feel joy again, ever feel the pull of lust or the shiver of anticipation. Whenever she realises she's being self-pitying, she gives herself a sharp lecture on how lucky she is, reciting all that she should be grateful for, condensed into bullet points.

The one thing that does make her happy is Fran. She's more like the girl she used to be when Andrew was alive. Of course, it's not a magic spell – she hasn't transformed overnight into a Disney princess, and her locker-room language is as foul as ever – but it feels ... normal. More than that, for the first time ever, the two of them have formed an alliance against the world.

In Luke's absence, the house has become unapologetically female. The sour smell of his old socks and sweaty T-shirts has gone. His bean burgers and mushroom sausages and cans of Coke are no longer taking up space in the fridge. Cora and Fran curl up together on the sofa on Saturday evenings, snug as cats, watching *Strictly*, sharing a bar of chocolate and commenting on the dancers, without Luke rolling his eyes and asking when supper will be ready because he's *starving*.

'How's Luke?' Helena pants over her shoulder, as if she's read Cora's mind.

'Fine. I think.' Cora's legs are concrete. She wills herself onwards, focusing on the Peter Pan statue just ahead. 'After a series of urgent text messages asking how to use a washing machine and how long he should boil pasta for, he's gone kind of quiet on us. You know what he's like.'

'Yeah. Not really a chatterbox,' Helena says, pulling away from Cora down the path leading towards the lake.

Cora uses all her determination to keep up. 'I'm looking forward to the Christmas holidays,' she puffs. 'Having him home again.'

However much she's appreciating the time with Fran, she can't wait to have Luke back. She wants his bedroom full of his stuff again, carefully arranged in neat lines, his colour-coded charts pinned to the wall. And Luke at his desk, lanky legs splayed, headphones on, with his sweet smile and gentle hands. She won't mind about the fast-disappearing food from the fridge, or his absurd trainers like small boats left lying on the hall floor. She just wishes he'd be more communicative. Weeks go past and she doesn't hear a word. She can't stop a little knot of anxiety gathering. It'll be more than good to have him home. It'll be a relief.

After the run, they skip coffee, as Cora has to get into work early. It's not exactly a lie. She always likes to get into work early, although it's not absolutely necessary this morning. But there have been weeks of suppers and Friday mornings full of

Helena's questions and observations and orders, and she can't face any more. She knows her friend means well, that she loves her, but she also knows that Helena can smell out her hidden misery, can tell that she's not really over him, and that's why she won't shut up about it.

The two women hug, Helena's arms tight and protective around Cora's shoulders, then Helena turns towards Knightsbridge, and Cora to the Queensway Underground station to jump on the Central Line for home, to shower and change before work.

As she heads for the Bayswater Road exit, she sees something that makes her stop and stare, her eyes focusing on the figure of a bullet-headed man tramping along a nearby path, his own gaze fixed to the open paperback splayed in his hands, a brindled Staffie trailing behind. Nobody else walks and reads like that, not with a dog at their heels. 'George?' He looks out of place in Hyde Park, and she can't understand what he's doing here, so far from his narrowboat and the canal. She calls his name again and jogs over the grass towards him.

He looks up, expression glazed, still caught in the story he's reading. She's ridiculously pleased to see him. She's missed him – his blunt kind words, his sudden wry sense of humour, his steady presence. She smiles. 'What are you doing here?'

'Oh, we walk all over, don't we, Claude?' he says. 'We've covered all the London parks at some time.'

'It's miles!'

'One foot in front of the other. Surprising where it will get you.'

She crouches down and gives Claude a scratch behind his ear. He wags his tail, as if to please her.

'Have you ... have you seen Jacob?' she asks, concentrating

on the dog's benign face, his amber eyes. 'Is he ... all right?' She looks up.

George rubs his head, rasping at grey stubble. 'Doesn't complain. But I can tell he's cut up about something.' He looks at her with a meaningful gaze.

She stands. 'It was his choice, George,' she says quietly. 'I don't think he could cope in the end, seeing me as well as his son. Think he got caught between two worlds.'

'His son?' George raises an eyebrow. 'That's news to me. You sure?'

She swallows. 'I saw his photo. And Jacob – he ... he said so. Not in so many words. But ...'

George's eyes disappear in the folds of a narrowed squint. 'None of this adds up, if you ask me.'

'So ... you've never seen a child at the boat?'

'Never seen anyone go in or out. Nothing except that bird. Jacob's a loner. You were the first woman I saw set foot.'

'Really?' Cora can't help herself asking. 'No other girlfriends?'

'Not that I saw.'

She frowns, puzzled.

'He's not the usual narrowboat type. And although he's always willing to muck in, he keeps himself to himself. Not that he's stand-offish. Just ... private. I see him going off in the middle of the night sometimes, looking like the world's on his shoulders. But,' George scratches his head again, 'he's a decent bloke.'

His words release the doubts she's kept shored up; and a tumbling of unanswered questions begins to churn inside, making her unsteady, nauseous. She manages to control her face, keep her mouth from trembling. 'It's good to see you, George.' She bends to pat the dog's muscled flanks. 'And you, Claude.'

'Stay out of trouble.' George lifts his paperback in farewell and turns back to the path.

Cora goes in the other direction, cutting across the grassy slope towards the Bayswater gate. Her trainers are damp, her skin tight with dried sweat, salt on her lips. She lets herself remember that night on the boat, the sketches of the boy, Jacob's anger, his hot white pain. But he wanted her gone, that much was clear. *It would be better if you go now.* And he hasn't contacted her, not once. There's no space for her in his life. *I'm not free*, he said. *I never was.*

Whatever the truth of the identity of the child in those pictures, she'll never know it now.

Notting Hill

Fran's on her way to her favourite vintage clothes shop in Portobello Road when she stops outside a small bookshop. There's a sign in the window advertising for an assistant. She bites her thumbnail. She doubts the money will be great, but it would be a start. At least she'd be surrounded by books. But the job might have gone already, she thinks. A nagging doubt starts up – other people applying will know about book prizes and the names of the latest literary authors; will probably have English degrees, will be cleverer than her. She hears Zac's voice in her head: *You're not stupid. You're perceptive and interesting and passionate. Don't let anyone tell you differently.*

She pushes at the door. It's a tiny space. Shelves packed with coloured spines reach from floor to ceiling. A man with bottle-top glasses sits behind the counter, reading a novel. There's a smell of paper, of books.

She approaches, and waits. He ignores her. She clears her throat. He looks up with an irritated expression. 'Yes?'

'I've come about the job,' she says. 'The advert in the window?'

He looks at her through greasy lenses, and scratches his head as if she's said something incomprehensible.

Fran is wearing a short skirt; her green tights have a hole in the left knee. Her T-shirt says *I'M NOT ALWAYS RUDE, SOMETIMES I'M ASLEEP*. She tugs her jacket across her front. 'Okay then,' she mutters, 'I guess it's taken,' as she turns away.

'What's the last thing you read that made you feel *and* think?'

Surprised, she turns back. '*King Lear*.'

'Why?' He pushes the bridge of his glasses with one finger, nail bitten to the quick, smudged with ink.

'Because ... it made me feel something unspoken, because it's about things you can't explain, because at the end, you know that despite things finding a new order, the world has become a colder place.'

He leans over the counter. 'And is there a novel that does that too – makes you feel something unspoken?'

'Um ... lots, but recently I got lost inside what-his-name's *House of Leaves* ... Mark Z. Danielewski. It was a total head-fuck. Full of unspoken stuff. Kind of pretentious. But his ideas gave me vertigo – like the ground was falling from under my feet.'

She wants him to ask her something else. Talking like this is unexpected. She likes it. It feels like a challenge. She can't tell from his expression whether she's giving answers he approves of, but he's listening intently. She waits for the next question.

'Can you work a computer?'

She was hoping for further interrogations about books. Can she work a computer? Duh. She nods.

'Do you understand how to read spreadsheets?'

She nods again. Actually, she hasn't a clue. But she could learn.

'Five afternoons a week. Mondays and Wednesdays off. Can you start tomorrow?'

'What? I've got the job?' She stares at him, afraid that he's joking.

'Write your name down here.' He pushes a scrap of paper and a leaking pen towards her. 'Your number, address – all that jazz. See you tomorrow. Twelve on the dot.'

As she gets to the door, he calls out, 'I'm Les, by the way.'

'Fran,' she says, grinning. 'Fran Pollen.'

Fran has worked at the bookshop for over two weeks now, and her confidence has grown. She steps forward to help customers while Les sits at the counter, head buried in a book. When someone innocently asks about the latest rom-com novel or popular blockbuster, he crinkles his face in disgust, glaring at them through his bottle-top glasses, so Fran takes over, looking it up on the computer while she smiles at the customer, asking them to pop back the next day to collect it. She's taken to doing the window displays, likes rearranging the card selection. Turns out she's good at doing the ordering-in, the system open on the computer, the Excel spreadsheet ready. Les is happy to leave it to her – says computers are the devil's work. 'I don't know how you've survived all this time,' she tells him. 'You're a bad-tempered Luddite. You know people can get all of this on Amazon for about half the price?'

'I'm a character,' he growls. 'A surly one. Holden Caulfield or Mr Darcy.'

She raises one eyebrow. 'Scrooge more like.'

He glowers at her. 'Point is, people love to hate me. Gives

them something to moan about. It's bonding. If they get a smile out of me, it's like winning the lottery. You don't get that on Amazon, do you?'

She earns a pittance, but she's catching up on her reading, and she has time to look for other jobs – longer-term, things with career prospects. She tries not to be depressed when she realises she doesn't have the right qualifications for any of them.

'How are you, babe?' Alesha is radiant. Her skin flames under the downlighting, borrowing scarlet tones from her figure-hugging dress. Nearly every man in the place is giving her wolfish stares. As soon as Fran has perched on the bar stool, Lesh is dangling her left hand in front of her. A diamond glints.

'What the fuck?' Fran stares at the ring and then at Lesh. 'Engaged?'

Alesha nods, grinning. 'Wedding next summer.'

'I thought . . . I didn't know you wanted to get married.'

'I love him.' Her shoulders rise and fall, implacable in her good fortune. 'It feels right.' She grins, 'Right man. Right time.'

Jealousy twists in Fran's belly; not because Alesha's getting married – Fran has no desire for that – but because it'll give Carl a special hold over her, an official hold. Even as the feeling enters, it's erased by a flush of shame, and she grimaces, angry with herself. *Be careful with other people's hearts.*

'Wow, Lesh!' She leans across and hugs her friend. 'That's . . .' she raises her brows, widens her eyes, 'that's amazing. Hope he knows how lucky he is.'

'July the twenty-fourth next year. Save the date.' Alesha holds up her drink so that Fran can clink with her.

'Congratulations!' Fran says over the chime of glass. 'I'll even be bridesmaid if you want.'

'Yes! Of course I want,' Lesh says. 'We'll discuss clothes another time. I'm thinking simple and elegant, butterscotch and ivory. But how about you? What's going on?'

Fran sips her beer. 'Nothing much. Les is a miserable old sod. But I like the job. Mum's doing better, I think. But she's . . . fragile. She needs me.'

'I think it's good for you,' Alesha says gently.

'What?'

'Being needed.'

'Hmm.' Fran crosses her legs, dips into a bag of crisps and munches. 'Maybe.'

'What about your love life?' Lesh persists. And Fran knows that Lesh wants the same thing for her as she has for herself – she wants Fran settled with the right man.

'I don't have the patience,' Fran says. 'Not now. Me and Mum, we're single girls together, and I think that's best for the moment. It's . . . it's kind of nice, actually. Neither of us wants the upheaval of all that bullshit – meeting someone, getting to know each other, then finding out they're a lying bastard. Except you, of course,' she adds with a smile. 'You're a rarity – you've found a good one.'

'The only one,' Lesh says happily.

There's a sense of an ending, Fran thinks as she walks to the Tube. It's come with Alesha getting married. Things will never be quite the same again. Lesh is moving into a new phase of her life, while she, Fran, is still living at home. It's like being on a train journey and never arriving at your destination – just going around and around and arriving back at the beginning. She digs her hands into her pockets. There's a chill in the air, the pavement slippery with rotten leaves. Looking after Mum has been keeping her sane, keeping her from freaking out about her future – her non-existent prospects. But Cora will get herself back on track; she's a survivor. She has her job, and Helena. She won't need Fran for much longer. Fran sniffs, the cold air catching at the back of her throat.

Shepherd's Bush

Cora and Fran are having a night in. There are crisps and olives in bowls on the coffee table, and caramel ice cream in the freezer. Cora has noticed that Fran tempts her with treats and snacks at every opportunity – her daughter is trying to fatten her up. Cora's touched. She eats whatever she's offered obediently, gratefully.

She brandishes a bottle of wine. 'I'm guessing you want a glass?'

'Does the Pope wear long dresses?'

Cora pours Pinot Grigio into two glasses. 'I've noticed that you're drinking less, Fran,' she says. 'I can't tell you how relieved that makes me.'

'Yeah. Sorry. I . . . I got kind of wild, didn't I?' Fran raises her glass towards her mother. 'I guess it must have been frightening for you, especially as you're a bit of a control freak.'

'Believe it or not, I used to be pretty easy-going.' Cora smiles. 'I've never been a big drinker, but your dad thought I was a slob when we met at university. I wasn't too fussy about keeping things clean. I'd rather have my head in a book than my hands in a washing-up bowl. My parents teased me about my daydreaming. My teachers were less amused.'

'And that all changed after you had me?'

'You were premature . . . this tiny, fragile little creature. I was so frightened that I was going to hurt you by mistake. That I wasn't able to care for you. I swung the other way – from someone who didn't mind about a few dirty mugs to needing everything to be immaculate and scrupulously clean. And . . . well . . . I became very depressed, as you know.' Cora holds her wine glass tighter, remembering those days.

'Seriously!' Fran's face has widened in amazement. 'I never knew that becoming a parent could cause such a dramatic personality change!'

'Oh, believe me,' Cora says, 'it's the most dramatic thing that can happen to a person. Never mind the mystery of hormones, your whole world changes the moment your child is born. It's also the most wonderful thing that can happen to you,' she adds softly. 'Even if we had a rocky start, I always loved you more than I knew it was possible to love anyone. More than myself.'

Fran smiles and dips her face. 'It's been nice having this time to ourselves, just the two of us.'

'Yes, it has.' Cora glances at her daughter on the sofa beside her, long legs tucked up, and thinks how young she looks without her usual scowl, her blackened eyes and red lips. She watches Fran nibbling an olive, extracting the stone and putting it in a bowl.

'You never mention Zac any more,' she says cautiously. 'Have you stopped being . . . friends?'

Fran sits back with an impatient sigh. 'I could never be

friends with someone like him. He's such a know-it-all.' She shifts her legs, fiddles with her hair. 'Anyway, he wasn't a boyfriend. So it's no big deal.'

'Fran,' Cora says quietly. 'You like him, don't you? You came home with your face all lit up after you'd seen him. You seemed happier when he was in your life.'

Fran groans. 'Maybe. Yeah. I don't know.' She hugs her knees to her chest. 'I suppose I do like him. But he thinks I'm a selfish brat. And he's right.'

'You're not selfish,' Cora says. 'You've had it really tough these last years. It's been one thing after another: Dad dying ... letting go of a career you've wanted your whole life.' She leans forward, touching Fran's arm. 'But you've always been a fighter. Even when you were tiny. Did I ever tell you that when you were born, you had jaundice? The cure was to put you in a heat box, naked and blindfolded. You were just days old, and yet you somehow dragged yourself around that box, looking for food, for comfort. Your survival instinct was ... extraordinary. One of the nurses told me not to get upset, that the heat would knock you out. But you didn't sleep for what felt like ages. You kept searching – little fingers creeping forwards, inching yourself into the corners of that box.' She squeezes Fran's arm. 'At ten days old, you did the impossible.' She nods. 'If you want Zac, go and find him.'

Fran turns her head, and her eyes glisten. 'But I've tried to talk to him. He won't listen. He ignores my phone calls and texts. And I don't know where he lives – don't even know the address of the care home where he works.'

'Isn't there somewhere else? A club or café that he goes to?'

Fran sits up. 'There's a theatre group ... Cat's Eye. He told me the address once. He's connected to it. They meet a couple of times a week.'

'There you are, then!' Cora raises her glass. 'Don't lose him – not without at least trying to talk to him.'

'I like this fighting talk, Mum,' Fran says. 'It suits you.'

Fran lifts her glass and touches it to the rim of Cora's. Their eyes meet, each reflecting the other inside the mirror of their pupils.

Hanger Lane

Boleponds Community Centre is a bleak grey building on the edge of an estate. Fran pushes inside quietly, unnoticed by a group of about fifteen people caught up in discussion in the centre of the room; there's lots of gesticulating and laughter. They're surrounded by orange plastic chairs placed in a wide circle around the edges of the room. A woman with short silvery hair, wearing a voluminous patterned dress and a chunky wooden necklace, sits on one of the chairs holding a sheaf of printed pages on her lap, reading through them with a magnifying glass.

Fran stares around at the scuffed magnolia walls, high ceilings crossed with rafters, a withered balloon caught behind one of them, silver string hanging down. She's searching for Zac, but can't see him. She notices that the group are mostly teens to late twenties, a couple of older people, perhaps in their forties. There's a variety of styles going on, from colourful flowing trousers and tops to jeans and sweatshirts. 'Shall we start?' a voice says. Three young men stand shoulder to shoulder in a row. One begins to talk. The rest of the group have moved back to sit on the chairs. Fran sinks onto a nearby step, trying to be unobtrusive, but the silver-haired woman notices her and inclines her head in greeting. Fran gives a brief nod back.

A girl on one of the orange chairs begins to tap out a rhythm softly on a drum she holds between her knees; a man joins in, strumming a guitar held across his lap. The three performers sway to the music. They break apart, dancing through the circular space, interweaving their limbs. Fran realises that the rest of the group are standing now, silent, rigid and straight as soldiers. They form a large ring around the dancers, hands joined; and as the music becomes louder, the group shuffle forward so that they concertina inwards, compressing the three men into a tighter and tighter huddle, until they collapse, hands over their heads, almost hidden between the legs of the crowd. The guitar has stopped; the drum pounds in a frenzy, then falls silent.

She's not sure if she's walked into a workshop or a rehearsal. Whatever it is, it's rough, probably partly improvised, but she finds herself caught up in the drama, strangely moved.

'Great!' The woman in the patterned dress stands up and claps her hands. 'Let's have a quick break,' she calls.

There is laughter. People pat each other on the back, small groups and couples drift towards a table by the wall, where Fran sees there are plates of biscuits and jugs of juice and water waiting.

'Naomi?' The silver-haired woman has come over. She stands in front of Fran and smiles. 'I'm Carol.' She gestures to herself. 'Can we talk?'

'Um. Sorry. You've got the wrong person. I'm Fran.' She looks around the room. 'Actually, I was wondering if Zac was here?'

'Not Naomi? Oh dear.' The woman rattles the beads around her neck. 'I was expecting backup. A volunteer. Someone to help organise.' She scratches her head, ruffling her silvery crop. 'It's a bit much for me on my own. We usually split the group up – focus on different parts of the script . . .'

'So . . . Zac's not here?'

'Oh, sorry.' Carol gives a small smile. 'He doesn't come to many of our meetings. He's more on the admin side of things. Sorry.' She rattles her beads again. 'I'm a bit distracted.'

'Well . . .' Fran says slowly. 'I could maybe stand in till Naomi gets here?' She settles onto her heels. 'I went to drama school.' She shrugs. 'I don't have plans for this evening.'

'Oh my dear.' Carol clasps her hands together. 'That would be wonderful. We're in the early stages of the production. Here.' She shoves a couple of pages into Fran's hand. 'A scene between an asylum seeker and their caseworker.' She looks towards the table and calls out, 'Yara and Adrian, could you come over? This is Fran, she's going to listen to you read your scene.'

Fran's insides contract with embarrassment. Yara is the same slight, dark-skinned girl who was talking to Zac at the party. From her expression, Fran can tell that Yara recognises her too.

'I saw you with Zac,' Fran says quietly. 'And I was really rude to you. At the party. I'm sorry.'

Yara nods. 'It's okay.'

'It isn't,' Fran says. 'Not really. I was drunk. And . . . jealous, I guess.'

'I can understand.' Yara touches her arm, and smiles. 'He's handsome. Even more without the beard.'

'Yeah.' Fran gives a small smile.

'It's okay,' Yara says again.

Fran blinks. She has that feeling again. The one she had in

Rachel's kitchen. A squirming in her belly. It's as if she's standing outside herself, watching her mistakes.

Adrian has pulled three chairs into a circle. The girls join him. Fran reads the short script to herself, and then listens to Yara and Adrian speak it aloud. Adrian is a tall, heavyset young man with a pale, square face; he scoops out caverns of space with large, uncoordinated gestures and a booming voice.

She asks them both if this is something they've experienced themselves. Yes, they say. It is. Fran keeps her face as blank as she can – she doesn't want them to see the shock ringing inside her. She's not here to feel pity; she's been given the task of helping them get the best out of the words on the page. She stares at her feet, examining her DMs, the red and green embroidery around the laces, until she's got some control and can meet their expectant faces.

She suggests they swap roles, so that Yara plays the caseworker and Adrian the asylum seeker. She sees at once that this gives the scene a different edge; it takes on the energy of the unexpected. She leans forward, watching the pair of them perform, holding her breath. 'That's so good,' she says. 'Let's do it again. Try speaking slower, Adrian. Yara, maybe see what happens if you look away when he's delivering that second line.'

When Carol stands and claps her hands, calling 'Session's over,' Fran can't believe the time. She glances at her mobile to check that it's really 10.30.

'It goes fast,' Yara says, grinning. 'I know. Wednesdays and Fridays are the best evenings of the week.'

'Will you be here next time?' Adrian asks.

'No. I don't think so,' Fran says. 'I was just filling in.'

But Carol catches her at the door. 'Naomi never showed.

297

Would you like to come back next week? It's unpaid, I'm afraid, so I'll understand if . . .'

Fran clears her throat. 'Why not? I enjoyed it.'

Carol angles forward, beads swinging, and puts her warm hand on Fran's arm. She squeezes. 'I'm glad. Welcome to Cat's Eye.'

And behind her, Adrian grins, making elaborate thumbs-up signs.

Shepherd's Bush

'Well, that was awful!' Cora says as they walk home from the local cinema. It's a cold evening, and she pulls her coat tighter. 'What were we thinking?'

The film they've just seen was a shoot-'em-up with a clunky script and no plot – just an acceleration of frenzied violence. She'd wanted to book tickets for *Portrait of a Lady on Fire*, but that fell under the banned romantic category. Except, she realises, maybe she's ready to watch people falling in love on screen again. It's been nearly two months of no contact with Jacob, and although everything still hurts – not just her heart, but her brain, liver, lungs; even her teeth – she needs to face up to the world in its entirety again, and that includes love.

'Yup.' Fran is laughing. 'So bad it was funny.'

They turn off the main road. 'Have you got rehearsals again tomorrow evening?' Cora asks.

'Yes. We're putting in more hours. The show's getting close. Still a lot of work to do.'

Cora smiles at the enthusiasm in Fran's voice. 'And Zac still hasn't turned up?'

'No,' Fran says. 'I asked Carol for his address, but she couldn't give it to me, you know, for privacy reasons. So I gave her a note to pass along to him. But he hasn't got in touch, so I guess it's over – even though it never really began.'

'I'm sorry.' Cora touches her arm.

Fran nods. 'Yeah.' She swallows and looks away. 'My loss.'

'Why is it called Cat's Eye Theatre? I don't think you ever told me?'

'It's named for the cat's eyes in the road,' Fran says. 'You know – the reflective glass that guides you home, keeps you safe.'

'Is it very hard to listen to their stories?'

'Of course.' Fran makes a considering expression, lips pursed. 'But what I feel more than anything when I'm there with them is ... I don't know ... we're all just people, aren't we? It could be any one of us in their place, forced to escape from horror, seeking a new life. We don't choose where we're born – what time and place, what parents, religion, culture.' She shakes her head, and then grins as if remembering something. 'We have a laugh. Every time. Although there's a fucking major tragedy behind each person, there's all this joking around. And ... so much generosity.'

Cora stops and touches her daughter's gloved hand. 'I just want you to know that ... that I'm proud of you.' She swallows.

Fran's eyes shine. Her lips quiver. Then her face darkens and she blinks and looks down. 'I wish ...' She bites her lip, seems to hold her breath. A shiver runs through her. 'Let's not stand around,' she says abruptly, walking on. 'I'm freezing my arse off out here.'

Cora stares after her, puzzled. She's still a mystery, this child of hers. It seemed as though she was going to make a confession or say something profound, but then changed her mind. The street light catches the gold and bronze in her hair, sparks flying as she marches into the darkness.

At home, they sit at the kitchen table with warming cups of hot chocolate, their cheeks still flushed from the cold.

'Carol asked if I'd take on the role of assistant director,' Fran says casually, turning her mug in circles on the wood.

'That's brilliant, darling! You're really enjoying being behind the scenes, aren't you?'

Fran nods. 'It never occurred to me when I was trying to act – I didn't think I was clever enough to be a director or writer.' She grins. 'But it's so satisfying when something I suggest gives the actors' performance more meaning.'

'So will you stay with this theatre company? With Cat's Eye?'

'If I can keep on at the bookshop, then I'll do an unpaid year with Cat's Eye, and then either they'll start paying me, or I'll look for a similar role with another company.'

'Sounds like a plan.' Cora leans forward, raising her cup to clink against Fran's.

Fran laughs. 'Yeah – finally, I have a plan. Damn. I might even start to write lists next. I'd better not tidy my room – it could all be too much for you.'

Cora holds up her hands. 'I'm not saying anything!' She goes to the sink to let down the blind over the dark window. 'Luke will be coming home in a few weeks.' She stares at the vague wintry shapes of the garden, remembering Jacob and Luke out there, the bike in pieces on the ground. 'Let's have a big Christmas tree this year, celebrate Luke's first term and your success at Cat's Eye.' She unfurls the blind and turns back to Fran. 'Have you heard from him recently? Luke? He hasn't emailed for ages and he didn't answer last time I tried to call.'

Fran shakes her head. 'We usually just WhatsApp each other, but I haven't heard anything for a while.'

The small knot of worry is back in Cora's gut again, but she doesn't want to voice it. This evening should be about Fran – it's wonderful to see her excitement, her confidence in the future.

'What about Jacob?' Fran says, her voice dropping. 'Is it really over with him?'

Hearing his name is a shock. Cora is rigid, hands clasping each other for support. 'He ended it, Fran. And . . . I haven't heard from him.' She unclasps her hands and puts them briefly over her face. 'I do still think of him. All the time, if I'm honest.' She attempts a smile. 'But I'm lucky. I have you and Luke. I have Helena. I have a lot to be grateful for.'

'You're so positive,' Fran says.

'I don't have much choice,' Cora replies quietly.

Fran yawns. 'Sorry. Shattered.'

'Yes.' Cora covers her mouth, yawning herself. 'We should go to bed.'

As she rinses the cups in the sink, a noise starts up. An unfamiliar ringing. It's the house phone. Nobody ever calls it. Except salespeople. Or wrong numbers. She thinks she'll ignore it. But it must be too late for cold calls? Sighing, she picks it up.

'Hello, is that Luke's mum? Mrs Pollen?' An unfamiliar voice.

Her heart stops. The blood drains from her body. 'Yes,' she whispers.

'It's Will here. I'm on the same landing as Luke. I have the room next door.'

Cora waits, her fingers gripping the receiver.

'Thing is, we don't know where he is. He hasn't been back to his room for ages.'

'What do you mean?'

'Nobody's seen him in hall for days, maybe longer.'

'Have you told the university ... someone in charge?' Cora can't think who that person would be. Fran has stopped at the threshold, listening to Cora's side of the conversation. She widens her eyes questioningly at her mother.

'Yes. But they won't do anything because he's been to some lectures, apparently. And someone saw him in the library the other day.'

Relief washes through her. 'Maybe he's staying with someone, then? A girlfriend?'

There's silence. Cora and Fran stare at each other.

'He doesn't have a girlfriend. He doesn't have any friends.'

Cora puts out a hand to steady herself against the table. 'Then ... where's he sleeping?'

'That's what I'm saying. We don't know. He's kind of disappeared.'

'I'm coming,' she manages. 'I'll be there as soon as I can.'

She puts the receiver back. Her hands are shaking. She looks at Fran. 'It's Luke. He's ... disappeared. He hasn't been sleeping in his room.' She clenches her fingers. 'I need to go there. Now. I ... I'll get the car ... I'll—'

'Wait.' Fran puts her hand on Cora's arm. 'Just hold on. We should both go. But tomorrow. We can't do anything now.'

'The car!' Cora wails, remembering. 'It failed its MOT. It's at the garage.'

'Then we'll get the train.' Fran moves away. 'I'll look up the earliest one. We can go from Liverpool Street.'

Cora nods, swallowing. She won't be able to sleep, won't be able to close her eyes until she finds her son, until she knows he's safe.

46

Liverpool Street

Fran and Cora emerge from the hot, crowded Underground into Liverpool Street terminus. Above them, the vast icy dome of the roof, the flap of pigeon wings. And everywhere, bustle and noise. Fran glances at Cora and moves closer, as if to protect her mother from the hectic assault of screeching trains, echoing public-speaker announcements and the slap and thunder of feet. Commuters are arriving on trains in dizzying numbers. Fran and Cora pull themselves to the side to avoid the hurrying mob clutching briefcases and takeaway coffees, rushing through the barriers, most of them talking on their mobiles or staring at screens in their hands.

'Shit. Over here,' Fran says, guiding Cora, a hand on her mother's elbow. 'Platform nine.'

It was still dark outside when Fran's alarm went off earlier that morning, and she was groggy, disorientated, fumbling for her mobile. But when she got downstairs, Cora was already waiting in the kitchen, neatly dressed, buttoned into her coat, her bag on her lap, ready to go. She looked brittle, dark circles bruising her eyes, an untouched cup of cold tea before her. Fran wondered if she'd been there all night. Since then, she's hardly spoken a word.

Now they shuffle close to Platform 9. Through steel turnstiles, Fran can see that their train is there, but people are still getting off; a cleaner with a bucket on wheels disappears into one of the carriages. She scans the surrounding crowd expectantly. She hasn't told Cora what she did last night, and she feels a tug of doubt in her belly. Has she done the right thing?

Her heart thumps a warning as she recognises a familiar figure emerging out of the mass of strangers. Beside her, Cora isn't aware of anything. She's biting a fingernail, staring blankly at the departure board – at the flickering names and numbers, the endless rearranging of information.

'Mum.' Fran pulls at her sleeve, alerting her, drawing her attention to the tall man approaching.

As Cora turns, Fran feels her mother's body stiffen, senses the buckling of her knees. She stares at her mother's face worriedly, watching as she speaks his name with disbelief. 'Jacob?'

Questions crowd inside that one word.

He stands before them. He looks only at Cora. His speckled green and gold gaze is even brighter than Fran remembers. 'Cora,' he says, his hands hovering in the air between them. 'I'm so sorry. Of course I want to help,' he goes on with a choke, as if in the middle of a conversation, putting his hands in his pockets. 'In any way.'

Cora swings round, her eyes wild. 'Fran?' The syllable twists in her mouth.

Fran inhales, guilty. She clears her throat. 'I called him last night, Mum. I knew he could help. And . . . and I knew he'd want to know. He cares about Luke.' She touches her mother's sleeve again. 'The three of us can cover more ground.'

'You didn't know?' Jacob flinches, a ripple at his neck as he swallows. 'I thought . . . I thought you'd asked Fran to call me.'

Fran hears a lurch of disappointment and wonders if her mother heard it too. Cora shakes her head. 'No. No. I . . . I didn't ask her.'

'Ah, that's . . . awkward.' He collects himself, tries for a reassuring smile. 'I'm sorry. I . . . I'll go. Leave you to it. Unless . . . you think I could be useful?'

'I'd never have asked you in the first place,' Cora says shakily, almost as if she's talking to herself. 'But now you're here . . .' She looks at him directly for the first time. 'Fran's right. It would help to have another pair of eyes and hands. The only thing that matters is Luke. Finding him.'

'And you can't get through on his phone?' he asks.

Fran frowns. 'We've both tried his mobile. But it goes to voicemail every time.'

'Don't worry.' Jacob glances towards the waiting train. 'We'll find him.'

Fran remembers Jacob in Marble Arch. How he came straight away on his bike. How he listened without judgement and took control, sorting out her mess, getting rid of Hugo. It took one conversation. The evening seems like a lifetime ago, the girl she was then a distant relation. But Jacob is the same as he was. And she's glad she called him.

On the train, Jacob sits opposite Cora and Fran across a small table. The three of them make nervous, halting conversation. They talk about Luke, trying to guess what could have happened. When they fail to come up with any positive answer, the conversation falters and falls into uneasy silence. Fran snatches glances at Jacob, wondering if Rachel told him why she'd been at the house that day. She hopes not.

She puts her forehead against the glass, closing her eyes, letting the rumble of the wheels on the tracks lull her into a half-sleep. She wants to give the two of them some space. The tension between them is a physical thing – a twisting rope tugging them together, even as they strain apart. Whatever reason Jacob had for ending the relationship, Fran's certain he still has feelings for her mother, still desires her, loves her even. She's disappointed when she opens her eyes to find them both studiously avoiding each other, looking at their phones, flicking through emails, checking the weather. Her mother scrolling through details about UEA and the layout of the campus.

At Norwich, they get out and find a taxi, going straight to the UEA campus, to Luke's hall – the Ziggurats, an iconic jumble of concrete and glass pyramid shapes marooned in a field. They go up to Luke's landing, and Cora knocks on his door. There's no answer. She pushes at the handle, and to her surprise, the door swings open. Fran walks over to the window and pulls the curtains. Cora sees that the bed hasn't been slept in. The pristine-looking sheets are pulled tight; the navy waffle blanket is wrinkle-free.

'This isn't like any student room I've ever seen,' Jacob says slowly. 'It doesn't look occupied.'

'He's always been weirdly neat,' Fran says. 'But this ... it's something else.'

Cora sniffs the scent of lemon, the bite of bleach. The carpet is immaculate. She can see marks where the hoover has mown through the pile, pushing it into darker stripes. She runs a finger over an empty shelf, then Luke's desk. She finds a slight trace of dust on her skin. He hasn't been here for at least a few days, she guesses. The window sparkles, framing the watery grey sky and distant green and purple trees without a smear or blemish. What kind of teenage boy polishes his window? The posters the two of them put up on his walls that first day have been removed. His bin is empty. His desk is bare, apart from three black pens lined up in a row, the spaces between them exactly the same.

Cora goes to his drawer and pulls it open. She suppresses a gasp. His clothes are here, folded neatly in colour order. She lifts a sweatshirt to her face and inhales, but although she hopes for a whiff of her child, longs for the scent of boy sweat, all she can smell is fake lavender fabric conditioner. She goes to the bed, dropping onto the mattress. She clutches the sweatshirt to her chest. 'He's taken his laptop. His books.' She gazes at Fran and Jacob. 'He hasn't worn any of his clothes.'

There's a brief knock at the door and a boy enters, muscled forearms visible in a tatty short-sleeved T-shirt, dark hair pushed into a quiff. 'You're Luke's parents?'

'I'm his mother,' Cora says quickly. 'You're Will? Can you give us any idea where he might be?'

Will scratches his head. 'Like I said before, someone from his course saw him in the library a couple of times. He was there yesterday afternoon apparently. But he hasn't been back to Ziggy for ages. When he was here ...' He pauses and shifts his weight from one foot to the other. 'He ... well ... he never stopped cleaning his room. It drove me crazy. The sound of the hoover. The smell of cleaning products. He'd be cleaning at three in the morning sometimes.'

Cora puts her knuckles to her mouth and closes her eyes. She thinks of his minimal, tidy room at home. Keeping his space just-so has always been important to him; now it seems it's the only thing he feels he has any control over. All these weeks, why didn't she sense that something was wrong? Too caught up in her own grief over Jacob, she answers herself angrily.

Jacob sits down beside her, his shoulder touching hers. She wants to lean into him, instead stays bolt upright.

'Thank you, Will,' he's saying. 'If you think of anything else that might help us find him . . .' He gets up and goes over to the student, exchanging numbers. Then he turns. 'Shall we all go to the library to start with? Seems like that's our best hope. If he's not there, we can split up.'

Cora nods, and struggles to her feet.

There's no sign of him at the library. Cora and Fran show people his image on their phones, but students shake their heads and shrug. Fran says she'll wait in case he turns up. She takes a seat near the entrance. Cora and Jacob hurry through other buildings on campus, peering into rooms, checking the lecture hall and canteen, showing his photo to anyone who will stop and look.

'Should we go to the police?' Cora asks. Her eyes hurt with the effort of staring at every face, searching every shadow.

Jacob rubs a hand over his face, as if his eyes ache too. 'I don't think they'll do anything,' he says. 'Technically Luke's not missing. He's been seen as recently as yesterday afternoon. It hasn't been twenty-four hours yet.'

'But he's vulnerable. I'm worried about his state of mind.'

'Yes, that's true.' He nods. 'Shall we go together, or do you want to go alone and I'll keep searching?'

Cora bites her lip. 'I'll do it. I'll call you when I'm done.'

'Right. Good luck.'

Her worry over Luke is using up most of her feelings, and yet she can't stop the pull towards Jacob, the ache in her heart, in her belly. He's here for Luke, not her.

At the police station in town, once she's explained Luke's mental state, she's taken into a small room to talk to an officer, fill in a missing person report. She finds a photo of Luke on her phone and downloads it. The constable tells her that in the first instance, they'll coordinate their enquiries at the university itself, interview the students in his hall, check CCTV footage.

Cora leaves the station feeling impatient, needing to get back to the search herself – as if she can't trust anything but her own eyesight, the radar of her maternal instinct. She checks her phone. Nothing from Fran or Jacob. She calls Jacob, and he answers at once. She can hear the roar of traffic in the background. 'I'm in town,' he says. 'It could be a red herring, but someone said they thought they might have seen him near the cathedral.'

'I'll meet you there,' she says.

It's a short walk from the police station to the cathedral. The spire rises into a bleached sky. Jacob is waiting at the entrance, hands in his pockets. He hasn't seen her yet. He's completely familiar and dear to her, and yet they must behave like polite acquaintances. It hurts. It hurts almost as much as her terror for Luke.

'Shall we go in?' he says when he sees her. 'Have a look around?'

As soon as she's inside, she senses that her son is close – it's almost as if she can smell him. She walks into the washed light of the interior with her breath caught in her lungs. She goes up the central aisle towards the altar, padding across honey-coloured flagstones, her hands trailing wooden pew ends. The place shimmers with reflections from limestone walls. She knows why Luke chose to come here. It's filled with light, a sense of peace. She tilts her head back, gazing into the slender curves of the vaulted ceiling, and then round to the vast coloured-glass window at the end. She blinks, her vision filled with a blaze of reds and greens and blues. There are gaggles of people, tourists, wandering about, cameras at the ready. Out of the corner of her eye she sees a figure bent as if in prayer, a mop of dirty-blonde hair falling across his face. Her heart skips. But it's not Luke in human form, more like a memory, a smudged shadow left behind. As soon as she recognises him, he's gone.

'He's been here,' she tells Jacob breathlessly. 'I know it. We need to look outside.'

He doesn't question her, following as she hurries onto the pavement. The surface is pockmarked with dark spots. It's beginning to rain, a light drizzle making the road slippery, the air damp and misty.

With a jolt, her brain understands that she can see him again, about twenty feet away, and for a second she fears that this Luke is a mirage as well. But she notices the details of his dirty trainers, the scuffed and bulging rucksack hanging from his shoulders. 'Luke,' she breathes, tugging at Jacob's arm. 'He's there. At the junction. By the traffic lights.'

Jacob gathers himself, urgency mobilising his body; she senses his knees tensing to stride forward, muscles firing to raise an arm. He's filling his lungs to shout.

'No,' she says sharply. 'Wait. We mustn't startle him.'

But it's too late. Luke has turned, is staring at them, and

behind the blind glare of his glasses, Cora sees confusion warp his expression, sees it turn to panic, to fear. 'Oh God,' she says. 'He's going to run.'

As the words leave her mouth, the traffic lights change to green, but Luke is lifting off from the pavement, his heels peeling away from the surface, his body suspended in space.

She moves. She has no conscious thought. Her legs power forwards, sinews on fire, reaching and reaching through space, fingers stretched to snapping point. Luke's head bobs as his leg extends, his foot leaving the edge of the pavement. There's a squeal of brakes, the long blare of a horn like a scream. Her fingertips brush the edge of his backpack, scrabble to grasp a shoulder strap. She yanks down, her fist tight as a vice, heels scuffing concrete as she brakes and skids. Luke is jerked to a halt. His weight topples backwards, and she's thrown off balance, the two of them tumbling in slow motion towards the ground, the pavement rising up at ferocious speed to strike them hard. She feels all her bones judder at the impact, landing in a crumpled pile, Luke sprawled on top.

The stopped world cranks into action: she's aware of people shouting, and a huddle of concerned bystanders collecting around them. But she's only interested in her son, in gathering him into her arms and holding on tight. Luke is panting, sobbing, 'I'm sorry, I'm sorry.'

'Hush,' she says. 'You're safe now.'

They sit up. She takes his face in her hands. A lens has cracked on his spectacles. She lifts his torn palms and inspects tiny beads of red. 'Are you hurt anywhere else?'

Luke shakes his head, eyes wide. 'Don't think so.'

Someone reaches down to pull them up. She lets herself be hauled to her feet. She expects to see Jacob. But she's staring at a stranger, a woman who's talking fast, telling them what a near-miss Luke had, gabbling, 'My Lord, I nearly had a heart attack. That car was coming right at him.' Cora nods, not listening.

She cranes her neck, looking for Jacob. He's standing a few feet away, staring at her and Luke; his face is stretched into a mask of shock. Tears roll down his cheeks. His hands hang by his sides as if he's lost the use of them.

'Jacob?' She walks over, wincing as she realises her left hip hurts. 'Are you all right?'

He nods, but then convulses as if he's been punched in the stomach. Bent over, his body shudders with ragged breaths as he snatches gulps of air. She leans down and puts her arm around his shoulders. 'Jacob? What's the matter? Look – Luke's here. He's fine. He's not hurt.'

He straightens, his face wet. 'Yes ... thank God.' He puts shaking fingers on Luke's shoulder. 'Thank God.'

'Shall we get out of here?'

Jacob nods, but doesn't move. His sobs continue. She has never seen a man cry with such violence, or with so little noise, as if his grief is tearing him apart from the inside and this outward misery is just a reflection, ripples hitting the surface. The storm is raging deep down, unseen.

'What's wrong with him?' Luke whispers.

She shakes her head at her son, and leans towards Jacob. 'Jacob,' she says gently. 'Let's go and find somewhere quiet to sit down.'

With Luke's hand in hers, she links an arm through Jacob's and guides them both away from the stares of the remaining curious strangers. Traffic is flowing onwards as if nothing's happened, the moment of crisis already erased.

Luke rubs his eyes with a balled-up fist, and shudders. 'You saved me, Mum,' he tells her. 'You saved my life.'

Jacob swallows. 'You did,' he manages. 'You were . . . amazing.'

Shepherd's Bush

Cora shepherds Jacob and Luke to a nearby park, where the three of them slump onto the damp wooden slats of the first empty bench. She can hardly hear anything except the racket of her blood in her ears. Her hands are shaking. She gets out her mobile to call Fran, managing to give her a brief, stilted update, explaining where to come. Then she phones the police station, telling them to call off the search.

Jacob has stopped crying. His face is grey, drawn. He seems exhausted and unable to respond to anything. This is a new Jacob, this vulnerable, traumatised man, staring with unseeing eyes. He sits beside her with his fingers placed carefully on his knees.

On her other side, Luke seems compelled to speak. 'I couldn't go back to my room, you see,' he's saying. 'Every time I set foot in it, I knew I'd tracked germs inside, brought in filth and muck from the outside. So I had to clean it again. It . . . it was exhausting.' He pushes a hand through his hair, his words coming fast, tumbling over each other. She holds his hand, listening. 'So I thought I'd lock myself in to stop the contamination. But I needed to eat. I needed to get books and go to lectures. And anyway, my body was polluting the space. Old skin. Dead cells. Sweat. Hair.' He shudders. 'And . . . and every time I had to touch or use something, I needed to wipe it clean and put it back in its exact place, and that was exhausting too.' His voice stumbles on. 'So then I realised that I could just stay away – not go into my room at all. Problem solved.' He gives a short laugh, his eyes dead. 'I didn't plan to sleep rough. It just happened . . .'

Cora thinks of her child alone on the street all night, while she was sleeping in her bed, unaware of the danger. She presses her fingernails into her palms, little half-moons of pain.

Luke takes a deep, shuddering breath. 'I tried to sleep on the landings in Ziggy at first. But people kept telling me to go back to my room. So I left campus, went into town. It was horrible. Cold and uncomfortable, and I was frightened of sleeping in case someone attacked me and stole my stuff.' He touches his bag. 'My laptop's in here. Everything important.'

He's taken his cracked glasses off and put them in his pocket. His eyes look naked without them.

'I went into the cathedral. But they close it in the evening. Sometimes I found a bench. But I didn't lie down. I was so tired.'

'And you were still going to lectures?' she asks.

He nods. 'And the lab. I worked in the library. Sometimes I slept there with my head on the desk.'

'And none of your tutors knew?'

He shakes his head. 'I don't think so.'

'I wish you'd told me, darling,' she says gently.

'I was ashamed.' Luke hangs his head.

'You have nothing to be ashamed of,' Jacob says, his voice hoarse, adamant. His first words.

'Jacob's right,' Cora says. 'None of this is your fault.'

Fran arrives, hurrying towards them with a cardboard tray holding cups of tea. She puts it into Cora's hand and extends her arms to her brother; he stands up, leaning into her embrace, and she hugs him tightly, her long hair falling around them like a curtain. 'Jesus,' she murmurs. 'You scared the crap out of me.'

The tea is very strong and very sweet. Cora cradles her cup; the warmth is comforting. She's cold, cold to the bone. Luke's teeth are chattering as he raises his cup to purple lips.

'We should get out of the wet,' she says. 'Let's find a taxi, catch the next London train. Go home.'

'Do you need anything from halls?' Fran asks her brother.

He shakes his head.

'Jacob, I think ... I think you should come home with us,' Cora tells him.

He opens his mouth to protest, but closes it again. He doesn't have the strength to resist, she thinks. She's never seen him like this. She doesn't want him to be alone on the boat, surrounded by water. She thinks that if necessary she can sleep on the sofa or with Fran, and let him have her bed. There's a sharp sensation inside her chest; she puts her hand over the stab of pain. It's not being able to behave naturally, not being allowed to let her body fit with his, or slip her hand inside his for comfort.

At home, they troop through the front door, kicking off shoes and hanging coats at the bottom of the stairs. Fran goes to put sheets on Luke's bed. Cora makes more sugary tea, and pours whiskies for her and Fran and Jacob. Luke says he'd rather have a Coke. But there are none in the fridge. 'I'll get some tomorrow,' Cora tells him. 'Stock up on all your favourite stuff. And I'll contact the university to explain and tell them you won't be coming back until at least after Christmas.'

'I don't want to get behind in my work,' he says anxiously.

'They can send you work. You're not going back until you feel ready. We'll sort it out together. I don't want you to worry.'

She notices a twitch in his left eye.

'Why don't you go up and use the bathroom?' she says. 'Take as long as you need.'

He nods, and disappears from the room. While they wait for him, Cora rustles up a quick tomato pasta. None of them talks. Luke returns, his skin pink and glowing, wet hair slicked down. They eat, Luke yawning and blinking, hardly able to swallow. Cora thinks she must remember to make him an appointment to get replacement spectacles.

Luke gets up to go to bed. As he passes Jacob, he stops and puts his hand on the older man's shoulder, and Jacob rouses himself enough to reach up and place his hand on top of Luke's fingers.

'Night,' Luke says.

Jacob's mouth twitches. He pats Luke's hand. 'Sleep,' he says. 'You need to sleep.'

Cora accompanies Luke into his room. 'Will you be all right in here tonight?' she asks. When she checks on him five minutes later, his face is pushed into the pillow and he's snoring. She pulls the door to, leaving a gap.

Fran has cleared the table. 'I'm going to bed too,' she says, yawning. 'If there's nothing else I can do?'

Cora kisses her daughter's forehead. 'Go,' she says. 'You've been amazing. Thank you.'

After Fran has left the room, Jacob raises his head. 'How's Luke?'

'He's asleep.'

'Best thing for him.'

'Yes. I'll make some calls tomorrow. The university. The doctor.' She sits at the table next to him. 'Thank you,' she says. 'For coming with us – for everything you did.'

'I'm sorry,' he says quietly.

She leans forward. 'What for?'

'For breaking down. For ... for losing it.' He squeezes his eyes shut. 'You didn't need that. Not today.'

The moment opens like a door – there's darkness inside. She takes a sip of whisky for courage. 'Do you ... do you want to talk about it?'

He avoids her gaze, looking down at his hands, staring at them as if he's never seen them before. He gives a little shake. 'I'm sorry for hurting you, Cora,' he says in a husky voice. 'I didn't know what to do. Before. On the boat. I didn't want to pull you into my mess. Into my life. It wasn't fair on you.'

'Jacob,' she says. 'It doesn't matter now. But I'd like to know what ... what happened today. It was as if you disappeared ... went into another place, another world.'

He sighs, and a shudder runs through him. 'I thought Luke was going to die.' He flattens his palms over his eyes. 'If you hadn't caught him in time ... the car would have hit him. It brought it all back.'

He compresses his lips tightly, his jaw tense. The clock on the wall ticks. She hears a motorbike rev and roar somewhere in the distance.

'I haven't let myself go there,' he says. 'Not for years. I've stopped myself from thinking ... about that day.'

'What day?' she prompts quietly.

'The day my brother was hit by a car.'

'Natan?' Cora feels cold.

He nods. 'I was fifteen. He'd just turned fourteen. We'd had a row. Over something stupid. I can't even remember what now. But I was angry with him.' Jacob places his fingers on his thighs, curls them into fists. 'We were on the pavement near the park, and he was holding his football. I snatched it from him and threw it.' He looks at her, his eyes dark. 'Just for spite. To tease him. I don't know.' He takes a jagged breath. 'He ran. He ran straight into the road to get it back, without looking. And there was a car.'

Cora puts her hand over her mouth.

'It hit him. He went into it head first. I watched – it seemed like slow motion.'

'It was an accident ...'

'No.' His voice is hard. 'No. It was my fault. He nearly died. He was in a coma for a long time and they didn't know if he'd make any kind of recovery. He looked so small on the bed, except for his swollen skull. All the wires.' He stops, closes his eyes, squeezes them tight.

Cora waits, hardly daring to breathe.

'Then months of rehab,' Jacob continues, his voice a husk, 'months of hoping. He fought to survive, but he's severely brain-damaged. Unable to walk or speak.'

She swallows. 'I'm ... I'm so sorry.' All the words she can think of are inadequate. She bites her lip.

'He needs me. I need him. That's why I don't leave London. He's in a care home here. And I have to be able to see him as much as I can.'

A sudden knowledge comes to her. 'Your Saturday afternoons?'

He nods. 'I collect him and take him to my parents for the afternoon, and at the end of the day, I take him back. If he has an episode at the care home, they know to ring me, any time of the day or night.'

'The phone calls,' she murmurs.

'I can calm him. I can help. You see,' he looks at her, 'you see why I can't have a relationship? Why I couldn't ask you to share this with me? I was wrong to invite you for that drink.'

She doesn't disagree with him out loud, even though she does disagree. With all her heart she wishes that he'd told her before – that he'd at least given her a chance. But this isn't the time to speak to him about it – not now, not when he's trembling, wiped out, almost incoherent with strain and shock.

He's hunched over the table, and she thinks the natural thing would be to hug him. It's what she longs to do, but something about him makes her hold back. As if he might break if she touches him in the wrong way, or says the wrong thing. But she needs to know who the child is.

'And the boy?' she asks quietly, tentatively. 'In the sketches?'

'Natan. As a child, as the boy I remember before . . .'

The truth of this takes her breath away. She judged him, made assumptions too quickly, when she should have waited. She should have trusted him. And he should have trusted her. She looks at the kitchen clock. 'It's late. You need to sleep. You can have my bed.'

He starts to argue.

'You don't have a choice in this,' she says. And when he doesn't move, she dares to take his hand to lead him from the room. 'I can bunk with Fran.' She feels the texture of his skin against hers.

In the bathroom, she runs a sink of warm water and sets out

a bar of soap. A flannel. They don't meet each other's eyes. The gurgle of water and their breathing are the only sounds. 'There.' She steps away from him. 'I'll fetch a clean towel.'

She ducks out of the room, needing to hide her trembling fingers, the longing that must be blazing from her. She takes a towel from the airing cupboard and folds it into a square, then again and again, rearranging the creases, buying herself time to breathe.

He appears out of the bathroom, slow steps across the landing towards her. 'I borrowed your toothbrush,' he says. 'Hope you don't mind.'

'Of course not.' She's glad of the normality of his confession. She offers him the towel, but he shakes his head; she drapes it over the banister. 'Well . . .' She's finding it hard to look at him without touching the hair flopping across his forehead, without kissing his heavy-lidded eyes. 'Get some sleep,' she says, trying for a practical tone. 'I'll leave you now.'

She opens the door to her bedroom for him. 'Hope you'll be comfortable. I'll be in with Fran if you need anything.'

'Cora?' The word is a line of tension.

He's shivering. He holds out his arms. The mute question rebounds inside the space between them like an echo.

She's in his embrace without knowing how. She leans against his chest. His breath is minty. His lips in her hair. 'I've missed you,' he murmurs, and light vibrations hum through her skin into her solar plexus.

'Me too,' she says, a catch in her throat.

They stay in each other's arms until she disentangles herself and leads him by the hand into her room. Without speaking, they undress, stumbling in their exhaustion, and slide between the sheets in their underwear. They roll together, holding each other again, skin against skin. The physical reality of him is overwhelming, her senses alive with the slide of his body against hers, the prickle of his leg hair, the undulation of his muscle beneath her shoulder. His toes brush her shin. She leans into the bones and flesh and weight of him. 'I wish you'd trusted me,' she whispers.

'It's not just you, Cora. I've never told anyone what happened that day. Not even my parents. From the moment the car hit him, I felt like . . . like a criminal. I was so ashamed and frightened. I've never had the courage to admit what I did – not to anyone.'

'You've lived with this all your life?' She struggles up onto one elbow to look at him, at his face shadowed in the half-light. 'You've been alone with it since you were fifteen?' She is full of incredulity.

His head moves slightly. 'It's why . . .' His voice breaks. 'I suppose I've been a loner all my life. It was like . . . like a wall between me and the world.'

'Jacob,' she murmurs, pressing her lips against his shoulder. She has no words. She thinks of him as a teenager, a boy younger than Luke, living with this fear and guilt, the weight of it heavier with each day that passed.

They lie in each other's arms and he strokes her hair. Her lips rest on the warm ridge of his collarbone. She smells the musk of his skin, the hint of the lavender soap he's just used on his hands. 'I thought about telling you lots of times,' he says. 'I knew we couldn't have a relationship worth anything without me confessing it to you. But when you told me about Andrew's accident, I thought it would be too hard for you to hear about me and Natan – to meet him. The parallels with your husband are just too close. It felt impossible to tell you – I didn't want to bring those memories back. I couldn't do it to you.'

'I'm more resilient than that,' she says gently.

'I wasn't just being . . . noble.' He gives the word quotation marks with his voice. 'I was a coward. I was terrified that if I told you the truth, you'd be disgusted by me, horrified by what I'd done. I thought I'd lose you.'

She turns her face into his neck.

'From the moment we met, I've been torn in two. I don't usually get close to anyone. That way I don't have to make any decisions. But with you, it was different.' He takes a shuddering breath. 'I guess I just panicked. I was scared by how much you'd come to mean to me.'

'Jacob, I think you need to tell your parents the truth about what happened that day. You can't carry this alone.' She pauses. 'I'd . . . I'd like to meet Natan,' she says.

He squeezes her hand. A silent affirmation. Then he sighs. 'I got it all wrong, Cora. Got myself into such a muddle.' He pauses. 'Thank you for listening. For not hating me. I'll never forgive myself . . .' she feels a tremor run through him, 'and I suppose I've . . . I've never believed that I deserve to be happy.' His voice is a whisper. 'It's strange to think that I am.'

'You do . . . deserve . . . to be happy . . .' Her mouth doesn't work any more. Words break apart. She's consumed with tiredness.

'You were incredible today,' he murmurs. 'Like a . . . tiger . . .'

She falls into nothingness, feels him falling with her, their hands clasped as they tumble over the edge together, letting go at last of secrets, of fear, as they sink into unconsciousness, too shattered to dream.

*

When she wakes, it's early. Jacob is awake too, his head on the pillow, looking at her. His eyes are full of tenderness, sunrays around his pupils. She smiles, and he moves his hand to touch her face, to stroke her cheek. She turns her head, pressing her nose and mouth into his palm, into the salty warmth of his skin. They roll towards each other, embracing. She takes off her bra, wriggles out of her knickers. They laugh, inhaling one another's morning breath. The sour, sweet fug of the night. He hugs her to him, scooping her close, ribcage to ribcage; her lips press into the dip in his shoulder; she licks the delicate hollow. They fit together, soft angles filling spaces, shapes inside shapes like an extraordinary puzzle. He kisses her breasts. She trembles. They explore slowly, each re-finding the other, reclaiming what was lost. Cora's face is wet. There's salt in their mouths. Tears mingling. The ache of missing him is replaced with another kind of pain: the pressure of her heart, swollen with the relief of having him in her arms again, in her bed, in her body.

Hanger Lane

The theatre is brightly lit as the audience arrive. Fifteen minutes to go until curtain-up, but the auditorium is already nearly full. All the seats have been sold for the opening night. Fran supposes that Jacob, Cora and Luke are there somewhere, taking their places, waiting for the lights to dim and the show to begin. The chatter of overlapping conversations and shuffling feet makes an anticipatory hum. She doesn't have time to peer at front-of-house; she's too busy helping the actors prepare, to dress, to remember lines forgotten in a last-minute panic of stage fright. She's trying to find a lost prop – a life jacket that's integral to the performance – and at the same time shout instructions to the guy doing the lighting.

She's never felt so overstretched and stressed out. So happy.

Only a minute late, the lights go down. The audience falls silent as the first actors enter the stage. The theatre has been set up as a thrust stage, with half a hexagon extending into the audience. 'For more intimacy,' Carol said. They're also making use of all three stage entrances at the front, to access the aisles running between the audience, bringing the action to those sitting down, 'To snap them out of the complacency of being voyeurs.' She wants the audience to be able to reach out and touch the players as they brush by, see the beads of sweat on their foreheads, hear the rasp of their breath.

Fran stands behind the scenes, eyes fixed on the performance. She knows every line by heart, the script etched into her memory. It reels through her mind in bed at night – the whole performance – with her speaking all the parts, organising imaginary replicas of the actors going through their gestures and actions. Now her muscles quiver, ready to help, to prompt anyone who clams up. But the play runs exactly as she hoped, and she can sense the effect it's having on the audience. They are absolutely motionless, stunned inside the darkness. And who could fail to be affected? The piece is alive, raw and bloody with the truth; every word holds the passion and bravery and humour of the people who have lived through the story they tell.

Afterwards, the audience are on their feet, the actors gathering for bows, for praise and whistles of appreciation. They are all grinning, relieved, elated. Carol is beckoned on stage and a huge bouquet is thrust into her arms. Fran is clapping and smiling, and then she's being half pushed, half pulled centre stage to join everyone else. Adrian steps towards her and gives a little bow, presents her with a bunch of white flowers. She presses her nose into the petals to hide her blush, then puts her free arm around his neck, hugs him tight.

When the clapping has stopped and the audience begin to leave, there's a muddle of people backstage changing and dismantling scenery. Fran is busy checking props off on her list when Cora, Jacob and Luke appear. 'Well done,' Cora says, squeezing her. 'I loved every minute. Couldn't stop crying at the end.'

Jacob is nodding. 'It was very moving.'

Luke's face opens in a tentative smile. 'Yeah. It was great.'

She knows how hard her brother is working to get better. She admires him. It was a shock to realise that he'd been struggling for a long time in silence. She feels a stab of guilt, knowing she's always taken up so much air in the house, so much space.

She gives him a gentle punch on the arm. 'Thanks for coming.'

She promises that she'll meet them in the local pizza restaurant after she's finished up at the theatre, and hands her flowers to Cora for safekeeping. 'Don't feel you have to come,' Cora says. 'If your group are going on somewhere, just text me.'

Fran is folding three large blue sheets that are used in the sea scene when she feels someone watching her. She glances over her shoulder.

'Want a hand with that?' Zac is standing behind her. She'd forgotten about his lack of beard. The clean lines of his face are shockingly naked.

She starts. Feels a blush burning her cheeks. 'You were in the audience?'

'Of course.' He takes up the hem of a sheet and they step together and apart in a kind of dance, folding edge to edge. He stops folding and looks at her. 'It was one of those performances that stays with you. It was life-affirming. Life-changing.'

'Carol's a genius.' She stares down at the sheet in her hands, taking it from him and placing it on a chair, picking up the next one so they can repeat the whole thing.

'You can take some of the credit, you know,' he says. 'Carol thinks very highly of you. The whole group does.'

She nods, not sure of her voice if she speaks.

'I got your note,' Zac goes on. 'Thank you. For the things you said.'

'I should thank you,' she says, as she gathers the second folded sheet into her arms. 'You tried to get me involved with Cat's Eye. You tried to introduce me to Yara. You knew I'd love it here, didn't you?'

'Yeah,' he admits. 'I thought you might want to get involved . . . if you saw what they were doing.'

'Thank you,' she says quietly. 'It's the best thing that's ever happened to me.'

'It's all you, Fran,' he says. 'You did it. If it doesn't sound patronising . . . I'm proud of you.'

'No . . . not too patronising. Although you are. Of course.'

'Of course,' he says. They smile at each other, finishing folding the last sheet in silence. Fran places it on top of the pile.

'Well,' he says, 'I should go.'

She can't look at him, can't hide the longing in her eyes. She wants to touch his hand, curl her fingers around his, press her lips to his. How could she have taken him for granted? All those weeks of not understanding who he was, who she could be with him, until it was too late.

'Zac . . . I wondered if—'

But he's already talking, and their words cross. 'I'm meeting some friends,' he's saying. 'They're waiting for me.'

Her question falters, falls away. 'Yes. Sure,' she says, flicking her hair over her shoulder. 'See you around.'

He puts his hands in his pockets, half turning. 'But . . . if you'd like to come along? A quick drink, maybe?'

She takes a deep breath. In the old days, she would have made a joke, or pretended that it didn't matter, but this is too important – she's not afraid of admitting that any more. Her heart is beating very fast.

'Yes,' she says. 'I'd like that.'

Bethnal Green

Jacob and Cora are shopping for dinner at Broadway Market, shuffling at a snail's pace with the crowd, everyone wrapped in scarves and hats against the cold. There are stalls either side of them laden with iced cakes and pots of jam and tubs of glistening olives. At a fruit and veg stall, Jacob pounces on an aubergine, holding it up for Cora to admire the taut purple skin, leaning over to pick out some red peppers, a handful of shallots. They are hosting a meal for Jacob's parents – the first time Cora will meet them. Jacob's father has agreed to come, and knows all about Cora. 'My mother prepared him,' Jacob explains. 'Not sure what she said exactly, but when I broke the news, he was surprisingly reasonable.' He points to a cauliflower, stretching to take it from the stallholder.

Cora makes a mock-fearful face, belying the fact that she really is nervous. 'Don't worry. It'll be fine.' Jacob grins and hugs her. 'My father can be difficult, but he has a big heart.'

The market is full of mouth-watering smells. People are

queuing for the hog roast, sizzling stir-fries, pizza slices, rock oysters; small groups stand eating with concentration out of paper bags. Cora hears snatches of different languages. A busker is playing Beatles covers; Cora starts to hum along to 'Penny Lane'. They stop in front of a stall selling local honey, and Jacob buys a jar of gleaming liquid. 'Good for allergies and hay fever,' he says.

'Sometimes, I find it hard to believe you come from the city,' Cora says, slipping her arm through his. 'I can picture you living in a cottage in the middle of nowhere, sketching the animals in your garden, growing herbs.'

'Only if you'll come and live with me.'

Cora smiles, and says lightly, 'I might be persuaded.'

'Except,' he stops and looks at her, 'I couldn't be too far from Natan.'

She squeezes his arm. 'I know.'

'How's Luke doing?' he says as he slows in front of a bakery stall, choosing a sourdough loaf dusted with flour, and two baguettes.

'Better,' she says. 'The university are being helpful and sending work. When his OCD took over, it must have been a nightmare for him.'

'Yes,' Jacob agrees. 'But give him some time and he's going to be more than all right. He's such a bright kid.'

'Mmm,' Cora agrees. 'I've been reading about it. Apparently OCD affects some of the most able, sensitive and talented people. High achievers, too. Historians think Samuel Johnson might have been a sufferer.'

'Really?'

'Something to do with the way he leapt across thresholds and had to touch every post in whatever street he went down.'

They wander past racks of second-hand denim jackets, and a

stall selling woven baskets in candy shades of pink and lemon and orange – like sweets for giants.

'And this therapist he's seeing – what kind are they?'

'Behavioural. Luke might need to take some more time out of university. But his therapist says he's already doing well.'

'I have a surprise for him.' Jacob stops, his eyes bright. 'I rented a car and drove up to UEA yesterday and brought his bike back. I know he's been worrying about it. I was going to cycle it over tomorrow – if you think it's a good idea?'

'Oh!' Cora stares at him. 'You did that? He'll be so happy!' She hugs him, pressing her lips into the place just behind his ear where his skin is soft and warm. 'Jacob ... thank you.'

They head back to the boat along the canal, carrying bags of produce. A large London plane tree stands next to the path, tiny seed pods littering heavy branches. Jacob puts down the bags and lays a hand on the jigsaw bark. 'You know why it looks like this, like camouflage?'

She shakes her head, setting her bag down, flexing her aching fingers.

'It's the tree's way of dealing with city life. The bark peels away to rid itself of pollution. The roots don't need to dig deep. It can grow in any soil.' He pats the trunk. 'Maybe I'm a bit like a plane tree. I belong in the countryside, but I've adapted to city living.'

She stares up into the silvery branches. 'We have plane trees lining our street. And I never knew that about them.'

'Stick with me.' He kisses her nose. 'I'm a fount of knowledge.' He grins mischievously and rolls his eyes, then picks up the shopping. 'Here. Let me carry your bag.'

She shakes her head. 'I know my biceps are invisible. But they're surprisingly powerful!'

*

334

The boat is rich with the smells of cooking, aromatic with spices and herbs. Jacob has taken charge of the main course, and Cora has made a cake at home, an orange and almond torte. 'Does your mother do much baking?' she asks casually as she gets the pudding out of its tin and puts it on a plate.

'Is a rabbi Jewish?'

'Oh. I hope this turns out to be a good one. I've made it a hundred times, but it would be typical if—'

He cuts her off, grabbing her hand and holding it to his chest. 'Hey!' he says. 'Stop worrying. My mother already loves you, and she hasn't even met you yet. Everything you've ever made has been delicious. This isn't a test, you know.'

'Okay.' She nods and grimaces. 'Sorry. Just feeling the pressure.'

'Cora ... my mother is the kind of woman who's generous with the word love,' he says quietly. 'But I use it more sparingly.'

She catches her breath. He's still holding her hand to his chest, and she feels the thunder of his heart. Her pulse quickens, an echo of his.

'I love you, Cora Pollen.' His voice is as certain as his words. 'I loved you the moment you opened your front door. I've never stopped. Never will.'

'I love you too,' she says.

And suddenly it doesn't matter about orange tortes or even whether his parents like her. All that matters is him, and the way he's pulled her close, their hands entwined. The way he's looking at her now.

There are voices outside, one male and one female. They are arguing loudly. Claude starts to bark next door. Jacob raises an eyebrow at Cora. 'I should have warned you.' He makes a wincing expression as there's a scuffling noise. 'My parents know how to make an entrance.'

He goes to the front hatch and throws open the door. 'Ma. Pa. Be careful stepping onto the boat.' He jumps up the steps. 'Wait. Let me help you.'

There are pants and grunts and complaints outside. Cora stands with her hands folded, waiting nervously.

A woman with a mane of grey hair comes down the narrow steps into the galley, stepping sideways, clinging to the rail. She's shaking her head. 'What a place to live,' she exclaims. 'I still can't understand what's wrong with dry land.'

She's adjusting her long floral skirt, but stops when she sees Cora. She gives a beaming smile and holds out her hands. 'There you are,' she says, stepping across and taking Cora's cheeks between her palms. Her touch is dry and warm; her eyes, looking into Cora's, shine with the same brilliant colours as her son's, golden flecks around her pupils. 'You are as beautiful as he said.' She nods. 'Maybe a little thin. But lovely.'

'Ma!' Jacob reprimands her. 'Don't start.'

She waves her hand. 'I'm on my best behaviour. I'm allowed to be excited to meet the woman my son's been telling me about for months.'

'And this,' Jacob says, 'is my father, Isaac.'

A short, stocky man with grizzled hair, black-framed spectacles perched on his nose, is regarding her with a stern expression. His small mocha eyes are watchful behind thick glass. He takes off his hat and steps forward, takes her hand, places his other hand over the top. 'Cora, I'm pleased to meet you,' he says gravely. He shakes his head. 'I won't pretend that you're the woman I'd hoped my son would choose, but . . .' he's still holding on to her hand, and he squeezes it, 'man makes plans, and God laughs.'

Cora's lips twitch uncertainly. Should she smile? His expression remains serious, focused on her face. She gives a brief nod and he releases her hand.

'Come and sit down. I'll get everyone drinks,' Jacob says, ushering them inside to the small table, taking coats, pulling out chairs.

Cora accepts her glass of Chablis gratefully, and takes a nervous gulp. But the meal is a success. Both his parents eat heartily and compliment Jacob and Cora on the tagine and the cake. Apart from his appreciation of the food, Isaac doesn't talk much; it's Rachel asking question after question, listening intently and then, just as Cora prepares to ask her something, launching into another. She wants to know about Cora's job, about her parents, about Andrew and Fran and Luke.

'Give her a break, *sheifale*,' Isaac says gently. 'You're wearing her out.'

'Am I?' Rachel sits back in her chair. 'I'm sorry. I've been storing up all my curiosity for so long.' She puts a finger to her lips. 'I'll be quiet now.'

'Nobody wants that, my love.' Isaac leans over and kisses her cheek. 'But I will talk now. I have something to say.' He holds up his glass. 'First, a toast to Jacob and Cora. Despite my misgivings, I can see they make each other happy.' He stands up, clearing his throat. 'Another man says it better than me, and we must all remember his wisdom. He said that the salvation of man is through love and in love.'

'Viktor E. Frankl,' Rachel says in a whispered aside, beaming. 'It's his favourite quote.' She raises her glass. '*L'chayim*,' she calls out, with Isaac repeating the toast. They clink all four glasses at the rims, a splash of wine falling onto Cora's wrist. She licks it off.

'You see, Cora,' Isaac says, setting his drink back on the table, 'you must forgive me my early doubts. Jacob is the last in our male line, and I wanted the family to go on. Natan will not have children. I'd hoped for Jacob to meet a nice Jewish girl, and have Jewish children who bear the name da Costa. But,' his eyes glitter with tears, 'I see that it's not meant to be.'

'Papa,' Jacob says gently. 'I've never wanted children. Ever since Natan's accident, I knew that he had become my responsibility. I didn't even think I could have a relationship, let alone a family.'

'And this is what we'd like to talk to you about,' Rachel says, pushing her hair behind her ears, rolling up her sleeves and beginning to pile up plates.

'Leave it, Ma,' Jacob says. 'You're our guest.'

'You must let go of this guilt of yours,' Isaac is saying. 'It does not belong to you.'

The words are spoken softly, but they slice through the atmosphere. Cora suppresses a gasp, and holds her breath; she feels Jacob and Rachel holding theirs too.

'You are not guilty of anything,' Isaac carries on, leaning towards his son, his chin jutting. 'Let it go.' His fingers strike the tablecloth, his voice wrung tight with emotion.

Cora shivers at this unexpected order. She glances at Jacob, sees him flinch and sit up. 'You're wrong, Pa,' he says in a low voice. 'I can never let it go. Because I *am* guilty. Natan didn't drop the ball. I threw it. That's why he ran in front of the car. Because of me.'

There is silence. Cora hears herself swallow.

'We always wondered what really happened,' Rachel says

gently. She looks at her husband. 'But we knew you'd never do anything to deliberately hurt your brother. We didn't want to pry, because you were already in so much pain.' She shakes her head. 'Perhaps we should have got the truth out of you sooner. We should have had this conversation long ago.'

'How can you forgive me?' Jacob's voice breaks.

'There's nothing to forgive,' Isaac says gruffly.

Rachel dabs at her eyes. 'This isn't about blame, *hayim sheli*. It's about your brother and you. We all love Natan. But you insist on doing so much for him. Too much. You pay for everything.' She puts a hand to her heart. 'For which we will always be grateful. But you get up in the middle of the night, rush there when they call you. You feel only you can satisfy his needs, can calm him and reassure him. It is . . . a kind of selfishness, a kind of ego, to feel only you are good enough.'

'What?' Jacob's eyes widen. 'Is that what you really think?'

'Your mother is right, Jacob. We've been worried about you for a long time. We didn't know how to help . . . how to tell you what we're telling you now. We were afraid it would break you.'

'But now you have Cora. You have enough . . . balance for us to say it,' Rachel says. 'You must live your own life. Properly. Not this half-life. Spend time away from the city. Think of yourself, of Cora.'

'Natan needs me.' Jacob's voice is very quiet.

'I know, darling,' Rachel says, gathering his hands to her and kissing his knuckles. 'He does. But he doesn't need you to sacrifice everything for him.'

Jacob's eyes fill with water; he stands up abruptly, staring at his parents. He tries to speak, and fails, shaking his head. Cora curls her fingers into her palms, wanting to go to him. But she watches him turn and blunder towards the bedroom, shutting the door behind him. She looks at Rachel and Isaac.

'Give him a minute,' Rachel says, her mouth trembling. 'We'll go now. It's getting late. You two can talk better without us. I know my words were harsh.' She wipes her face with a large hanky. 'But they are true. He's not the only one who can be there for Natan. While we're alive, God willing, while we have days on this earth, we want to do more.'

'I think … I think I understand,' Cora says, getting to her feet and following Rachel and Isaac through the galley.

'It's not good for anyone to be alone,' Rachel says. 'Especially a man. I prayed he would find someone – someone like you.' She kisses Cora's cheeks, her lips resting for a moment each time against her skin. 'Get him out of London if you can. He needs to enjoy himself. God knows, this self-sacrifice has been going on too long. Get him to change his routine. Even if only a little.'

'*Zei gezunt.*' Isaac kisses her hand gravely before he puts on his hat and helps Rachel into her coat.

Cora guides them off the boat, making sure they step safely onto the towpath, and stands with her hand up. She hears them talking loudly as they disappear along the canal, admonishing each other, complaining, teasing, until their voices fade and there is nothing but the plop of a fish rising, the rustle of invisible night creatures.

Winter

Woodford

Cora and Jacob take the Tube to Woodford. It's raining when they emerge into daylight, and Jacob unfurls a large umbrella over them. Cora links her arm through his.

'It's only five minutes from here,' he says.

She nods, not wanting to talk in case her voice betrays her. Meeting Natan feels like a huge event. Even bigger than meeting his parents.

The care home is a graceful building covered with a climbing creeper, gnarled and bare now that it's winter. But Cora can imagine the wisteria flowers in the summer: an abundance of lilac frothing around the windows.

'Such a beautiful house,' she murmurs as they crunch over wet gravel.

'Apparently, years ago, royalty hunted in Epping Forest,' Jacob says. 'So from early on, grand houses have been built here. Some of them have been turned into schools and care homes, like this one.'

Inside, there's the usual institutional smell of bleach and cooked food. And Cora sees that the place has been adapted with mobility rails and ramps. But as she and Jacob make their way past the reception desk into the heart of the building, she glimpses private rooms through open doorways, with pictures on the walls and personal ornaments on shelves. They pass smiling staff in the corridor, pushing residents in wheelchairs or helping them make their way along, holding elbows, giving encouragement.

Jacob turns into a large, airy common room. Cora expected people to be gathered around a TV, but instead there are small groups engaged in art activities or games, and a nurse in the corner is playing a guitar.

They approach the group gathered around the music.

'Natan,' Jacob says quietly as he bends to look into the face of a man sitting in a wheelchair. 'Hey, how are you?' He squats down. 'Do you mind if we go somewhere quieter? There's someone I'd like you to meet.'

He stands and nods at one of the nurses as he takes hold of the wheelchair. 'We're just going to Natan's room for a bit.'

'I'll get someone to bring you all a cup of tea,' the nurse says.

Natan's room is full of colour. A home-made mobile hangs from the ceiling. There are family photos all over the walls. The bed is covered with a crocheted blanket in rainbow shades. Jacob arranges two chairs in a semicircle next to Natan, and Cora slips into one.

'This is Cora,' he tells his brother. 'She's very special to me.' He smiles at Cora. 'And this is my brother, who you've heard so much about.'

'I certainly have,' she says, leaning forward to smile at Natan. 'He never stops talking about you.'

'She actually likes me,' Jacob says to Natan in a stage whisper. 'So don't tell her any of my secrets, okay?'

A slow grin spreads across Natan's face and his fingers tremble on the armrests of the chair. Cora can see that he's happy to be with his brother, but that it's a struggle for him to listen. He blinks often. Sometimes his eyes slide away, as if he doesn't have the strength to focus.

'I love your room,' she says. 'Did someone make the bedspread? It's gorgeous.'

'Ah, that's Mum's work, isn't it, Nat? She's the queen of crochet. Blankets. Cushions. Rugs. We had to be quick on our feet to avoid being press-ganged into her latest creations.' He shakes his head sorrowfully. 'You can't get away with orange and brown crocheted trousers when you're a twelve-year-old boy.'

Natan's smile widens, taking over his face.

Cora laughs. 'You're both lucky to have her. She's a powerful woman. And powerful women make strong sons.'

'Yes,' Jacob says. 'That's true. In Nat's case, anyway. He's as strong as a lion. Never known anyone braver, either.' He takes his brother's fingers and kisses them.

Cora blinks, a tear escaping. She brushes it away with her thumb, and takes the opportunity to jump up as a woman bearing a tea tray knocks at the door. She takes the tray with a nod of thanks.

'Shall I pour?' she asks, as she sets it down on a side table.

Shepherd's Bush

The house smells of Christmas – brandy, pine, spicy cinnamon and cloves, with scents of frankincense and orange zest drifting from the candles in the hall. It reminds Fran of her childhood in Suffolk. They used to gather huge garlands of glossy ivy and red holly berries in the woods with Dad, twist them through the banisters and loop gold-ribboned swags of green across mantelpieces. They had a gigantic glimmering tree in the sitting room in front of the French windows, an angel on top, presents piled beneath. Christmas in London has always been a more subdued affair, with just the three of them, her and Luke squabbling over what to watch on TV and Cora going through the motions of producing the perfect lunch. The small tree perched on a table in the corner always seemed, somehow, apologetic.

This year is different. For a start, they have a tree whose topmost star nearly touches the ceiling, just as Cora promised, its thick, luxuriant branches loaded with decorations and white lights. Jacob went with them to help choose it and bring it home, and joined in the decorating, even though Christmas isn't on his calendar. He's spending today with his brother at the care home, where the residents are having a pre-Christmas party, with a magician and mince pies and carols. 'Religion doesn't matter to Natan,' he explained as he passed Fran silver and red baubles to hang on the branches. 'It's human connection and care that make all the difference to him.'

Zac came to help decorate the tree, too. He's studying hard on the days he's not working; he stays up late with textbooks, frowning over pages, chewing the end of his pen. Fran reads novels or scripts while he studies; she lies with her head on his lap, or his head on her lap, both of them with books or screens open in their hands. They feed each other chocolate and biscuits, take it in turns to make cups of strong tea.

It's Saturday, two and a half weeks to go till Christmas. Fran sits at the breakfast table with Cora and Luke. The sound of the letter box snapping open makes Cora start. There's a slide of envelopes onto the mat, Luke leaps up, a piece of toast in his mouth, and goes to fetch them. He comes back, chewing, and dumps a small heap of mail onto the table. 'I'm off,' he says. 'We've got a long one today – out to Box Hill.'

'Have a lovely time,' Cora says. 'Don't forget your reflective top.'

He grabs another slice of toast and waves over his shoulder. 'See you later.'

'Not if we see you first,' Fran calls out.

Cora shakes her head and smiles, pouring more coffee for them both.

'He seems almost back to his usual nerdy self,' Fran says.

Cora nods. 'The sessions with his therapist are really

helping – and just being able to step away from the pressure of university for a while has made a difference.'

'So how long are you and Jacob going on this trip for?' Fran asks, taking a sip of scalding liquid. 'Your journey up the canal?' She pretends to shiver. 'At this time of year! You're both mad. It'll be freezing.'

'But the boat's lovely and toasty inside, and we'll wrap up. We've only got five days,' Cora says. 'We're going to head up the Lee towards Waltham Abbey, see how far we get. It'll be the first time Jacob's taken the boat anywhere, so it should be a bit of an adventure.'

'What if you get stuck in a lock?' Fran teases. 'Or sink? You'll miss Christmas Day.'

'I'll swim back if necessary, with a branch of mistletoe between my teeth,' Cora laughs. 'Don't worry. But I do need to make sure I get everything done before I leave. Lots of jobs to check off the list.'

'Mum,' Fran says, 'I ... I need to tell you something.' Her chest is suddenly full of butterfly wings, her mouth dry.

The smile fades from Cora's lips, and she puts her head on one side attentively.

'You know when we first met Jacob, and I had a mad crush on him?' Fran flashes a look at Cora to stop her from interrupting. 'Then it got awkward and weird when I realised you liked him too. But I ... I don't know ... I guess I was a bit crazy. I thought ... I thought I could take him away from you—'

'We've talked about this before,' Cora breaks in. 'None of it matters.'

'No,' Fran says. 'It does. Just listen. What you don't know is that I went to see his parents.'

'What?'

'One afternoon, when you were at work, I went to Leytonstone and knocked on their door.'

'You went to see Rachel and Isaac?'

Fran gives her another look. She has to talk fast. Get it over and done with. 'I had this stupid idea that I should tell them about you.' She can't look at Cora; her shoulders hunch. 'I knew how upset you were about him hiding you from his family, and I thought . . . I thought if I just confronted his parents, got it all out in the open, it would help to fix things.' She balls her fingers into fists. 'But I should never have tried to interfere. After you split up, I understood how much you loved him, and how wrong I'd been about the two of you in the first place.'

Cora takes a breath. 'Oh Fran.' She puts her hand over her daughter's. 'I'm not angry. It was complicated for all of us. But we've moved on.' She rests her palm on Fran's cheek. 'And thank God for that.'

Fran's lungs push out stale air, as if it's been trapped inside with her guilt.

'Now, I should start on making the mincemeat for the mince pies,' Cora is saying, pulling her hair back into a ponytail with a businesslike twist. 'We need to get the rest of the cards in the post today,' she goes on, 'and do you want to feed the cake with brandy? Oh, and I must remember to put in an order for bread . . .' Fran can tell that she's consulting an invisible list. 'And we can do present-wrapping later.'

She starts to hum 'Hark! The Herald Angels Sing' while carefully easing envelopes open with her finger, pulling out festive cards and reading them to herself. 'Where's Zac spending Christmas?' she pauses in her humming to ask.

Fran picks up one of the opened cards featuring reindeer with snow on their antlers and looks inside, squinting at scrawled signatures. She puts it down. 'I was going to ask if he could come to us – his father doesn't do Christmas, and he's out of the country anyway.'

'Of course,' Cora smiles. 'The more the merrier. I've ordered enough food to feed an army.'

Bethnal Green

After Jacob's parents had disappeared into the night, Cora turned back into the boat, going straight to Jacob. He was sitting on the bed in the dark, his hands clasped between his knees, head bowed.

'Do you think it's true?' he asked in a low, gravelly voice. 'Do you think I've been selfish?'

'No.' She knelt before him and put her hands on his. 'No. Not in the way you're thinking. You've been wonderful, years and years of putting your brother first, being consistent and caring. It's just … I don't know, maybe it's like those times when we feel shy, unable to join in a conversation. We're aware of our own emotions, our own perceived inadequacy, but we're not thinking about other people, how they might be feeling.' She paused, pressed on. 'I suppose it's an ego of a kind. A back-to-front one.' She rubbed his knuckles with her thumb. 'Maybe that's more what your mum meant – you've been so caught up with Natan and his needs, so caught up in playing your part,

351

that you've forgotten that your parents need a role too – a bigger one than they already have. And maybe you've forgotten that they've been deprived of watching you grow up to be happy and fulfilled, so they've had to watch both sons give up their lives in different ways. It's not selfishness on your part; it's more like . . . tunnel vision.' She squeezed his clenched hands. 'It's been your way of surviving. But maybe they're right – you need to let go a little, think about yourself more, and in that way, you'll be giving something important to your parents.'

He groaned, running his fingers through his hair. 'I thought it had to be me. I was the one who threw the ball. I was the one—'

'It wasn't your fault,' she said, slipping onto the bed, close beside him. 'You did something a million kids do every day. You didn't do it with malice or intent to hurt; it was bad luck, terrible timing that Natan stepped off the pavement at that precise moment.'

'I would give anything . . .' his voice broke, 'do anything to turn the clock . . .'

'I know.' She put her arms around him, his breath warm against her neck. 'I know,' she breathed, their wet faces pressed together.

The next day, he told her that he'd try to step back a bit – that he'd start by doing a short trip on the boat, let his parents be the point of contact while he was away. 'Will you come?' he asked. 'I promise not to shout when we get stuck going through a lock.'

So here they are, it's early morning on the day of their depart-ure, and they're piling boxes of provisions on the side in the galley, packing bags of pasta and tins of beans away onto the shelves, stocking up on wood for the stove. Jacob has already given the engine the once-over. They've spread the map out on the table and followed the blue line of the Lee, counted the locks they'll need to go through, marked the places on the journey where they hope to stop and explore.

Cora has brought a small bag of things with her – not much more than a change of clothes, a novel, and her coat, hat, gloves and boots. It's going to be cold on deck.

Through a porthole, she glimpses the towpath, rimed with frost. Skeletal trees make lacy silhouettes against the low sun, and there are thin panes of ice floating on the canal.

As they're finishing unpacking the provisions, there's a 'helloooo' from outside the boat. And another. Jacob stops with his hand raised to place a jar of coffee on the side, his ear cocked. 'Was that someone calling us?'

Cora tries to look innocent. 'Hmm,' she says. 'Maybe. Let's take a look.'

She lets him go up the steps first, hearing him catch his breath. 'Ma? Pa? Natan?' There's a smile in his voice. 'What are you doing here?'

Cora comes out onto the stern. Jacob's parents are there with Natan in his chair, wrapped up and snug in a red scarf and matching hat. Jacob leaps off the boat to greet them, bending to kiss his brother, ruffling his hat. Hugging his mother.

'We came to wave you off,' Rachel says. 'Didn't we, Natan?'

'We wanted to see the maiden voyage,' Isaac says, handing over a bottle of red wine. 'Here. To toast the first night of your travels.'

'Thanks, Pa.' Jacob is squatting in front of Natan, holding his hand, looking into his face. 'Hey,' he's saying, 'it's great to see you. When it gets warmer, we'll see if we can find a way to get you on board, maybe take you for a trip if you'd like.'

With a whirring of feathers, Scout drops from the sky, landing on Natan's knee. Natan blinks, then a crooked smile transforms his face. Scout cocks her head. 'Look at that!' Jacob puts his finger under the bird's throat, scratching. 'She likes you, Nat.'

There's another shout, and Cora glances into the wintry light. Fran and Zac are coming towards them hand in hand along the towpath, Luke pushing his bike beside them.

'I can't believe it!' Jacob is rubbing his nose and laughing, striding to greet the new arrivals. 'You're all here!'

'We've only come to watch you make a mess of it,' Fran grins. 'Rescue you when you fall in. If you're lucky.'

'Then I'll be sorry to disappoint you,' he says, winking.

'Why is your boat called *Pica Pica*,' Luke asks. 'Does it mean something?'

'It's the scientific name for magpies,' Jacob tells him. 'In honour of Scout.'

Rachel produces a flask of tea and passes around small cups. The group stand close on the path, their breath making clouds, chatting to one another and exclaiming over the narrowboat, asking questions about how cold it will be on board ('Not at all,' Cora assures them, 'not in the cabin') and whether Scout will go with them ('Only if she wants to,' Jacob says).

'So you two will be all right while I'm gone?' Cora asks Fran and Luke. She knows she shouldn't fuss, but she can't help it. The freezer is stocked with meals. Luke's appointments are marked on the calendar. And as Helena keeps telling her, *they're grown-ups.*

Fran hooks her arm through Luke's. 'Rachel's threatening

to send us food parcels. And Zac's practically a doctor, so all emergencies are covered.'

'Think I have a few more years to go before you can call me that,' Zac murmurs.

'Okay.' Cora relaxes into a smile, and looks at Jacob. 'Then we're about ready to go, aren't we?'

He wraps his arm around her shoulders. 'We are, my love.' He gives her a squeeze. 'Cora's written out a timeline for the trip. I'm going to do my best to deviate from it.'

'Ha!' She smacks his arm lightly.

'So,' he says, gesturing towards the boat. 'Shall we step aboard? Give these people a show, now they've come all this way?'

She jumps up before him onto the stern, and when he's aboard, he starts the engine. It judders into life. Luke uncoils the mooring rope and throws it to them; it rears through the air like a living creature, and Cora stretches to catch the unspooling weight. She arranges it neatly on deck, secretly relieved that she didn't drop it.

There's a burst of clapping. Jacob grins at her from his place at the tiller, steering slowly away from the bank and out into the canal.

George pops out of his cabin, Claude at his heels. He puts up his weather-beaten hand. 'They're off!' he shouts. 'Thank God. Thought you'd never leave!'

At the sound of his voice, the rest of the boat people emerge to stand on their decks, waving, calling out goodbyes. There are cheers, wolf whistles. Laughter. Claude is barking.

The boat moves slowly away from her mooring spot, leaving the other vessels and the little group on the path behind, nosing through faint swirls of mist. It occurs to Cora that she met Jacob because of the Underground, with its dusty web of tunnels, its tracks rushing blindly through the bowels of the city, but here they are taking a very different kind of journey. Travelling for the pleasure of it, enjoying the slow unfolding of the landscape, breathing fresh air, noticing the details of the world as they glide forward.

A familiar black and white shape flutters out of the sky. Scout settles on Jacob's shoulder, then flaps down onto the rail of the boat, ducking her head, eyes glittering. Cora strokes the bird's shining back, and she preens, chirrups, and takes off, skimming the dark water in a long swoop. 'I did wonder if she'd come along with us,' Jacob says. 'But I saw her with a tiding of magpies yesterday. Perhaps she's found herself a mate.'

'A tiding?'

'A better collective noun than a mischief, don't you think?'

She grins, wrapping both her arms around his waist, her nose in the fuzzy warmth of his jumper. They stand together, watching the group on the bank get smaller and smaller. Jacob holds up his hand in a salute. The very last thing to disappear from view through the swirling haze is the bright red of Natan's hat and scarf.

As the shouts from the towpath grow fainter, it's the river they hear calling to them: muted city sounds mixing with bird cries. A flock of geese fly overhead, their beating wings like applause. London slips past, glimpsed through wreaths of white, graffitied walls, the tangled green of the bank, and further off, rooftops and towers. The engine rumbles and thuds and the water flows on, carrying them deeper into the silver of the morning.

Acknowledgements

Many thanks to my editor, Emma Beswetherick, and to my publisher, Hannah Wann. It's a joy and a privilege working with you both. Thanks as well to the talented team at Little, Brown and Piatkus: Jo Wickham, Brionee Fenlon, Kate Hibbert, Sarah Birdsey, Andy Hine, and Helena Dorée. Thank you to Jane Selley for eagle-eyed copyediting, and Hannah Wood for the stunning cover. To my agent, Eve White, and Ludo Cinelli, thank you for your support and good counsel.

For thoughtful, useful feedback, thanks to: Alex Marengo, Mary Chamberlain, Viv Graveson, Laura McClelland and Cecilia Ekback.

Thanks to Lilli Matson for being kind enough to talk to me about her job at TFL. Thanks to Gary Hagen for his one-liners, and to Claude for being himself.

Love and thanks as always to my partner, Alex M, my sister, Ana, brother, Alex, and my wonderful children: Hannah, Olivia, Sam and Gabriel. And to Sara Sarre for sharing the writing journey with me, and everything else besides.